Y
Goldsworthy, Sandy.- Aftermath

Springport Branch
Jackson District Library 7/07/2

W9-CNV-150

WITHDRAWN

WITHDRAWN

A Novel By:

SANDY GOLDSWORTHY

Clean Teen Publishing

THIS book is a work of fiction. Names, characters, places and incidents are the product of the authors' imagination or are used factiously. Any resemblance to actual persons, living or dead, business establishments, events or locales is entirely coincidental.

NO part of this book may be reproduced, scanned, or distributed in any printed or electronic form without permission. Please do not participate in or encourage piracy of copyrighted materials in violation of the author's rights. Purchase only authorized editions.

Aftermath

Copyright ©2014 Sandy Goldsworthy

All rights reserved.

Cover Design by: Marya Heiman
Typography by: Courtney Nuckels

ISBN: 978-1-940534-88-6

Y
Goldsworthy, Sandy.- Aftermath /

Springport Branch
Jackson District Library 7/07/2015

For more information about our content disclosure, please utilize the QR code above with your smart phone or visit us at www.cleanteenpublishing.com.

Chapter 1
Ben's Story

Tell me you didn't go back to that lake again, Benjamin.

Molly's piercing thoughts jerked me back to reality. I shook my head and cast a second line into the murky waters of Lake Bell. The narrow passage on the backside of the island was home to the largest northern pike in the county.

You're pretending to be fishing, but you're really sitting in that tin can of a boat that's decades older than you would be, if you were still alive.

After a long mission, I should be entitled to some time off.

I can read your mind. Or, has that human disguise made you forget our world?

I chuckled and nodded to the electronic device humans called a phone. It sat on the bench in front of me. The hologram of my brunette partner appeared. We were alone, but I glanced around anyway.

Maybe Molly was right. I was on earth far longer than any other time since I died.

"Relax, Benjamin. No one in their right mind would be out at this time of the morning."

"Hey! I used to fish in this spot every day when I lived here."

Molly's eyes widened. "That proves my point!"

"Nice. I've been gone for almost ten years, and this is how you welcome me back?" Our laughter was muffled against the thick vegetation lining the shores around us. Molly and I were undercover agents in the Afterworld's Bureau of Investigation.

"Tell me. How was your mission?" Molly flashed a telling smile.

"We both know you came here to lecture me." Molly shook her head and started to respond. I held up my hand. "No. Before you tell me it's time to let go, it's time for me to pick up the pieces of my existence and look to the future, I want you to know I've done some serious thinking."

"Benjamin—"

"Nope. You should know this is my last trip. I visited the bait shop in Riverside, said goodbye to the owner this morning, and drafted papers to sell my folks' house on the other side of the lake… I'm ready."

Molly wrinkled her forehead for an instant.

"Don't worry. I'm okay with it."

Molly looked down, her hands clasped together. "You should really think about what you're doing."

"I did. And I moved on."

"Don't make any rash decisions, Benjamin."

"Rash? I've been looking for Elizabeth since 1941, and you've been nagging me ever since."

Molly's face went pale. I peered into her mind, but her thoughts were clear, an obvious sign she was shielding me. It was a game we used to play when I was in training at The Farm. As a rookie, my skills were constantly tested. At first, Molly was stronger than I was, blocking me out of her mind. Eventually, I learned to break her barriers. All I had to do was concentrate…

"Benjamin, stop! We got a call," Molly blurted out.

"Huh?"

"While you were on assignment, a call came into dispatch."

"So? Hundreds of calls come in every second."

"A girl broke her arm. She was rather distraught, I'd say. She was only six years old. Poor thing. Else, I'd never known. Dispatch would have assigned her case to a patrol unit to investigate and then filed it away." Molly took a deep breath before continuing. "Did I tell you I was assigned to office duty? I can't say I enjoyed it. Of course, giving tours wasn't bad. I had a chance to meet some new recruits. Not that I'd want to partner with any of them. Oh! I heard you met Bianca. She told me to say hello."

"Molly!"

She jumped in response. "Oh, yes. My apologies for drifting." For a slight moment, Molly looked uncomfortable.

"What are you trying to tell me?"

After a moment of hesitation, she whispered, "I found Elizabeth."

The movement of my fishing pole distracted me. I stared at the spot where the line pierced the water and hung the bait precisely twenty-eight feet, five-and-a-half inches below. Pointing my index finger, I moved it in a slow, circular motion. The line stopped twitching, and the fish moved on.

Silence lingered in the crisp, predawn air.

Out of habit, I lit up a cigarette and took a long drag. Regrets suddenly hit me. She was gone. Lost. All those years I looked for Elizabeth, the years undercover I searched for her... Instead, she was living another life?

"Benjamin?" The water's surface shivered when Molly spoke.

I took a second hit and held my breath for a moment.

Memories of my wife, Elizabeth, warmed me. Her bright blue eyes and gentle smile had caught my attention back in 1931. We were young, innocent, and alive. I didn't know it then, but that Saturday, at Hudson's Grocery in Riverside, I met my soul mate. We married a few years later and welcomed a son, Danny.

Did you hear me?

I ignored Molly and recalled the last time I saw Elizabeth.

"These eight months will go by quickly. You'll see." It was my last tour of duty on the *USS Arizona*. "I'll be home soon. I promise." They were words that still haunted me today.

I never made it home and never saw Elizabeth again—not on earth or in my world, either. I died on December 7, 1941 at Pearl Harbor. It was the reason I chose to join the Bureau and train as an undercover agent. It gave me a chance to search for the love of my life.

"Benjamin, she couldn't contact you. There was a breach of contract." Her tone was soft. "It wasn't your fault, or hers."

Thoughts circled silently between us. I was numb. Emotions I expected, words I wanted to speak, failed me.

A fish nibbled on my bait again. This time, I didn't move to stop it. I watched the tapping of the line in the calm water, one, followed by another. The fish grabbed hold and the line tightened, bending the pole downward. I reeled in my catch and released the fish back to the waters below, in one automated motion.

To the east, the sky turned a dark purple—the dawn of another day.

Chapter 2
Emma's Story

Four Years Later, Present Day

I got out of my car as the first bell rang.

Parked in the last row, furthest from the building, I was sure to be late. Wonderful. Monday morning, the third day of school, and I felt like crap for arguing with Dad.

It wasn't really an argument. He told me his opinion, which didn't match mine.

I raced to the doors of Highland Park High School, haunted by the image of Dad's bright red face. "No way. I'm not letting you and your girlfriends drive two hours to a party at some campground," he said.

"Dad, I'm a senior, and it's not just any campground. It's at Lake Bell."

"I don't care where it is. There are no chaperones," he argued. "Besides, we're going to Lake Bell this weekend as a family. Did you forget?"

How could I forget? Ever since Mom died, Dad and I went to visit Aunt Barb every holiday and most weekends in between. She lived in Wisconsin and owned a fancy resort on Lake Bell. Weekends consisted of me being bored out of my mind while Dad and his sister drank wine and talked with her friends. It was different when I was young. There were other kids my age to hang out with.

Dad's angry tone still echoed in my mind when I reached my locker.

I wasn't trying to lie to him. I thought he knew about the senior trip to Lake Bell each Labor Day weekend. It had been the tradition for years.

"Damn it." I couldn't get my lock open on the second attempt.

"Whoa! I never heard you swear before." Matt's smile broke my crabby mood and eased my frustration.

I grinned in response and finally opened my locker.

"You didn't answer when I called this morning." Matt Bishop and I had known each other since sixth grade, even though we had only been dating for a few weeks. Bishop followed Bennett, which put Matt next to me in every class we had together. Our teachers liked alphabetical seating.

"Sorry. It's just... Well, I was talking to my dad. That's all."

He raised an eyebrow as if expecting more of an answer. I didn't respond, and he looked away. Could I tell him my dad had ridiculously strict rules?

After picking out my books and shutting my locker, Matt and I merged with the stream of students in the hall. A few people looked at us. I wasn't surprised. Matt was the starting quarterback on the football team since sophomore year and hadn't ever had a serious girlfriend.

"I called because of the senior trip," Matt said.

Great. Just what I wanted to talk about.

"Lewis' parents offered to have a cookout," he continued. Lewis Warner was one of the super-rich kids in our school and Matt's best friend ever since I could remember. "They have a cottage—well, more like a huge house—on Lake Bell. Lewis said everyone could hang out at the lake, go Jet Skiing, play volleyball... whatever."

"That's nice." I wondered if Dad would be okay with that.

"Best of all, we can stay there. You know, instead of the campground." We reached my classroom and stopped outside the door.

Was that an invitation?

"I heard there aren't enough cabins, anyway," he added.

"Oh. Really?" Aimee Wilkinson glared at us. She was Junior Prom Queen and rumor had it she was interested in Matt. She was a super-rich kid, too, and anything Aimee wanted, Aimee got.

"Yeah. So what do you say?" Did I imagine eagerness in his tone?

"Um... yeah," Of course, I'd need Dad's approval.

"See you in Spanish." His voice was low, almost in a whisper. He stood close enough that our arms touched. I hoped he would kiss me. Instead, he said goodbye and left.

***

The first three class periods flew by, compared to history, which dragged on.

There was nothing more monotonous that listening to lectures on World War II and the attack at Pearl Harbor. Instead of paying attention, I sent Dad a text and told him I was sorry I upset him. Not telling the whole story was no different than telling a lie, I realized.

Aftermath

My best friend, Melissa Ryan, was waiting in the hall after class.

"So? Did you hear about the party at Lewis' house on Lake Bell?" Melissa's energy was in overdrive. "I'm so excited. I can't wait!"

"Matt told me," I answered, when she finally took a breath.

"Like, omigod. You and Matt, me and Lewis." She smirked, raising an eyebrow.

"Uh-huh." Melissa and Lewis started dating junior year. Even if she and Lewis were getting close in that way, this weekend wouldn't have the same meaning for Matt and me. He wouldn't even hold my hand in school.

"This is going to be sooo great!" She squeezed my arm when we reached Spanish class.

"Listen, my dad freaked out on me this morning," I blurted out.

"What? Why?" She stopped in the doorway.

I shrugged. "You know. His strict rules."

Students pushed past us as the bell rang.

"Don't worry. I'm sure we'll figure something out." She grabbed my arm. "Come on."

Senora Gonzalez was talking to a student when Melissa and I took our seats beside Matt and Lewis. Matt greeted me with a smile and suddenly, I felt better.

"You've got lunch next. Right?" Matt whispered.

"Yeah."

"Maybe we could sit together." It was a statement, not a question.

"Yeah, that'd be great." My cheeks warmed. Matt had dark eyes and a warm smile, and he knew when to use it. No wonder girls like Aimee were after him.

"Did Matt tell you about this weekend?" Lewis asked.

"Ah, yeah."

"Good. My parents are cool with a few people staying over."

"Thanks, Lewis. I'll check with my dad."

"Yeah, sure," he said, like I was rejecting him. "You know, he's welcome to call my parents. They'll be there. They got rules, you know. No beer. No smoking. It's cool, though. The locals party on this island… we can join 'em for a bonfire. I've got some friends there."

"Emma's aunt lives there," Melissa said before I could answer.

"You've been to the island parties?" Lewis seemed interested.

I shook my head. Dad barely let me out of sight as it was. There was no way he'd allow me to go to a party on an island.

"Makes Friday nights around here seem tame." He laughed, referring to the huge parties a few football players hosted every weekend. "There's a nice beach there. And a resort my parents go to. Only place in town they'll have dinner."

I nodded. "The Carmichael Inn."

Senora Gonzalez called the class to attention. I should have said my aunt owned the inn, but when the teacher hushed the class a second time, I lost my chance.

Class dragged on for eternity. Quiz tomorrow. Review of last year. Study group today after school. Eleven minutes left in class.

"Abran sus libros en la página diez," Senora Gonzalez said, handing out packets to each row. *Open your books to page ten.*

A knock on the door interrupted Senora Gonzalez from her presentation. When she went to answer it, Melissa brought up the trip again.

Ten minutes left.

"You can ride up with us, Friday night," Lewis offered after Melissa told him I couldn't drive.

When I looked up, Senora Gonzalez was headed toward me. "Emma, can you come with me?" Her piercing eyes stared at me. "Grab your things, please."

Melissa shrugged. "I'll see you at lunch."

I gathered my books and followed Senora Gonzalez to the door.

Why was I singled out?

At the doorway, I paused. All eyes were on me. Matt smiled before I turned and walked out. The office secretary greeted me with an unusual look and escorted me through the maze of hallways to the waiting police officer, Principal Davis, and the school nurse.

What did I do?

Chapter 3
Ben's Story

Pete Jorgenson waited at the gate, like usual.

"Good to see you. How was your trip?" He matched my stride.

"Uneventful." We walked past the long lines and through the maze of security in the Admissions Center in the Northern Hemisphere. We called it the Hub.

An older man with a scrappy, peppered beard, wearing a shabby, tan overcoat tried following us through the invisible field that authenticated our identities. I heard the sparking sound of the neon-blue web that prevented his access into my world, temporarily paralyzing his movement. It stirred unrest amongst the pending admittents, those people waiting in line for acceptance. Fear filled their minds, but they didn't flinch. Within seconds, calmness overcame them again.

A security officer waved his hand in the direction of the man, and the sparking vanished. The web disappeared, yet the old man did not move. The swarming crowd retreated as an unseen force separated them from him.

I stopped and glanced at the suppressed chaos. The disruption was so commonplace that Jorgenson didn't react. Most pending admittents understood they died. After all, their Admissions Guide told them. It was the first words a Guide verbalized to the deceased when they hovered over the remains of their human body. But with so many thoughts, emotions, and memories running through them, it was hard to understand what was happening, and unrest was expected.

"Molly checked in a short time ago," Jorgenson said. We followed the crowd. Most everyone was approved for entrance.

"I didn't realize she came home for a visit."

Jorgenson nodded as we passed slower-moving people in front of us.

A quick update with her would be good before we were engaged in our assignment, and time in our world would be limited. Molly was placed in the field a human-year earlier. Time passed faster in my world.

"Libertyville went well, I trust." Jorgenson referred to the few hours I spent in the small Illinois town for a group compulsion at a high school football game. It was the easiest way to quickly plant memories in humans. Claire, a rookie, was assigned with me. We simply compelled the student body into remembering us before kickoff. Minutes later, we were greeted like long-lost pals by teens we never saw before.

"Claire did well," I said, looking Jorgenson in the eye. "She was a bit apprehensive at first, but the cover worked." It gave us a backstory, should some idiot kid question who we were at some point in our mission. Now, we could legitimately say we were Ben and Claire Parker, two teen siblings previously enrolled at Libertyville High School, active in soccer and well liked. It worked, in case anyone wanted to check up on us. Given today's technological advances and social networking, we needed to connect the dots ahead of time.

"Good. I'm sure her handler will be happy. I'll pass along the news. Claire chose not to come back with you?"

I shook my head. "No, she wanted to stay." I chuckled. "She's enjoying the life of a high school student. Doing better than I expected. She's made friends."

Jorgenson's smirk was understood without my need to read his thoughts. Claire was a cute kid that spent a number of years in rehabilitation before entering the academy. Her past life ended tragically when she overdosed. It was a breach of her life contract. "She's young, Pete."

Not that young, he said in thought.

Young enough. She's only been here a few decades... And she's a rookie.

We aren't old. We're just more experienced. Pete Jorgenson transitioned decades before me. He was forty-eight years old the day his third contract expired, when his human body died, and he stood in a similar admission line as the pending admittents we passed.

"I'll tell her that," I said aloud.

"By the way, Bianca asked about you."

I rolled my eyes.

"She wants in on your assignment."

"Of course she does. Bianca is a very persuasive woman." And she didn't take no for an answer, despite the numerous times I told her I wasn't interested in her romantically.

She's also very attractive. Most agents would jump at the chance—

I'm not like most agents.

But—

Look, if you're interested in her, go for it.

She's requesting you.

"Not interested," I said. We walked through the last checkpoint in the long tunnel called the Bridge. It connected the Hub with our world and provided a database purge or download, if that was necessary. An admittent, one who was approved for entrance to my world, would regain knowledge lost during their human life, here on the Bridge. Those taking on a new human life would lose our world's memory as they walked the tunnel's length on their way out. It was a good filtering system, but one that did not apply to me.

I was an immortal agent.

Chapter 4
Emma's Story

My heart began to race when I saw the police officer.

He stood with the principal, school nurse, and a man in a gray sport coat. Despite being two classrooms away, an uneasy feeling came over me when the cop looked in my direction. This couldn't be good.

The man in the suit motioned his hands, exposing a badge and gun hanging on his belt. He looked like the detectives I saw on TV, and I guessed he was in charge.

Two cops? Omigod. What did I do?

Even though I tried to slow my breathing, my body took over. My chest rose and fell in extreme sways like the metronome I used to play with on Aunt Barb's piano. A lump formed in my throat.

What could I have done and what I would say in response?

I didn't even drink that beer at last weekend's party.

The secretary continued walking toward them, and I kept pace. I wondered if my knees would give out before we got there.

What if I got kicked off the soccer team? How could I explain that to Dad?

I took a deep breath. I didn't do anything wrong. They had to believe me. Right?

I have no idea who was drinking, I rehearsed in my head until Principal Davis motioned me inside the administrative office.

The uniformed officer and the detective followed behind me.

My heart thumped, and I couldn't hear the words they spoke. Everything sounded like garbled mumbles. The nurse led the way past the reception counter, around the corner, and into a small conference room on the right. When she held the door open, I saw my aunt sitting at the table. Her eyes were bloodshot and puffy. Aunt Barb rose to hug me, but I stood stiff, emotionless.

I felt the weight of the air around me. They didn't have to say a word.

Suddenly, I knew.

Instinctively, I touched my phone in my pocket. Dad never texted me back.

Principal Davis suggested we sit. The door was shut, cutting me off from the outside world. Introductions were made, but I didn't hear anyone's name.

My head started pounding.

Aunt Barb sat across from me. The principal was to my right, the detective to my left. I looked around the room and noticed the uniformed officer at the door. His eyes were somber.

The detective spoke first. His expression was serious, but his tone sympathetic. As he spoke, Aunt Barb's eyes swam with tears. Mascara streaked across her cheek when she tried to catch the runaway river. She looked like hell.

I couldn't hear them.

I didn't want to know.

My head hurt.

My heart ached.

I was in a trance. This couldn't be real.

I watched the detective's lips move, but I only heard a few words. He spoke of an accident in the city, a car, and my dad.

Aunt Barb sat with her arms crossed, her well-manicured fingers curled into fists. She periodically dabbed a torn-up tissue to her eyes. Her golden-brown hair was tousled, not in its usual, perfect form. She was a beautiful woman, always well dressed and physically fit, except today.

Today, she was broken.

"Emma?" The detective called my name, more than once, I thought.

"Huh?" Was he talking to me? He looked familiar. Should he? My mind wandered. I couldn't concentrate.

"I know this is difficult," he said.

I heard noises in the hall. Voices, footsteps. The bell must have rung. Flashes of color passed the window, separating me from my life on the other side. It was lunchtime. Matt was going to have lunch with me.

Wait.

Was that Melissa's voice? I caught a glimpse of blonde hair and a purple shirt through the partially opened blinds. What was Melissa wearing today?

I had to get out of here.

"Emma, is there anything I can get for you?" Principal Davis put his hand on my shoulder.

"I… uh… I don't know."

I heard Aunt Barb's voice answer for me, but I couldn't register what she said.

The detective apologized for my loss. The uniformed officer nodded in consensus.

Dad was gone. Hit by a car on his way to work. Aunt Barb identified the body.

My dad's *body*.

"We'll gather your things from your locker, if you'd like," Principal Davis said in the same monotone voice he spoke with during announcements each morning. "Then you can head home." He paused, looked at me, and then to Aunt Barb for response.

"That would be nice, Mr. Davis. Thank you." She turned to me and reached for my hand. "Is that okay with you, Emma?" She hesitated for a moment. "Or would you like to do it yourself?"

I shook my head. Tears began to spill over the edges of my lids and down my cheeks. Aunt Barb pulled me to her, holding me while I cried. I closed my eyes tight and hoped this would all go away.

Everyone made small talk. Everyone that is, except Aunt Barb and me. The detective assured the uniformed officer he would drive us home. The principal offered condolences.

When the secretary came back with a bag full of the contents from my locker, it was time to go. While they could all go back to work, back to their daily routines in their normal lives, I could not.

My life, as I knew it, was over.

Chapter 5
Ben's Story

I watched her from the borrowed police car in the sweltering heat.

It wasn't noon, but the thermostat on the squad's dashboard registered 88 degrees. Officer Scott Michaels wasn't on duty—until I dropped in at the police station, that is. His uniform with badge and name tag hung neatly in his locker beside his gun belt. I slipped into his clothing, altered my appearance, and impersonated an officer. I had a discussion with the garage manager and took a squad for a few hours.

Discussion was my term. In reality, I compelled him. It was a tactic I seldom used. Molly did it all the time. It was a tool available to undercover agents, but one we weren't encouraged to use often. Even though the human had no residual effect, the remorse I felt lasted longer than it was worth. Of course, there were times I had no choice.

Today seemed like one of those times.

It was the date circled in thick, red marker on my calendar. The day I waited for since I learned the details of Emma's life. Today, Brian Bennett would transition. In my world, that meant he would move on. In Emma's world, it meant her father would die.

Sometimes, I hated knowing the future.

I drove around the neighborhood outside Highland Park High School. It was a series of dominos falling in sync that morning. First, there was the accident that killed Brian when he crossed Madison Avenue in downtown Chicago on his way to work. Then there were the phone calls to the various police departments looking for next of kin, and finally the one that reached his sister, Barbara Carmichael, in Westport, Wisconsin.

When a squad was requested to accompany another municipality on a notification call, I responded, being the closest to the high school.

I had to see Emma.

I adjusted the rearview mirror in the police car and watched the detective load Emma's things in the trunk. The reflection staring back at me was far different from my normal look, or any disguise I ever used. I had to resemble Officer Michaels, in the rare event I ran into anyone that knew him. He was thirty-eight, six-feet tall, and about ten pounds overweight. A little shorter than my actual height and older than I was when I died.

Disguising our appearance was one of the benefits of being an immortal. It was something Molly enjoyed. She enhanced her looks every chance she got. Of course, not all missions allowed her to resemble a runway model. For the most part, immortals chose an appearance they were happy with when they were alive.

Crandon, the detective, waved and drove out of the school lot. Emma didn't make eye contact with me as they passed by.

I heard her thoughts and felt her emotions long before I saw her in the hallway. It was a perk of the job, but it could also be a curse. Emma was cautious, nervous.

I couldn't blame her, knowing what she would face in the aftermath of this tragedy.

When she turned the corner and saw us clustered at the doorway, her feelings changed to fear with thoughts flashing quickly between insignificant teenager things. She didn't put it all together until she saw her aunt.

There was nothing I could do but witness her reaction.

Crandon explained how Brian Bennett was killed by a drunk driver, but Emma wasn't paying attention. Her thoughts swirled with recollections of her dad, her friends, school, and someone named Matt.

At one point, when our eyes locked, I almost blew my cover. Despite the look of pain on her face and the bloodshot eyes swimming with tears, she was beautiful. Deep down, behind the layers of innocence, she was the woman I once knew. It was my opportunity to compel Emma, to alleviate the sorrow, to release the block that prevented her from remembering me. It was my chance to save her. Instead, I looked away and did nothing.

Molly's voice screamed in my head, distracting the thoughts of my past life with Elizabeth. *Are you seriously at her school? Of all times to stalk her, Benjamin, what are you doing?*

I sighed.

Don't ignore me, Benjamin! How do you expect to get away with this? She was right. I crossed the line. *The commander will not condone this, and you know it,* Molly continued.

Being here was a mistake.

Chapter 6
Emma's Story

Detective Neal Crandon placed my things in the trunk of an unmarked police car.

Like a criminal, I sat in the back behind a Plexiglas divider.

"We're friends," Aunt Barb said. She sat in front. The emblem on the dashboard read Westport, Wisconsin. "The Highland Park Police Department called him this morning." Her tone was low. I didn't answer. Instead, I stared out the window during the short drive to my house.

Dad's house.

We pulled in the driveway on Cavell Street, and Neal shut off the engine. Even though I knew the house hadn't changed since I left a few hours earlier, it suddenly seemed different.

Aunt Barb got out of the car and retrieved the house key, leaving me alone with Neal.

"I forgot my car at school," I blurted out.

"I know. Barb and I'll take care of it." He turned to face me. "Right now, the most important thing is to get you home. I'll handle the rest."

I nodded when our eyes met.

Neal carried my backpack inside. I stood firmly on the concrete step, refusing to enter. The house was oddly silent. Chester, our four-year-old English Mastiff, didn't bark. He came bounding out to greet us, his tail wagging more sluggishly than normal. It was like he already knew.

Thoughts circled in my mind so quickly I had trouble sorting them out. I was frozen in place. Regret for arguing with Dad hit me hard. I gasped for air. Aunt Barb wrapped me up in her arms. Chester sat at our feet.

Then it dawned on me. Aunt Barb was all I had.

"Emma, I want you to know that I will take care of you." Tears poured down my cheeks. "I know this is the worst possible thing that could have happened, but you're not alone." She attempted a weak smile. "We're in this together."

I wanted to run and hide, but I knew I couldn't get away. I walked across the backyard and sat on the swing. Aunt Barb followed, sitting beside me.

"We'll need to make funeral arrangements… and then you'll come live with me." She swung slowly, lifting her feet so her heels wouldn't drag in the dirt.

Suddenly, I realized the impact of her words. "But—"

"I know. Your life is here."

My life here was over. I knew that back at school. "I'll have to move?"

"Yes. I'm sorry. Your dad and I talked about it, once. It was so far-fetched. I never thought it would happen." She gazed at the house. "He wanted me to take care of you… if anything ever happened. I promised I would." She wiped her eyes with a wadded tissue.

Aunt Barb was the only close family I knew. Living with anyone else was something I couldn't comprehend. But living with Aunt Barb meant giving up the only life I had ever known.

We rocked back and forth. Our feet barely left the ground. Aunt Barb told me what to expect over the next few days. Neal would be leaving and her friend, Lisa Lambert, would be coming to stay with us. "To help out."

It didn't matter to me. Nothing did. Not anymore.

When a black sedan pulled into the driveway minutes later, Aunt Barb greeted the blonde I remembered from visits to Lake Bell.

Lisa stood a few inches taller than Barb did, probably at about my height. She was slender with shoulder-length platinum hair and as kind as I remembered. Grabbing me, she hugged me hard. Her strength was infectious. "Honey, you'll be fine. I know it seems like the world is ending right now, but it's not. You'll see." She released her grip on me.

Was she for real?

Aunt Barb cleared her throat, and I noticed her glare. She squinted, lifting her eyebrows. Remembering my manners, I mumbled a thank you.

"Emma, can I have your car keys?" Neal interrupted. "Lisa and I will get your car." He turned to Aunt Barb. "A Jetta, right? Did you say it was silver?"

Why couldn't he ask *me* the type of car? I grabbed my keys from my bag and handed them over without saying a word.

Chapter 7
Ben's Story

Downtown Westport hadn't changed much.

A few storefronts were painted brighter colors, and a few eateries switched names and menus. For the most part, the four-block strip on the shores of Lake Michigan looked the same.

I parked atop the hill in front of Holy Name Church. It was where Elizabeth and I were married back in September of 1934. The carved-stone church was the largest in the area and the only catholic parish in Westport.

Father Richard Cornwell waved as I locked the borrowed silver Mercedes. He was the local priest assigned to Holy Name for over thirty years. He recognized my mid-forties disguise from frequent visits here when I searched for Elizabeth all those years.

The evening air was cool for late August. I walked the short distance to Rusty's Anchor on the harbor. My new assignment was a vacation compared to what Molly and I worked before. Serial killers, drug dealers, and other unsolved crimes were common missions for us. We aided victims and directed authorities to the culprits. We were decorated agents, a team with more tenure than any other officers on the force had. Most worked shorter assignments and lost interest after their loved ones joined our world. Not us.

Molly and I were the exceptions. She didn't have any loved ones to think about, and I spent years searching for Elizabeth, only to realize I missed her transition.

The last few years, however, were different. It was at a much slower pace. Commander E understood and concurred, allowing Molly and me to spend the next year or two in Westport.

"I can't afford to lose my top agents. If you both need some downtime, consider this an extended R and R," he said after the call came that Elizabeth had been found.

With that, plans were made, staff was assigned, and backstories structured. Molly and her fake parents, Grant and Ava Preston, moved to Westport from the East Coast a year earlier. At least, that was their cover story. Her parents were staff Sleeper Officers. In my world, that meant dormant duty. To me, that meant boring.

SOs, as we called them, infiltrated society, held jobs, owned houses, and participated in normal everyday life, except they were not human. They were dead, like me.

Dormant officers were in every city, ready to engage when called upon. Most spent their days like ordinary humans. Contracted for a decade or two, they were nurses or doctors, teachers or police officers. Empty nesters, they traveled in pairs, a husband and wife team. It allowed their term to be extended if needed, though most officers dreaded the aging disguise. It meant they had to be conscious of their appearance on a daily basis. Adding a wrinkle here or there, packing on a few pounds, and graying their hair, all little by little each day, so no human noticed a drastic change.

Dr. Grant Preston took a position at the county hospital. Ava Preston was a science teacher at Westport High School. Both were strategically placed where their special talents could be put to use.

For the next 730 days, I would be an SO, too.

Rusty, Jr. nodded when I walked into the bar and grill. I was disguised like a typical customer, middle-aged and well dressed. Rusty's Anchor had been around for generations. I took a seat at the bar and pulled out a couple of twenty-dollar bills. Rusty was the original owner's son. At fifty-eight years old, he wasn't in great health. He smoked, drank, and ate like shit, too many bar burgers and not enough exercise.

"Whadda'll ya have?"

I ordered a gin and tonic, and he hurried off to mix it up. It was a slow night, even for a Monday, eighteen minutes past nine o'clock. Small towns had a way of shutting down early, and Westport was no different. Aside from two rough-looking guys shooting pool and a man in his seventies paying his tab, the place was dead.

Rusty put the drink in front of me and made small talk. Was I in town for business? How long was I staying? Where was I from? I responded with made-up answers fitting for my designer silk shirt, trousers, and expensive penny loafers.

Aftermath

Time ticked away, slower on earth than where I was from. Minutes were seconds back home. I glanced at the clock behind the bar when Rusty filled a pitcher of beer for the tattooed man in the sleeveless black t-shirt.

Six minutes until Rusty's heart attack.

I sipped my drink and watched the football game on the TV above the bar. At least there was some entertainment to pass the time.

Rusty was oblivious to what the future held. He washed a few glasses and wiped down the counter. The cook and waitress checked in with him on their way out. I read their minds and his. *Good workers*, he thought. *Dedicated.*

Three minutes left.

The job of a Sleeper Officer was easy. Wait and observe. Observe and wait. It was nothing like the missions I worked all those years waiting for Elizabeth. This was simple. All I had to do was bring Rusty back to life. If it weren't for one of my kind, Rusty would die tonight. But it wasn't his scheduled time. His transition was set for 2024.

Two minutes left.

When the Chicago Bears scored, Rusty groaned. "I wanted them to lose."

I nodded. We were in Packer territory, after all.

"Ready for another?" He noticed my drink was almost empty.

"Sure." It would give him something to do.

One minute left.

The tough-looking guys were busy chugging beer and watching the game, in between shooting pool. Rusty put the drink in front of me, reached for my money on the counter, and turned toward the cash register. He never made it. Rusty slumped to the ground as the Bears scored again, and the tattooed man cheered.

I walked behind the bar and heard Molly's voice in my head.

Need any help?

I shrugged. *Why not? I always enjoy your company.* She was the sibling I never had.

I placed the palm of my hand on Rusty's chest, just above his heart. Molly slipped through a portal and crouched beside me.

Molly, you just can't pop in like that. There are some guys over there. I nodded in the direction of the pool players, though the bar blocked our view of them.

They can't see me. Besides, you wanted my help!

I rolled my eyes and lifted my forefinger, tapping it gently on Rusty's chest. I felt the gentle start of his heart under my hand.

Once it was beating at a steady pace, I looked at Molly.

I thought you were here to help. I waited for Molly to breathe oxygen into Rusty's lungs. *Or did you want me to do it?*

She shook her head. *No, I got it,* she said, and then hesitated, wrinkling her nose. *Man, he smells like an ashtray. What the hell?*

What the hell? I mimicked her words slowly. *You sound like a teenager.*

And you put me in this role, remember? She tilted her head and blinked her hazel gray eyes at me.

I chuckled aloud, accidentally.

The tattooed guy and his buddy heard the noise and called, "Hey, Rusty?"

Molly, you gotta get out of here. I don't feel like explaining your sudden presence, since you didn't walk through the door. Even though we were out of view, I knew it was a matter of time before someone peered over the bar and saw what was going on.

Hold on. She leaned down, about two inches from Rusty's face, and gently blew air toward him.

Ten seconds to disclosure, I said, knowing the tattooed guy was headed our way.

He's not breathing yet, Molly replied.

I stood up. "Call 911! Rusty had a heart attack."

The guy with the tattoo pulled out a cell phone, while his buddy finished his shot, as if nothing out of the ordinary was going on.

Rusty opened his eyes and looked at Molly, then at me.

I held his hand, flooding his mind with my thoughts. *This is your second chance. Make the most of it.*

He blinked rapidly. *Thank you.*

You're welcome, I answered, happy for a simple assignment.

Chapter 8
Emma's Story

My room used to be my sanctuary. Now it reminded me of what I lost.

Framed family photos lined my dresser. Ticket stubs from my first Chicago Bulls game were posted on the bulletin board next to my last birthday card from Mom. Brochures from colleges Dad and I toured were scattered on my desk. Printouts of applications and essays rested on top, including the form for Dad's alma mater. I told him I didn't want to attend Wisconsin. I wanted to go to Northwestern, like most of my friends.

That seemed trivial now.

When I noticed the flyer for the senior trip at Lake Bell, I remembered the argument with Dad. Tears flowed as I punched the feather pillow on my bed and buried my face in it. I hated this. Why did this happen to me?

Chester nudged my limp arm about an hour later. I must have dozed off. Rolling over, I stared at the ceiling. Chester lay beside me on the bed and rested his head on my stomach. We heard muffled voices coming from downstairs. Neither of us moved.

I glanced at the picture of Dad and me. It was taken on Lake Bell at Aunt Barb's house earlier that summer. Dad and I went Jet Skiing while Aunt Barb made dinner. It was the first time Dad let me drive a ski myself. Aunt Barb scolded him for being so protective. That was probably the only reason he gave in. I remembered his lecture about not speeding on the lake. I was impatient as he walked me through the instruments and attached the kill switch cord to my wrist.

Now, I'd give anything to have him lecture me again.

The buzz of my phone distracted me. I sat up and read through a handful of texts, most from Melissa. *Where did u go? Were you really talking to the cops? What happened? WHERE R U? Text me back.*

The last one was from Matt. *Did you leave?*

"Well, Chester... what do I do?" He tilted his head to one side, his dark ears slicked back. "Yeah, you're right. I need to tell them." Chester put his head down, letting out a loud sigh.

Formulating the words in my mind was easier than speaking them aloud. I typed, *my dad died*, and hit send.

Aunt Barb knocked gently on the door, opening it before I responded. "Just checking to see how you're doing." She looked better than before. Her eyes weren't as red and puffy.

"I'm okay."

"Neal and Lisa picked up Chinese. Come downstairs and join us."

I nodded and followed her to the kitchen. Placemats were already in position on the table. Aunt Barb pulled out plates and silverware, while Lisa filled glasses with wine. Neal waved her off, declining. The three of them interacted, opening boxes of takeout and scattering chopsticks and fortune cookies on the table. A cake sat on the counter, a fruit basket beside it. Things that weren't there when I left for school suddenly appeared.

For a second, I felt like a visitor in my own home. Anger struck me like a slap to the face. Tears ran down my cheeks without warning as the day's events sank in.

Lisa saw me first. She pulled me in her arms. "It's okay," she whispered through tears of her own. Aunt Barb joined in the waterworks, rubbing my back while I cried. After a few minutes, our tears dried up and we were able to compose ourselves.

Neal made himself scarce until everyone sat down for dinner. They made small talk between bites of Egg Foo Young and Mongolian Beef. I pushed rice around my plate, but no one seemed to notice. Lisa said she would stay with us for a few days, but Neal had to get back to Westport. Dad's wake was set for Thursday and the funeral for Friday morning. Lisa reported that Father Cornwell agreed to give mass.

"He's an old family friend," Aunt Barb said when she saw my glance.

Lisa spoke of Father Cornwell as if he were the Pope. I wanted to yell that he was just a priest from a small, hick Wisconsin town. Aunt Barb seemed pleased and the longer I sat there, the more I didn't care.

When the doorbell rang, Neal jumped up to answer it.

"Your neighbors have been dropping by all afternoon," Aunt Barb said.

"They have? Why?"

"It's what people do... in times like this," Lisa answered.

Aunt Barb nodded toward the fruit basket I noticed earlier. "They drop off food because they don't know what else to say, besides *sorry*." She shrugged as if that was acceptable.

I had no idea what I would say if this happened to someone I knew. Was that what people did when Mom died? I couldn't remember. I mean, what *did* you say? Sorry certainly wasn't it. I didn't want to hear "I'm sorry."

Sorry wouldn't bring my dad back, or my mom, for that matter. It wouldn't reverse the accident that killed Dad or cure the cancer that ended Mom's life. Sorry didn't make up for me having to leave my friends and move to Wisconsin. Sorry didn't dry up my tears or take away the ache in my heart.

Sorry just didn't cut it.

By the time Neal walked back into the kitchen, I was sick to my stomach with anger. He carried a red box from the Highland Park Bakery.

"Emma, you've got a friend here to see you," he said.

Tears poured out of my eyes when I saw Melissa in the doorway. She gave me a hug and whispered, "I'm so, so sorry."

Suddenly, that silly little word was comforting.

Chapter 9
Ben's Story

In all the years I spent undercover, I was never a high school student.

Hey, you structured this cover. Molly's voice rang in my head, as I followed the flow of annoying adolescents in the hallways of Westport High. *You could have waited to meet Emma when she was in college, or working her first job. Instead, you decided seventeen was the right age to introduce yourself.*

It wasn't her age. I timed it in the aftermath of her dad's transition, I responded in defense. I took a seat near the window in calculus. It was my first period of the first day of school.

Yes, yes, whatever! You dragged me along into this assignment, she muttered. *And I'm not any happier than you are, sitting through the secondary education system.*

You volunteered, I rebutted. *Remember? 'I could use a bit of down time, Commander'.* I mimicked her meeting with our leader when I came up with the idea several years earlier.

Molly sighed in defeat. I acknowledged Drew Davis. He took the seat behind me. Mr. Vieth called us to attention. Molly was greeted by her Spanish teacher in another classroom.

Are you two done bickering? Pete Jorgenson's voice interrupted Vieth's roll call.

We don't bicker, Molly replied.

Jorgenson knew better. As our handler, he was privy to every thought, comment, action, even feeling, our human disguises encountered on earth. It was part of our contract, succumbing to the tether, the bond between our world and an agent on assignment. It was an invisible leash that allowed him to keep tabs on our whereabouts at all times.

Right. And you were Mother Theresa in your last life, too, Jorgenson joked.

Ever since the pioneer field agent Victor Nicklas went rogue over a century ago, the tether was required. It didn't bother me.

Good luck in your senior year of high school. Jorgenson's chuckle echoed in my mind as Vieth called my name. I raised my hand, acknowledging my attendance.

Thanks.

And, stay out of trouble this time, Jorgenson curtly added. *I don't particularly like explaining your stupidity to the commander. It makes* me *look bad.*

What trouble?

Molly snickered.

Well, for starters, your compulsion of the garage attendant wasn't for the betterment of the case. And while we're on the subject, this assignment is a vacation for you. In other words, behave. I'd hate for Emma to get a bad impression of you.

I wanted to laugh, but I kept my composure. *Okay, okay. I'll make you proud.*

I'll check in on you later, Jorgenson said and signed off.

Even though Jorgenson closed the communication line, it was only in a hibernated state. He could still listen in. If I really wanted privacy, I'd have to break free of the tether. My rank gave me top-level security clearance and, with the skills developed over the years, I could easily do it. Of course, going off grid like that could only happen for a short period before a search team would be deployed.

Mr. Vieth began his first-day-of-school lecture. It consisted of the welcome-back, here's-who-I-am and here's-what-we-need-to-do-this-year speech. I already knew the ins and outs of calculus and of Vieth. I read his file weeks earlier when my schedule was posted. Born and raised in Westport, he was the son of two teachers, the great-grandson of Henry Nichols of the Nichols farm on Summit Road, where I worked back in the 1930s. Vieth was thirty-six years old, married, and a father of two. He had a dog, a cat, and a hefty mortgage.

Doing the math, I guessed old-Henry had to have transitioned by now. I rarely kept track of any humans I knew back then. Most immortals only monitored their loved ones until the last one passed. Very few lingered beyond one generation, the way Molly and I did. Molly was a career-agent. She enjoyed the excitement of being undercover more than experiencing life firsthand.

I, on the other hand, waited for Elizabeth.

Chapter 10
Emma's Story

The next few days were a blur.

Aunt Barb pulled out old albums and spread pictures all over the kitchen table. At first, my eyes started to water, but when she told stories about each photo, my tears dried up.

People continued to stop by as the news spread. Platters of food, baskets of fruit, and boxes of pastries filled the counters and refrigerator in our small house. Aunt Barb was right. No one knew what to say, even though the phone rang off the hook. Instead, most people just dropped off stuff.

Matt stopped by after football practice, but he didn't stay long.

Neal came back the day of the wake. I heard his footsteps as I sat on the couch, wishing this were all a dream.

"She's upstairs." I assumed he was looking for my aunt.

He paused for a minute. I could tell he wanted to say something.

"Emma, I want you to know how sorry I am. To have been the one to break the news." He hesitated, took a deep breath, and continued. "Your aunt wasn't ready to talk, that day." He looked sincere, and it dawned on me how much he must care for her.

"It's okay. Someone had to tell me."

"Well, what happened is not okay." Neal sat down on the edge of the cushion next to me. "What you've experienced is… well, it's unimaginable. Unfortunately, none of us have control over that. We can only pick up the pieces and try to put them back in some semblance of order."

He looked me in the eyes and I saw concern, like the look my dad used to give me. The thought brought tears to my eyes. "I don't know if Barb tells you this enough, but she loves you. I mean, she really loves you. You're like a daughter to her. She talks about you all the time—about your soccer games, about how well you're doing in school. She's really proud of you. Did you know that?"

I shrugged.

"Well, she is."

The silence that followed made me realize he was human, just like me. He wasn't the intimidating police officer I expected him to be. He attempted a weak smile. "I didn't know she talked about me… to you."

"Not just to me—to Lisa, to her friends. You're a big part of her life."

I guessed I already knew that.

"You know, Westport isn't that bad of a town to live in. It's smaller than what you're used to, but I think you'll like it." He grinned. "I hope so, anyway."

***

Zimmerman Funeral Home looked the same as it did when Mom died. The deep red carpet with gold pattern made me nauseous. I remembered it from being there six years earlier.

I made my way to the same chenille wing chair and sat down. Aunt Barb spoke to the sad-looking, heavyset funeral director. He wore a dark suit and looked vaguely familiar.

Neal sat in the matching chair beside me. We were separated by a small, round, marble-top table with a tall lamp, and prayer cards fanned out in a perfect semi-circle. I looked at the rich colors of the saint pictured on the cards, but I didn't dare touch them. Neal must have sensed my stare. He picked one up and told me what I already knew. "There's a prayer on the back, for your dad. See?" He flipped over the card and showed me the written confirmation of why we were there.

When the funeral director opened the double doors, it was time. Aunt Barb nodded to me, "Ready?"

Ready was far from my state of preparedness.

My stomach started to ache. I crossed the threshold and saw Dad's casket at the back of the room. It was surrounded by plants and flowers of all sizes and colors. They were everywhere—on the casket, on the floor, and on stands that lined the walls of the room. The mixed floral scents stopped me for a moment. My nausea returned, and I contemplated turning around and running away. When my knees started to buckle, I was suddenly happy Aunt Barb talked me into low heels instead of the strappy, black sandals with four-inch spikes I wanted.

"It'll be okay," Neal spoke softly behind me, while Aunt Barb proceeded ahead of us. I felt his hand on the back of my shoulder. "Are you alright?"

My body began to shake, and I couldn't stop it. I turned quickly, hoping to escape to the safety of the foyer. Instead, I ran straight into Neal's chest. He smelled of cologne. A different scent than my dad wore, but a nice, comforting smell that I breathed in deeply. "It's okay." Neal held me until my shaking stopped.

Aunt Barb and Neal waited patiently for me to pull myself together.

Dad's casket was beige with small flower accents carved into the corners. It was the same casket Dad picked out for Mom.

It was like time stood still.

The room was absolutely quiet. No music, no hum from a fan, no voice from a soul.

I focused on the shiny finish of the casket and the bouquet of red flowers that rested on it. I refused to look at him. Like a Ping-Pong match, my eyes scanned back and forth, but never settled on Dad. I noticed the photo collages Lisa helped us make, the gold drapes that matched the chairs in the room, and the cards attached to each plant nearby. But when Aunt Barb touched Dad's hand, I was finally forced to look at him.

Dad doesn't look like Dad, I thought. His skin was discolored and thick, like candle wax. He had wrinkles I never saw before. His hair was combed back and gelled in perfect lines—not the way he usually wore it, messy with a few strands off to the side.

I looked at Aunt Barb in hopes my glare would convey my concern that this wasn't my dad. This body wasn't her brother, Brian Bennett.

Instead, her tearful eyes told me I was wrong.

***

Father Cornwell was the first guest to arrive and the most talkative. He held my hand the entire time he recited stories from when I was little. As much as I didn't want to listen, I had no choice. When he finally moved on, a surge of strength came over me.

Odd, but for a split second, things didn't seem that bad.

The Lamberts were next. Having spent a few days with Lisa, I was happy to see her again. She gave me a tight hug and whispered kind words in my ear. Tom, her husband, did the same.

When TJ Lambert came through the line, I didn't recognize him. He was taller than the last time I saw him and offered condolences in a deep man's voice. He was the opposite of the skinny boy I kissed all those years ago.

TJ's sister, Hannah, stood a few inches shorter than her mom did, but she had the same blonde highlights and bubbly personality. She practically bounced in place while waiting her turn. If she wasn't a cheerleader, she missed her calling. She gave me a huge hug, like we were long-lost friends. Then again, we were friends all those summers ago on the lake—TJ, Hannah, and me—but with time and distance, those friendships faded, and now they seemed like strangers.

Keep them moving, a voice in my head said. *Just keep them moving and you'll be fine.* I nodded, responding to my own thoughts.

People came and went for hours. Melissa came with her mom, other friends showed up in a group, and distant cousins strolled through. It was tiring.

When visitation was almost over and the line was winding down, I saw Matt. I lost it the minute our eyes met. Tears flowed in a constant stream. Like everyone else in line, Matt offered sympathy but, instead of a handshake, he pulled me into his arms and let me cry. I buried my face in his chest and concentrated on not hyperventilating. Breathing in his fresh scent slowly, I tried to calm myself while he held me.

"Hey," he whispered. "It'll be alright."

Matt hugged me twice as long as anyone else did and when he was ready to move on, I still wasn't.

Chapter 11
Ben's Story

"Whatever you do, don't order the casserole of the day," Drew Davis said when we reached the cafeteria entrance.

I glanced at him. "That bad?"

He shook his head. "Not if you like left-over leftovers with some cheese sprinkled on top." A smirk crossed his face.

I would have laughed, but I knew he was right. Even the lunch lady that scooped a heaping spoonful had sympathetic thoughts when she handed the plate to the kid in front of me.

Claire, my undercover twin sister, acknowledged me with a grin from the salad bar. Drew took notice of her, but he didn't comment. I didn't need to be an immortal to know where his mind was going. I tuned out the idea and moved forward in line.

I grabbed a sub and a coke and paid my bill. Justin Zore and a few other soccer teammates slid over on the bench when they saw Drew and me headed their way. Claire smiled at Drew as we took seats near her. She sat with Hannah Lambert and a couple of cheerleaders. As if on cue, the girls turned to look at us. Justin smiled at Hannah, who blushed in return.

Drew finished his first slice of pizza before I had my pre-packaged sandwich unwrapped.

Molly walked past my table with a strawberry blonde-haired girl and waved. The blonde wore short shorts, exposing her long legs. She paused, smiling at me, and then followed Molly to Claire's table.

"Only a few days here and you already know the hot, popular chicks?" Drew was being sarcastic.

"Who? *Molly*?" I asked in a surprised tone, knowing she was listening in.

"Molly *and* Stephanie," he answered. They were out of earshot, but both girls turned to look at us anyway.

"Molly lives down the street from me."

"I'm moving to your neighborhood." Drew bit into his second slice of pizza.

Stephanie chewed on her lower lip, and then broke into a full smile, while Molly grinned.

Drew elbowed me just as I was about to take another bite of my sandwich. "Hey, looks like they're interested."

"I wouldn't go there if I were you," Justin commented between forkfuls of spaghetti. Justin was our team's goalie and from what I could tell, he was the most sensible kid among them.

Drew let out a laugh before Justin finished his sentence. "Why not? Steph's available and with legs like that?"

"They're both taken. That's why not," Justin explained, and then took the last bite of his lunch.

Huh? Molly's taken?

"Not from what I heard," Drew said. "Lucas and Steph broke up."

"Again? They break up every other day." Justin pushed his empty food tray to the side. When he looked at me, he continued. "If they're off today, they'll be back together tomorrow."

I nodded.

"This time, it's real," Drew said.

"Who can keep up? And who cares?" Justin took a drink of Gatorade.

Drew lowered his voice. "He picked up some chick in Riverside. I heard he stayed at her place last weekend."

"Her place?" I asked. "How old is this girl?"

Drew glanced around before he answered. "Like twenty-something. Blonde hair, big boobs, drives a sports car. Has a condo on the west side of town."

"You're crazy." Justin laughed.

"Shhh…" Drew scolded. "I was sworn to secrecy, man. He didn't want Stephanie to get wind of it. You know… in case it doesn't work out. He wants to keep in good graces with her."

I shook my head, finishing my sub.

"So you *actually* believe this?" Sarcasm oozed out of Justin's serious tone.

I chuckled, and Justin laughed.

Drew shook his head and finished eating. "Real funny."

"He's making up stories. You know he's living with his mom, right?"

Justin added.

"His mom's a whack job," Drew said, staring at Justin. He turned to me and whispered. "He got busted with some pot this summer. His dad freaked and threw him outta the house. Now he lives with his mom. Or, he's supposed to, anyway. I don't think she knows if he's there or not."

"There's no way some hot chick with a condo and a sports car is into Lucas," Justin said in a hushed voice.

"I'm telling you, there is."

"Have you seen her?"

I cleared my throat before Drew could answer. He looked up. Molly and Stephanie stood in front of us.

"Hey, guys," Molly said. Drew and Justin mumbled hellos. "Ben, I was wondering if you could give me a ride home after school."

"Yeah, sure."

"Oh, and this is my friend, Stephanie Carlson. Steph, this is Ben Parker," Molly said. "He's the new neighbor I was telling you about. You met his sister, Claire. They just moved here."

"Nice to meet you, Stephanie."

"Hi, Ben." Her smile was intense. "Where did you live before?" she asked after an awkward pause.

"Libertyville, Illinois."

"Oh, I haven't heard of it." She twirled a lock of her long hair as she spoke.

"So I'll meet you out front?" Molly asked. *Will you be back from Emma's dad's funeral by then?*

"Yeah. I'll catch you later," I answered to both of her questions. They smiled and turned to leave.

I'm so sorry. Stephanie begged me to introduce you, Molly explained.

Great. That's all I need.

Drew elbowed me again, and I made a mental note never to sit beside him again. He let out a low chuckle. "Man, Stephanie's into you!"

I took a drink of coke to avoid his annoying topic of conversation. Stephanie glanced over her shoulder when she reached the door. I felt another set of eyes on me and turned to see a light-haired guy staring back. He looked away as our eyes met.

"Who's Lucas, anyway?" I asked, guessing I already knew.

Justin looked around, and then nodded toward the door. "He's over there... walking out of the cafeteria. The tall, blond guy in the blue shirt."

That was what I thought.

Chapter 12
Emma's Story

We arrived at St. Mary's Catholic Church an hour before the scheduled visitation.

When I was a kid, I thought the church looked like a huge ship pulling up to shore. Her vast wall of windows angled back like the bow of a ship, stopped only by hedges and sidewalks that circled her shores.

It was a large parish, Mom used to say. That was when we went to church. We went every week when I was a kid, before Mom died.

There were two parking lots, one on each side of the massive windows. Dad always parked in the lot on the right. The North Lot, he called it. We came in from that side. It was the closest parking spot he once told me, when I asked why we always parked in the same place. That morning when Neal pulled in, we parked in the south lot, on the opposite side of the church. A different spot than normal.

That was what I was now, I realized. Different.

The church looked the same as the last time Dad and I went to mass at Christmas, minus the decorations, of course. After Mom died, we only went to mass on holidays or when Aunt Barb was in town. Dad didn't suggest going, and I didn't ask why

I noticed Dad as soon as we walked in. His casket was against the wall in the church entry, between religious paintings and glowing sconces. A kneeler was placed off to one side of the casket with tall candles on the other. Aunt Barb walked right up to Dad, made the sign of the cross, and stood silent. Neal was an arm's distance away. I, on the other hand, loitered as far from the casket as possible. I couldn't bring myself to move.

Memories of Mom's funeral flooded my mind, as Aunt Barb and Neal greeted the parish priest, Father Cornwell, and the funeral director.

I blinked away tears and looked around. *You can do this,* a deep voice in my head said. I repeated the words. I *could* do this.

Dad's casket had a few bouquets nearby, and others scattered around the church. Aunt Barb said we could pick a few plants to take home, if I wanted. The rest she would donate. I didn't care. I didn't want them. Why would I want to be reminded of where they came from?

A few people busied themselves preparing for the mass. Photo collages were set up next to bouquets of flowers. A book guests were expected to sign was placed on a podium, and pamphlets were arranged on rolling bookcases.

Before I knew it, people streamed in and greeted Aunt Barb, while Neal stood with me. He didn't say much, though at one point, he asked if I wanted a glass of water or an Altoids mint from the tin he pulled out of his coat pocket. I shook my head. I never liked Altoids.

***

When Father Cornwell gave the last prayer, the congregation was dismissed. It was eerily quiet as we proceeded down the aisle following the casket containing my dad. Few words were spoken on the drive to the cemetery, either.

The air was still when we arrived. Aunt Barb, Neal, and I followed the pallbearers to the open gravesite. Light dew remained on the grass and wet my toes as we passed through areas of shade. The moisture beaded on my sandals.

When Dad's casket was properly positioned over the open gap in the ground, the funeral director placed a floral bouquet on top. The wide, white ribbons with gold letters spelling out "Loving Father" and "Loving Brother" swayed in the gentle breeze.

We took seats in front row, graveside. More people came than I expected. The last car in the procession was an expensive-looking silver sedan. A tall man with gray hair and a dark suit got out. I recognized him from the church, though I had no idea who he was.

Father Cornwell stood near the red granite headstone that was so familiar to me. Dad and I visited here often, every Saturday at first, right after Mom died, but less often lately. I stared at the cross and streamlined single flower engraved in the center of the stone, remembering when Dad and I picked it out. He originally wanted other flowers, a bouquet, he told me. I told him Mom would like this one better. The lady at the stone place called it some kind of lily. It was long and thin, with a trumpet-shaped blossom on a single stem. "Are you sure?" Dad asked me that day. "Are you sure she wouldn't like this basket of flowers engraved on the stone?" he pressed.

I shook my head. "No. She'd like the lily."

When Dad tilted his head to the side, I knew he was considering it. He always had the same look when he was deep in thought. He pinched the bridge of his nose with his forefinger and thumb for a just a second before outlining his cheeks and jawbone with his fingers in one quick swoop. When he completed the invisible drawing on his face, and his finger and thumb met once again at his chin, the decision was made. "We'll take the lily," he told the lady at the counter. Then, he winked at me.

Dad and I would bring lilies to Mom every Saturday after that. Well, at least in the beginning. When my Saturdays got booked with sports and school activities, and when Dad was busy running me around, our weekly visits to Mom's grave lessened.

Things changed.

Our Saturday routine changed. Instead of going to the diner downtown for breakfast, then to the small flower shop on the corner, I grabbed a granola bar and ran out of the house, while Dad ordered flowers from the discount supercenter. The order changed from a weekly spray to a monthly sprig. Then winter came, and no order was placed at all.

The last time Dad and I came to visit was Mother's Day. Even then, we just checked that the floral shop delivered the flowers as scheduled.

I couldn't pull my gaze from the headstone with the names of my parents carved deeply into its surface. I stared so hard, my eyes burned. When tears erupted again, the letters blurred together as one. I wiped quickly, hoping no one noticed. I looked around, trying to focus on something—anything—to distract me from the stone, the grave, and from Dad.

My eyes settled on a brown-haired man near a large oak tree.

I blinked, squinted, and looked again.

He hovered around the trunk, slowly pacing back and forth with his hands in his pant pockets.

When Aunt Barb gave my arm a gentle squeeze, I lost sight of him. I scooted forward in my seat to get a better view, but he was no longer walking. Instead, he stood facing the tree. He tilted his head to the side like he was deep in conversation. It was oddly familiar.

Father Cornwell raised his hands to the gathered crowd and began to pray. Everyone stood and bowed their heads. I found myself unable to concentrate. There was something intriguing about the man in the distance.

The brown-haired man brought his hand to the bridge of his nose, and

I began to feel sick to my stomach. When he quickly slid his hand to his chin, my heart raced.

Father Cornwell continued his prayer, but I didn't listen.

There was pressure in my chest, and I had a hard time catching my breath. I concentrated on inhaling and exhaling and watched the man. I focused on him, staring until he turned to look at me. I was convinced he saw me.

I was afraid to move, afraid to blink.

Then he smiled, and I knew.

The man at the tree was my dad.

I glanced at Aunt Barb for just a second. I wanted to nudge her, to tell her I saw Dad. But when I looked back at the tree, he was gone, replaced by a dark-haired woman in a black suit.

Was my mind playing tricks on me?

The tall, gray-haired man from the expensive car walked beside the woman from the tree. She leaned into him, clutching his arm as they reached the back row of guests.

"Eternal rest grant unto him, O Lord," Father Cornwell said.

"And let perpetual light shine upon him," Aunt Barb whispered beside me.

"May he rest in peace."

"Amen," the crowd responded in unison and slowly began to dissipate.

The service was over.

Aunt Barb reached for my hand. It was time to go. I looked for the man but didn't see him or the woman he was with.

When I got a good view of the road, I realized his car was already gone.

Chapter 13
Ben's Story

My blood pressure was still elevated.

"What the hell was Brian Bennett doing at his own funeral?" Molly and I sat in a corner booth at a diner in downtown Highland Park after the cemetery service. The restaurant was empty, except for a well-dressed couple at a table nearby.

"From what I understand, his case worker turned her back for a second, or so she says. She's new. First solo assignment." Molly opened a menu.

I shook my head in disgust. Having been a Field Training Officer years before, I knew the first rule was never to release an agent prematurely. Today's incident was cause for a citation. "Who's the FTO?"

"You didn't look?" She glanced at me and then continued, not waiting for my reply. "I'm sure it's in the file. I didn't pay much attention. If you want my opinion, she was released from training too early. These rookies today aren't what they used to be."

I ignored her.

"Are you even hungry? Didn't you have lunch at school?" she asked. It was a little after two o'clock.

I shrugged. "You really can't call the cafeteria food a good lunch. Besides, my teenage body needs all the nourishment it can get."

"Hmm. Except, you're disguised as a fifty year old right now, wouldn't you say?" She smiled, put the menu down, and glanced at the specials written on the chalkboard.

"Nice." I shook my head.

"So about Brian Bennett—" I began, after the waitress took our order.

"You seem to have forgotten how new admissions are. They rarely want to leave their life behind, so they find a way back."

I sighed. She was right. Almost every admittent looked for an escape and Brian did just that, slipping through a portal at the cemetery that morning. Molly appeared after I pulled Brian behind a tree. I heard him coming. He sounded like a freight train chugging its way through a sleeping town.

"I'm glad you came when you did," I said. Brian's thoughts were loud, full of anger and confusion. Admittents were rarely stable, their energy volatile. I didn't want to startle him, but leaving him unattended had the potential for worse consequences, like human detection, which happened. "Emma saw her dad. She recognized him," I said, though Molly already knew that. She heard my page to dispatch. It was standard protocol for an unsupervised, untrained immortal on earth. "Fortunately, you got there in time to deceive her."

"Yes. She'll get over it. After all, she's full of emotions right now. In a few days, she won't even remember seeing him," Molly answered.

"Nice disguise, by the way."

Molly aged herself a couple of decades older than her natural age when she died. In the pencil skirt and blazer she wore to the cemetery, she reminded me of how she looked on our first assignment together, back in 1947. I was undercover as an adolescent boy. She played the role of my mother that cold February evening when we boarded the Red Arrow train in Detroit.

"What are you saying? I'm completely presentable for the cemetery service." She glared.

"Yes, very appropriate," I agreed. Molly had a thing for always looking her best. She was meticulous with her choice of clothing, hairstyle, and makeup. I told her not to worry about her appearance that night, as our train crossed into Pennsylvania. She patted her cheeks with pressed powder and applied red lipstick, anyway. Molly was never a mother in real life. Pretending to be maternal on assignment was a stretch for her.

"Benjamin Parker Holmes, why is that smirk on your face?"

"Wow. Full, formal name. You know I shorten it for assignments, right? I must be in trouble." I chuckled, and then remembered the first time she called me by my human birth name on our first assignment. It was after our passenger car derailed and tumbled down the embankment outside of Altoona. I wasn't prepared for what I saw. I was fresh out of the academy and inexperienced. Cries from the injured pinned amongst the wreckage distracted me from my mission to lead the newly deceased to their waiting guides. Molly's piercing voice snapped me back to attention that night.

"Not yet. It's still early," she said with a smug smile.

The waitress delivered our drinks and left without a word.

"Bianca says hello," Molly said.

"Is that right?"

"She's still upset." She took a sip of her iced tea. "She doesn't understand why you didn't pick her."

I took a deep breath, attempting to remain calm. This wasn't the first time Bianca expressed disappointment, and I was quickly tiring of it.

"She reminded me that she graduated top of her class and should have been awarded this post. After all, she's spent time in the field, like you suggested. She said she's paid her dues… And Claire… well, she's fresh out of the academy."

"We both know why Claire is here," I answered, firmly.

"Yes. You made that very clear. Bianca doesn't understand. That's all."

"What's to understand?"

"Ben, she's convinced there's chemistry between the two of you."

"Never. You know that. And I chose someone else for the job. Period."

Molly was quiet for once, both verbally and mentally.

"Besides, you know I have a soft spot for—" I began.

"I know, I know. You like reconciling families," she mumbled.

Molly didn't understand the importance of family. She never left anyone behind. She never searched for a loved one or waited for them to join her in our world. My need to find Elizabeth was completely foreign to her.

"Then you need to explain that to Bianca the next time she's here," she blurted out.

"I don't owe Bianca Beringer anything," I answered as our food was served.

"May I trouble you for another slice of lemon?" Molly asked the waitress. Her British accent hinted in the air, so I knew I was getting on her nerves. Molly was born and raised in London, though she told no one of her past life. None of the other agents we worked with ever heard her history and never would, if she had anything to say about it. Of course, no other agent worked with her as long as I did.

I sprinkled a good dose of salt over my meatloaf and mashed potatoes, but I avoided the pepper. Piperine had an adverse effect on our immortal powers. "Ena-thin' else I can get cha?" the waitress asked when she returned.

"No, that will be all. Thank you." Molly stared at me as she responded. Annunciation was her biggest pet peeve. The "cha" was nails on a chalkboard, scratchy and whiny.

"Are you sure you weren't an English teacher in a past life?" I whispered after the waitress was out of earshot.

"Okay, I'll tone it down." She took a bite of her chicken wrap.

"It's fine for your current disguise. But I'm hoping your *popular* friends at Westport High School never saw the formal side of you. You wouldn't fit in." I raised my eyebrows and smiled.

"Right. *My* high school *friends*." She grinned as images of students she met over the past year filtered through her thoughts, then into mine. I wondered which guy was her boyfriend, but thought to keep that under wraps until another time. "Your friends too, I might add. As soon as you get to know them and we get out of this disguise." Her tone on the latter part confirmed her disappointment with me when I requested a middle-aged character at the cemetery.

You couldn't show up looking like a teenager, I thought. *It was a funeral. And Emma will run into you in high school.*

Eventually. Her firm tone echoed in my head.

"Sooner than later." I took a bite of my meatloaf. Not as good as my mother's cooking when I was a kid. Then again, I never found human food to be as flavorful since I died.

Molly was silent for a moment, and then said aloud, "I heard you were pretty impressive on the soccer field. I guess your training went well."

I nodded, swallowing the gravy-covered meat. "I had a great time. I can't say Claire enjoyed it." My partner and I had to train in soccer, Emma's favorite sport. One of the requirements in any undercover assignment was to get to know your target's likes and dislikes. Learning soccer was a requirement that Claire knew when she took the assignment. She just didn't like it.

"I gathered that," Molly said. "She's not terribly athletic, but she's stirred some interest amongst the young lads since she's arrived. Her golden-blonde hair and long, bouncy curls turned a few heads."

I put my fork down and looked into her eyes. "Jealous the attention's off you?" I waited for a response. Molly was exceptionally attractive. Her dark hair and gray eyes made many men go weak in the knees. Both humans and other immortals, including other agents we had worked with.

She remained silent, though her thoughts were teetering on anger.

"This oughta be fun. I can't wait to be a seventeen year old again." I smirked, and then realized that being seventeen was probably not the age most people would want to repeat.

I, on the other hand, enjoyed it. It was when I first met Elizabeth.

Chapter 14
Emma's Story

There was a brief moment when I first opened my eyes that I forgot.

I was me again—a high school senior looking forward to homecoming and graduation, applying for college, and hanging out with friends. That tiny split second of time disappeared as quickly as it came. The happiness and security I felt were suddenly replaced with pain and uncertainty.

I remembered.

It was the day after Dad's funeral. The day the rest of the world went back to normal. Everyone returned home and back to school. My world was turned upside down.

I heard clinking noises downstairs and found Aunt Barb putting a pan into the oven. She couldn't sleep either, she said. It was six o'clock, yet she was already dressed in khaki shorts and a pale pink polo shirt with some embroidery on the sleeve. She looked like she was headed to the golf course with her long, light brown hair pulled loosely back. She wore a slim pair of blue-framed glasses resting low on her nose, but removed them when she explained our plan for the day.

It wasn't the first time I heard it, like I didn't remember our discussion the night before, or the morning before that. The plan, she told me, was to pack up enough stuff to last me a week at her house. Then we'd come back and officially move. I got it. I had to move. Nothing else mattered. I had to leave everyone I knew here behind.

She must have sensed my mood because she suddenly became quiet. Clutching her coffee cup with both hands, she laced her fingers together.

"I've been thinking, Emma," she began. "Did your dad ever tell you about the old house I renovated on Lake Michigan?"

I shrugged. Aunt Barb always fixed up old houses. She practically renovated every house on Lake Bell, especially those around the Carmichael Inn. It wasn't until I was older that I realized she and Uncle Rob owned the inn and that the homes Aunt Barb fixed up were rentals on their property.

"Rob and I bought the house years ago. We planned to live there."

I nodded, encouraging her to continue.

"I let it sit after my husband died." She hesitated, her eyes focused on the contents of her mug. A moment later, she continued. "Then one day, your dad talked me into fixing it up. I think he knew it would be good for me. You know, to get my mind off Rob." She took a sip of coffee. "Anyway, I think it would be the perfect new beginning for us." Her smile was contagious. I saw the excitement in her eyes and realized I couldn't be grumpy anymore.

The wild, fun aunt I used to shop with was back.

Aunt Barb pursed her lips, raised her eyebrows, and tipped her head to one side. Dad used to call it her mischievous look. She proceeded to tell me about the Victorian on a bluff overlooking the shores of Lake Michigan.

"It needed a lot of work when we bought it," she said. "You should've seen it. It was a disaster!"

I felt the pride she had in her work. She was an accomplished architect with an eye for interior design, pairing period homes with modern amenities. At least, that was what the Midwest Architectural Digest reported on her work last year, when they highlighted a few of her homes on Lake Bell.

I wasn't sure if I would like the house, but with her excitement for it, I couldn't help but hope.

Chapter 15
Ben's Story

I couldn't sleep.

It was the third time in the past hour I woke up. The sun wasn't out yet. I prepared for this since Molly called me at the lake to tell me she found Elizabeth.

I should be ready, yet nerves got the best of me.

Numbers flowed through my mind. 12219212129605102016. In my world, the numeric series represented a call dispatch received. Millions of requests came in annually. Human thoughts, pleas, and wishes were logged. Few cases were investigated.

This sequence of digits was different. It identified a seventeen-year-old girl named Emma, the woman I loved and lost. My wife Elizabeth's life contract was scheduled to terminate in 1972. Except, it didn't happen that way. Elizabeth died in 1954, along with 71,046 others that same day.

I didn't know it at the time.

The day she died, I was stationed in Plainfield, Wisconsin, covering Ed Gein, a serial killer the world came to hate. I was oblivious to what was going on back in my world. Molly and I were deep undercover. We were part of an exclusive division of the Special Investigative Unit.

We were activated once Gein stopped robbing cemeteries and started engaging in abduction and murder. We knew it would happen. It was simply a matter of time.

Molly was one of his first victims. As an immortal, however, no human reported her missing. No newspaper reported her amongst the victims. No name was assigned to the body parts police found years later, remnants of her fake human corpse.

By 1957, our mission was complete, and Molly and I were reassigned.

I didn't realize Elizabeth had already transitioned. I didn't even alert anyone in Admissions to look for her, to let her know I was waiting. After all, I still had fifteen years.

While I waited for her, I chose cases in Wisconsin. I wanted to be close to where I thought Elizabeth lived. I expected her to be in Wisconsin, near Lake Bell, where we met. Finding her should have been easy. All I had to do was listen for her voice. It was how immortals kept track of loved ones, or our targets. If only I found her voice.

With the prosecution of Ed Gein, Molly and I were awarded assignments that were more delicate. It was a tough job being assigned to one serial killer case after another. Of course, there was no pain in the torture our immortal bodies endured during any attack. Instead, the mental trauma endured by human victims we befriended affected our spirits as we read their thoughts and felt their emotions.

It was a stressful division for an operative. My partnership with Molly grew stronger over those years, and our senses hardened. We were no longer quietly sobbing for the pain victims felt during their deaths. Instead, we looked the other way.

I hated myself on those occasions I couldn't protect the innocent. I imagined how disappointed Elizabeth would be if I didn't help. That was when I took matters into my own hands. It promoted me to higher profile cases. Molly and I were given authorization no other agents had. We were suddenly exempt from the rules and regulations other divisions abided by.

The power and recognition meant nothing without Elizabeth. Between cases, I continued my search.

I was confident Elizabeth was alive in Wisconsin, and I expected to find her.

Chapter 16
Emma's Story

"Your friends miss you already, huh?" Aunt Barb asked after my phone buzzed.

It was the fifth text from Melissa in the first thirty minutes of our drive to Westport.

"Yeah," I said, and then confessed my friends were headed to Lake Bell for the annual senior trip. I told her about the party at Lewis' house, but intentionally left out the part about staying overnight and the fact that Dad and I argued about it the morning he died.

"Hmm… I never realized Kathy's son was your age," Aunt Barb said. "Or, that he went to your school, for that matter. You know, I should call her."

I shot her a sideways glance.

"It might be good to surround ourselves with people. You know. Get back into some kind of routine." She focused on the road, looking at me occasionally out of the corner of her eye.

"Ah, yeah." I was anxious to see Melissa, but I wasn't sure I wanted to spend a lot of time with anyone else. Even Matt.

Was that wrong of me?

Aunt Barb dialed before I realized what she was doing. She juggled her phone against her shoulder as she drove. It was obvious she reached Kathy Warner as one-sided conversation filled the air. Aunt Barb seemed sad one minute and then laughed the next. Clearly, they were friends. Was that was good for me or not?

"We'll stop at home for a few minutes. Then I'll drop you off at Kathy's, okay?" Aunt Barb asked after a series of phone calls.

There was a brief silence after the word "home" fell off her tongue. She appeared to grip the steering wheel tighter for an instant before she spoke again. She probably hoped I didn't catch on. "Kathy said a few of the kids were staying overnight at her house." Aunt Barb looked at me briefly, and then turned back to staring at the road in front of us. "The rest are staying at cabins. Did you know that?"

I nodded, though I wasn't sure she saw me.

"She said you could stay at her house. I understand Melissa will be there." She changed lanes, and then continued. "I don't mind. I mean, I'll probably go into the office. I might work late. You know… having been gone a few days."

"Yeah, okay. That would be great." Wow. Did she just say I could stay overnight? Dad would have never offered that.

We rode for a few minutes in silence before Aunt Barb turned on the radio. A familiar beat filled the air and put me in a better mood. It was my favorite song. I wanted to turn it up, but I didn't dare touch the control. Glancing over at my aunt, I noticed she was mouthing the words. When I started singing, she smiled. She turned up the volume, and we sang loudly. I had no idea Aunt Barb knew the words or liked my kind of music.

Maybe living with her wouldn't be so bad.

The thought came and left quickly, leaving me with a layer of guilt. Was I betraying my dad? When Aunt Barb smiled again, I knew Dad would want it that way.

The ride to Westport went faster than I expected. Our conversation and singing off-key helped pass the time.

When we reached Aunt Barb's house on Lake Bell, I let Chester out of the SUV. Back home, he knew the boundaries of our yard and didn't venture outside of them. I wasn't thinking when I let him loose in new surroundings.

Chester ran nose to the ground around the side of the house and out of sight before I could get his name off my lips. "Chester!" I took off in pursuit. He was never a bad dog, just adventurous. By the time I caught up with him on the lakeside of the house, he finished his job and ran to the patio door at the lower level. Aunt Barb must have heard me because she was already opening the door for both of us to come in.

Inside, Chester was just as nosy. He went from room to room, though Aunt Barb didn't seem to mind. "He'll settle down. He's just curious," she said when I tried calling him back. It wasn't the first time he'd been at her house. We brought him every visit. I just never paid attention to what he did, before.

Aunt Barb's house looked the same as it did the last time I was there. Except that this time, things were different. "Put your suitcase upstairs," she said while she flipped through the mail on the granite kitchen counter.

"Okay."

I put my bag on the floor between the side-by-side guest rooms. After Mom died, Aunt Barb painted both rooms and replaced the furniture in the one where Dad slept. She didn't want him to be overwhelmed with memories of Mom was what she told me when I asked why. Dad's room on the right was painted a textured denim shade that resembled the weaves in his favorite worn-out jeans. The wooden-framed bed was replaced with a black, wrought-iron headboard and dressed with fluffy, white bedding and sheer curtains that blew with the breeze.

By comparison, the room we called mine had lavender walls and bedding with delicate purple and blue flowers that Mom used to call Laura Ashley. It took me a long time to realize that was the name of the bedding, and not the room's name. After Mom died, I wouldn't let Aunt Barb replace the comforter. Mom liked it too much.

I sat on the floor between the doors and drew my knees up to my chest. The Laura Ashley room seemed suddenly juvenile or old lady-like. Add a lace doily and I'd be in a grandma's house. I almost laughed aloud with the thought.

Dad's room was crisp and clean. I used to climb in his bed before the sun came up on mornings we stayed here. He'd tell me to go to sleep, and then roll over, facing away from me. A few minutes later, I would hear his gentle snore and knew I could put the television on low. The massive, black armoire housed more than just a few drawers for his clothes. Aunt Barb placed a TV in it for nights Dad couldn't sleep. I overheard her tell him. Sometimes, I would hear muffled laughter and guessed he was watching some talk show well after the house was dark and quiet. That was right after Mom died, and I figured he was lonely without her.

I walked into Dad's room and ran my hand along the thick wood trim of the armoire. It was heavy and masculine, yet full of details in its trim with dents and scratch marks that made it looked loved. I pulled open a drawer, checking what was inside. There, beside a clean set of sheets, was a dark gray t-shirt. I touched it gently, as if it would break. Tips of letters in navy-blue ink peeked from around the fold. I didn't need to open it to know. The words read *Just Do It*. Dad wore it with swim trunks almost every time we visited. It was his favorite shirt. He had it for years. The band on the neck was frayed and the letters were starting to fade, but he didn't care. I suggested he get a new one. He didn't listen. He probably didn't realize he left it behind.

Suddenly, I didn't feel so alone.

"I'm running to the Inn for a minute," Aunt Barb called from the stairs. "I'll be right back. Will you be ready?"

Her voice snapped me back to reality, and I quickly shut the drawer. "Yeah… yeah, sure," I answered, stepping back into the hall. "Aunt Barb?"

"Yes?"

"I want to stay in my dad's old room. Is that okay?"

"That's fine, honey. That's completely fine."

I fought back tears, as Aunt Barb gave me a hug.

Chapter 17
Ben's Story

My phone hummed on the counter in a low pitch no human could hear.

I glanced in its direction and tilted my head. A transparent hologram appeared, hovering over the island in the gourmet kitchen where I sat.

"Good morning, Commander," I said out of respect, and then sipped my morning coffee. I glanced at the time on the microwave. 8:42.

Benjamin. I heard a voice in my head and saw the dark-skinned man nod in the hologram image above me. Ezekiel Cain was smoking a pipe. His feet were propped up on a mahogany desk with a wall of shelves behind him. The room didn't look familiar to me. "I trust you've settled well and are fully prepared for today." His spoken voice was deep. Freshly polished auburn-tanned shoes reflected the light from his desk lamp.

"Yes, sir, I am."

"Cut the protocol. It's me," the commander said. His casual, relaxed tone didn't fit with his formal white suit with black pinstripes. He was an odd character to say the least, always in disguise, changing appearances regularly because he could. He preferred generational periods, reflecting on past eras and lives he lived or visited. "Are you ready?" His voice turned from rigid military tone to friendship. He was a century older than I was, if not more, though he rarely spoke of age.

"Yes, I am." I nodded, glancing up at him, my nerves a bit on edge. "I've been briefed… staff's in place. I'm ready."

"Well, you've had time to monitor and train. I suppose the soccer camp was nothing compared to The Farm." Commander E, as he was called by his direct reports, chuckled. His mind filled with combat exercises I endured under his training program, and then turned to images of me in a soccer uniform. He had a subtle way of pushing recruits to be the best agent they could be. Not everyone succeeded, but everyone respected him. A few called him the agency's filter because he weeded out those incapable of handling difficult situations.

I laughed. "No, nothing by comparison!" Even though he was known as one of the toughest officers The Farm ever had, he was like family to me.

"Seriously, seventy years is a long time, Ben."

"I know."

"I'm sorry you were on assignment when Elizabeth surfaced." Commander E's eyes looked droopy, as if the topic aged him twenty years. "Off the record?"

I nodded.

"I was torn about pulling you. I knew how much she meant to you. The officer in me couldn't do it. You were making such progress in your mission… more than any other operative was. I couldn't jeopardize that."

"You did the right thing." I could read his thoughts, and I knew he was sincere. It wasn't often that Commander E released his shield. When he did, his genuine personality was exposed. "Elizabeth had to finish her contract, and she agreed to take on a new life immediately following her conditioning." Her new life as Emma Bennett. "I saw her file." It was filled with video clips and short briefs. The images burned in my mind. I had no idea the suffering she endured during her remaining years without me. It was no wonder she took her own life when she did and transitioned much earlier than scheduled.

There was a short pause. I saw images of Elizabeth in Commander E's mind while she prepared for departure to this earthly world. She looked timid, her eyes sunken. Not like the Elizabeth I knew, the fun-loving, spunky girl that captured my heart back in 1931. Then again, she just finished years of counseling, part of her rehabilitation between lives, and was headed out to a troubled contract already outlined for her. She knew what she was getting into. She knew ahead of time that she'd be orphaned.

She just didn't remember that now.

"You're a good agent. One I want to get back on assignment as soon as possible." Commander E flashed a grin and I felt the shield fall back into place, camouflaging his thoughts.

I nodded. *Not too soon, I hope.*

"I promised a year or two, Ben. Nothing more. There's something brewing out west. The forecast looks like a recon squad will be issued in about eight to ten months. Probably need an operative undercover soon after that."

I was silent. I knew my time was limited, but I didn't like hearing the deadline before the project began. Couldn't another operative go?

"And, Benjamin? One more thing. Don't use compulsion unnecessarily again."

Damn. I thought I got away with it.

"I'll overlook it this time. Don't make me regret it."

"Yes, sir."

"Make the most of your time with Emma," Commander E replied. "You'll be there for her through this aftermath. Then you move on and let her finish her life. I'm counting on you for this next job. I've got SOs in place. They'd make a good team for you." A female voice in the background distracted him. I watched him motion his hands to someone out of sight, then direct his attention back to me. "Take advantage of your time."

I knew he wouldn't share more on the topic, so I dropped it. "Where are you exactly?" I asked, realizing the time and hearing music in his background.

"I'm out west."

I raised an eyebrow. Commander E was always secretive with his agents, though more open with me.

His shield lowered again. "I'm in Honolulu."

I glanced at the time, less than fifteen minutes passed since he called. "That's about what? Four in the morning by you?" To say Commander E was social was an understatement. He was known to party all night. He'd tip a few back and enjoy the company of a lady, or then again, sometimes several ladies. They were all human, and he was not. Back then, a few guys talked about less-than-complimentary actions. Rumors flew about relationships he had that were kept under the radar. In the end, it didn't matter. No one got hurt.

A scantily dressed brunette carrying an open bottle of champagne sat on Commander E's desk in the hologram above me. Her high-pitched voice whined, "Aren't you done working yet? I've been waiting for you!"

Commander E cleared his throat and nodded in my direction, though the sudden tilt was over before her human eyes could register the movement. He wished me well, shielded his thoughts, and shut down the link. The hologram hovering in my kitchen vanished in an instant with a sound only my immortal ears could hear.

Before he shielded me, I read his thoughts. He was encouraging me to cross that invisible barrier between professional and personal. Other agents crossed it. I knew that. Molly did it all the time and never thought twice about it. I used to tease her about her love-'em-and-leave-'em attitude. But, she was right—no one got hurt. Everyone moved on.

I didn't know if I could do that to Emma.

Knowing our time together would be limited meant potential heartbreak for both of us if I let her back into my heart.

Chapter 18
Emma's Story

My palms were sweaty when Mrs. Warner opened the door.

Aunt Barb stood by my side with an armful of things I'd normally be embarrassed to bring. She loaded up a wicker basket filled with a casserole the Inn prepared, a couple loaves of French bread, some cheeses, and a bottle of Mrs. Warner's favorite wine.

I never met Mr. or Mrs. Warner before, but they welcomed me like I did.

"I didn't know you were related to Barb Carmichael. She's really cool," Lewis said after my aunt offered up Jet Skis from the Inn, for the day. Lewis led me outside to where our classmates congregated.

For a single second, I felt proud.

But when a guy I barely knew stopped talking mid-sentence to look at me, I realized I was that girl, the orphaned girl that left school abruptly a few days earlier.

Lewis didn't seem to notice the silent stares I got, as he leaned over the deck railing in search of Melissa. Flagstone paths led past a volleyball court and wrapped around a fire pit. Mature trees and picture-perfect flowerbeds scattered the meticulously landscaped yard.

"She must be in the boathouse," Lewis said.

I followed him down the stairs to the path. We were still a distance away when I saw Matt. He had his back to me and, suddenly, I found myself nervous to see him.

A football player at the table with Matt crushed a can in his fist. Frank was the type of guy that didn't care what people thought of him. He partied a lot, told obnoxious jokes, and made a scene, all for fun. Aimee laughed at whatever was said, throwing her head to the side in an overdramatic motion.

Melissa and I labeled it her signature move. The way she tilted her head was annoying, like time stood still and the spotlight was all on her.

The uncomfortable feeling I had earlier swept over me when Aimee leaned across the table and touched Matt's arm.

Was she flirting with my boyfriend?

Omigod. What was going to happen after I moved?

Thoughts swirled in my head, and all I wanted to do was leave. I had to look away. I didn't want to see if Matt flirted back. I focused on the boathouse and searched for Melissa. When I finally got the courage to glance at Matt again, he was no longer sitting with Aimee. Instead, he was on the pier talking to a blond-haired guy on a Jet Ski.

By the time Lewis and I reached the lakeside patio, Melissa saw me. She screamed my name and ran to greet me in a strong-gripped hug. Frank did the same, repeating the same words I'd heard for days, the words that triggered the resurface of tears—I'm sorry.

Melissa asked one question after another. When did you get here? How long can you stay? Did you hear about the island party? She rattled them off faster than I could answer, not to mention she barely took a breath.

When she finally paused, I told her I could stay overnight.

"Oh, I'm so happy." She gave me another tight hug.

I lost track of where Matt was and if Aimee was watching him. Before I could worry about it, Lewis suggested we pick up the Jet Skis from the Inn.

Matt was untying the ropes at the bow of boat when we reached the pier. He didn't notice Melissa or realize I was there. He stood and turned into me.

"Hey!" His tone was low, and I realized I startled him.

"Hi," I said. The nervous feeling I had before went away when our eyes met.

I stepped into the boat, and Lewis started the engine. The gentle chug as it came to life and the sound of bubbling water made me feel at ease. The familiar scent of exhaust and mildew calmed me. I was suddenly content. I felt at home.

Lewis slowly backed away from the pier. The sun was hot on my skin. I took off my cover-up and settled into the bench seat at the back of the boat. Melissa sat in the bucket seat next to Lewis. The water glistened in the sunlight off in the distance, until a boat's wake disturbed it. I was me again, out on the lake. All those happy memories of my parents and summers at the Inn came flooding back. I was in my own little world when Lewis increased the speed in the open waters. After Matt stored the ropes in pockets on the inside of the boat, he sat down beside me.

He reached for my hand and smiled.

"I'm glad you're here," he whispered in my ear.

"Me, too."

I wanted things to be the same, but deep down, I knew everything between us was different. When I looked into his eyes, I could tell he felt it, too. We were silent most of the ten-minute ride to the Carmichael Inn. Matt held my hand, his thumb rubbing gently on my finger. I guessed he didn't know what to say any more than I did.

We rounded the point across from the island, and the Inn came into view.

"That's my aunt's house," I said to Matt, pointing to a row of similar houses with matching siding and trim.

"Which one?"

"Third from the left," I proudly answered. "All the houses are part of the Inn. Most are rentals. Except my aunt's."

When we neared the harbor, Lewis reduced the boat's speed and Matt let go of my hand.

"Is Melissa taking a Jet Ski back with you?" Matt asked. His eyes were somber, and I guessed knowing I was moving was just as hard on him as it was on me.

"Can you come with me?"

When he nodded, his eyes seemed to smile. He began pulling out the boat's ropes and prepared to dock.

The marina at the Inn was a friendly sight. Colorful shops lined the shoreline. Piers jutted into the water from a whitewashed boardwalk. There were enough slips to moor a couple of dozen boats at a time, and usually they were filled. The Carmichael Inn had great food, from the five-star restaurant to the Sports Pub 'N Grill to the small stands on the beach that served Chicago-style hot dogs and deep-dish pizza slices.

Aunt Barb and her late husband designed the lakefront shops similar to Disney's Boardwalk, Dad once said. Of course, a very scaled-down version with a contemporary coffee bar, convenience store, newsstand, and sporting goods shop for boaters and guests. The shed at the end of the beach offered paddleboats and windsurfer boards, not to mention Jet Skis for rent.

I never really thought about it before, but I guessed Aunt Barb was well off. I remembered Dad once saying she was taken care of financially. I looked around at everything labeled 'Carmichael Inn' and realized Dad was right.

I was lost in thought when Lewis docked the boat, and Matt jumped onto the pier.

A brown-haired guy in a boat nearby called to Lewis. The guy climbed out of his boat in a quick leap and shook Matt's hand. Lewis similarly greeted the boy he called Drew.

"Island party tonight. You comin'?" Drew asked. He looked to be our age, with a tan, lean chest. His hair was long on top and trimmed short on the sides and he wore faded swim trunks that looked like they'd seen better days. I wondered if he lived on the lake and spent his entire summer in the sun.

"Wouldn't miss it. I got some friends up, but we're there, man," Lewis answered with a smirk.

"Matt, we missed you on the fourth," Drew said. "Huge-Ass-Party. You'd have loved it." Drew was shorter than Matt by several inches, but his posture made him seem taller. He held his chin upward at an angle when he spoke. I wondered if he knew TJ or Hannah and if he went to the high school I'd end up at. Someday.

"I told him what he missed," Lewis answered.

Melissa rolled her eyes at me. That was the weekend she was on vacation with her family and before Matt and I started dating.

"I'm having some people at the house tomorrow night. If you're still in town." Drew's invitation was quiet and in a lower tone than before. I couldn't help but wonder if he didn't want Melissa and me to hear it.

"Hey, I'll catch you later. Bring your friends," Drew said when he finally noticed Melissa and I were standing on the pier.

"Yeah, for sure," Matt answered, reaching for my hand. We walked along the water's edge, weaving through sunbathers and kids playing in the sand.

"Thanks for coming with me," I said and looked up at him.

"Yeah, no problem… I wanted to." Matt squeezed my hand gently.

"So how well do you know that guy… the one at the pier?"

"Who? Drew?"

"Ah, yeah... I think that was that his name." The sun was hot on my shoulders.

"He's friends with Lewis. I met him when I came to visit this summer." I nodded, and he continued. "He's a big partier." He shot me a look, and I knew exactly what he meant.

"Yeah, I got that part. You missed this year's party on the Fourth, huh?" I asked. Waves gently rushed in, covering our feet.

"Apparently so. I heard they got busted. Some guy got caught with drugs.

Drew said everyone laid low after that. Just a few parties at his place. Not like what they used to be."

"Drew lives on the lake?" My feet began to sink in the wet sand when the water retreated.

He nodded. "Yeah… on the opposite end. There's only a few houses by him, and I think he said they were vacant or something."

I stumbled. My right foot got bogged down in the clumpy, wet sand. Matt waited while I regained my step. He chuckled, but he didn't say anything. I couldn't help but laugh, as I caught myself from falling a second time. His arms were around me before I knew it, lifting me up. When our eyes locked, I realized how much I would miss him. I was sure he would kiss me until some kids ran past us, interrupting the moment.

When we reached the equipment rental office, we were third in line. Matt crossed his arms tight against his chest while we waited. I glanced around. Wake boards and skis were stuck in the sand, propped against the small building. Weathered white shutters were folded back, exposing a window where a bronze-tanned brunette girl stood behind the counter.

The girl stared at the couple in front of her as they completed paperwork. The middle-aged man asked her a question and when he wasn't looking, she rolled her eyes.

If she didn't like her job, why didn't she quit?

I was sure Aunt Barb wouldn't be happy if the girl didn't at least fake it in front of customers. I wondered if Aunt Barb would let me work here. I was lost in thought when Matt's voice startled me.

"So when are you moving?" His voice was soft, and he uncrossed his arms. It was a topic I didn't want to think about, even though he deserved to know.

"Next weekend. I think."

"That quick?"

"Yeah." I focused on the dirty-white sign above the rental window. The Carmichael Inn logo was neatly printed in navy blue with Rentals Here in red capital letters. The customer at the counter pushed the clipboard to the bronze girl. She handed the man a receipt and pointed the couple toward the beach.

"I guess I'll have to visit Lewis more often," Matt said as we moved up in line.

"Do you come up here a lot?" I couldn't help but wonder if he did and if I'd get to see him after I moved.

"A couple times a summer. Not as much in winter," he said. Then he quickly added, "We were here that week you were on vacation. Before football started."

"Oh… yeah." I remembered him sending a text about it.

The bronze girl giggled. I noticed how she hovered over the dark-haired guy filling out paperwork. She had a bright smile with exceptionally white teeth against her dark skin. Interesting… she didn't smile at the older couple.

I barely noticed the guy in front of us before, but took a look at him while the bronze girl continued flirting. From the side view, I agreed he was attractive. He stood several inches taller than Matt did, but seemed to carry himself with more confidence. When he smiled, his eyes squinted and his jaw tightened. It was a masculine look I never saw on Matt or any other boys at my school. It was a more mature look, like a grin on a man, not a boy, and I guessed he was probably much older than I was.

He couldn't be from here, I thought.

I didn't realize I was staring at him until he turned and looked at me. Heat crept up my neck, and I focused on the sand around my feet. My heart began to race. He was much more attractive than I originally thought. He wasn't cute like the boys at school. He was handsome like the Prince Charming I dreamed of when I was little. Like the fantasy characters in all of those sappy Disney stories Mom used to read to me.

When I felt normal again, I glanced back at Prince Charming. He wore a white T-shirt with the sleeves cutoff and the seams torn at the side. As he filled out the form on the clipboard and his left arm moved, I caught a glimpse of his tanned chest. I felt like a middle-schooler staring.

The bronze girl perched herself in front of him. Her elbows rested on the counter with her chin sitting in her hands. I could tell she was talking to him, but her voice was low, so I couldn't hear what she said. I wondered what Prince Charming thought of the brunette, as he pushed the clipboard back to her. Then, an instant later, he glanced in my direction.

Busted again.

The same tingling I felt earlier, returned. I caught my breath and stared at my feet, pushing sand around, hoping my face wouldn't redden. How ridiculous. He was clearly older than I was and staying at the hotel. He obviously wasn't from around here, so the odds of me ever seeing him again were slim. The idea lessened my embarrassment. I focused on my surroundings, on anything to avoid looking at him. I stared at the sign hanging on the building listing the ten rules of the lake, and I wondered if anyone ever read them.

"Hey man… sorry for the delay," a deep voice spoke, jolting me from my daydream. I looked up. Prince Charming was talking to Matt. "Paperwork." He tilted his head toward the open window as if in further explanation. The brunette was no longer in view.

"No problem." Matt shrugged.

Don't look at Prince Charming, I told myself. But I wanted to. My eyes were drawn to him like a magnet to metal. I wanted to look, but when Matt leaned toward me and his upper arm gently touched my shoulder, I snapped back to reality.

I felt like a kid again.

Chapter 19
Ben's Story

Sand crept between my toes, as I stood waiting to rent a Jet Ski.

It was my first official day undercover as Ben Parker. Normally, I was a confident person. Molly called me arrogant at times.

I was never nervous, until now.

Seeing Emma brought back all those insecurities I left behind in adolescence, when I was still alive. I stood at the counter, waiting for the brunette to get approval for my rental. I was under eighteen she told me when I handed her the paperwork and my undercover driver's license. If only she knew how old I really was. I could have convinced her to release the Jet Ski without the hassle of paperwork, but with Emma standing behind me in line, I was in no rush.

Of course, Brinn, as her name tag clearly read, wanted to stall my application as long as possible. She took her time making the call to my fake aunt, Marty McMann, who worked in the office. Minutes passed as Brinn moved slowly. Her thoughts of me were initially flattering while she hovered, as I completed the form. But after a few overdramatic eye gestures and fake giggles, I had enough and blocked out her thoughts. Besides, they interfered with eavesdropping.

Emma and Matt talked about meaningless stuff while I waited for my rental. How long are you staying? When are you moving? Are you coming back to Highland Park? Topics that made Emma immediately tense up. I felt her pain, as she mentally relived the notification at school and the days that followed. I glanced at her as she tried wiping away her tears before Matt noticed them.

Stupid punk. He didn't even realize the impact his words had on her.

I turned to face him, locking my eyes with his. I knew what I was doing.

He stood paralyzed, his eyes focused and unblinking. I could manipulate him any way I wanted to right now. The power I had as an immortal was far greater than any human could imagine.

I wanted to kill him for hurting her. For being with her. I had the ability.

No one would know.

A simple heart attack or accidental drowning all came to mind, as I held him in my mental grip. I never did anything like that before. My phone buzzed in my pocket, but I ignored it. I never killed anyone for no reason, or without just cause.

But I could.

And part of me wanted to. I wanted to protect Emma and that meant eliminating anything or anyone that hurt her. Getting rid of anyone that stood in my way of protecting her, even if the pain she felt was unintentional.

Ben-ja-min! I heard her screech my name in my head before her hip bumped into mine. "Hey neighbor. Renting a Jet Ski?" Molly said aloud. Her thoughts were less bubbly as she yelled in her British accent, *Exactly what the bloody hell are you doing?*

My focus was lost, and Matt was released from my stare. I turned to look at Molly.

You can't possibly think compulsion is the answer, she said firmly.

"I'm just waiting for the paperwork right now, Molly," I said, pretending we weren't having a private mental discussion. *I wasn't going to hurt him.*

You wanted to. You thought about it.

But I didn't.

Didn't your reprimand for that compulsion teach you anything? She was referring to my borrowing of Officer Scott Michaels' squad car the day Emma learned her father died.

What reprimand?

You're kidding, right? I thought Commander E would have you doing community service by now. After all, you left that garage manager in a compelled state for hours.

Molly, he was fine. I shook my head.

Yes, but your spell didn't wear off as quickly as you guessed it would, Benjamin. You overdid it. Your emotions are running on steroids right now, and you need to tone it down.

I looked over at Emma and realized Matt was holding her in his arms. Maybe my subtle thoughts helped push him along. *Or, maybe he isn't so bad after all.* Molly's thoughts crept in. At least Emma felt better. I could sense that.

Marty waved at Molly and me, as she entered the rental office and signed the papers Brinn had waiting for her. "Want to go for a spin?" I asked Molly.

"Maybe later," she said aloud. *Join me first?*

I shrugged, waiting to hear what she was talking about.

We need to resuscitate a young boy that is about to choke on a pecan in his turtle sundae at the ice cream shop by the marina. Poor clerk. Some young lady new to the job... Didn't get her CPR certification yet. Perhaps this will light a fire under her ass, as they say.

I raised an eyebrow.

Come with me. It'll be rewarding. She smiled, her gray eyes convincing.

Brinn's expression turned to disappointment as she handed over the key to the Jet Ski.

Fine. But you're buying ice cream.

Deal.

Chapter 20
Emma's Story

The Carmichael Inn employee walked us through proper use of a Jet Ski.

It wasn't the first time I rode one, but I listened anyway. After he ran through the boating rules for the lake, he left Matt and me to attend to others.

I snapped the buckle on my vest and climbed onto the black-and-red trimmed watercraft. The seat was slightly hot to the touch. Matt stood beside me as if I needed help, but he didn't offer it. "Hey, I didn't mean to upset you earlier," he said when I was finally settled in place.

"It's fine. I mean, it's not your fault. I try not to think about it. That's all." I looked down at the water.

He stood next to me for a minute in silence, and then lifted my chin so I couldn't avoid eye contact. When he bent down and kissed me, I was somewhat surprised. I shouldn't have been. I mean, the signs were there and we almost kissed on the beach earlier. His eyes locked on mine as our lips separated.

"Ready?" he asked.

I nodded and started the engine.

Matt climbed on the Jet Ski beside me and started it. "Should we head back to Lewis' place, or ride around for a while?"

"Let's ride around," I answered. Matt led the way into the lake. The water was calm and peaceful until we reached the widest part of the lake, past the island, on the end closest to where Lewis lived and where most of the boat traffic was.

Matt crossed the waves left behind from other watercraft, and then circled back around for a jump. I followed. There was enough activity between boats and other Jet Skiers that we had plenty of waves to ride. Lake Bell was a long lake with the island and sandbar off center, hugging the southern shores. Anyone that knew the lake knew where to ride and how close to get to the island without beaching their vessel. Those that didn't know the lake hung out on the western end, where the lake was deeper. Matt was one of those people.

I chuckled, remembering how I blushed when Prince Charming busted me staring at him. He was great looking, but I realized he was completely out of my league when I saw his girlfriend. She was model pretty with bright eyes and long, dark hair she wore pulled back in tight ponytail. Everything about her was classy. Even in Highland Park, most girls didn't have the confidence she seemed to have as she clung onto Prince Charming's arm. They were a perfect-looking couple.

I was lost in my daydream, as I trailed Matt around the lake. For a slight second, I thought about how Matt and I looked together and wondered if anyone—besides Melissa—thought we looked good together. Before I could dwell on the thought, a Jet Ski flew past me at speeds far greater than what I was accustomed to. The blond driver sped past Matt and wove in between other boaters. He wasn't really being reckless. He just took more risks than I would, like a stunt driver. Risks Dad would never approve of, if he knew.

Good thing he wasn't here to see this. As soon as the thought entered my mind, regret followed. I slowed my speed and wiped my eyes, fighting back the tears. I would give anything for Dad to be back, even the punishment I'd get for being reckless on the lake.

Matt was ahead of me when a boat towing a tube neared us. I slowed down and veered away, but Matt didn't notice. He followed in pursuit of the blond Stunt Boy and the bigger waves. When the tube flipped, losing the riders in the water, I was further detained.

In the distance, Matt took one wave, and then another. Each time, he got a little more air. He and the blond were jumping in tandem, Stunt Boy taking more risks than Matt was.

With all the traffic, the water was no longer calm. A series of large waves separated me from Matt and the risk-taker. I tried to catch them. I sped up, taking the first wave faster than I should have. The lift I got was more than I was comfortable with. My stomach ached as I landed and leaned in the water, almost losing my balance. I knew this should be exhilarating, but I wasn't feeling it.

I didn't notice a third Jet Skier until after he did a flip. I let go of the throttle and watched a dark-haired guy do a complete somersault in the air, hovering over the water. I was pretty sure I held my breath. I never saw anyone do that on Lake Bell before. When he landed gracefully with a beautiful spray behind him, I knew he couldn't be from here.

I was mesmerized by the sight, but Matt and Stunt Boy were challenged. I sped up in time to see Stunt Boy take a series of waves. He was shaky and off balance, separating from his Jet Ski mid-air. He landed several yards away from it, giving a thumbs-up sign. I hadn't caught up to them yet when Matt gunned it in pursuit.

Matt hit the wave the same way. Mid-flight, I could see he was off-center, though he landed first, and then tipped off his Jet Ski. I chuckled after I knew he was all right. X-treme Sports on ESPN wasn't better than this.

As I neared Matt, I realized I was headed toward the same waves at a speed I couldn't slow in time. Dad wouldn't be happy with me right now, if he were alive, I thought.

But he wasn't. And I was alone out here.

I was sick to my stomach with nerves, as I held my speed firm and took the wave at an angle. The Jet Ski got some air, and my fear increased. My arms and hands felt weak and prickly, and I was sure I couldn't hold on. I closed my eyes for a moment and took in a deep breath. I squeezed the handles tight. I felt an arm around my back, shifting my body, turning my head and dipping my shoulder to the right. I couldn't move. My body was rigid in its new position. The Jet Ski shifted below me. The handles turned, and the nose tipped upward.

Suddenly, I felt in control. It was like the Jet Ski moved on its own, centering and balancing over the water with me gripping the handles. My body lifted off the seat only by a few inches, but I felt like I was flying.

It was exhilarating.

The fear suddenly dissipated, and I landed gracefully in the water. I understood now why people were drawn to larger waves. My heart raced with the adrenaline rush and I wanted to do it again, but the boats were no longer nearby and the water began to calm again.

***

Stunt Boy and the dark-haired guy floated next to Matt and his Jet Ski. When I reached them, I realized the guy that did the flip earlier was Prince Charming.

Figured. I knew he couldn't be from around here.

"Nice jump back there," Stunt Boy said.

"Thanks," I answered. When I looked at Prince Charming, he had a slight grin.

"I'll catch you later," the blond guy said. Then he and Prince Charming left.

"Need help?" I asked Matt.

"Yeah." He reached for my extended hand. "That was an incredible jump you had. Where did you learn that?"

"I don't know. It just came to me." Who was I kidding? I had no idea. I expected to fall off, not land perfectly. Matt grabbed my hand, and a smile crept up on his face. I saw it for an instant, just before he pulled me into the water beside him.

When I surfaced, I splashed water at him. He caught my hand, pulled me into his arms, and kissed me. This kiss was better than before, and I found myself feeling that slight tingle as our lips separated.

Chapter 21
Ben's Story

Molly nudged my arm as she walked past me.

I was sitting on a boulder at a teenage bonfire. It was expected, though I didn't want to be there. Waiting for Emma and hearing her thoughts while that boy, Matt, flirted with her all afternoon, wasn't what I had in mind for my Saturday plans. I'd rather catch a college football game instead of torturing myself.

I got up and followed Molly down the tall grass path, giving sufficient space so it wouldn't appear peculiar.

How are you doing? she asked.

Bored, but fine. And you?

It's a typical Saturday night. She shrugged. *By the way, quick action on that Jet Ski this afternoon. Emma didn't have a clue she was being helped.*

That's what I'm here for. She would have gotten hurt if one of us didn't intervene, I answered.

Molly reached a cooler partially hidden behind a tree and some brush.

I came up behind her, as she flipped open the cover and searched for a beverage. "Anything good in there?" I asked. She pushed cans around like she couldn't find the right one.

"Just looking for a light beer," she said.

A high school-aged boy with short, almost shaved, dark hair, approached. Even without my immortal skills, I could tell he played football by his stocky build.

I dug my hand in, mixed up the selection, and pulled out a lower-calorie beer. *It tastes like water,* I said, handing the can to Molly.

I know. But I need to watch my girlish figure. Being human isn't all it's cracked up to be. I heard her chuckle in my head.

I pulled out two other beers and handed one to the guy behind me.

"Thanks," he said. I recognized him from school. His formal name was Thomas John Lambert. He was a senior and a family friend of Emma's aunt.

"Yeah, no problem," I replied, noticing a glance between him and Molly.

"Ben, this is TJ," Molly quickly said. He extended his hand, as Molly continued. "Ben is my neighbor... Ben Parker, Claire's brother."

"Yeah, moved in with your aunt, or something, huh?" TJ added as we shook hands.

I nodded, reading his thoughts of Molly as I downloaded his memories. I noticed Molly cringe when my hand touched TJ's. After a second, I understood why. "My parents, ah... my dad, actually, got transferred to China for a few years. My sister and I wanted to finish high school here in the states, so we moved in with my aunt." I repeated the cover story we had in place.

"That's cool. I hear you play soccer."

"I do."

"So you know Justin," he said. I glanced at Molly. Images of her on TJ's arm flipped through my head, as the downloaded data was categorized in my mind. My brain was like a computer storing information for later extraction. This data on Molly would definitely be used again, even if only as bribery.

"Yeah, I know him. Goalie," I answered, ignoring Molly's mental pleas.

"Yup, that's him. My sister's been dating him for about a year. Good guy. You play defense?"

Benjamin, you can leave now. Molly's thoughts were getting louder.

I nodded for both of their sakes. "Left defender."

"Nice," TJ said. Molly reached for his arm, "Well, it was good meeting you."

"Yeah, nice meeting you too," I answered, and they walked away.

Seriously, Molly. You hooked up with him already?

What do you mean already? *I've been here for well over a year, Benjamin, and who says I can't have a little fun while I'm at it?*

I shook my head and returned to my new group of friends.

Chapter 22
Emma's Story

The afternoon sped by.

Before I knew it, classmates staying at the campground said goodbye. Even though I wasn't sure when—or, if—I'd see them again, it wasn't a tear-jerking send off. I would miss my soccer teammates, but I didn't really like Aimee Wilkinson and her posse of clones.

After a typical parental lecture from Mr. Warner about not drinking and no co-habitation when we returned, we were free to go to the island bonfire. Lewis started the engine, Matt untied the ropes, and Frank helped Melissa, Jenna, and me into the boat.

The sun sank into the tree line as we docked on the sandbar, and the guys secured the boat to a nearby tree. A group of people, about my age, sat on boulders surrounding an oversized pit with roaring fire. The comforting smell of burning wood filled the air.

"Glad you could make it," Drew said. Lewis introduced everyone, but Drew barely glanced at us girls. "Good timing. Fireworks are at sunset."

"Fireworks on Labor Day?" Frank questioned. "I thought that was only done on the Fourth of July."

"You bastards never had fireworks on Labor Day?" Drew asked.

Frank smirked, and Matt shook his head.

"Hey, man… Us bastards spend a lot of money in your little hick town." Lewis chuckled.

"Spoken like a true rich boy," Drew answered and nudged Lewis. Laughter erupted between them, and I realized they must have known each other for years to put up with the friendly banter. "So you seriously don't have fireworks for Labor Day?"

Frank shook his head this time.

"The fireworks are actually a lake thing," I intervened. All eyes turned to me. Even Drew, who barely noticed me before, stared. I felt my cheeks warm, but I continued anyway. "The Inn sponsors them. They started it back when it was a dormitory for factory employees, way before it was a resort. Now it's an annual tradition... There's an employee appreciation party tomorrow. This is the kick off."

"How'd you know that?" Drew asked. His blank stare and arrogant nod made me feel uncomfortable, and I suddenly lost my voice.

"Her aunt owns the place, man. You didn't know that?" Lewis answered. "Joke's on you."

Drew shook his head and smiled.

I eased into a grin. For the first time since I could remember, I wasn't the poor Highland Park kid on Cavell Street. Instead, I was one of the rich kids.

If only Aimee Wilkinson could see me now.

"Let's party!" Frank said. "Where's the beer?"

Drew pointed toward some tall grasses. "Cooler's down that path, around the bend. You'll see it."

As I glanced in the path's direction, Prince Charming came toward us, a beer in hand. I looked away before I got busted staring again.

"Want something? Water?" Matt asked. "I mean, I know you don't drink—"

"I'll take a beer," I answered quickly. "I mean, why not? Everyone else is."

Matt looked stunned, but he didn't say anything. He and Frank took off down the path and passed out beers a few minutes later. The guys continued chatting about everything and nothing that mattered, at least to me, anyway.

"Come on." Melissa pointed to an open boulder near the fire, and Jenna and I followed. Jenna spread out a blanket on the sand, while Melissa and I shared the oversized rock.

"Check him out," Jenna said, referring to the dark-haired guy I called Prince Charming.

"I know. I saw him at the rental office," I whispered back. When I looked in his direction, he looked up. Our eyes met for an instant before I turned away. "He's got a girlfriend," I added, remembering the brunette that looked like she belonged on the cover of the Sports Illustrated Swimsuit Edition, not on the shores of Lake Bell.

"Too bad," Jenna responded. For the tiniest of moments, I felt like I knew him. Like it wasn't the first time I saw his face at a campfire. But for the life of me, I couldn't recall a time that I'd ever see him before today, or when I'd ever been on the island, especially at a bonfire.

"Hey, what about Frank?" Melissa asked. We watched Frank slam a beer as if in competition with Drew, and then crush the can in his hand. "Ah, never mind." When I looked back at my prince again, the same feeling returned. I felt déjà vu a few times in my life, mostly here at the lake, if I remembered correctly. But I never figured out what was so familiar.

"Yeah. I know." Jenna laughed. She popped open her beer and raised it. "Cheers," she said and clinked cans. I chugged a big gulp of Coors Light. It bubbled and burned down my throat. I didn't like beer, but I kept up appearances anyway.

By the time Matt, Lewis, and Frank joined us at the fire, my drink was almost gone and I felt completely relaxed.

"You okay?" Matt asked, as Jenna eagerly accepted another beer.

"Yeah." I couldn't tell him how I really felt. Could I?

"You're not mad or something, are you?"

I shook my head and realized my vision was a bit blurred.

"Come on," he said, reaching for my hand.

"Where we going?" I asked when I stood.

He smiled. "Let's go for a walk."

"Okay," I answered.

He stared at me, not blinking. "You sure nothing's wrong?"

"Yeah, I'm sure." I smiled weakly. There was everything wrong. I just wasn't mad.

He leaned down and kissed me gently. I wasn't used to public displays of affection. I could feel my cheeks burn before our lips parted.

Matt held my hand and led me down the beach. It was quiet and secluded where Lewis docked. Matt helped me inside the boat and then climbed in behind me. He pulled two beers out of his sweatshirt pocket and placed them in cup holders between the front seats.

"Want one?" he asked, popping open one for himself.

I shook my head.

He took a drink and sat down.

Away from the fire, with the sun fully set, I shivered and wished I wore jeans instead of shorts. I took a seat beside Matt and tucked my legs beneath me. An explosion of color in the sky distracted me from the chill in the air.

"Hey, that's cool," he said, pointing to the starbursts in red and blue above us.

I agreed. His eyes never met mine, as he took another drink.

Popping sounds echoed in the dark before shades of pink spread across the sky, illuminating the boats parked beside us. A silver pontoon with a raised fishing chair, a couple of Jet Skis, and a shiny, new-looking ski boat lined the shoreline. Minutes passed as we watched the fireworks and listened to the "oohs" and "ahs" let out by friends and strangers at the fire pit nearby. The quietness between splashes of light was both peaceful and uncomfortable.

Was it me? Why was being with him suddenly so awkward?

When the grand finale rumbled above us and the sky brightened in rainbow colors, Matt finished his beer and put his arm around me.

"Are you cold?" he asked.

"A little." A lot, actually.

Matt stood up quickly and returned with two blankets in hand. He wrapped one around me and tossed the other on the seat. "Better?"

I nodded.

When he sat back down, he put his arm around me again and gave me a kiss.

"I didn't mean to make you cry earlier," he said.

I looked away. I didn't want to think about earlier—or the day before, or the day before that. I didn't want to remember why I cried.

"It's okay," I mumbled.

Matt lifted my chin and shook his head. "No, it wasn't. I'm sorry."

His apology was simple and touching, but it wasn't his fault I was a sobbing mess the past few days. "I'm going to miss you," I whispered.

"Me, too," he answered. The air thickened between us in the quiet, dark night. When Matt kissed me again, he didn't pull back. Instead, he moved me into his lap. I tasted beer on his tongue, as the kiss intensified. His hand wandered to my back and even though I was kissing Matt with the same energy I used to, it wasn't the same and I wasn't into it.

Things weren't supposed to be like this.

I fidgeted, but Matt didn't notice.

I shouldn't be thinking of moving and leaving my friends behind. My mind shouldn't be filled with thoughts of the recent days and past memories of Dad and my life in Highland Park. I should be ecstatic to be on the senior trip, to be here, alone with Matt. But I wasn't.

Would everything really be all right?

It was what everyone whispered when they went through the receiving line at Dad's funeral. "You'll see. It'll all work out." Except, I didn't really believe that.

Aftermath

The rev of an engine startled us, ending our kiss abruptly. A Jet Ski sped off into the lake, and the quiet returned. A bit of relief came over me.

"You're crying again," Matt said, wiping the tears from my cheek. I wanted to tell him I was sorry, and that I didn't mean to ruin the moment, when I glanced up at him, I could tell he already knew. "This is it, isn't it?" he asked.

I nodded and stared at my lap.

"Maybe we can visit. It's only two hours," he said. His tone was weak.

"Yeah, maybe," I agreed. Even though the words were said aloud, we both knew it was over. He pulled me close for one last goodbye.

***

A distant ring woke me the next morning. Light peered through the partially opened blinds. It took a few seconds for my eyes to adjust and realize I was in the guest room of Lewis' home. Melissa was on the phone. When she ended the call, she nudged Jenna.

"Wake up," Melissa said. "My mom's gonna be here in a minute."

"Already?" Jenna whined from under the pillow.

I rubbed my eyes and glanced at the clock beside the bed. It was almost nine-thirty. Crap. Aunt Barb said something about errands this morning. I reached for my phone, as it buzzed with a text from her.

"What time's your aunt coming?" Melissa asked.

"Um… she's here. I guess," I answered and cleared my throat. I was barely awake. Memories of the night before came back hard—the tears shed with Matt, then the beer I decided to chug after we rejoined our friends at the bonfire. We stayed out late, and I was exhausted.

By the time I got downstairs, Aunt Barb was having coffee with Mrs. Warner in the gourmet kitchen, and Melissa's mom was waiting in the car. Jenna said goodbye and gave me a hug before she walked out the door, tears streaming down her face.

I fought back my own tears and turned toward Melissa.

"I'm not saying goodbye," she said firmly. "I'm spending the weekend with you when you're back to officially move. So, I'm just saying see you later. Okay?"

I nodded, tears now flowing freely. Melissa squeezed me tight, then turned quickly and left without looking back. Aunt Barb wrapped her arm around my shoulder and stood with me, as I watched my friends climb in the car and drive away.

"Come. Let's get your things," Aunt Barb whispered. She chatted with Mr.

and Mrs. Warner while I picked up my bag and wondered where Matt was. After thanking them for their hospitality, I got up the courage to ask.

"Oh, dear. The boys left already," Mrs. Warner answered.

"They left?" I was confused.

"Well, yes. They had football practice this morning." She glanced at her watch and continued, "About eight-thirty this morning, but I'll let Lewis know you said goodbye."

"Yes. Thanks."

I choked back the sadness I felt.

Chapter 23
Ben's Story

The walls in my bedroom were builder bland and boring.

Marty McMann bought the model home on the tenth hole of the Carmichael Golf Course five years earlier, when her undercover sleeper assignment began.

Marty was Barbara Carmichael's executive assistant and my aunt in our cover story. She was willing to let Claire, my undercover sister, and I live with her. At least, that was the story we told humans.

I touched the cream-colored wall and watched a caramel shade spread outward, floor to ceiling and around the room. As it reached the cherry wood trim, I realized it was wrong. I rubbed my hands together for a second, trying to visualize a better color choice, and then touched the wall again. An ugly light brown spread outward in a similar pace.

As the color finished flooding the walls, Claire stood in the open doorway. "Hey, you painted!" she said, glancing around the room.

"I painted?" I was stunned by her enthusiasm. Could a rookie be so naïve?

"It's a great color."

"Great?" Melted chocolate ice cream looked good in a parfait glass, with remnants of hot fudge and a sprinkling of chopped nuts, but it looked terrible on walls, especially in my room. I could feel the heat emanating from her embarrassment before I saw her cardinal-red face.

"I just… I, ah." Claire stumbled over her words. She'd have to get over the intimidation she felt around me before our classmates sensed it.

"Ben, are you embarrassing poor Claire already?" Marty stepped into my room, and then looked around. "Horrible color. I hope you're planning on changing it."

"We were just talking about that. Good timing, Marty," I said, touching my finger to the wall again. A gray-toned taupe spread around the room, covering the past shade.

"Much better." Marty smiled. She was sixty-two years old in human years. It was her age when she died, back in April of 1966, the age she preferred to be undercover. She was a bubbly woman with a lot of spunk. "What do you think, Claire?"

"What?" Claire asked aloud, but her thoughts were swirling. "How... how did you do that?"

"Oh, honey, how long have you been in the field?" Marty put her arm around Claire.

"Well, um... this is my first assignment... outside of training," Claire reluctantly answered. Claire was thirty-one years old when she died in 1944. It was a breach of contract, which was not looked upon favorably in my world. Souls that returned to my world prematurely endured decades of rehabilitation and counseling before new lives or assignments would be considered.

I couldn't help but laugh. Claire's inexperience would be a comic relief on this assignment. Much better than the serious, violent missions I'd grown accustomed to.

"Now that you're both here... Barbara Carmichael invited us to her cookout this afternoon. Well, I should say, I've gone for years, but she's extended an invitation to both of you," Marty said matter-of-factly. She carried herself younger than the age on her fake birth certificate. Her hair curled out at the tips, barely touching her shoulder. The various shades of gray mixed with blonde gave her a youthful appearance that humans her age envied.

"I've got plans," I answered.

"What? You're not going?" Claire questioned. Her thoughts were more confident now. She didn't have Molly's humor. I could see that. I'd have to be more careful not to offend her.

"That's fine," Marty said.

"Well, if you're not going, it wouldn't look right for me to go," Claire replied. "At least you've met Emma."

I shrugged. I didn't care if Claire went or not. "Where have you been, anyway?"

"I spent the night with my new group of friends." Claire put her hand on her hip and shot me a smirk. "Hannah Lambert invited me over."

"Hmm. Good to see you're fitting in."

"What happened to you last night? You left before the fireworks were over," Claire commented.

"Actually, they were over when I left. And, trust me, I saw enough."

"Well then, if you two kids aren't going, I'll just tell Ms. Carmichael you had plans," Marty intervened.

A beep from a car horn in the driveway interrupted us. It was Lucas, the kid I met on the lake the day before. We agreed to spend the day Jet Skiing again and considering there was something about him that bothered me, I couldn't pass up the opportunity.

Being an immortal had its perks, but there were limitations when I was undercover in human form. Namely, I could only hear current thoughts or conversations. I couldn't retrieve memories from humans, unless there was skin-to-skin contact.

Even though Lucas and I spent several hours together, I didn't have a chance to shake his hand. A handshake was the fastest, most universally accepted hand-to-hand contact that offered the proper amount of time to download a human's records. Well, for most humans, that was.

Not only did a handshake download recollections of special events and transcripts of prior conversations, it also gave me the network of relationships that person experienced during their life.

In the case of Lucas Crandon, it was that network I guessed to be disjointed. It wasn't that I just disliked Lucas. There was something different about him, but I couldn't pinpoint it. Not yet, at least. His thoughts were limited, mostly of girls, parties, and Jet Skiing. And in most of those, he put himself high on a pedestal. The boy certainly had an ego.

"Hey, Lucas! Thanks for picking me up," I said, extending my hand toward him.

When he shook it, I began to understand. "No problem. Ready?"

I nodded. "Let the fun begin."

Chapter 24
Emma's Story

After hours of running errands, we finally returned to Aunt Barb's house.

It took several trips to unload bags of snacks, bouquets of flowers, and cases of beer and soda.

"Can you take that downstairs?" she asked when I carried in two cases of Coke.

"Sure," I answered, heading to the lower level. It wasn't the first time I walked freely around Aunt Barb's house. I used to come and go all the time, when Dad and I visited. They would sit upstairs while I hung out in the rec room and played board games with TJ and Hannah. But as I looked around the picture-perfect family room, nothing was like it used to be.

I put the soda on the table and glanced from the stone fireplace with a chunky wood mantel that Mom admired, to the weathered leather couch I used to nap on. Bright orange and green pillows in various patterns and textures were added since then, as were the tall, copper candleholders on the end table.

Everything looked different.

Bookshelves lined the walls of the long, rectangular room, filled with old and new books. Bright-colored spines stood at attention next to old-looking leather ones in drab tones. Photos and trinkets, memories of Aunt Barb and my uncle's travels, were selectively placed throughout. A carved wooden elephant sat beside an album with "Safari" written on the burlap cover. Two shelves over, a miniature Eiffel Tower rested next to a picture of Aunt Barb. A shiny, navy-blue frame held a photo of her and Uncle Rob embarking on a cruise. They stood beside a white life ring with "Welcome Aboard" printed on it. It was the last trip they took, a few months before he died. I took a deep breath and shook my head.

How could I have been there hundreds of times, but never seen what was right in front of me?

Then I noticed it, sitting on a shelf. A larger image, about the height of the tallest book, caught my attention. As I stepped closer, I realized it was Dad and me. My hand automatically rose to touch the glass separating me from him. I stood frozen for a minute, and then it hit me. He was gone, really gone.

Dad was dead.

I felt a pain in my chest before my body began to shake or tears reached my cheeks. It was a deep, aching burn, like something was boiling inside of me. My throat hurt, and I suddenly couldn't swallow. I sobbed uncontrollably, as I tried to catch my breath.

I wasn't sure how long I sat on the floor between the bookcase and the wooden table before Chester found me.

He licked my face and nudged my arm until I lifted my head and opened my eyes. Chester barked once, sharp and deep, before lying down beside me. He was too large for the small, confined place, but he squeezed in anyway. His oversized body rested against the shelves, while he placed his head on my lap.

"Emma?" I heard Aunt Barb's voice.

I didn't answer. When I opened my mouth, no sound came out. Aunt Barb found me in the corner and helped me up. She hugged me tight to her chest until my shaking stopped.

Chapter 25
Ben's Story

I didn't like Lucas from the minute I met him.

Of course, after downloading his memories, I saw him differently. His father, Neal Crandon, was a detective for the Westport P.D., and the officer that brought Barbara Carmichael to Highland Park the day Emma's dad died. A decent dad, by all accounts, at least from what I could tell. He was strict and lawful, while Lucas was not.

Even with the broken-home scenario he lived in, I still didn't like Lucas.

I parked my Toyota Cruiser on Main Street, in front of Priscilla's Diner. It was the building that used to house Hudson's Grocery back when I lived here in the 1930s. But years later, it changed hands and names so many times that I couldn't keep up. The oak sign with black scripted font proudly stated the name of the current restaurant, named after a stillborn Carmichael, buried decades before.

Priscilla Carmichael transitioned the day she was born. Sad, but it happened more often than people knew. Most humans didn't talk about it, but we did. Priscilla was a beautiful soul. She accepted a human life as a new contract, knowing it would last mere months, in vitro. She had long since moved on to other contracts, to other human lives, completely unaware of the past lives she lived, of who she was and what she was a part of.

The streets were quiet and bare. It was early, pre-dawn, with most residents sound asleep. A dog barked in the distance, though I knew it wasn't because of me. Lucas lived with his mom in a brownstone house in the least desirable section of Riverside. I walked along the sidewalk beside the factory that old man Carmichael started well before my time. It was the main manufacturing company back in the day that employed most of the town.

All the Carmichael kids worked there, and even ran the place after the old man died, except William. He was the youngest and the least interested in stainless-steel products.

William worked in the factory just enough to pocket some cash and buy the old, vacant monastery on Lake Bell. It was the right decision for him, though everyone in his family and the town, for that matter, thought he was crazy. William proved the critics wrong. He created a legacy and now, a century later, the Carmichael Inn had a reputation of its own.

A chain-link fence topped with three rows of barbed wire separated the sidewalk and small neighborhood from the plant. As I walked the two blocks to where Lucas lived, I could hear the thoughts and dreams of local residents, but like most useless dialogue that cluttered the sounds waves, I ignored it.

When I turned the corner onto Leonard Street, I could hear Lucas' thoughts. He was asleep. Knowing his voice, however, I could filter it out amongst the others within the current radius of my location.

The thoughts that ran through Lucas' mind were disturbing at best. He was a selfish, loveless individual, with a speckled past. He was surrounded with emotional trauma and violence, which was why I chose to find him.

I had to see how he lived.

As I reached house number 312, I could sense something. I heard the thoughts of his neighbors next door and downstairs. But there was only one other person in the upper flat in which he resided. A woman. Her name was Charlene, and I knew she was his biological mother. Her Nevada-issued driver's license listed her as Charlene M. Tillman. She took the last name of her second husband, the third surname she had during this lifetime.

There was another spirit hovering, I could feel it, but it was not present.

I pulled the hood of my sweatshirt tight over my head, as I loitered on the street in front of his house. The sky was still dark from night, and no soul was awake within blocks.

I scanned the surrounding houses and blocks around that. I visually canvased the roads that encompassed those, and the ones around them. A woman hit the snooze on her alarm clock. A man woke up for a bathroom break, but nothing appeared out of the ordinary.

Yet, there was something out of place.

There was something definitely wrong. I just couldn't figure out what it was.

Chapter 26
Emma's Story

I was walking amongst strangers.

The street was crowded, and skyscrapers surrounded me. I didn't recognize the buildings, or know exactly where I was, but I wasn't nervous or scared.

It was Chicago.

People of all ages were around me. Most were headed in the same direction. Only a few walked toward me, against the flow. Traffic moved on the street. Car horns beeped and whistles blew. I overheard muffled conversations, though I couldn't say I saw where the sounds came from.

The weather was chilly. I pulled my hat down over my ears and lifted my collar a bit higher.

At first, I barely heard his voice and when I did, I was sure it wasn't directed at me. But the next time he spoke, he was clear.

"You need to give him time," a masculine voice said behind me. I couldn't explain why, but I slowed my pace. People around me slowly began to disappear. *They must have found their destination*, I thought. However, when everyone was suddenly gone, I realized I didn't know where they went.

I was alone on the street. The buildings around me seemed smaller, and the traffic went away. The voice behind me got louder. I stood still on the sidewalk, frozen in a suddenly unfamiliar place.

"It may take some time. Be patient with him," he continued. He wasn't familiar, yet I wasn't afraid.

I turned to face him. I had to know where the voice was coming from.

The man was older than I expected. I noticed a light graying above his ears, in contrast to his dark skin. He wore a charcoal wool overcoat, belted high at the waist, with a faint plaid pattern that looked out of style. A red scarf was neatly tied and tucked at his neck and his black fedora was trimmed with a small, red-and-gray feather. In a different era, I would have guessed him quite fashionable. The wool looked thick and firm, like good quality material went into his coat, and he carried himself well.

He spoke to me as if I knew him and who he was talking about.

I did not.

"He will come back to you. Just give him time."

I stood still and looked at him. I wanted to absorb everything about him, to recognize him.

He brought a pipe to his lips and took several short puffs. Smoke exhaled from his mouth in small bursts circling around us.

"What? Who?" I asked, watching the expression on his round face. I felt at ease around him.

"Elizabeth, he's been looking for you for quite some time. Be patient." The smoke from his pipe increased and lingered, despite the wind that picked up around us.

"My name isn't Elizabeth," I started to say, but the words didn't come out completely before he was gone and I was awake. "My name is Emma," I said aloud, realizing it was all a dream.

I sat up in bed and tried to put his face together in my mind. He vaguely reminded me of an actor on TV, on one of those police shows my dad used to watch. The more I thought about the dream, the less I remembered. And soon, reality came flooding back and the dream was completely forgotten.

It was barely light outside. Streaks of reddish purple were rising in the east, as I peered out my window in Aunt Barb's house. I crawled back in bed and pulled up the fluffy, white comforter around me. I couldn't help but feel awkward in my new surroundings. The only thing that belonged to me was the small suitcase in the corner and the iPad on the dresser. Everything else was new, strange.

My thoughts wandered to Aunt Barb's cookout, as I tried to fall back asleep. I'd been to her parties since I was a kid. It was an even mixture of friends and employees. Of course, I never paid much attention before. Most years, I brought a friend along, or busied myself with Hannah and TJ when we were younger. But yesterday was a different experience for me.

Hannah proved to be as friendly as her mother was. She quickly chatted like we had been friends forever. Of course, we were. It was just forever ago that we really spoke to one another, like friends. She helped me cut lemons and limes that Aunt Barb wanted at the bar, for mixed drinks she said, when she handed Hannah and me bags of fruit. As we washed and sliced them, Hannah brought up the board game, Life, we used to play. At first, I felt a bit uncomfortable, but when she made fun of herself and her addiction to the game that summer, we both laughed. That was the summer I kissed TJ. It was my first kiss and one that Hannah witnessed. She ran off and tattled to our parents. Reminiscing of that day was the icebreaker in our conversation.

"TJ's got a girlfriend, Molly Preston," she said. For a minute, I thought we were twelve again and she was busy telling me gossip.

"Do you like her?" I asked, attempting to make conversation.

"Yeah, she's really nice. Really pretty, too."

I nodded, not sure what else to say. I opened a jar of Marciano cherries and poured them into a bowl. "What about you? Do you have a boyfriend?"

"Yup. Justin. He was supposed to come to the cookout, but he can't. He plays soccer."

Soccer? Now she had me interested. "For Westport?"

"Yeah. He's a goalie."

"I play soccer… well, I did. Back home, I mean," I answered.

"Well then, you need to meet Brinn… she plays. Hmm, I wonder if she'll be here. She works for your aunt at the Inn."

I nodded. "What position does she play?"

"Sorry, I'm not sure. But she's really good. She made varsity as a freshman." I listened, but I didn't reply. "Oh, and there's this new girl. Claire. I think you'll really like her. I've hung out with her a few times. Molly said she plays soccer, too."

"Claire?"

"Yeah. You know what? I think she just moved here from Chicago. She was at the island party last night."

"Really? What does she look like?" I asked.

"Long, light brown hair. I would've introduced you, but—"

"I didn't see you last night," I interjected.

"I know. I saw you, but you were walking the beach with some hot guy. Is that your boyfriend?"

I felt my cheeks warm. "Matt. Um, we broke up." It was the first time I said it aloud.

"Oh, I'm sorry." Hannah's tone was sincere.

After a few moments of silence, she asked, "So when do you start school?"

"I'm not sure. Barb and I didn't really talk about it." I hesitated. "I mean, I just got here yesterday."

"Yeah, I suppose it's pretty soon. Well, I think you'll like Westport. I'll introduce you around. And of course, TJ will too."

I wasn't sure that TJ would agree to what Hannah committed him to. But it would be nice to have friends.

The sky turned a deep orange, as I fell back to sleep.

Chapter 27
Ben's Story

"That'll be eight dollars and thirty-one cents."

I dropped a ten-dollar bill on the wooden counter next to a coffee, an energy drink, the Westport Gazette, and a tin of cinnamon-flavored Altoids. The older, gray-haired man at the register stared at me for an instant before picking up the money and counting out my change. Even though I frequented his bait shop and convenience store for decades, he shouldn't recognize me. After all, I changed my disguise every time I stopped in.

"Thank you, son," he said. He touched my hand, as he handed back some coins and a dollar bill. Our eyes met briefly, as files downloaded and I was able to read his past. A surge of happiness came over me, until the distinct ring of an old-fashioned bell distracted my thoughts.

"Good mornin', miss," the man said, looking toward the door as he bagged my items.

"Good morning," a familiar voice answered.

I didn't need to turn around. I knew she was behind me.

"Aren't you here bright and early?" Bianca asked when I picked up the bag with my purchases, grabbed my coffee, and turned to leave.

"And aren't you surprisingly where you shouldn't be?" I retorted under my breath and headed to the door. I knew she followed me. Her mindless thoughts filled the airwaves between us.

"Benjamin, are you angry?" Bianca questioned.

I unlocked my Toyota with the remote, threw the bag into the front seat, and turned to face her. I took a sip of the steaming java before answering her. "What do you think, Bianca?"

The stunned look on her face wasn't what I expected. After a moment of silence, she gathered her thoughts and said, "I'm sorry. It's just that I've always wanted to work on a case with you. I thought… in my free time, right now… that I could. I could be here, if you need me. If you saw me here, you'd find a spot for me."

I shook my head. "Where are you staying?"

She pointed to a four-story building across the street. Retail shops were on the lower level with patio railings lining the floors above. The condos were new and a bit more upscale than residents on Leonard Street, behind the factory.

"There isn't a safe house in that building," I stated.

Bianca shrugged. I noticed her glance toward the street where a red Corvette slowed, as if contemplating pulling into the lot where we stood. Instead, the car crept to the corner at a snail's pace and eventually turned.

"So you've set up home in a non-agency-issued dwelling? What did you do? Take out a lease, like a human?"

She stared at the ground. The spunky girl that begged to be part of my mission suddenly lost her assertiveness. "Um, yes."

I glared at her. As an agent, we had access to resources for whatever we'd need on earth. Anything was available—birth certificates, driver's licenses, even cash. Lots of cash. "Is this even a sanctioned trip?" I couldn't help but ask.

Bianca looked up at me, confidence returning to her eyes. "Yes."

"And, they're aware you've chosen to set up your own residence? Not stay at a safe house? Why not? Why aren't you at the safe house?" I pointed in the direction the Corvette turned. "There's a three-bedroom ranch a couple blocks up. That's *legit*."

Bianca shrugged. Again.

"You're sure the agency is aware of your presence here in Riverside?"

She nodded. "Yes. Ben, I'm in-between assignments. I requested time off, here… and it was approved."

"When's your next post?"

"January."

"You intend to stay here 'til then?"

"I'd like to," she answered, her tone weak at first. "Yes. I plan to."

I took a deep breath. She was right. In between missions, agents were free to take vacation, and there was nothing I could do to stop it. Of course, I'd sure remember to give Jorgenson hell for it.

"Maybe we could have breakfast?" She smiled and touched my arm. "You know, there's this cute diner down the street, Priscilla's. Have you been there?"

"No. I'm not having breakfast with you. And while you're here, you're staying away from me. Got it?" I took a step back, and she removed her hand.

"Ben, I really want in on this."

"Bianca, there is no assignment here. This is my vacation, too. Nothing more."

"But you picked—"

"No. It's dormant duty, Bianca. There's no hidden mission. I've stopped a heart attack and saved a kid from choking. That's it. Got it?"

She looked away, but I knew she understood.

"Maybe we'll bump into one another, then," she answered, defeated.

"Yeah, maybe," I said aloud, but I sincerely hoped not.

She said goodbye and turned to leave. When she approached the crosswalk and I opened my car door, I noticed the Corvette again. The dark-haired driver slowed mid-block and watched Bianca cross the street. As if waiting for her to recognize him, he sat idle at the corner, but Bianca didn't look back. Once she was inside the building, the Corvette turned the corner, glancing at me as he passed.

Was he just a curious bystander checking out an attractive woman? Or was there something more? Then the conversation with Drew dawned on me—a blonde with a sports car and a condo in Riverside.

Could Lucas have met Bianca?

Chapter 28
Emma's Story

Aunt Barb took the next two days off work.

She said she was entitled to a vacation. Even though she never went into the office, every time her phone beeped she answered it quickly, regardless of where we were. I should have known she was a workaholic. So was Dad.

We kept busy. So busy, I could barely catch my breath. Somehow, I thought that was intentional. We shopped, we laughed, and we cried. We had lunch at the Inn one day and in Westport the next. We picked up odds and ends at the pharmacy and ordered groceries online for delivery. We rented movies one night and watched TV another. We had ice cream for breakfast and ordered dessert before dinner, but we didn't talk about Dad, and she never mentioned me going to school. It was an active and tiring couple of days, like a typical weekend at Aunt Barb's.

Except that it wasn't.

When Aunt Barb suggested we visit the house on Lake Michigan, I agreed. After all, it was the house we would soon live in, the old Victorian she renovated months earlier.

Aunt Barb was unusually talkative on the drive to Westport. She pointed out landmarks at practically every corner, which was good, I guessed, since it was a different route than Dad used to take. By the time we reached North Avenue, I felt pretty comfortable that I'd find my way back on my own.

"There's Westport High School." Aunt Barb pointed to a contemporary building with a wall of glass and stone. The building was over two blocks long. The student parking lot was full of cars. I forgot it was a school day. As Aunt Barb circled the campus, I noticed the soccer field alongside the football arena. "Not as bad as you thought, huh?"

"No, not at all," I answered. Even though Westport was a small town and in the middle of nowhere Wisconsin, the school wasn't much different from mine back home.

"So... what do you think about starting school next week?" she asked, turning back onto North Avenue. The topic I wanted to avoid finally surfaced.

"I, ah—"

"After the move, of course. Maybe give it a few days to settle in. Start Tuesday? Then the first week will be over before you know it." She glanced at me and smiled.

She was right. It would be a quick, short week. Then again, her life would return to normal, while I had to start over.

"It'll be a piece of cake. You'll see," she said before I could respond.

"Um, yeah." Piece of cake. My stomach did a flip when I thought about facing hundreds of new students. Being *that* girl—the pathetic girl that transferred because her parents died.

Great.

"And the best part," she said, two blocks from the school, "is that it's close to where we'll live." The road curved a sharp right, giving way to a spectacular view of Lake Michigan. An observation deck overlooked the endless water, while a narrow stretch of grass hugged the bluff, a block long. A wooden sign read, North Pointe Park.

Seconds later, Aunt Barb turned into the first driveway, lakeside. The Victorian-style house was narrow and deep, with a round tower in the front, next to the front door. I was silently relieved it was tastefully painted in beige and cream, and not in some god-awful pink or purple that I would be embarrassed to live in. The driveway was long with an attached garage and a barn-like building at the back of the property. A row of dense trees clung to the bluff, lining the left side of the driveway.

"Wow. Huge yard," I said after the car came to a stop.

"I know. It'll be perfect for Chester." He whined at the mention of his name. We turned to look at him in the back of my aunt's SUV. He barely fit across the seats, but somehow managed to poke his head through the open window.

"Ready?" she asked after turning off the engine.

"Yup."

A long, skinny porch ran along the side of the house. Aunt Barb walked up the four steps and unlocked the door. Small bushes separated the porch from the driveway, with oversized planters flanking the stairs. Baskets of geraniums and petunias hung between each supporting pillar.

It was welcoming.

We walked into an open-concept first floor, with the dining room in front of us, the kitchen to the left, a great room to the right, and a den off the front foyer. Cherry wood cabinets and cream-colored trim filled the house. Aunt Barb proceeded to give me a tour and recount the home's history, from its original construction for a wealthy town resident's daughter, to the 1950's conversion to a multi-unit rental. She pointed out little changes she made, and big ones that emphasized the pride in her work.

Aunt Barb led me up a mahogany staircase to a loft.

"What do you think?" she asked as we stood in the open space overlooking the foyer.

"The house is beautiful, Aunt Barb. And, it's huge! Much bigger than it looks."

"I know. I agree. But what I meant was—what do you think about this space?"

I shrugged. The area was about the size of a bedroom, with two doors off to the left and a long hallway heading toward the back of the house.

She explained her idea of setting up a TV and Dad's leather couch in the loft for me to hang out with friends. She talked with her hands and moved around the room to help me envision her thoughts. I smiled as I remembered her doing the same thing to Dad when he looked at buying that brown leather couch.

When she was done, I said, "I love it. Thanks, Aunt Barb." I gave her a hug, but it was temporary. She quickly pulled back, reached for my hand, and continued the tour, ending in a bedroom overlooking the lake.

"This will be your room," she said, referring to one of the doors off the loft space. "Right next to mine. Unless you want one of the others," she added.

The room was almost double what I had back home, with a walk-in closet and private bathroom, not to mention an incredible view of the never-ending water.

"It's perfect," I answered. The closet could hold three times the amount of clothes I had, and the bathroom was bigger than the one Dad and I shared on Cavell Street.

"I was thinking we could paint the walls, and maybe put a chaise lounge chair here." She motioned with her hands again, walking around the room, pointing out where she thought the bed and desk would work.

This time, when she finished, she let me give her a hug.

"I just want this to be our home," she said.

I nodded and whispered, "Me, too."

After we wiped away tears, she suggested I look around while she took some measurements and checked on a few things. I wandered through the rooms upstairs, and then found Chester in the great room on the first floor.

"Come on, boy. Let's check out the lake," I said, opening the side door.

Hidden behind overgrown bushes and tree branches, a whitewashed railing peeked out. I pushed a low-hanging branch aside and found a staircase to the water. The paint was weathered, though the steps seemed sturdy. As I descended the stairs, the trees thinned and the wind increased. The breeze was much cooler than the temperature I felt in the driveway above. I jogged the last flight of stairs to the flat boulder about the size of my bedroom back home. Two Adirondack chairs faced the water, waiting for visitors. Bits of dirt and bird droppings spotted the chair's finish. I guessed they hadn't been used in years. I slipped off my flip-flops and sat down on the boulder.

The water looked inviting.

If only I could reach it with my toes. I stretched and re-stretched, scooting my butt closer and closer again, to the edge. The water appeared within reach, but it was no use. Waves rolled in and splashed against the rocks. A mist surrounded me.

I wondered if it was as deep and cold as it looked. I sat content for a minute. It was peaceful here. Pretty. The extent of the water was endless, reminding me of the ocean and its great vastness. Its music was hypnotizing. I closed my eyes and listened to the rhythmic flow of its beat. I felt the pulsations in my chest. Water crashed again.

Thump and splash. Thump and splash.

A chorus rang in my mind. Sprays of cool mist met my skin and comforted me. It beckoned me.

I had to touch it. I had to try again.

Balancing my weight on my arms, I lowered my body to the pile of rocks below. The water receded as the tip of my toes reached the jagged edges of the stones. I waited. And waited again. But the water was not cooperating.

Impatience won as I leaned down further, stretching and lowering. When my foot touched the wetness below, a sharp, prickly sensation shot through me. It felt like needles stabbing my toes.

The water was shockingly cold.

But as quick as it came, it went. The water recessed to the vast openness of the infinite Great Lakes pool, and I waited. Lesser waves strolled in and out, leaving me with a longing for the power I felt when the striking chill pierced my skin.

Wave after wave, yet no force.

I clung to the boulder that doubled as a lakeshore patio. Only a few inches below, the stones gave way to a sandy bottom. All I could imagine was touching it. I wanted to dig my feet deep into its surface. I wanted to touch it.

To be part of it.

A distant voice and the sound of a deep bark distracted me. When I looked up, Chester was sprinting down the stairs. I lifted myself back on the boulder before Aunt Barb reached me.

"Are you okay?" She was out of breath. "What were you doing out here?"

"I just wanted to wade in the water." I could tell she didn't believe me.

"Honey, the water is so dangerous." She pulled me into her arms and repeated how worried she was.

"I wasn't trying to hurt myself. Really, I wasn't."

"Oh honey, I didn't think you were. You just made me nervous, that's all," she said. "There are too many stories of people losing their lives in these waters."

I sat silent, not sure what to say. Luckily, I didn't need to.

"One story right here, actually. Well, it's a legend. They say a woman died in these waters about a hundred years ago."

I looked at her, but I didn't interrupt.

"The legend says she was a young woman in love with a sailor. He never returned home, and his ship was never found. It was thought his ship sank during a storm. Years went by and her life was miserable. Since he promised to return for her, she would come here to the water's edge looking for him, night after night, convinced he would someday return.

"One day, she simply disappeared. Her sister knew she was slipping out each night to the lake and claimed the sailor came back and took her out to sea. To be with him."

"Really?"

"Well, it's just an old legend. I'm not sure how much truth there was in it."

I nodded.

"But they say if you ever see a sparkle in the middle of the lake, it's her."

"Huh. So this shoreline is kind of haunted?"

"I wouldn't say that. Or at least, I don't believe that," she said, looking off toward the water. After a few minutes of silence, she continued. "I could use a good burger. How 'bout you?"

"Yeah, that'd be good."

Chapter 29
Ben's Story

Chester's frantic bark broke my concentration.

Coach Vieth had us running drills on the soccer field. Dribble, dribble, pass, pass, shoot. Next pair up. Repeat. Forty-seven minutes left in practice.

Mentally, I searched the airwaves, listening for Emma. I could pick out her voice a million miles away, even if it was just her thoughts and not a spoken word.

A second later, I found her on the shores of Lake Michigan, by the Victorian house she'd eventually live in with her aunt. Emma seemed focused on the water, wanting to feel it.

Damn it!

What was she doing?

I finished the run with a teammate and intentionally twisted my ankle. I dropped to the ground and clutched the lower portion of my left leg.

I grunted as if in pain when the coach and a few players reached me near the goal. Envisioning swelling, I watched as my ankle mimicked my thoughts.

"Looks bad," Drew said.

Coach shook his head. "Better get that checked. Trainer's inside. We gotta get you back and healthy. We gotta game in a few days."

I nodded. "I'm sure I'll be fine, Coach." Drew helped me up and let me lean on him as we walked toward the building. After several feet, I lessened the limp-act and told him I could make it on my own. With him out of sight, I jogged to the back of the building and slipped into the nearest portal.

I had to see if Emma was really all right.

Chapter 30
Emma's Story

Aunt Barb never left my side, or at least not for long.

After the incident at Lake Michigan, she had contractors add a gate and reinforce the set of stairs, but stopped short of fencing in the boulder patio. "It wouldn't look right, aesthetically," she said. "Besides, it's not like we've got toddlers living here that could accidentally fall in."

I agreed. After all, I knew what I was doing and I didn't want to hurt myself.

Really.

By mid-week, the renovated Victorian house was looking more like a home. Our home, Aunt Barb reminded me. Painters finished coating neutral colors throughout the first floor, just in time for the delivery of new furniture. Decorators hung draperies, while technicians installed a security system.

Things were coming together quickly. It didn't surprise me. Aunt Barb seemed to have a lot of connections. Every day, a crew was at the house doing something, which meant we were there, too.

I sat on the plastic tarp that covered my new ivory chair in what would be my bedroom. The walls were painted once, but needed a second coat the middle-aged man said when I walked in. "Paint's almost dry." It was a pale shade of aqua and complemented the comforter Dad and I picked out last year. Even though Aunt Barb said I could decorate my room however I wanted, I decided to keep the furniture and bedding I had back home.

My room had an oversized window and glass door leading to a long, narrow deck. From here, I could see over the lush trees that lined the bluff's edge. The dark shades of blue water extended far off into the distance. It was a spectacular view. Nothing like the telephone pole I saw outside my bedroom in Highland Park.

When Chester nudged my hand, I realized he probably shouldn't be in my room wagging his long tail on wet walls. "Chester, come on. Let's go," I said, and stood in attempt to coax him out, but he sat in the middle of the room on the painter's drop cloth. "Come on!" I repeated.

Chester tilted his head and lifted his black ears. It was the pose he gave me when he wanted something. His fawn-colored forehead wrinkled as if deep in thought. Back home, I would yell, "treat" or "who's here" to get him to move. He would jump, bark, run, and bark again, like a mad dog on a mission. It worked every time. Except, in a newly painted room, I didn't think that was a good idea.

I surveyed the room to see what Chester could destroy if he suddenly got energetic. An empty pail sat alongside the opposite wall, with the painter's tray and some remaining paint, nearby. There wasn't enough stuff to do damage. Still, an oversized dog in a hyper state of mind could always do damage. I walked slowly to the doorway and turned toward him. He was watching me. "Want to go for a walk?" I asked in a low tone.

Chester barked and ran past me without knocking over the pail. He sprinted down the stairs, leaving only the echo of each woof behind. For a split second, I wondered if the workers downstairs would be afraid of him. Even a small English Mastiff running at full speed through the house would scare most people. Then I realized how Chester warmed up to the guys when they got here earlier. The heavyset man even called him a gentle giant.

It wasn't that Chester wasn't a nice dog. He was just cautious with strangers. At least that was what Dad said when Chester yelped at Matt every time he came to visit or picked me up.

"Call him protective, Emma," Dad said, the last time Matt stopped by and Chester wouldn't stop barking. Matt stood outside his car at the curb, while Chester stood near the front door. He didn't growl at Matt, but he did stand tall with his ears back. It was his Don't-Mess-With-Me face. When Matt took a step, Chester would speak. Chester was funny like that, although he was just a snuggler at heart.

"Aunt Barb?" I called when I got to the empty great room. I heard voices toward the back of the house and followed the sound. I found her with the contractor in the laundry room. "Excuse me, do you mind if I take Chester for a walk?" I asked when she looked up.

"Go right ahead. Are you okay? Did you want me to come with you?" she asked.

"No, I'm fine. Chester seems antsy, that's all."

"Okay. Have fun." She smiled before turning her attention back to the man with the tape measure.

I walked the sidewalk toward North Pointe Park with Chester obediently on my left. The leather leash draped in my hands the way the dog trainer taught Dad and me when Chester was in puppy class. Even though he was a huge dog, he was well behaved. Well, most of the time. Funny, but he loved Melissa and Jenna, and most any other girlfriend I brought over. He just didn't like Matt.

The park was small, too small to be called a park as far as I was concerned. It consisted of a wrought-iron bench and a set of stairs to a gazebo built into the bluff overlooking the lake. Chester and I descended to the roof-covered deck and stood at the railing. It was the same view I had from my new bedroom. A gentle breeze cooled my arms and brought a lake scent, different from Lake Bell. A subtle fish smell filled the air, as waves crashed against the rocky shore and small whitecaps formed and dissipated in the distance. It was welcoming, comforting.

It was the kind of place I could visit every day. I saw myself sitting on the bench in the gazebo. Watching or waiting. I belonged here.

When Chester barked, I jumped. This wasn't my home, not yet at least.

"Okay, okay," I whispered to him. "Let's go," I said as he led me back to the sidewalk. I promised Aunt Barb I wouldn't venture near the water again, but as we headed down North Avenue toward the high school, I couldn't get the calm feeling out of my head. I felt at peace staring at the lake.

Before I knew it, Chester and I were at a full sprint, ending at Westport High School's campus. Chester directed which way to go. Even though it wasn't like him to take the lead like that, I followed without question. When we reached the vacant soccer field, Chester lay down in the goal and I sat beside him. A soccer field was like my second home. The grass was thick, vibrant, and smelled freshly cut.

I was always content within the white painted lines of a soccer field. When I looked at the bleachers, I almost heard the cheers from parents and fans. Teammate's calls filled my mind. Memories of games and practices, friends and opponents, flooded my thoughts, and I found myself wondering if I would ever play soccer here. Or, ever again, for that matter.

Girls' high school soccer season didn't start until March. I knew if I wanted to play for Westport, I'd have to play now, for a club team in the off-season. That was what I did back home. That was what my friends were doing right now. Everything back home was set. I had a coach, a team, and a position.

Here, I had nothing.

I let go of Chester's leash and lay on my back beside him. A week ago, I would have never thought about quitting soccer. Now, it seemed like I had no choice. Then again, a week ago, I didn't expect Dad would die, either.

I stared at the sky and watched the clouds merge and change shape. Mom and I would call out what they looked like when I was young—a ship, a butterfly, a dinosaur. I was just as content staring at them now, as I was back then.

Maybe I fell asleep, or was just lost in a daydream. Either way, when Chester barked and took off running, I realized where I was and that we were no longer alone. A flash of his fawn-colored fur sped away. Shit!

I snapped to attention and chased after him.

"Chester!" He sprinted toward someone coming through the open gate on the opposite end of the field. I called his name again, but it was of no use. He was ignoring me, charging toward a tall boy with dark brown hair and an athletic build. The boy dribbled a soccer ball toward the far goal and seemed oblivious to the impending approach of Chester.

"Stop!" I cried in warning, uncertain of what Chester would do to the boy when he reached him. My calls went unnoticed.

As I got closer, I realized Chester didn't run after any ordinary boy. He ran toward the Prince Charming I saw at Lake Bell. Chester jumped on the prince, but he didn't bark.

I was out of breath and at a loss for words by the time I reached them.

"Sorry," I squeaked out between deep inhales. I hadn't run that fast since coach had us doing sprints last season. Guess I needed to start working out more.

Prince Charming never looked up, but he said, "No problem." He was kneeling and, with both hands, he was scratching Chester's ears. Chester was in heaven, wagging his tail uncontrollably. It was as if they were long lost buddies.

"Hey, my dog likes you," I managed to say. I didn't know what was more embarrassing—my inability to control my dog or the fact that I was so out of shape. Either way, I probably looked ridiculous.

"Yeah, I see that," he said.

"Ahhh... sorry..." I mumbled. "He's not usually like that."

There was an awkward moment of silence before he spoke. "He usually doesn't like people? Or he usually doesn't charge toward them?" I saw his smirk, though he still didn't look up at me. He was focused on Chester, who was now licking him in the face.

I was too nervous to laugh. That was a pretty stupid thing for me to say. "Ah, both."

"Really? Seems pretty nice to me," he answered, still petting Chester. I couldn't believe what an attention seeker my pup turned out to be.

I reached for Chester's leash on the ground and inhaled deeply. "He's usually more protective… More standoff-ish, I guess." Chester proved me wrong. "Chester, stop." I tried to sound firm and tugged on his leash. "Come here."

"It's okay," Prince Charming said, standing up. He was suddenly looking directly at me.

My chest ached. His brown eyes were focused on mine.

"Maybe he just likes me," he said and flashed me a grin.

My palms began to sweat, and I could feel my heart beating faster. He was the most beautiful boy I had ever seen. Say something! I lost my train of thought. "Yeah… I guess."

I sounded stupid. I looked stupid. What was I even wearing?

"Well," he said. Could the moment could be any more awkward?

"Yeah, sorry… again…. I'll get him outa here." I tugged on Chester's leash, but he was firmly planted on his butt.

Prince Charming nodded. The silence was uncomfortable.

I wasn't sure where I got the confidence, but I finally said, "My name's Emma."

"Nice to meet you, Emma. I'm Ben." He smiled.

I felt a tingle in the pit of my stomach and found myself grinning in return.

Ben kicked the soccer ball up and caught it with one hand. "You play? Or just lounge in the goal?"

"Yeah… I mean, I play."

"Nice," he answered.

My cheeks burned, and I could tell I was turning red.

"Maybe I'll see you around, then." He turned to walk away.

Chester sat obediently by my side. "You were pretty friendly with him," I said and chuckled. Prince Charming had a name.

Ben.

Chapter 31
Ben's Story

I KNEW IT.

I expected Molly to give me grief about my first meeting with Emma, but I didn't expect her in my head seconds afterward.

You're unbelievable, Benjamin. You could have been kinder to that poor girl.

Claire's thoughts were softer. *She really likes you, Ben. It was obvious.*

I ignored them both, as they carried on a conversation in my head. *He should sweep her off her feet,* I heard among other comments, like how they needed to correct the damage I'd done with my attitude.

The guys on my team weren't much better. From the minute I joined them on the field for warm-ups, I was questioned about who she was. The girl with the huge dog, they called her.

"Her name's Emma," I finally said, juggling a soccer ball with my knees.

"She's the new girl Lewis said was transferring from his school," Drew added.

I wasn't supposed to know that, so I shrugged.

"Hannah knows her. She's got some sad story, doesn't she, Justin?" Drew asked, kicking a soccer ball to him.

Justin jumped and caught the pass, then rolled it back. "Yeah, her parents died. She's moving here, or maybe already has, I guess," Justin told us. "I haven't met her yet. That's her over there?" he questioned, pointing toward Emma at the gate.

I nodded. "She didn't tell me much. Just that her name's Emma," I answered.

"Well, don't get interested, man. She's got a boyfriend," Drew said as the coach called us over.

Benjamin, are you ignoring us? Molly's stern voice pierced my thoughts. *Have you heard a word we said? We gave you some great ideas. What do you think?*

I think you need to get out of my head.

Molly kept babbling, the coach had a few announcements—scrimmage tomorrow, meeting in the gym before practice on Friday—and more comments between the guys about the cute girl with the huge dog.

See, you're going to have competition for her, Benjamin. If I were you, I'd ask her out before someone beats you to it.

Molly, stop. You know I only have a year here. Maybe I should just let her meet a human.

Commander E said a year or two. Don't waste your time. You'll end up—

I know, I know… I'll end up regretting it, I answered her thought.

Yes, you will.

The trouble was… I already did.

Chapter 32
Emma's Story

The next day we were back at the house.

Aunt Barb monitored the contractor's work and made calls, while I loitered around, trying to text friends who couldn't respond back because they were in class. By mid-afternoon, I was bored. It was almost three o'clock when I checked my phone. The same time I saw Ben on the soccer field the day before.

I convinced Aunt Barb that Chester needed exercise and headed to the high school. The walk to the soccer field seemed longer than yesterday, but I was also preoccupied with the anticipation of seeing Ben again.

When I arrived, it looked like most of the team was already there. I spotted Ben juggling almost immediately, but he didn't see me. I kept Chester on his leash, as we jogged the track circling the field. Ben appeared to be deep in concentration when I rounded the bend near him and his teammates. He didn't even look up.

And the next day, same thing.

On Friday, Aunt Barb had a full schedule planned for us, all of it at the new house. We unpacked boxes of plates and cookware, hung pictures and folded towels. After the cleaning crew was finished, I decided to take Chester for another walk. Aunt Barb was putting sheets on the bed in her room when I told her.

"Okay, I'll just finish up here, and I'll come with you," she said.

"No... that's okay. I'll just walk up to the school and back. We've done it before, and we had fun. You can stay... if that's okay, I mean. I'm fine."

"Alright. Take your time. I've got a few more things to do, anyway."

Chester seemed to know the route to school better than I did. Instead of obediently staying on my left, he charged ahead. It wasn't often that Chester possessed such energy. Then again, I had more enthusiasm since I met Ben, too.

The soccer field was empty when we arrived. Chester and I walked the asphalt track twice, but there was no sign of Ben and no one resembling a soccer player showed up. I checked my phone and noticed it was already after three o'clock.

Just as I was about to leave, a brown-haired boy walked through the gate, with a few others behind him. This time, I had a good grip on Chester's leash. I recognized him as one of the soccer players from before.

"Hey, are you Emma?" the boy asked, as he approached the bend in the track where I stood.

"Um, yeah. Do I know you?" I questioned.

"No. I just guessed," he answered, and then smiled. "I'm Justin. I recognized your dog."

"My dog?"

"Yeah. Well, Hannah talked about him. I figured a girl hanging out on the soccer field with a dog that… well, *that* big… was probably Emma."

"Oh." I laughed. "You're Hannah's boyfriend, right?"

He nodded. "That's me. I think Hannah was going to introduce us at your aunt's last weekend, but I couldn't make it. Anyway, Hannah told me you play soccer and have a cool dog. Chester, right?"

With the sound of his name, Chester snarled. It was a low growl, not a loud bark, but not a vicious warning either. It was his Get-the-Hell-Away-From-Me look. It was similar to his Don't-Mess-With-Me look, but more serious. I tugged on his leash hard, until his ears perked up and he looked apologetic. "Sorry, he's not usually like this."

"Don't worry. I'll stay away. I don't need a huge dog like that mad at me." Justin smiled, and I could see why Hannah liked him. He was cute, but not my type.

Out of the corner of my eye, I could see a soccer ball mid-air headed where we stood. Justin had his back to the kicker and didn't see it coming.

It was gut instinct.

I really didn't think about it, I just reacted. Dropping Chester's leash, I jumped as the ball came closer. My head made contact, and I aimed it back to the kicker. It happened so fast, I didn't realize what I did.

"Wow!" Justin said before my feet landed back on the ground. I heard cheers and whistles from people behind me. "Great header. Hannah said you played, but I really didn't expect much."

I shot him a look.

"I mean, most of the girls I know… well, let's just say they don't play very well."

"Justin, who do we have here?" A deep voice spoke behind me.

"Coach Vieth, this is Emma," Justin answered.

"Emma, tell me where you learned that," Coach Vieth said.

"I played in Illinois," I answered. "Highland Park."

"Are you visiting Westport? Or what brings you here?"

"No, sir. I'm transferring."

The coach proceeded to ask questions about the position I played and whether or not I planned on trying out for the high school team. "We could use someone with your skills. The girls practice twice a week in the off-season, if you care to join them. It will give you touches on the ball until spring. That is, if you want to play."

"Yeah, thanks. I really appreciate it," I said. Suddenly, Westport didn't seem so bad.

I glanced around and noticed Ben on the opposite side of the field.

"Come on, Chester. Let's go," I said. I shook his leash, but he was firmly planted on the ground. I had to coax him to move. As soon as he stood, he started walking toward Ben. I yanked on his leash harder this time, and said, "No Chester. We're going home."

Then, I realized I used the word home.

Chapter 33
Ben's Story

I wasn't sure why Molly picked Rusty's Anchor to meet.

We already resuscitated Rusty and I heard he was doing well, but I didn't question her motive. I was just happy to be out of the bleachers. After all, it was Friday night, which meant high school football in Westport, the social event of the week for every teenager in town.

As instructed, I showed up promptly at 9:35, disguised as a thirty-six-year-old man. Old chunks of driftwood adorned with fish netting and seagulls sat in the entryway, with an oversized, partially rusted anchor. Last time I was here, I never noticed the dingy-looking life rings on the paneled walls.

The hostess sat me at a window booth, told me they only served until ten o'clock, and then left. I felt the presence of an immortal like myself, as I opened a menu.

It was faint and could be from a distance or shielded by a barrier, a skill only experienced agents possessed. Claire, I knew, would never pick up on the sensation I had. It was both a blessing and a curse.

I scanned the place mentally from a bird's eye view, as I pretended to read the menu. It was my favorite ability. I simply left my body for a nano-second to get a different view. No human would ever notice my rigid body for that split second of time when I left it frozen in place. I could visually cover the entire building before anyone noticed I left my body behind.

There was only one table of guests in the dining area and one middle-aged guy at the bar. Rusty made small talk with the dark-haired man. The hostess left her podium station and was punching out in the kitchen. The cook was grilling two burgers, one with Swiss cheese, the other plain. The food-prep girl fixed condiments on white stoneware plates and began wrapping and storing tomatoes and pickles. She stopped mid-path to the commercial refrigerator when the hostess told her about me.

They couldn't see me. I was invisible in spirit form outside of my body. Of course, I couldn't be free from my body for long. A minute or two at most.

I glanced around the kitchen and noticed the back door open. I perched myself higher to get a view beyond the confines of the building as Molly sat down in the booth, across from my body.

"You were propelling, weren't you?" she asked when I returned.

The sensation I felt had to be her. "Yes."

"Bored?"

"You were late."

"It's 9:36. I'd hardly call that late." She tipped her head the way she always did when she was in a snippy mood.

"Okay, so why the meeting?" I asked. "Nice disguise, by the way."

She held back a grin. "You like?"

I laughed. Molly would change her height, her hair color and style, but she would never pack on pounds or add wrinkles. She was a bit vain. Wrinkles that came with the age of her disguise were always camouflaged with makeup, like the abundance of eyeliner she had on.

"There's no reason a thirty-something-year-old woman can't wear something attractive. Is there?" She blinked in slow motion, her long lashes swooping to her cheeks like a monarch's wing in flutter.

I shook my head. "Nope. No reason you can't wear something attractive," I repeated and chuckled. Molly would never change. She was a fashion statement with her fitted black dress, double strand of pearls, and slick hair pulled back into a neat bun.

She rolled her eyes at me, as she heard my opinion.

"Ready to order?" the waitress asked.

I looked at Molly, who seemed flustered, and then turned to the waitress. "Yes, we are," I said. "Honey, would you like me to order first? You know, they only serve until ten o'clock." I touched Molly's hand as I spoke, and then glanced up at the thirty-two-year-old waitress, who smiled back. She wasn't in the kitchen when I propelled.

Molly's thoughts were pointed. She hated being called honey as much as I hated saying it aloud. "I'll have the grilled chicken, please," she spoke to the waitress. "And a glass of Chardonnay."

After I ordered Rusty's famous fish fry and a beer, the waitress left.

"She's pretty," Molly said.

I nodded. "Is she why we're here?"

She glanced around and then continued silently, *Yes. She would have left a few minutes ago and been attacked and killed.*

Is this a sanctioned assignment? Or are you going rogue? It wasn't usually our mission to change the life path of a human, but it was something we could do. Sometimes it was without consequence, but not always.

She shot me a look. "Jorgenson sent me."

"You know the hostess punched out a few minutes ago," I said.

She shook her head. "She'll be fine."

I was confused.

"The waitress' ex-husband is sitting in his car, drunk and angry, with a loaded gun in his lap. Give him twenty minutes and he'll be passed out. When Maria's done with her shift, she won't even see him."

"Why didn't Jorgenson call your parents to handle this? We're missing an underage high school party right now." I smiled.

She paused while Maria served our drinks.

"Well, let's see. Ava is at a medical event at the Carmichael Inn, where Grant was until he was paged to the hospital. Marty is covering for Barbara Carmichael, so she could be with your beloved Emma. Which means Marty can't leave the Inn until the event is over." Molly took a sip from her wine. "This situation with Maria came up rather suddenly. I don't mind, really, Benjamin."

I nodded and raised my glass in a toast. "And it gives you a chance to be an adult again."

She smiled and clinked her glass with mine.

"Jorgenson could have called Bianca. I'm sure she wouldn't mind."

"Bianca?" Her tone expressed her surprise.

"Yes, Bianca. She's here."

Molly turned to look around the restaurant. "What, pray tell, do you mean by *here*?"

"You didn't know?" I told her Bianca rented a condo and planned to stay until January.

"I'm sorry. I had no idea she was that extreme. She clearly doesn't understand your bond with Emma."

As soon as Emma's name came up in conversation, Maria brought our food. Her hand accidentally touched mine, as she placed my fish fry before me. I could tell she was an abused wife and a mother of three that was trying to make ends meet. She finally had the courage to get a restraining order after

Rusty gave her a job waitressing.

After Maria brought a side of mayonnaise, Molly ordered another drink, and later a glass of water. When Maria returned to our table a third time, Molly struck up a conversation with her. Despite Molly's repetitive requests, Maria was pleasant. She smiled and chatted with us like we were the only customer she ever had.

Suddenly, I understood why Molly enjoyed these simple assignments.

Chapter 34
Emma's Story

Aunt Barb woke me before my alarm went off.

"I want to get on the road early," she said as I strolled into the kitchen, dressed and ready to go. Aunt Barb put two slices of bread in the toaster. "Neal will be here any minute. Oh, and Marty's agreed to watch Chester while we're gone."

"Marty? From your office?"

She nodded and sipped her coffee.

It was Saturday, the day of my move from Highland Park to Wisconsin. Neal volunteered to help move the delicates. It was what Aunt Barb called the fine china and other valuables she didn't trust to the moving company. "I want to make sure your mom's precious things stay that way," she said.

Going back to my old house made me both nervous and excited. I was looking forward to seeing my old friends and spending the night with Melissa, but I also knew it would be the last time things would be the way they used to.

The drive flew by, as Aunt Barb and Neal talked the entire ride. I put in ear buds and turned on some music to drown out their conversation.

What could they possibly talk about for two hours? They just saw each other the night before, at the high school football game. Westport won against some school I never heard of. TJ played and so did Neal's son, though I didn't know his name, or what number he was. Hannah was there. As I suspected, she was a cheerleader and simply waved at me when we walked in.

When we reached my house, it looked different. The swing set in the backyard seemed small and vacant. Flowers were wilted in the pot beside the door.

Stepping inside, a chill ran through me.

I swore I saw Mom cooking at the stove, stirring a huge pot of chili. Dad kissed her on the cheek and asked for a taste before it was done. In the family room, I saw Dad reading the paper with his feet propped up on the oversized ottoman that doubled as a coffee table.

"It's the new thing," he said to me. "Impressed that I'm not old and out of touch?"

I smiled to myself, almost convinced they were there with me.

When Aunt Barb called my name, images of Mom and Dad vanished, leaving me with memories of a distant past.

"You okay?" She smiled weakly as if ready to give me a hug.

"Yeah. I'm good," I answered quickly and turned away. I didn't want to remember. I wanted to focus on getting this over with so I could be with my friends.

Aunt Barb had a plan and immediately put Neal and me to work. She had labels and boxes for us to sort what was staying and what we would bring with us. The movers were scheduled to pack things we were taking. The rest would be donated, Aunt Barb told me.

I went to my room and began filling a small box with the mementos I accumulated over the years. The soccer and basketball trophies that meant so much to Dad and me at the time seemed suddenly more important.

Hours passed quickly. Before I knew it, all we had left were cartons stored in the basement—holiday decorations, silver platters Dad hated polishing, and my old collection of American Girl dolls. I paused for a moment when I saw the outfit Mom bought my doll at the store in Chicago. It was way before Mom got sick, back when she and I would go shopping downtown, or take in a movie on a Sunday when Dad watched football. Memories flooded my thoughts and suddenly, I wanted to keep the collection of dolls and accessories.

"Honey, you keep whatever you want. Okay?" Aunt Barb said. "Even if you're not sure, keep it. For now. You can always part with it later."

We packed, labeled, and organized the house, while Neal sorted tools and moved the patio furniture that would sell with the house.

When Melissa's BMW pulled in the driveway a little after five, I was relieved. I ran out the side door, as she shut off the engine. She gave me a hug in between squeals of "Omigod, I'm so excited to see you" and "I've got so much to tell you."

I felt like we were in middle school again.

Melissa greeted Neal and my aunt like she knew them for years. She navigated their questions in a confident tone that matched a middle-aged woman. Melissa was always good at impressing adults, and she certainly wowed my aunt with her interest in the Inn and how the packing was coming along.

"Have a great time, girls," Aunt Barb said as we headed to the door. "Emma, don't forget the moving truck will be here early."

I nodded. How could I forget? She told me a dozen times.

"So, your aunt and Neal, huh?" Melissa asked as she pulled onto the street.

"What? No. I don't think so."

"Really? I would swear they had body language. You know, like a couple."

Couldn't be. I shook my head. "Uh-uh. No way. My aunt isn't dating Neal. They're just friends. Neal knew my uncle. That's all."

Could they be? I shook the thought.

"So, The Grill or Norton's? What do you feel like?" Melissa asked.

"The Grill."

She smiled. "I was hoping you'd say that." It was Melissa's favorite restaurant, mostly because it was next to her favorite jeans shop, a little boutique with designer brands. "The guys are going to Frank's later tonight." She glanced at me, as we rolled to a stop at an intersection. "Lewis said we could stop by. If you want to, that is." Her elevated tone made it sound inviting.

I hesitated before I agreed to go, but Melissa didn't seem to notice. I wondered if Matt would be there and if it would be awkward seeing him. Obviously, he didn't tell anyone that we broke up, either.

Melissa pulled into a parking spot in front of the restaurant. I checked my reflection in the mirror and put on a fresh coat of lip gloss.

"Um, Em? Isn't that Matt?"

I flipped up the visor and looked in the direction where she was pointing. Walking down the sidewalk, Matt was holding hands with Aimee Wilkinson.

"What the hell?" Melissa asked and looked at me.

My heart pounded in my chest. "I, ah… we… we broke up."

"What? When? Why didn't you tell me?" She was staring at me now. I felt her eyes on me as mine were fixed on Matt opening the restaurant door and following Aimee inside.

"Mel, I'm sorry. I should have. I wanted to," I whispered. "I guess I… I didn't think it was real." I shook my head, still staring at Matt. "I can't go in there. I just can't."

Melissa started up the car and shook her head. "Neither can I."

We spent the rest of the night at her house. We talked about school,

Matt, and which colleges to apply to. We ate ice cream out of the tub and watched *Saturday Night Live*. Melissa swooned over the host, an actor she crushed on since his first movie came out when we were in middle school. It brought back memories of earlier days, before boyfriends and high school, before Mom got sick and before Dad died.

"Do you think we'll stay this close? You know, after I move away?" I whispered after Melissa shut off the TV. Even though it was almost three in the morning and I was exhausted, I didn't want the night to end.

"Of course we will, silly," Melissa mumbled. "You're my best friend."

I smiled to myself in the pitch-black room and slowly fell asleep.

***

The moving truck was already in front of the house when Melissa drove me home the next morning. Two men in gray uniforms loaded Dad's leather couch, as she parked the car. Neal's Jeep and my Jetta were both filled with boxes and framed prints.

"Good morning, girls," Neal said when he met us in the driveway. "Glad you're here. We're ready to go."

I glanced toward my aunt. She stood by the garage, talking to a woman in a deep red suit. The woman had blonde, perfectly shaped hair and wore an abundance of jewelry. Dressed like that I doubted she was with the moving company.

"She's the realtor," Neal said, when he caught me staring.

I tensed with his words, but Melissa's immediate hug changed the subject.

"Text me every day, okay?" she asked, her eyes beginning to water.

"I will." Tears ran down my cheeks. Saying goodbye was harder than I thought it would be. "Come visit, okay?" I asked in between deep breaths.

Melissa nodded and wiped her eyes. She smiled briefly, then turned and left.

Neal put his hand on my shoulder and mumbled something about it being all right. I knew he was just being nice.

Nothing about this would ever be all right.

Chapter 35
Ben's Story

Claire and I drove to school together each day.

It was expected of siblings, I assumed. She was settling in well, making friends with Hannah Lambert and a few others that I couldn't name if I had to. I didn't care. She was fitting in. In other words, she was working out.

Rookie or not.

Molly never took a liking to young agents. Not that she didn't like them, personally; they just brought a level of additional responsibility to any mission. Like an untrained dog you kept on a leash, rookies should never venture too far alone.

"Are you ready for today?" she asked on our drive in that morning. It was Emma's first day of school, and we were already running late.

I nodded. Of all days, Claire picked today to get picky about her appearance.

"I'm sorry it took me so long to get ready," she said. "I just can't get the hang of these newfangled hair irons. We didn't have them, back when… well, you know."

Yeah, I knew. Back in the late 1930s when she lived in Chicago.

We drove in silence until we got stuck at a stoplight. When the light turned green, I gunned it. I had to get past the railroad tracks before the gate dropped. A train was a few miles away, and timing was everything.

"What are you doing?" Claire's voice distracted me and broke my concentration. I lifted my foot from the accelerator pedal, and the car immediately slowed to a more manageable speed. Sixty miles an hour was fine on the county highway, but frowned upon on city streets with a posted speed limit of twenty-five.

My change of pace meant we got stuck by the train.

"This is my fault, isn't it?" Claire asked. "I'm really sorry, Ben."

I calculated the precise speed necessary based on the distance to the tracks, the speed of the train, and the time school started. I had it. I was set. We would have made it on time.

Then, Claire's distraction interfered, and we sat idling. In other words, we would be late.

I took a deep breath and realized Molly's point about rookies.

"You know, Claire, you don't need to use a *curling* iron to fix your hair in the morning."

Her bright blue eyes looked up at me, but she didn't understand.

"Shape it. With your hands. It'll turn out like you envision."

She gave me a blank stare.

I shook my head, realizing we had a long way to go on the training of basic immortal abilities. Maybe Molly had the patience to teach her.

I certainly didn't.

Chapter 36
Emma's Story

"Of course I'm driving you," Aunt Barb said.

I thought she was kidding, but when she pushed the issue, I realized she was serious. As much as I appreciated what my aunt did for me, I didn't need a hovering pseudo-parent holding my hand like a kindergartner on the first day of school.

I was nervous enough as it was.

Ten minutes later, she dropped me off curbside and, after a brief wave, I was on my own. I headed to the office, picked up my schedule, and blended in with other students walking the halls.

When I rounded the corner, I saw Hannah standing at an open locker. She smiled and waved.

"My mom told me you were starting today. Where's your first class?" she asked.

"Room 132. Calculus with Mr. Vieth."

"He's good. You'll like him. He's the soccer coach, you know."

"Oh… that's why his name sounds familiar."

"Um, yeah," she said, reaching for my schedule. "What other classes do you have?" Before I could answer, she scanned my list and pointed out subjects we had in common. "Looks like I'll see you second hour."

"Okay."

With that, she headed to class, and I located my locker. It was down from Hannah's and just outside Mr. Vieth's room. Huh. *Very convenient*, I thought.

The bell rang, as I walked through the door.

Mr. Vieth was friendly. I guessed he recognized me from the soccer field the week before, but he didn't say anything about it. Instead, he handed me a textbook and directed me to an open seat, then continued writing problems on the board. I was grateful he didn't make me stand in the front of class and introduce myself.

I settled into the chair and opened the book to the page number he listed.

It was then that I saw Ben. He walked in late, heading toward an open desk two rows over from mine.

"Welcome, Mr. Parker," Mr. Vieth stated loudly. "Good of you to join us today."

Ben sat down without a word, and I held my breath.

The classroom buzzed with conversation, but Ben sat still staring forward and Mr. Vieth continued writing examples I guessed we'd discuss, eventually. Ben was more attractive than I remembered. He was taller than Matt was, and broader. Most importantly, when I looked at Ben, I felt a tingle that I never experienced with Matt.

You're being ridiculous, I thought.

Ben didn't know that I even existed. Well, not really, anyway.

I watched him out of the corner of my eye. When Mr. Vieth called the class to attention, I only partially listened. I couldn't get Ben out of my mind. I wondered if the brunette I saw was his girlfriend and if we'd get a chance to talk again.

Then, suddenly, Ben looked at me.

Busted. My cheeks burned, and I quickly looked away.

"We have a new student in class today," Mr. Vieth said.

Oh shit.

"Emma Bennett just transferred from Chicago," he said, motioning in my direction. "Please make her feel welcome."

"Whew!" someone whistled from the back of the room.

"Okay, now. Let's open our books to page thirty-two, please," Mr. Vieth continued.

I looked toward Ben and saw a slight grin on his face, though he never looked away from Mr. Vieth. Ben seemed focused on the teacher and the examples he was covering. As I turned to look away, I thought I saw his beautiful brown eyes turn in my direction.

He couldn't possibly be looking at me, could he?

Chapter 37
Ben's Story

Her rosy cheeks gave it away.

I didn't have to read Emma's thoughts to know Coach Vieth had embarrassed her. Hearing her heart pound rapidly when she noticed me was gratifying. Emma had Spanish second period and art fourth hour, both with Claire. She had history and gym class with Molly, and literature, physics, and study hall with me. And lunch with all of us.

I knew her schedule well. Then again, I set it up. Emma took tough classes and got good grades back in Highland Park. Convincing the school administrator in Westport to put her in classes with undercover agents was simple. Of course, I didn't ask him to do this—I compelled him.

Best of all, there would be no consequence for this compulsion since it wasn't out of the realm of possibilities. In other words, I didn't over-exaggerate Emma's abilities to earn it on her own. I simply helped expedite the thought process.

I tuned into Claire's thoughts, as I took my seat in art history. It was an easy class, not only because I was an immortal and knew everything already or could find it, but because I lived during most of the periods on the syllabus, starting with the Renaissance period. Of course, my favorite artist was Renoir from the Impressionist period.

It was the first time I met Elizabeth.

Claire took her seat in the middle of the classroom in Spanish. With her thoughts in my head, I was able to get a view of the room, students, and Mrs. Garcia. After the bell rang, both the Spanish teacher and art history teacher, Mrs. Benoit, called the class to attention.

Sometimes, it was difficult monitoring two conversations and locations at once.

I saw Emma in Claire's thoughts. She sat one row over and two seats forward from Claire. Mrs. Garcia introduced her before she began the day's lecture.

Molly interrupted my thoughts with her own. *So much for you talking to Emma in calc first hour. Though I noticed her interest in you.*

I nodded, but I kept my thoughts silent as Mrs. Benoit started a slide presentation with her lecture.

Ben, she's finally here. When are you going to make a move?

Mrs. Benoit was covering the 1300s and the Italian Renaissance.

Mrs. Garcia asked the class questions in Spanish.

It's her first day. Let it go. My tone was firm.

Fine. I get it. But don't complain to me when things don't work out for you. Molly's thoughts rang in my head. I needed to give Emma time to settle in. Then, well, then I'd see if I fit into her life.

For now, she was just a human that had no idea who I was, and I intended to keep it that way.

Chapter 38
Emma's Story

Spanish class seemed easier than in Highland Park.

With a backlog of homework, Mrs. Garcia suggested I stop by her room after school to discuss making up the assignments. I guessed I knew starting over wouldn't be easy.

When I reached my locker, I was lost in thought and fumbled with my lock. I tried the combination three times before it finally opened. The light brown-haired girl at the locker beside me didn't say a word, but she knew I was having trouble. She glanced at me out of the corner of her eye while I struggled. I was grateful she didn't make a snide comment. I had enough embarrassment with both teachers announcing me as the new kid that morning already, and I still had six more classes left.

"Hey," the girl beside me said after I opened my locker. "You're the new girl in Spanish."

"Guilty," I said, grabbing a new notebook for US history class.

"I could tell." She laughed.

I nodded. "It's my first day."

"I'm Claire Parker," she said, extending her hand. Her smile was big and bright, and I immediately felt comfortable.

"Emma Bennett," I said and shook her hand.

"It's good to meet someone else that's new," she said enthusiastically.

I tipped my head to the side. "You're new, too?"

"Yeah. Well, I've been here since the start of summer," she added. Claire proceeded to tell me she transferred after school let out in June, so she was new to the high school. When the warning bell rang, she quickly asked, "What class do you have next?"

"US history."

"Upstairs?"

"Yeah."

"We better hurry. I have government, and I think history is in the classroom next door."

I shut my locker door and rushed to class, arriving just as the bell rang. I noticed Stunt Boy from Lake Bell in the back row when I handed the teacher my schedule. Mr. Dunn studied the sheet the office gave me, then finally looked up and told me to take a seat. The only open desk was toward the back of class in front of the blond boy I recognized. I sat down, as the teacher started to address the students.

"Hey, you're the crazy Jet Ski girl, aren't you?" Stunt Boy asked.

I chuckled at the absurdity of his words and shook my head. "I thought you were the crazy driver," I whispered, facing forward.

He tapped my shoulder with his pen, "No, I'm pretty sure you took flight."

I couldn't help but smile as I remembered how much fun I had that afternoon.

I tried to pay attention, but Mr. Dunn's low-toned voice and the boring subject let my mind wander. Funny, but Dad loved history. When he wasn't watching ESPN, he was browsing the History Channel. I suddenly missed him. The realization of where I was and what I was missing back in Highland Park flooded my thoughts.

I shook my head to avoid tearing up and let my mind wander to Ben. I wondered what class he had and whether I'd have him in more periods. When the teacher turned his back to write on the white board, the boy behind me tapped on my shoulder again. "What's your name?" he asked.

"Emma," I answered, hoping no one else could hear me. "And yours?"

"Lucas."

Mr. Dunn continued his soft-talking, monotone lecture. I wanted to ask Lucas if the teacher was always so boring, but I was afraid I'd get caught, so I quietly took notes.

Class dragged on. Lucas didn't say anything else during the lecture, and he hurried out after the bell rang. I was convinced I would be late but finally found my way to art class. I felt like a fish swimming upstream, fighting my way amongst the students in the crowded hall.

I was pleasantly surprised to see Claire and Hannah when I walked in, and quickly made plans to meet them for lunch.

Lucas came late and passed my table. He smiled and said, "Hey, Emma."

He wasn't my type, but I started to feel like I was making friends.

Chapter 39
Ben's Story

Emma's emotions rode a rollercoaster her first day at school.

She laughed, chewed on her lower lip, and even teared up when recalling her dad, but she made it through the day without even texting her friends from Highland Park. Claire made sure she had someone to sit with at lunch, though I noticed Emma didn't eat. Reading her thoughts, I realized she hated the salad she ordered. I couldn't blame her. It was a wilted mess.

After school, she joined Claire at the track for a quick run, and then headed to a soccer meeting. When Claire got home later than evening, she thanked me for letting her join our undercover team.

"Emma is so nice. I really like her," she said. "I think we'll be great friends."

Reading Emma's mind, I knew she felt the same way.

***

The next two days flew by. Emma worked diligently to get caught up on missed assignments. She studied for hours while her aunt adjusted to their new house. Neal stopped by after Emma's first day, but not the next. I knew he wanted to spend more time with them, but gave in to Barb's request to slow things down. "For Emma's sake," Barb told him, and even though he respected and understood that, he still wanted more.

I could relate.

***

It was Friday, first-hour calculus, my first class of the day with Emma.

Jorgenson's voice reached into my thoughts. It was his way of calling me, of making contact from our world to the human world. But as Coach Vieth called upon Emma to solve an equation, I found myself listening to her response and forgetting about Jorgenson until Molly reminded me after art history, hours later.

"Jorgenson said you haven't returned his call," Molly whispered. We walked into the crowd of kids in the hallway.

"I didn't get a chance yet."

"You forgot. Admit it." Molly's tone was sharp.

I shrugged. Okay, so I did.

He wants to make sure you saw the bulletin, she explained.

I didn't.

The bulletin on the RA. Her thought had a tone of irritation.

Yeah, so? A rogue agent isn't likely to be off-grid more than twenty-four hours... if that.

She glanced at me out of the corner of her eye and remained silent.

I'm not worried about it. Even if the agent's here in Wisconsin—and frankly, if you're gonna go rogue, you need to pick a city like Chicago or New York. No one in their right mind would pick some small town in Wisconsin. I waved at a guy on the soccer team whose name escaped me and then continued. *But, if they did, so what?*

Molly raised her eyebrows, though I didn't give her an opportunity to speak. *We both know agents are tethered to their handlers and have been for years. I mean, how far can they really go without being detected?*

I didn't understand the big deal. I'd call Jorgenson in due time. I was undercover. I had things to do besides hand holding his whimsical questions.

"Are you done yet?" She smiled at me coyly.

"Yes," I answered, defeated.

"Something eating at you?"

"No."

Well, whatever. This is our job, Benjamin. And Jorgenson said the commander has called a meeting this afternoon.

I cut her off. *Because of a rogue agent? Are you kidding? Agents go off the grid all the time. There was a bulletin last week in Houston. The agent turned up an hour later. Jorgenson's crying wolf, and he's got you wrapped up in it now.* I shook my head, disgusted. "I've got soccer practice. I can't make it to a meeting this afternoon. You can brief me on it later, if it's really important. Or I'll talk to Jorgenson at our scheduled check-in later tonight."

She stopped beside her locker and shot me a death look.

Look. Besides us, there are only a handful of agents that can shield their handlers for extended periods of time. She opened her locker and tilted her head at me. *Okay, maybe not even a handful of agents with our experience. So how dangerous can this rogue agent be? Every agent is monitored. There are*

Trackers in every community… have been for over a century. We're not talking about Victor Nicklas.

As I thought the words, the color drained from Molly's face.

"We *are* talking about Victor?" I said in a hushed voice. Victor was a highly advanced agent that ran several divisions centuries ago. He was known to have a temper and rumored to have been at odds with the commanding rank. He went rogue in 1842. Trackers were not in place at the time and handlers were not tethered as they are now. Teams spent years recreating Victor's meetings throughout Europe. They followed up on leads that went from cold to frigid faster than water could turn to ice in winter.

Molly nodded.

Why would Jorgenson notify us*?* I asked, confused.

Victor is rumored to be in Wisconsin.

Okay, so send a tracking team. I mean, how do they even know Victor's in Wisconsin? And wouldn't a larger city be easier for him to hide?

A hybrid was admitted to a Chicago-area psych ward yesterday."

Wait. What? A hybrid? The presence of a hybrid was like humans encountering dinosaur artifacts. Well, perhaps not exactly. Though hybrids were rare. Removal of a human's soul simply for the ability to control them as an extension of us was prohibited centuries ago.

She nodded. *He was initially in a drug-induced coma, and hospital staff thought he was an addict.*

It didn't make sense. The Bureau banned creation of hybrids when they realized agents abused them. Back then, agents were spread pretty thin. Too many assignments and not enough staff lead to the development and use—or abuse—of hybrids. Humans on their deathbeds were given a second chance at life. For the exchange of their soul, they were returned to a state of health. Only to learn they were controlled by their maker, the immortal that converted them. At the time, souls were only held for weeks or months, at most.

When I didn't respond, Molly continued. *Once he came down from his high, he began chanting Victor's name, saying he turned him into a hybrid. A sleeper notified the office, and a recon agent was dispatched.*

When was this?

Yesterday.

It was deemed immoral after some agents abused their powers by not returning the held souls in a timely manner, allowing these humans to transition into our world.

Where was this?

The guy was found in a back alley behind a dumpster in Chicago… outside some bar. People walked past him for hours before some guy stopped and called paramedics, Molly explained. *The recon agent extracted the meeting places between the hybrid and Victor. Most were in Wisconsin.*

This changed things.

"They met in old barns, country spots, mostly," she said in a low voice. *There weren't any witnesses, I guess. That, or he killed them. The hybrid had faint memories of conversations indicating additional hybrids, but no hard facts.*

"Okay, so I understand he could be around here and obviously, we need to be on the lookout. But, seriously, why would Victor come here?" I whispered, and then smiled at a classmate that walked past.

She looked down. "Jorgenson wants us on the case."

Why? There are other agents the commander can assign.

She lifted her shield, and I saw images of Victor with a dark-haired woman.

"Molly? What are you telling me?"

New pictures in her head zoomed in on a young, beautiful woman I guessed to be Molly, taken in the late 1800s in London. As I watched, the video replayed Molly walking down a narrow street. It was late at night and very dark. While she wasn't able to see the shadow of the man lurking in the alley, I did. Molly was caught off guard, beaten, and strangled. Her body was mutilated and organs removed, the remains discarded as if useless.

"Molly, why didn't you tell me this sooner?"

Tears welled in her eyes, and she looked away. I lifted her chin, forcing her to look at me. *I didn't know you were murdered.*

"I couldn't tell you. Or anyone for that matter."

Was it Jack the Ripper?

"It was Victor," she whispered, nodding.

"Victor was Jack the Ripper?"

"Shhh!" she scolded. "Yes."

I waited for her to continue, as a cluster of students passed us.

"Victor and I go way back," she said. Her dark eyes were full of pain. Even though we couldn't feel physical pain the same way humans did, we remembered it and felt the emotional trauma of others, or from our own past.

"You don't have to tell me right now, if you don't want to."

She shook her head and continued. *The first time I met him, we married in 1782. I was young. He was fifteen years my senior. Ben, I loved him with my whole heart. I had no idea he was immortal.*

Her thoughts ran through their courtship and marriage. Initially, he loved her and treated her like a princess. Once she became pregnant, his worship for her changed. He began beating her. He found other women and wouldn't come home many nights. She was alone and helpless.

Ben, I didn't know about our existence. I didn't realize we had life contracts. I only knew I couldn't take it anymore.

Reliving her story, she felt the pain from the beatings she endured, her heart heavy.

The night I died, I fought back. He beat me, and I shot him. When I transitioned, I learned he was immortal. I didn't realize that. I mean, how would I know?

You wouldn't.

We both ended up back in our world. I went to rehab, but you know how the good ol' boys' network worked. Especially back then. He was given a slap on the wrist—if that—and went back undercover. They didn't realize he was a double agent. It took another lifetime for them to figure it out.

I didn't understand until she explained that after rehab, she took a new life contract. She met Victor again, in London, in 1831. He was charming, they fell in love, and the story ended as it did the first time, with her death a year later.

After that, he disappeared, and I went into hiding.

I hesitated. The numbers didn't add up. "Molly, Jack the Ripper was late 1800s, not earlier in the century."

She looked down.

"That wasn't the last time you met him, was it?"

"No," she whispered. "I couldn't take it anymore. I trained some… but honestly, I wasn't allowed in the field. I lived in fear and wanted to forget."

"So you're saying you took a new life contract, to forget Victor?"

"Yes. I was stupid. I know. I thought he forgot about me. So I left."

So you had three life contracts, each meeting up with Victor?

She nodded. *And he vowed to—*

"To always find you." I finished the words she was thinking.

Chapter 40
Emma's Story

"Thank God it's Friday," I said, opening my locker after class.

"I know," Claire answered. "I have a quiz on Monday, so I'll probably end up studying all weekend." She rolled her eyes, as she put her books on the top shelf of her locker.

"Me too." Trying to catch up on missed Spanish and calculus assignments took hours each night, and I still wasn't caught up.

"I'm excited for tonight, though," Claire said. Even though I only knew her for a few days, I felt she was genuine, not like some girls I knew back in Highland Park, especially Aimee Wilkinson, who was really just a bitch. Melissa texted me a dozen times to give me updates on Matt since we broke up. She was right when she predicted Matt would ask Aimee to the homecoming dance. He didn't tell me that, of course. In his last message to me, he just asked about school. It was the only text I received from him all week.

I glanced in the mirror hanging on the inside of my locker door and freshened up my lip gloss.

"You're going, right? To the party after the game?" She flashed me a huge grin that lit up her eyes, too. Claire had a narrow face and huge smile that was always welcoming. I found myself wondering if she ever got mad or nasty like Aimee.

"Yeah, I'm going. Sounds like fun," I said, shutting my locker door. Claire was excited when Hannah invited us in art class the day before. I suspected Hannah's mom encouraged her to invite me. Going to a party with a crowd of people I didn't know made me nervous. At least Claire would be there.

"Good. I can't wait!" Her smile turned flat when she looked behind me. She seemed to fidget, glancing away, and then back to the busy hall out of the corner of her eye.

I turned to follow her glare and realized she was staring at Ben. I was suddenly grateful for checking my hair. I spent the better part of every morning critically selecting my clothes for the day, since Ben was in a couple of my classes. I wasn't sure why I bothered. He didn't seem to notice me, even when I jogged the track near his practice after school.

"I'm leaving now, but I'll be back tonight," Ben said as he approached us, his eyes intently focused on Claire.

Great. The only guy that I was interested in had a thing for one of the few friends I made.

Claire nodded in response to Ben. Her eyes were wide and her face pale. She definitely looked upset. They couldn't be dating. Could they? I thought he was with the dark-haired girl from the beach.

"Hey." Ben turned to me. Our eyes met briefly before he directed his attention back to Claire.

"If I'm back in time, I'll pick you up from school. Otherwise, I'll meet you later." Ben's tone was firm and direct, like he was giving her orders. I wondered if he was always like that.

Could they be *just* friends?

"Yeah, I'll find a ride if you're not back," she said in a mumble I almost didn't hear.

"You could call Marty, otherwise," he added with a slight glance in my direction. She nodded and, after he left, Claire's smile returned.

As we walked to class, a ton of questions came to mind, but none I felt comfortable asking, not yet at least. Instead, we made small talk until we parted ways, and I took my seat in front In the case in history class.

He leaned forward and whispered in my ear. "Going to the game tonight?"

"Yup," I said, turning sideways in my chair. "Are you?"

He chuckled and looked away briefly. For some reason, I found him cute. Not stunning like Ben, but easygoing and flirtable. He tapped his pen on his desk when our eyes met. "Yeah. I'll be at the game," he answered with an air of confidence, or arrogance. I couldn't tell.

"Maybe I'll see you there, then," I answered with a smile, as the bell rang and Mr. Dunn began speaking. Class was boring, as usual. Unlike the two days before, Lucas didn't say anything to me, or pass notes to anyone else nearby. I wondered if he was asleep during the dull lecture, but I couldn't bring myself to turn around in my chair and check. When I pivoted my body to look left, I only saw the empty chair where the pretty brunette sat the day before; the girl I saw Ben with at the beach.

I still wondered about Ben and whether he had multiple girlfriends. The brunette seemed awfully friendly that day, but Claire seemed angry, like a couple having a fight. I guess it was worthless worrying about any of it. Ben barely noticed me and never had a conversation with me after that first day at the track.

When the bell rang, Lucas followed me into the hall. Even though we weren't walking together, we were headed in the same direction, to the same class. He ended up beside me within a few strides. I glanced at him, and he smiled. We walked side by side down the stairs and into the next corridor. He kept pace with me, though he clearly could have gone faster. He acknowledged people we passed, but he said nothing to me. From an outsider's viewpoint, it probably looked like we were together.

I wasn't sure how I felt about that, but it definitely made strangers take a second look.

Chapter 41
Ben's Story

Molly and I took the rest of the day off.

Marty, my so-called aunt, notified the school that I had a doctor's appointment and Ava Preston, Molly's mother, excused her absence.

Claire stayed behind. She was uncomfortable at the mention of Victor's name and reputation, not to mention the meeting was classified and above her security clearance.

Pete Jorgenson met Molly and me at the Hub. Files of Victor's past were downloaded quickly, as we walked the bridge back into our world for the meeting with Commander E. What was known of Victor's transgressions during the century he went off grid was frightening.

Victor was thought to have been behind many crimes, though most agents were oblivious to his active existence. A separate division was put in place when Victor went rogue. It was a small group that consisted of home-based agents that monitored thousands of thoughts and tips that surfaced, field agents who were sent in to investigate tips worthy of our time, and other co-ops that investigated peculiar behavioral patterns in geographical regions.

Most of the division's staff never met Victor, or even got close, and none had combat experience. For the most part, they were all glorified sleepers, which is why Molly and I were called in.

Commander E was waiting for us in the boardroom when we arrived. His eyes were somber. He gave a weak smile when he shook my hand. "Good to see you," he said. He lowered his shield enough for me to feel his appreciation for my attendance. As soon as his emotions were released, however, he snapped the barrier shut and shielded his thoughts again.

The room was full of officers, representing every division within our organization. Molly and I took seats across from the investigator that got the tip and the field agent that interviewed the hybrid. They were the only agents in the room with a rank less than ours.

Commander E recapped the early years of Victor Nicklas' existence. "He was a prodigy back in the late 1600s," he said. "His work ethic and talent was exceptional. His involvement among humans was the foundation for our agency's undercover divisions today. He was the most decorated agent of his time and called upon for many, if not all, combat situations."

Victor's history sounded like the speech at a Hall of Fame award ceremony, not a criminal briefing. At some point, however, things changed, and Victor went rogue. His infractions were the foundation for advanced training, higher credential requirements amongst our staff, and new divisions to monitor and track all immortals authorized for earthly presence.

No agent could visit earth or exist in human form without a handler and without the tethering mechanisms we currently had. It was all I ever knew. Being mentally connected to Jorgenson whenever I was on earth was expected. It didn't bother me, but I wasn't doing anything against policy, either.

"Victor is cunning, deceitful, and very intelligent," Commander E said. "And, it would not surprise me if many of our undercover agents have encountered him in one or more of his chameleon-like disguises. He has adapted to the world for generations without discovery. While we have tethered our operatives to their handlers and monitored their activities, we are unable to penetrate the barriers he has in place."

It was known that Victor created the first hybrid. It was a tactic used back in the early 1700s, to expand our presence with the use of mortals at a time when our immortal force was limited. Our bureau was small. Agents were sent undercover for shorter periods of time, moving from one mission to another, sometimes leaving assignments prematurely. It was Victor's concept to create hybrids that would aid operatives during these lapses.

Hybrids were common back then. Field agents converted dying humans into a half-human, half-immortal beings with a simple second chance at life. Humans at the end of their life contract, literally on their deathbeds, were offered recovery for the exchange of loyalty and service. Good agents used the hybrid for the betterment of the world, but bad agents used them as slaves, creating an army.

A hybrid should have existed for months or a year at best. Unfortunately, many lingered for decades in this in-between period where their soul was no longer connected to their human body, yet not allowed to enter our world either.

"It was a time in our bureau's history that we regret," Commander E continued. "Hybrids grew in numbers, with the average field agent having ten or more at a time. It reached the point that hybrids were created unnecessarily and not released for transition timely. When our top agents were known to have hundreds of hybrids on staff at a time, we knew policies had to change."

Commander E explained that hybrids were banned in 1832. Several top agents were reluctant to the policy reform and kept hybrids on the side. Field agents were virtually untraceable and their indiscretions unknown. Internal Affairs officers were dispatched undercover, and agents not conforming to the new policy were terminated.

Victor Nicklas was one that slipped away, going off grid in 1842.

By this point in his career, Victor was thought to have been involved in hundreds of crimes, including robbery, rape, and murder. Commander E glanced at Molly, and I felt the sympathy he passed along to her.

"It took decades to track down the hybrids Victor and other agents created while in service. We were confident we had them all by early 1901," Commander E said. "But then, they surfaced again. Every few decades a hybrid or two was discovered. Until now."

An abundance of hybrids began to appear in recent years, some on the West Coast, others in the Midwest—the most recent being the hybrid that chanted Victor's name in a Chicago-area hospital earlier that morning.

When Commander E finished, an officer asked the whereabouts of the hybrid discovered.

"We have him in protective custody," Commander E answered.

"Wouldn't Victor realize that, if he is tethered to the hybrid?" another officer questioned.

"The hybrid was under the influence of narcotics at the time of his disclosure. Our agents stepped in and provided a protective shield so the hybrid is considered secure at this time."

"And if he isn't?" the officer asked. "What is your back-up plan?"

Commander E didn't need to say anything.

Molly and I already knew she would be used as bait.

Chapter 42
Emma's Story

"Touch-dooowwwnnn!" the announcer's voice sang over the loud-speaker.

Claire and I were on our feet, cheering with the rest of the students, sandwiched between a couple of girls I met at soccer and some of Drew's friends.

The crowd roared with enthusiasm, as Hannah and the cheerleaders led us in a chant. The base from the band's drums thumped, and the bleachers pulsed with its rhythm.

"Westport takes the lead with a catch by number forty-two, Crandon," the announcer continued.

Did he say Crandon? Number forty-two was Neal's son? I glanced at Claire, but she didn't notice my look, giving Drew a high five instead. I strained to see number forty-two, to get a glimpse of what Neal's son looked like, but between the helmet and shoulder pads, it was pointless. He resembled every other player on the field.

Three minutes later, the football game was over, and Westport won 21-14 against its rival, Riverside. As planned, Hannah drove Claire, a Hannah-look-alike named Courtney, and me to Drew's party. Like the first day at my new school, I was nervous. Everyone I met so far was nice enough, but going to a house party brought about a different set of concerns.

Drew handed each of us a small, plastic cup as soon as we arrived. Courtney and Hannah toasted each other and drank it before I could guess what the red concoction was.

It wasn't that I never drank. I tried beer. Once. I just didn't like it.

"Mmm, it's good," Courtney said and licked her lips.

"Yeah, you'll like it," Hannah added, staring at the untouched shot in my hand. "Go on."

I was suddenly warm, feeling like all eyes were on me. I could barely hear the music over the sound of my pounding heart. Claire nudged my arm, distracting me from the overwhelming peer pressure I felt.

"I'll try it, if you do. Can't be all that bad, right?" Her voice was low, almost like a whisper.

"Um, yeah," I mumbled, unsure of what it even was. I wouldn't have thought twice about saying no back home. Here, I just wanted to fit in.

"Hey, Drew. What's in this, anyway?" Claire asked, smiling at him. She waited for an answer with one hand holding up the shot cup, and the other on her hip.

Drew moved closer, stepping in between us, a smirk plastered on his face. "Now—now, ladies. Do you really think I'd serve you anything but the *very* best?" He put his hand on Claire's back, as he glanced at me and then focused on her. She seemed flattered but asked again what was in the drink. "It's just red gelatin and a splash of vodka. If you want more, the bottle's floatin' around, somewhere." His tone was low and soft. Even though I was nervous, I drank it down.

Once Claire realized I finished mine, so did she.

"Not bad, huh?" I whispered, feeling relieved that was over. She nodded.

"There's a cooler filled with beer on the porch. Lemonades in the fridge and some bottles of stuff in the kitchen. Help yourselves," Drew said, heading to the door when TJ and Lucas walked in with a group of guys I didn't know.

"I could use a water," Claire said.

"Yeah, me too."

We chatted with people as we worked our way through the house. Claire seemed to know almost everyone and eagerly introduced me. I knew I'd never remember their names, but it was nice to feel included.

An hour later, the house was packed. Guys chugged liquor from the bottle, passing it around and cheering each other on. When Trent pulled out a mirror, setting up a couple lines of cocaine, and someone else lit up a joint, I wasn't comfortable and looked for a way out.

Chapter 43
Ben's Story

The quietest section of Lake Bell was the inlet on the southwestern end.

Three houses were neatly tucked amongst the thick, dense trees. The Crandon family home, empty since Neal's dad moved to an assisted living center, was last on the dead-end road. The home beside it was vacant. It was where I grew up and came to visit, even years after my mother transitioned.

The house at the mouth of the channel was a rental ever since I could remember. It had the most waterfront, but the least amount of acreage. It was low, flat, and often flooded, but that was decades ago. Lake levels in recent years weren't as high as back in my day. Nonetheless, the property came cheap.

Drew and his mom were its current tenants. She was a workaholic single mom, a nurse who accepted double shifts at the hospital in Westport to make ends meet. It gave Drew plenty of unparented time for socializing.

That gave Drew the reputation most parents despised.

I stood on the wraparound porch. The water was calm and peaceful at this time of night. The moon shone bright, reflecting on the water's surface. Muffled music could be heard out here, but with no occupied homes in the vicinity, there was likely no chance Drew's underage party would get busted by the cops.

I sipped my beer and took in my surroundings. It was quiet now, but if the rumors were true and if Victor was lurking somewhere in rural Wisconsin, the calm serenity of lake living would soon change.

With the knowledge of Victor's presence came other problems. Claire was openly fearful of the infamous villain. Molly was headstrong and risky, despite his century-long threats to follow her. Then, there was Emma.

I had to protect her. No matter what.

My thoughts were blinded by her and overwhelmed by my duty.

What if Victor found Molly? With his chameleon-like disguises, he could impersonate anyone—including a teenager at an underage drinking party. He could blend in with them.

With us.

The thought of him and his motives were frightening, even to me. I took a long pull of my beer, but I really wanted a cigarette to calm my nerves. Old habits I developed undercover were hard to break. Drinking was easier to control than smoking. With alcohol, I could at least cure my hangover ailments.

That was what I told myself, anyway, when I played along with the guys earlier.

Drew passed around a bottle of Bacardi 151. It was a guy's drink, and the wimpy boys that made a face after taking a swig were belittled by the group of athletes. Grunts and cheers encouraged high school boys to chug-a-lug before handing it off. Guys tried to impress the girls and earn their place amongst the men-boys. As small as Drew was, he could hold his liquor.

When the bottle came to me, my competitive side kicked in, and I chugged double what any other guy drank before me. Of course, being an immortal, I could really hold my liquor. And when, or if, I ever let my human body get drunk, I simply fixed it. Placing my hand over my eyes would bring clarity to my vision. Running it over my stomach brought soothing sensations to any digestive issue, and gliding my hand over my arms and legs improved my stability and reduced my blood-alcohol content. I knew the tricks. I worked undercover with drug dealers for years. I could indulge with the best of them and come out sober.

Smoking, on the other hand, was a toxic habit. Even though I could cure the damage done to my lungs, I couldn't eliminate the addiction or the impact tobacco had on my senses. Instead, I took to chewing on toothpicks or eating Altoids.

The creak of the door and the increased volume of music brought me back to reality. I felt her presence, despite the darkness between us. Her blood pressure was elevated, and her thoughts swirled as she made her way to the railing. She stared up at the moon and across the lake.

I wondered if she remembered.

After a few moments of silence, I couldn't resist. "Not your thing?" I asked.

"Um, no. Well, I mean... you scared me. I didn't see you out here," Emma answered. Her heart raced.

"Sorry. I didn't mean to alarm you."

"No, that's okay. It's just warm in there. Hot, actually."

I nodded, though in the dim lighting, I doubted she realized it.

"Um, what about you? Not your thing?" she questioned.

Impressed, I chuckled. "Just getting some air. Like you."

"Oh, yeah. Of course."

"Hey, I meant to apologize for interrupting you and my sister this morning. I had a doctor's appointment and had to leave."

"Oh. No problem," she mumbled. "Did you say *sister*?" she asked. "I didn't realize Claire was your sister." I sensed relief.

"Yeah. Fraternal twins."

The door creaked and slammed open against the siding, distracting us. TJ charged past, pausing to ask if we saw Lucas.

"He left about ten minutes ago," I answered. "Took Steph home."

He grunted a response and took the path around the side of the house.

Ben, can we talk? Molly asked.

When I looked up, I noticed she was standing in the open doorway. Emma noticed too.

Sorry. I didn't realize, Molly mumbled. *Later,* she added. By the look on her face, I knew it was important.

I hoped it wasn't another bulletin from Jorgenson I missed.

Chapter 44
Emma's Story

Claire was Ben's sister.

The words were still sinking in when the brunette from my history class summoned Ben from the doorway. Well, she actually didn't say anything, but the look she gave him meant more than words and within minutes, he followed her inside.

They had to be dating. Right? I'd have to find the right time to ask Claire. At least, I knew Claire wasn't. When I headed back inside, I lingered in the doorway, between the kitchen and dining room. The house was still packed, and I couldn't see Claire, Hannah, or anyone I knew well enough to talk to.

Feeling like I didn't fit in was awkward. I pulled out my phone and checked for new messages, but there weren't any. Melissa already texted me about the football game and, last I heard, she was going to a party.

"Hey, how's it goin'?" TJ asked behind me.

"Hey," I said, startled. "It's goin'." I turned to look at him.

"You hiding, or bored?"

"Both." I was surprised with my honesty. "I just don't know many people yet, that's all."

He nodded and stared at the back end of the living room.

"Something wrong?" I asked.

He shrugged, though he didn't look at me and didn't answer.

I followed his glare. Ben was leaning against the mantel, talking to the dark-haired girl who summoned him. She stood with one hand on her hip, focused intently on Ben. He took a drink of his beer and glanced my way. As soon as he did, she turned and looked at me, too.

She had to be his girlfriend.

When I realized TJ was still staring at them, I asked. "What do you know about Ben?"

He was silent longer than normal for a conversation response, and when he finally answered, he didn't take his eyes off Ben and the girl. "Well, he's a good athlete... plays soccer. He and his sister, Claire, transferred," he said and paused. "...and apparently, he's making the moves on my girlfriend. Well, my *ex*-girlfriend."

"What?"

"We broke up tonight," TJ said. "She did it... said there were extenuating circumstances."

I turned back to look at Ben and the dark-haired girl, who were both staring at us.

"That's Molly?"

"The one and only," he answered.

Huh.

Chapter 45
Ben's Story

"You broke up with him *here*?" I whispered.

Molly stood in Drew's living room by the fireplace. *What did you expect me to do?* She had panic in her tone.

Seriously, Molly? Extenuating circumstances? What the hell does that even mean?

She shrugged. Her thoughts were silent.

Look at that poor kid. You dumped him at a party, in a crowd of peers. What's wrong with you?

It's for the better, she finally answered in thought. *Would you prefer I used you as the excuse? You know that's what they are thinking right now.*

I shot her a look of warning.

Besides, you and I both know I'm the bait to capture Victor.

Yes, I do. But I also know this kid's devastated. You just broke his heart.

What did you expect me to do? she asked in her British tone, the tone I seemed to hear a lot lately. *Should Victor find me, anyone close to me will be victimized.*

Molly, you should go back home and leave this problem to me and the rest of our team. You need to stay where you're safe.

Safe? How will I ever be safe from Victor Nicklas? Molly eyes were fierce.

You'll be safe back home. Victor cannot get through security, no matter what disguise he uses. He can't use the portals undetected.

She took a sip of her drink. *We both know he's not going to stop until he has me.* Flipping her long hair, she glanced at TJ. *And for the record, I will not go back home to hide. I'm staying here and working with you.*

That was just what I needed, two women to protect. I shook my head and took a chug of the cheap beer Drew gave me. Emma was staring at me.

She'd seen me with Molly too many times. I didn't need to read her thoughts to know she suspected something was going on between us.

TJ grabbed Emma's hand and led her to the kitchen. He handed her a beer and slammed one himself.

I knew it was a bad idea to get mixed up with a human, I said.

She was quiet. No comments aloud, no sarcastic thoughts. For once, I got the last word in and the peaceful feeling I had was overwhelming.

TJ drank a second beer slowly. Drew was flirting with Claire, who ignored him and whispered to Emma instead. Justin propositioned Hannah, while Trent was too high to proposition anyone.

It was the epitome of adolescence.

Is that what's holding you back from Emma? You're afraid of getting hurt yourself?

Molly's words were like a sharp knife to the heart. I should have known she couldn't be silent for long. I ignored her comment, but it didn't stop her.

Instead, I finished my beer, ready to go.

Chapter 46
Emma's Story

TJ HANDED ME AN OPEN BEER.

I didn't want to drink it, but he looked so sad that I didn't want to hurt his feelings, either. One beer wouldn't hurt, right? He must have recognized the look on my face.

"Not a big drinker?" he asked. We stood in the kitchen.

I shook my head.

"Drink slow."

I took a big gulp instead. I squeezed my eyes shut, as the cool bubbles burned my throat when they went down. TJ laughed at me, shook his head, and slammed his beer.

I couldn't get over that the dark-haired girl was Molly. I kept glancing at Ben and wondered how long they were together and keeping secrets from TJ. Ben had to know she was dating TJ, right?

When a popular song came on, Hannah and Courtney started dancing and singing into their beer bottles. Hannah's boyfriend, Justin, laughed, while TJ rolled his eyes and smiled. Not only was it the first time TJ smiled that night, but it was also the first time I remembered him smiling since we were twelve years old.

"My sister's drunk," TJ whispered in my ear.

"Yeah. It looks like it," I answered.

Great. Now how was I getting home?

Before I could think about it for too long, Justin handed TJ another beer and offered one to me. I passed, glancing around, looking for Claire, who was deep in conversation with Drew.

"He's been into her since she moved here," Justin said, noticing Claire and Drew.

"Oh."

"Yeah, Drew's got it bad," TJ added, and then glanced at Molly before sipping his beer. He had to have realized similarities in what he said, because a few seconds later, he turned his back and joined another conversation.

"Speaking of bad," Justin mumbled under his breath.

I glanced at Justin.

"So I see Molly's moved on, now that she's single," Justin added.

"Yeah, I heard. So what's the word on them, anyway?"

"Molly and Parker?" Justin grimaced. "Just neighbors. Parker's never said anything about her. I mean, everyone knows Molly is TJ's girl."

"Oh, yeah."

"You know Molly?"

I shook my head.

"Her mom's a teacher at Westport?"

I shook my head again. "TJ just told me her name tonight. I saw her before. She's in my history class."

"Who do you have for science?" he asked.

"Preston."

"That's Molly's mom… Molly Preston," he said.

"Oh… I had no idea."

He nodded.

"Hannah really likes her," I said and took a sip of my beer.

"Yeah. Molly's pretty nice. She lives on the cul-de-sac." He said it like that meant something to me.

"Oh, I… um. Should I know where that is?"

"Well, she lives on the golf course. You know, your aunt's place?"

"Yeah, I know what you meant." I was suddenly embarrassed.

Justin smirked. "She's on Snob Hill."

"Huh? I don't get it."

He laughed. "You've never been there, have you?"

I smiled and shook my head.

"It's just the richest section of the subdivision, that's all. My mom's a realtor."

"Oh."

"Mega-mansions are on Snob Hill," he said. Then, he quickly added, "I mean… there are mansions on Lake Drive, too. These are just the new ones."

It reminded me of Highland Park with the rich and super-rich kids. "I'll have to drive by," I said. "Do you live there, too? On Snob Hill?"

He shook his head. "No, I live near you, actually. Near Lucas."

"Oh… I don't know where Lucas lives."

He wrinkled his eyebrows. "Really? I would have thought you did." I must have had a bewildered look on my face because he continued. "Well, with your aunt and everything. I think she designed the renovation plans."

"Really? Well, she doesn't talk about work much."

"That surprises me," he said. "Well, maybe not. Lucas' parents are divorced, and his mom lives in Riverside. I doubt you would have met her, with your aunt and everything. But his dad got the house and started renovating it."

"What do you mean, *with my aunt and everything*?" I asked again, feeling stupid.

He squinted and scrunched his eyebrows. "Neal?"

"Yeah, what about him?"

"Neal Crandon?"

"I know, Neal Crandon. He's a police officer, my aunt's friend… or more than that, I guess. I don't really want to know."

"Lucas… Crandon." He led me where I hadn't gone before.

"Lucas *Crandon*?" How could I have not known this? "What? You mean… Neal is his *dad*?"

"Yeah… I thought you knew," Justin said.

"At your service," Lucas said, coming up behind me. "Did I hear my name?" He smiled at me and put his arm around my shoulder.

I shrugged away.

"Emma didn't know Neal was your dad," Justin jumped in.

"Yeah… Ems. How 'bout that? Your aunt… my dad... Nice, huh?" he joked. I smelled beer on his breath when he spoke. "Hey Drew! Got some snacks?" he yelled. Drew picked up a bag of Doritos from the coffee table and threw them at him. He caught it in his elbow, like a football. It was obvious he thought he was cool, having caught the winning touchdown.

I didn't.

Lucas opened the bag of chips and started to devour them. I wouldn't doubt he smoked pot and had the munchies. He offered the bag to Justin and me, but we both passed.

I couldn't believe I actually thought he was cute and flirtable at school. I glanced away and noticed Ben was no longer standing by Molly. Instead, he had a jacket in hand and was headed toward Drew.

"So, Em… what do you think of your aunt and my dad?" Lucas laughed.

"Yeah... I didn't know that Neal was your dad. He seems okay." I shrugged. "How long have they been together? I mean, are they a couple?" I was so clearly out of my element. I had no idea about the life Aunt Barb had here. I wondered if Dad knew all of this... or any of it, for that matter.

"I guess... He sleeps over." He said it so casually that it gave me the creeps.

"Huh. Like *often*?" I asked.

"I don't know, every couple of days, I guess."

"How long have they been together?" I couldn't believe it.

"Since last school year... sometime back then, I guess. It really doesn't matter to me. She keeps him off my case." Lucas turned to face me. His light blue eyes sparkled, as his lips curled into a grin. He was trying to be cute, but I didn't find him flattering.

"Hey, where's Steph?" Justin asked.

"I took her home," Lucas answered.

"She okay?" I asked.

"She's fine. Just really fucked up." He smiled at me, staring into my eyes, not breaking the gaze. I could see how some girls found him attractive, but I wasn't one of them.

When I finally pulled away from his stare, Ben was shaking Drew's hand and Claire was by my side.

"We're leaving," she said, giving me a hug. "Do you need a ride?"

"Ah..." I began to answer and nod.

"I got it," Lucas said quickly. "She lives a few blocks from me. I'll take her home."

"No. She's coming with us." Ben's firm voice startled me. "I'll get the car," he said before I could get nervous thinking about driving with wasted Lucas.

Instead, I got nervous thinking about being with Ben.

Chapter 47
Ben's Story

Lucas shouldn't have been in any condition to drive.

The amount of alcohol he consumed and the joints he smoked should have made him legally intoxicated, yet his heart rate was normal. I couldn't run diagnostics to confirm his vitals without touching him, but I didn't care enough to come up with an inconspicuous way to do that.

Emma was the only person I cared about that couldn't protect herself. If Victor was in Wisconsin, I had to keep her safe. His ability to disguise himself and infiltrate the social circles around Molly was too easy. I didn't want Emma anywhere near him, if that happened.

Removing Emma from the party eliminated any unnecessary exposure and took her away from Lucas. There was something about that kid that I couldn't shake. I knew Lucas was human and after following his actions, reading his thoughts, and propelling to his house, I knew he wasn't a hybrid, either. He couldn't be Victor in disguise. Impersonating humanity only worked on humans, not on other immortals.

But exactly what was different about Lucas, I didn't understand, either.

I pulled into Drew's driveway and sat idling waiting for Claire and Emma. It was my excuse to get out of the party quickly and to seem nonchalant about my insistence on taking Emma home. I read her thoughts to know she was confused about me. If the danger of Victor wasn't hanging over me, I'd probably be more attentive. Lord knows I only came here because I love her.

I just introduced myself to your girlfriend. Molly's voice ran into my thoughts.

What? I answered. *Emma's not my girlfriend.*

Well, your knight-in-shining-armor act got her heart racing. Molly's tone was sarcastic, though her words were flattering. *Besides, you pompous ass, she was under the impression there was something between us other than friendship. Something I suggest you clear up.*

I ignored the rest of her thoughts and listened for Emma's voice. It was the only one that mattered. I heard her say goodbye to Hannah before she emerged from the house with Claire.

Emma looked as beautiful as Elizabeth did, with long, honey-brown hair. Her eyes were the exact same shade of blue I remembered and, as she climbed into the front seat beside me, they sparkled.

Molly was right. I had to make things better.

"Where to?" I asked after Claire climbed in the back of my Toyota Cruiser. My guard immediately lowered in Emma's presence, like I was sixteen and it was 1931 again. Gone were the worries of Victor and Lucas.

"Ben, can you drop me off first?" Claire said before Emma could answer. "I promised Aunt Marty I'd get up early and go with her to the farmer's market in Riverside."

I almost laughed aloud. *Did Molly put you up to this?*

No, not at all, Claire responded.

"Yeah, sure," I answered, noticing her smirk in the rearview mirror.

A minute later, Claire said goodbye, and Emma and I were alone.

"Nice house," Emma commented as I backed out of the driveway.

"Thanks. Well, it belongs to my aunt."

"Did Claire say her name was Marty?"

"Yup. Marty McMann. She works for your aunt." No sense in beating around the bush.

"Oh."

"So which way?" I asked at the stop sign. I couldn't acknowledge I knew where she lived too.

"Sorry. Westport," she answered, hesitating as I turned left, toward town. "I live near school. Just a couple blocks past it on the lake."

"By Lake Park?" Like I didn't already know.

"Um, yeah."

The route from my house to Emma's was exactly 6.2 miles. I tracked it. Not that I ever used the two-lane county road to travel there. I used the portal that popped me into the old barn at the back end of her aunt's property. The building Barb Carmichael converted to a garage and office.

We continued for a few miles in silence. I didn't want to overwhelm her with questions and look pushy. Instead, I focused on the road, keeping my speed within the published limit. I wasn't worried about getting pulled over by a cop. I could easily compel my way out of a ticket. I just wanted to spend as much time with Emma as I could.

"So how do you know who my aunt is?" Emma asked. Her heart rate was on the rise.

"Everyone does." It wasn't a lie. Her aunt owned the number-one tourist spot in the area, if not in the state. She was smart, wealthy, and very connected.

"Wait. Your aunt dog-sat Chester when we moved me here." Her words ended in a whisper.

It was a statement I didn't feel needed confirmation. Her thoughts bounced from her dog to her aunt to the move from Highland Park. When her mind settled on memories of her dad's funeral, I interrupted.

"I saw you talking to TJ," I said. A vision of Molly came to her mind as soon as I mentioned TJ's name. She didn't answer, but I didn't give her much time either. "Molly couldn't stop talking about their breakup. Actually, she kept watching the two of you."

"TJ was pretty upset."

"You guys know each other well?" I asked, even though I knew the answer.

"Um, yeah. I guess. Lisa, um… his mom is best friends with my aunt. I knew him when I was little. You know… family parties and stuff."

I nodded.

"He was surprised Molly broke up with him."

"We all were. I thought they were a perfect couple." After a moment, I continued. "Molly's my neighbor. She lives at the end of the cul-de-sac."

"Oh, yeah. Justin told me."

Interesting. I didn't remember hearing that when I eavesdropped.

"Molly was looking for Stephanie. You know, Lucas' girlfriend?"

She shook her head.

"She was pretty drunk. Lucas took her home."

"Oh! I did hear that," she answered. "I didn't know Lucas had a girlfriend."

"Off and on, I guess." She was silent. "Molly wanted a shoulder to cry on, and Steph wasn't around." I turned to look at her. Even in the yellow glow from the streetlights, I noticed her blush when our eyes met. "I got stuck with her instead."

Benjamin! Stuck with me? Molly's thought interrupted.

As we passed Lake Park, I pointed to the first house. Emma nodded.

"Don't get me wrong, Molly can be nice," I continued, pulling into Emma's driveway. "Most of the time, I'd say she's high maintenance." I chuckled as the words were spoken aloud, blocking Molly's response.

Emma smiled.

That was all I needed to see.

Chapter 48
Emma's Story

I rolled over, half-asleep, half-awake.

An image of Ben came to mind. He had a casual smile on his face, like he did the night before when he said, "Goodnight, Emma." The sound of his voice lingered in my thoughts, as I squeezed my eyes shut.

I thanked him for the ride, smiled back, and left. He waited in the driveway until I was safe inside, door closed and locked. After I waved from the window, he slowly backed out.

If it were a dream, I didn't want it to end.

I rolled over again and dozed off. When I woke up later, I realized it was almost eleven o'clock. I jumped out of bed and went downstairs. It was much later than normal and the first time I slept this well since Dad died.

Aunt Barb sipped coffee and flipped through the newspaper sprawled out on the island. "Neal's invited us to lunch," she said when the doorbell rang.

It was just lunch, I thought. *I can do the piles of homework when we get back. Right?*

An hour later, the Carmichael Inn dining room host nervously sat us at a table near the entry. He tried seating us near the window for a better view, but Aunt Barb waved him off, telling him to save those tables for other guests. I could tell he was embarrassed by the gentle reprimand.

The menu was as impressive as the formal table setting with its multiple glasses and extra spoons and forks. I felt oddly uncomfortable when the waiter called me Miss Bennett.

It was a slow, drawn-out meal, which just delayed my plans to study. Not to mention, with Neal at the table, I had no chance of asking Aunt Barb anything I learned the night before. Neal was overly friendly and very attentive to my aunt. I hadn't heard her laugh since Dad died, but even back then, she was never giddy like this.

Great. An aunt with raging hormones.

By the time our entrees arrived, it was obvious she was happy with Neal, and I guessed this lunch was her way of showing me that.

"What's on your agenda today?" Neal asked me as he cut into his lamb.

"I have some homework, actually, and then I'll probably go for a run at the track."

"I have an idea, Emma," Aunt Barb said, checking her watch. "What if you and I do a little shopping first? I'd like a new pair of slacks for work, and I'm guessing you could use a new outfit. What do you say?"

That was the aunt I knew. "Yeah, I'd like that," I answered. I could always do homework tonight, right?

"We used to shop a lot," Aunt Barb told Neal. "We would come home with bags of stuff, and Brian would get so mad. We had fun, didn't we?"

"Yeah." I remembered how we'd spend the day at the mall and how I'd model my new clothes when we got home. Dad would tell me I looked nice, but he would have said that even if I didn't.

"Remember when I came home with those bunny ears?" Aunt Barb asked.

I laughed. It was the day we shopped for my first bra.

"Your dad thought I was crazy," she said and took a drink of her iced tea. "I had a blast. But that lady in the dressing room at Nordstrom's didn't like us very much."

I hoped she wouldn't tell Neal about it.

I was wrong. Not only did she tell him about bra shopping, she went into details about it. Even though we laughed about it when it happened, it suddenly wasn't funny.

Neal quietly listened, laughing at the appropriate times, and smiling as Aunt Barb talked. He appeared to enjoy spending time with her, and I wondered if he thought I was an intrusion.

"So Neal, I met Lucas," I said after I finished my salmon.

His smile turned flat, and Aunt Barb took a sip of her tea. Had I said something wrong?

"You did?"

"Yeah. I have him in two classes. US history and art."

There was a brief silence before he responded. "He's had a hard life, Emma. Just like you. You have quite a bit in common, I'd say." He glanced at my aunt, and then looked at me. "He lives with his mother in Riverside. I don't get to see him as often as I'd like."

"Oh. I'm sorry," I mumbled, not sure what else to say. What did he think we had in common? Both of Lucas' parents were still living.

"What if the four of us have dinner together sometime?" Aunt Barb suggested.

"Um, yeah," I replied.

"We could have you over tonight," my aunt continued. "Emma, we can shop this afternoon and be back in time to grill some steaks. What do you think, Neal? The Wisconsin game's on at seven."

Wrinkles in the corner of his eyes appeared, as a smile crept up on his face.

There went the idea of homework after dinner.

"Okay," Neal said. "But I'm grilling." His grin was warm and flirtatious, and my aunt blushed in response.

I didn't understand his comment, but somehow, it didn't matter.

Chapter 49
Ben's Story

It felt like hours slipped by, when only mere minutes passed.

She was usually here and gone by now. I stretched and re-stretched my calves before I gave in and ran three miles on the asphalt track. It wasn't my intention. I planned to casually bump into Emma, but she didn't show.

It was already after four o'clock. I twisted the pin on my vintage watch back and forth several times to wind it; something I'd done millions of times before. The old Hamilton kept time perfectly, despite a few scratches on the dial, some seventy years after I got it. It was a birthday gift from Elizabeth the year I turned twenty. We were married just over a year, with more nights apart than together. I flipped the watch over and read the engraving in block letters on the back. "Benjamin P. Holmes."

I was home on leave when Elizabeth gave it to me. It was two weeks before my birthday and days before I was scheduled to sail again.

Elizabeth packed a picnic lunch for our afternoon at the lake.

I rowed to my favorite fishing spot on Lake Bell, baited a hook, and dropped in a line. Elizabeth situated herself in the sun and pulled out a book to read—*A Farewell to Arms*. It was a clear, sunny, early September day. A slight breeze gently blew her hair, exposing her ivory neckline. Everything about her was inviting—the line of her chin, the shape of her lips, the color of her eyes. I studied her face every chance I got to keep her memory close while I was at sea.

Her hair was longer than the last time I was home, cascading well past her shoulders. She wore it pinned back with the blue-jeweled barrette I brought her on my last trip home. It matched her eyes and sparkled as bright as her smile.

Man, she was beautiful—prettier than the bent, scratched photo I carried in my wallet, more attractive than any movie star in any film I ever saw, and most importantly, she was mine.

Even though the navy was my job, leaving her was hard.

I watched her bright red lips move with the words she read to herself. She looked as delicate and innocent as the day we met. After several pages, she glanced up at me. Her cheeks were already pink.

"Are you watching me?" Her freckled, sun-kissed nose wrinkled when she grinned. Her flirtatious look brought out urges in me that were only appropriate behind closed doors.

"Why yes, Mrs. Holmes, I am." I couldn't stop looking at her.

"Benjamin!" She giggled. "You're making me blush."

"I'm sorry, but I can't help myself. I like watching you," I confessed.

Our eyes met and locked.

"I miss you when you're gone," she said after an extended period of silence.

As I leaned closer to Elizabeth, the boat rocked. I held the rim to balance myself as I kissed her lips, lingering longer than usual. They tasted sweet and salty as tears ran down her cheeks, meeting at our joined lips. "Ah, honey... I'll miss you too," I said, saddened by the spoken realization that my thirty-day leave was coming to an end.

I glanced away briefly and sat back. I couldn't bear to see her in pain, especially knowing I was the cause. The water was calm and peaceful. No one was swimming or fishing; kids were in school and the lake was quiet. We were completely alone. I looked back at her. She was watching me now, her tears gone.

I changed the subject to a lighter one, pointing to the book in her lap. "Haven't you read that book a hundred times?"

"Not a hundred." She smiled, her long lashes blinking slowly over those bright blue eyes that reminded me of the oceans I sailed.

"No? How many times, then?" I asked. "Even *I* know the characters by name. Henry and Catherine, right?"

"You're not funny. It's a fine story. Besides, I need something to read while you're busy fishing." She laughed, as she gently slapped my knee.

"Okay, okay. I get it. The fish aren't biting anyway," I said, pulling in the lines I had dangling overboard. I rowed to the island and docked the boat on the beach. It was the opposite end of the lake from the inlet where we rented a flat next door to my parents.

Elizabeth set up a blanket and picnic lunch for us, while I secured the boat to a nearby tree. The sun was lowering in the sky. It was after four o'clock, I guessed. I gathered some branches from the brush and built a small fire. The temperature was starting to drop, but it was still pleasant.

Elizabeth pulled out leftover ham, some cheeses, and a loaf of fresh bread she made that morning. She thought of everything, including a thermos of coffee, a flask of whiskey, and a birthday cake she baked before I woke up.

We ate and drank, talked and laughed. We reminisced about the first time we met, here on the island, and our first date when her father interrogated me. We talked about our future, how she would join me on base after this tour, and how we wanted children, lots of them. We dreamed of living on the lake when I retired, where our children and grandchildren would visit and play on the beach. We talked about growing old.

Together.

As the perfect day slowly came to an end, Elizabeth insisted on singing. Her soft, sweet, out-of-tune voice sang "Happy Birthday." She laughed at herself, wrinkling her nose as she attempted the high notes. She squeezed my hand, as I held back laughter. The more I held back, the more out of tune she sang. She giggled when it was over, covering her face with her petite hands.

"I'm lucky to have you," I said, reaching for her hand, pulling it off her face. I wanted to see her, to keep her face fresh in mind for the weeks to come when we would be apart.

"Oh, Benjamin!" She smiled, and then paused. "Wait, I almost forgot." She reached into the wicker basket and pulled out a small box wrapped with a blue ribbon. "Happy Birthday!"

Her enthusiasm was contagious.

"Open it! I hope you like it."

She sat on her knees, bouncing side to side.

"Open it!" she said again. I untied the ribbon and opened the hinged box. It was a handsome, black-and-gold watch.

"Well?" she asked. "Do you like it? I thought you could use a watch. You're always looking at the sun and guessing the time. Then you'd have a remembrance of me," she said. "See, I had your name engraved on the back." She pointed out.

"I love it. Elizabeth, I love it. Thank you." I reached for her. She was so beautiful. Cupping her chin in the palm of my hand, I leaned in to kiss her. Elizabeth wrapped her arms around my neck and kissed me back.

"I love you, Elizabeth," I said, pulling away to look at her. "I'll miss you," I whispered.

"Oh, Benjamin… I'll miss you too." Tears built up in the corner of her eyes.

I scooped her into my arms, leaning her back on the green plaid blanket. Our lips met again. The fire crackled, and the sun began to set. It was time to row back to shore, before it grew dark. I knew that, but I couldn't stop. I didn't want to leave. We made love by the fire, the day Danny was conceived.

I spent years wishing I hadn't joined the navy and left her, hoping and thinking she was alive, when she wasn't. Now I felt like I had a second chance.

Memories flooded my mind, as I stood in the school parking lot. When I eavesdropped on Emma's thoughts this morning, she planned to have lunch with her aunt, followed by homework and a run. That meant she should have been here around three.

For a brief second, I feared for her life, but as soon as I heard her voice, the thought dissipated. She was shopping with her aunt. A wave of relief swept over me. She was happy, content, and safe.

For now.

Chapter 50
Emma's Story

The fun aunt I remembered was back.

We spent the afternoon together, just like old times. I told her about Claire and Hannah and about school and homework. I even told her about the party at Drew's. Of course, I left out the drinking, and I downplayed my interest in Ben.

It was a great day.

When the doorbell rang, Aunt Barb asked me to get it. Chester beat me to the front door with sharp, piercing barks. Neal had a bouquet of flowers in one hand and a bottle of wine in the other. He greeted me with a hug and a kiss on my cheek before turning to Aunt Barb, who ran to the door when I opened it. I noticed their embrace before acknowledging Lucas.

Chester welcomed Neal, but barked at Lucas until I scolded him and covered his muzzle with my hand. "Chester, stop!" I said firmly. He looked at me, dropped his tail between his legs, and sat down.

"Hey," Lucas said with a weak smile. "Is he okay? He's not going to hurt me, is he?"

I laughed. "No, he's harmless... well, usually." I hoped. Lucas was dressed in jeans with a tucked-in pale blue shirt. He looked nice, but unusually preppy. Not clothes I would have expected him to wear, after his rumpled, dingy look at the party the night before. "This is for you," he said, handing me a shopping bag with vegetables sticking out of the top.

"Thanks." I shut the door and turned toward the kitchen. Lucas followed after Neal reprimanded him for not carrying the grocery tote for me. I couldn't help but snicker to myself at Lucas' lack of manners. Then again, I wasn't sure Matt would have carried it, either.

Lucas helped me unpack the groceries, while Aunt Barb put the flowers in a vase and Neal opened the bottle of wine. Chester stayed beside me. He was unusually clingy. Every time I tried to shake him off, he sat down with a deep sigh as if I bored him.

"Did you want something to drink?" I asked Lucas. "Barb's got Coke, Diet Coke, water, lemonade, or green tea."

"That's all?" he asked with a smirk.

"I know, right?" I laughed, but when he didn't answer, I continued. "There's also orange juice, grapefruit juice, tomato juice, coffee, or milk. Which do you prefer?"

He smiled and took a seat at the island snack bar. "Coke is fine."

"After that whole list, you pick the first thing I offered?" I teased, handing him a can of soda. I wondered if Lucas was hungover.

We sat at the island, while my aunt washed vegetables and Neal seasoned the steaks. They talked between themselves, mostly, including us only on occasion. Aunt Barb asked if Lucas liked mushrooms, and Neal wanted to know how I liked my steak prepared.

They interacted like my parents did when I was little. Just as thoughts of my past surfaced, Lucas nudged me. I looked up to see Neal feeding my aunt a taste of something he called demi-glaze.

"Want to try?" Neal held the wooden spoon toward me, as my aunt complimented him.

"No thanks," I answered. He looked at Lucas, who just waved him off.

When Neal and my aunt had their backs to us, Lucas rolled his eyes. It was the icebreaker that got us talking. He asked if I liked school and where I moved from. We talked about Lewis and Jet Skiing on Lake Bell. When he asked if I was still dating Matt, I answered, and then quickly changed the subject. Lucas admitted he and Stephanie broke up, too.

By the time dinner was ready, I liked him. Not the same way I liked Ben, but Lucas was nice and easy to talk to. He was completely different from the drunk, stoned guy I saw the night before.

Lucas sat across from me at the table. He had pale gray eyes and a lean build. It was almost opposite of Neal's dark features and broad shoulders. The only common characteristic I noticed was their square chin. I wondered if Lucas looked like his mother.

Neal grilled the steaks to perfection. Lucas seemed pleased with his and dug in like it was the first meal he had in ages. I wasn't very hungry and found myself full before I barely started. I pushed food around on my plate, as the conversation flowed between questions about school and classes Lucas and

I had together.

"I'll clean up the dishes, and then serve dessert," Aunt Barb said after everyone finished.

"No, I'll do it," I answered, anxious to get away from what seemed like formal conversation compared to before. Even though Neal was pleasant, he didn't seem like himself with Lucas around.

I loaded the dishwasher, while Lucas cleared the table.

"Are you going to Trent's later?" he asked.

"Umm… I don't think so." I actually wasn't invited.

Lucas was silent for a minute, and then said, "You can if you want. We can go together."

"Uh… Who's going? Anyone else I know?"

"TJ. Probably Hannah and Justin. I'm not sure. It'll be a small group," he said. "Don't worry; I won't leave you."

I laughed. "I wasn't worried about that," I lied. Although, I should be concerned he couldn't drive me home afterward.

"And I won't get drunk or stoned," he said with a brilliant smile. "Scout's honor."

"You were a Boy Scout?"

He shook his head and looked away. "Not a chance. I just heard the expression on television and thought it would impress you."

I chuckled. He was definitely a different person from the gross guy I talked with before. Instead, he resembled the almost-charming guy I met in history class three days earlier.

Chapter 51
Ben's Story

I was on the trail of a hybrid scent.

The pungent smell was one I couldn't forget. Sort of like that distinct odor marijuana had. Once your nostrils tasted it, you would always remember it, no matter what. When the scent arose again, your mind would take you back to that first time you smelled it. Like the scent of a new car bringing back the memory of your first purchase. Or the smell of autumn leaves reminding you of your first kiss.

I trailed him for hours, since late afternoon when I knew Emma was at home with her aunt. Of course, when I realized they invited Lucas for dinner, I put Claire on surveillance duty.

At first, I scoured the countryside, looking for buildings and silos that resembled the images in the hybrid's memory. Some looked familiar, but most were dead ends. I stumbled upon the sweet odor by accident in a cornfield. The scent alone would not alarm humans. They would find its aroma pleasing.

Immortals have a keener sense of smell, and the gentle cotton candy fragrance was much more pungent to us. Each hybrid had a unique perfume, yet all had the same sickly sweet foundation. It was their aftertaste, the bitter bite of green apple in our nostrils that sets hybrids apart.

I followed the trail from barn to barn, from one farm to the next, each with increasing depth of the odor. Some buildings were a conundrum of smells; a gathering place of numerous hybrids, I guessed. I wondered if Victor created a dormant army. And if he did, why?

Immortals gave off a presence. The soundless, scentless energy of their existence was overlooked by humans and most others of my kind. With years of undercover work on earth, I trained myself to sense them and pinpoint their location. It was like noticing a speck of dust on a radar screen, paying attention to it and recognizing what it really was. Most immortals would overlook it, assuming the speck was just dust.

When immortals left a building, a trail remained, similar to the exhaust from an airplane that humans could see in the sky long after the jet flew away. The difference was that the exhaust from an immortal was invisible to humans.

I felt a lingering presence in the last barn I visited. I was grateful Molly willingly stayed behind on my reconnaissance task. At first, she argued, but she knew it was best for me to go alone.

The presence led from the barn through rolling hills and a cow pasture to Summit Road, to a farm owned by the Kensington family in the town of Mosel. It was a small farm with no animals and few crops. The weathered, two-story house was across the road from the barn, perched on a hill.

It was the eighth farm I visited that day.

The barn had white, chipped-paint walls that were dirty and damaged. Many boards were missing and those that remained hung by a single nail. A short silo to the east of the barn provided the shelter I needed to propel. My body remained frozen, hidden from view by the overgrown, leafy brush surrounding the building. When I propelled above the barn, I realized a portion of the right side of the roof was missing. Moonlight came through the gaping hole, but around noon, I guessed the sunlight would brighten the barn like I saw in the hybrid's memory. The scent of multiple hybrids overwhelmed the air. Some were fresh, while other sour smells were much older. I scanned the property's interior before committing my body to enter. I couldn't tell if there was a portal inside and if danger lurked, I'd be trapped without one.

Portals weren't hard to find. They were located practically everywhere. It was just a matter of looking for them. Any building over a hundred years old had a portal. Most were in the cellar, or the attic. Humans couldn't see where two planes intersected, the wavering line we called portals. They only saw what we wanted them to see.

The west end of the barn was poorly lit and had a loft with messy stalls beneath it. The barn was home to horses, years before. I could sense the remains of their presence even though they transitioned. Their lingering energy directed me to a portal in the loft, in the corner where old hay was stacked, as if hiding the entrance to my world.

As I shifted my spirit closer to the portal, I heard a sound that resembled a twig breaking under the weight of a human foot. It took a fraction of a second to realize my human body was about to be discovered.

Chapter 52
Emma's Story

"I'm warning you. One more slip and I'll send you to boarding school."

Neal's voice was firm and elevated. I caught a glimpse of Lucas' nod as I descended the stairs. I was afraid to join them in the living room below, but as Aunt Barb heard my footsteps, she cleared her throat. The look on Neal's face was stern, not like the compassion I'd seen from him before.

"You look great," she said, giving me a quick hug.

Great? I had put on a sweater and jeans.

Neal smiled, as if that could erase the anger I saw in his face moments before. "Lucas was just promising to have you home early tonight. Isn't that right, Lucas?" Neal asked.

"Yes, sir," he answered. What was I getting myself into?

I gave my best fake smile and headed out the side door to the driveway. Chester tried to follow me, but I heard my aunt scold him and shut the door.

"Sorry about my dad," Lucas said as we crossed the street. "He gets like that once in a while."

"It's okay," I answered. "Parents can be like that… I guess."

Lucas sighed and then said, "I should consider myself lucky to have parents to yell at me, right?"

"I didn't say that." Of course, the thought *had* crossed my mind.

He led me to a red pickup truck with orange flames painted on the side. Twin exhaust pipes rose from the bed behind the cab. "Sometimes it sticks," Lucas explained as he opened the passenger door. He didn't wait for me to climb in. Instead, he went to the driver's side and had the engine started by the time I closed the door.

"Nice truck," I said, trying to lighten the mood. It was definitely unique. Nothing like it roamed the streets of Highland Park.

"It's Ray's, actually."

"Who's Ray?"

"Char… I mean, my mom's husband," Lucas answered. "He owns a used car lot."

The truck spewed exhaust and rumbled, as Lucas pulled away from the curb. We bounced through a neighborhood of old-fashioned mansion-looking houses before turning left, and then right, where the homes were smaller. When Lucas slowed in front of a brown brick house, he pointed. "That's where my dad lives," he said.

"Oh. Justin said Neal lived nearby. But you live with your mom, right?"

"Yup. In Riverside."

He didn't elaborate, and I didn't feel right asking any questions as we drove in silence. He pointed out Justin's house a block away before circling back to North Avenue and heading west like we were going to Lake Bell.

"Where exactly does Trent live?" I asked after he turned on an unfamiliar road.

"In the country."

The drive seemed long, and the silence between us was awkward at times. I was grateful when Claire texted me. She told me she was bored at home and asked what I was up to. When I told her where Lucas and I were going, she buzzed back with a "*What*?" followed quickly by a "With Lucas?" text.

I didn't want her to get the wrong idea. After all, Lucas and I were just friends but, when I suggested she meet us there, I realized it wasn't my place to extend an invitation. I thought Claire maybe felt the same because she didn't seem to like the idea, texting, "Yeah, maybe."

***

At the end of a long, wooded road, Lucas parked behind a beige sedan and shut off the engine. "Come on."

I followed him down the poorly lit driveway, hoping I wouldn't trip over anything. The moonlight that brightened the road suddenly diminished under the canopy of dense trees that separated the road from Trent's house.

"It's kind of creepy out here," I said.

"I told you. We're in the country, City Girl," Lucas said with laughter in his voice.

He kept the same pace we had in the road, despite the minimally visible asphalt. I barely trusted it was sturdy, as I took each step trying to keep up with his pace.

"Do I hear running water?" I asked when we reached the entrance.

"There's a river out back. Well, actually, it's a creek, I guess. Mosel Creek."

He opened the unlocked door and let us in without knocking or ringing the doorbell. I couldn't imagine leaving your house unlocked. Then again, Melissa and I were best friends since forever and I'd never walk into her house, either. Living in Wisconsin was definitely different from what I was used to.

"If you want to, that is," Lucas said, his eyes focused on mine.

"Huh?"

"Go with me. Canoeing."

"Oh, yeah," I answered quickly, hoping he didn't realize I wasn't paying attention.

After a wicked smile flashed on his face, it dawned on me that he didn't ask because he wanted to be friends. I followed Lucas through the dimly lit first floor and down a set of stairs. When we reached the lower-level family room, a tall, blonde-haired girl jumped up to greet Lucas. As I stepped beside him, Lucas put a gentle hand on my back, and the girl's enthusiasm deflated.

"Stephanie, this is Emma."

"Hi Stephanie," I answered, stepping forward so Lucas was no longer touching me.

She mumbled a hello and retreated to her spot on the couch next to TJ.

The Badger game was a tie with seven minutes left in the first quarter and we had the ball. Lucas was right. There were only a handful of people there. The guys didn't get up to greet us. TJ and Justin waved hello, but Drew and Trent were intently watching the play and making comments that peaked Lucas' interest. He joined them on the couch, as Hannah crawled over Justin and ran toward me. She gave me a welcome hug and whispered in my ear, "Oh-my-god, I'm so glad you're here. You came with Lucas? What's up with that?"

"Nothing. We just had dinner with my aunt and Neal, that's all."

She gave me a peculiar look, as if gauging the truthfulness in my comment. When it appeared she believed me, she said, "Steph's been waiting for him. She's probably pissed he came with you."

I didn't know Stephanie, but anyone could tell she was mad.

When a commercial came on, Trent offered Lucas and me beer. Before I could answer, Lucas said, "No thanks, man. Not tonight." He glanced in my direction and added, "You want one? You can drink, I'm driving."

I shook my head, shocked. "No, I'm good."

"Hannah, want something while I'm up?" Trent asked as he walked passed us to a small kitchen area tucked behind the stairs.

"Diet Coke," she answered. "I drank too much last night."

I looked around the room and realized only TJ was drinking beer. Everyone else had soda or water. It was a bit of a relief. As I glanced at Stephanie, she yelled, "Trent, can you mix up something for me?"

"Sure. Like what?"

"Surprise me. And make it strong," she added.

I felt her piercing eyes on me briefly, but when I looked in her direction, she turned away.

Chapter 53
Ben's Story

"What are you doing here?" I snapped at Claire in a low tone.

"I called you…"

"Shhh."

I called you, but you didn't answer me. What was I supposed to do? Claire spoke in thought.

Sorry. I was shielded. I was in pursuit… still am, I answered, realizing how stupid that was of me, not letting a rookie through my barrier. Would Molly have reached out to me? The mention of her name in thought brought a quick response from her, and I knew she was okay. I should have known. Her screeching voice would surely pierce any barrier I had in place, if she really needed me. *What did you need, Claire?*

She mumbled a thought about Emma, and my heart raced. *What do you mean—she's at Trent's house with Lucas?* I asked. *Then why are you here?*

Because, I… ah…

Claire, I can't leave. I'm on the trail of something… a hybrid and something else… an immortal, I think.

Victor?

I don't know for sure. Not yet. But I can't leave right now, I answered. *You need to handle this,* I added.

Her thoughts turned to Molly, who joined the mental conversation.

Absolutely not. I won't let Molly take this assignment, either, I interjected their discussion. I thought it might be a trap, but I shielded them both from my concern.

What then? Claire asked.

You need to handle this. I don't trust Lucas. You know that. That's why you were on call tonight. You need to be there.

How am I supposed to get invited to Trent's? Claire asked. I sensed a twinge of panic in her tone.

Molly began to think a snide comment, but I cut her off. *Claire, you're immortal. You have the ability to compel humans.*

But we were taught never to use that power, she answered. *There would be consequences.*

Unless it's the only justifiable course of action, or your director authorizes it. Either way, it's acceptable in this situation, I answered, continuing to ignore Molly's negative thoughts. With Victor back in the picture, she had less patience for rookies than ever before.

Claire was silent. She knew Molly was displeased. Not that they didn't get along, just that Claire understood her rank in comparison to Molly's. In other words, Claire was streetwise and knew when to keep quiet.

After a deep, cleansing breath, I released my shield and allowed Molly back into the conversation. Then, I calmly asked, *How did you find out what Emma was doing tonight? Did you propel to her house?*

No, I haven't solo propelled.

You haven't? Ever? Molly's question was almost a shriek.

Only in training… at The Farm.

Simulation exercises, I responded.

Yes.

Molly mumbled something I ignored.

Okay, Claire. So how did you know that Emma went to Trent's house? I asked calmly, though anger brewed within me. I couldn't believe the agency would graduate rookies without the basic field experience of propelling. A simple field trip would suffice to a rural area. The desert would work! I shook my head in disgust.

She texted me.

What exactly do you mean, she texted you? Molly asked.

Well, I texted her first. Then she replied that she and Lucas were going to a party at Trent's. She said it would be small… to watch the Wisconsin game on television.

And when I didn't answer your calls, you used the portals to find me, here, I said.

She said yes in a hushed thought.

Well, Claire, if you're not experienced in propelling, now's not the time to test your skills, Molly said. *You need to use your human talents to find your way there.*

What does that mean?

It means you need to flirt your way into an invitation to the party, I answered.

Chapter 54
Emma's Story

Stephanie was drunk.

I didn't pay attention to what she drank during the football game, but by the time it was over, I realized she had problems and not just with alcohol. Lucas ignored Stephanie even though she tried to cozy up to him on the couch. It seemed to be a challenge to her, like it was a game of playing hard to get.

The Badgers won in a play the guys called a Hail Mary. Cheers erupted after Wisconsin scored with forty-two seconds left. TJ and Lucas jumped to their feet, spilling a bowl of popcorn on the floor. Trent knocked over his beer, and Drew gave Claire a sloppy hug. Even Stephanie smiled, though it was brief.

Drew left at halftime to pick up Claire. The Badgers were winning, and he seemed in a good mood. Lucas said it was because Drew placed a bet on the game, but when they returned and we were losing, Drew still had a grin on his face. I guessed it was because Claire called him.

Trent poured shots of peppermint schnapps to celebrate our win. He placed three glasses on the table in front of Hannah, Claire, and me. Even though Hannah claimed to be hungover, she quickly reached for hers. Claire gave us her bright smile as the three of us clinked glasses and slammed the clear, minty liquid. It tasted like mouthwash, strong and refreshing. For some reason, I was more comfortable drinking at Trent's than I was at Drew's party. I wasn't sure if it was the smaller crowd, or the lack of drunken people pushing alcohol every time I turned around.

Maybe it was because it wasn't my first time.

When Trent held up the schnapps bottle in the family room, Stephanie grabbed it out of his hand. Claire nudged me when Stephanie chugged from the bottle. She wiped her mouth on the sleeve of her shirt and handed it back. TJ shook his head in disgust, and Lucas rolled his eyes.

I couldn't help but watch Lucas to see if he'd keep his promise and not drink. To my amazement, he did. Stephanie was visibly irritated and the more I watched her, the more I saw how trashed she was. When she stood, she swayed. Her eyes tipped back, and her gestures were overdramatic.

Lucas caught me watching her and shook his head. I looked away quickly, holding back a grin. When I glanced in his direction again, he smiled.

When Trent suggested a game of poker, Claire, Hannah, and I vacated the table and took seats on the couch across the room. As I settled into the open spot beside Stephanie, she sighed. It was deep and obvious. I didn't know if it was because of her intoxicated state or me. Either way, she got up within a few minutes and whispered something in Lucas' ear.

He shook his head in reply and picked up the cards Trent dealt him.

Without another word, Stephanie stormed off and up the stairs. The guys didn't seem to notice the vibration when she slammed the front door.

I gave Claire a look. She shrugged. Hannah spoke up, "It's not you, Emma. Stephanie's been out of control for months. Ever since Lucas broke up with her this summer, she's been begging him to take her back."

"Why? I mean, she's a really pretty girl. I'm sure she could find another boyfriend." Claire said what I was thinking.

"Yeah, I know," Hannah answered. "TJ told her that, too. But for some reason, she won't let go of him."

"Why'd they break up?" Claire asked.

"Well, I heard Lucas cheated on her. Some girl in Riverside. You know he lives there with his mom, right?" When Claire nodded, Hannah continued. "TJ found out and threatened to tell Steph, so Lucas broke up with her."

"Oh, wow," I mumbled.

"That poor girl. She's better off without him," Claire said.

"Yup," Hannah agreed. "Consider yourself warned, Emma."

"Huh? I'm not—"

"Emma came here with Lucas," Hannah told Claire, cutting me off. The smirk on her face reminded me of when we were little and she used to tattle to her mom. Now I remembered why TJ and I excluded her.

"Yeah, but your aunt's dating Lucas' dad, right?" Claire asked me. I nodded, but I didn't get a chance to respond before she continued. "So that doesn't mean you're seeing Lucas. Right?"

"Lucas and I are just friends," I said firmly.

A look of disappointment crossed Hannah's face, but she shrugged it off quickly and moved onto another topic. "So, Claire, where's your brother tonight?"

"Um, I'm not sure. At home, probably." Claire took a drink of her soda and looked down. She fidgeted with the metal tab on the top of the can.

"I totally thought he'd be here," Hannah continued.

"He doesn't tell me much," Claire said. Her usual, bubbly expression was suddenly lost.

"You guys get along okay, don't you?" Hannah badgered.

"Um, yeah. He just bugs me. That's all." When she looked up again, her brilliant smiled returned.

He doesn't bug me, I thought.

Chapter 55
Ben's Story

Summit Road had three farmhouses along it.

The Kensington farm was the furthest east and had the least potent scent, but the most variety. Claire visited me there. In the 1930s, it was the largest farm in the county. The family had four sons and three daughters, though most didn't finish high school because of chores. A few did, but I never kept in touch while I was alive, and I didn't bother to follow up after I died.

Standing on their property, I extracted the memories of life on these grounds from my time to now. Most of the Kensington kids from my generation moved away, except the one that died in the war, and the eldest son that stayed with the farm. He worked the acreage and prospered, passing it along to his only child, a son, who, at eighty-two years old, still lived there.

The farm was no longer active, except for a few fields he rented out. The vast land had been divided years before when Kensington sold a parcel of uneven terrain along the river to a developer who added a road and built homes.

Kensington was a widow, had been for a decade. He turned in early each evening, just after dark, and rose with the sun. Instant coffee was his morning drink that he preferred bold and black. Mondays, he did wash. Tuesdays, he paid bills. Each Wednesday, he drove into Riverside for breakfast at Priscilla's, a stop at the post office, and grocery shopping at the Park 'N Save mega center along the interstate. Each Sunday, he went to mass at Holy Name Catholic Church followed usually, but not always, by a visit from his daughter.

He followed a strict routine, with more days alone than with company. It made his homestead a perfect meeting place for the workings of Victor Nicklas, I realized as I made my way to the second farm on Summit.

Across from the entrance to the new subdivision stood a red barn with white-trimmed windows and stone footings. It was clean and well maintained, far different from the run-down building that stood in its place when I grew up here.

I bent down, grabbed a handful of soil, and concentrated on its history. The business was newly successful. The third generation farmer was in his mid-forties. He rented Kensington's land and grew corn and beans he sold to canning companies. Demand exceeded his supply.

Visions of staff working the fields surfaced. Equipment hummed in the barn. An outbuilding housed a few dozen Holstein cows. Grunts, moos, and snorts echoed in my mind. With the flurry of year-round activities, I was doubtful that Victor could hide his crew here or hold undetected meetings.

In other words, it was a dead end.

Dried granules of earth spilled from my stained palm, returning to the ground where they belonged. I stood up, wiped my hands on my jeans, and backtracked to the Kensington farm.

I picked up the hybrid scent in the barn and followed it closely, as it wound through uncultivated land in a zigzag pattern to the back of the property on the river.

The trail ended.

The river was their pathway of transportation. Since the water constantly moved, the fragrance dispersed and distributed in different directions to throw off any trackers. This was not the action of an inexperienced immortal. This had to be Victor.

I moved along the water's edge. The presence of an immortal was evident high in the air, at the tops of the tall trees. I positioned my body near a portal in the woods and propelled myself to the upper branch, no longer under the canopy coverage the dense trees created. The air was cooler here, as the wind picked up. The energy from the immortal passed, swirled, and led me mentally west.

I followed the presence to the bridge on highway M. Bittersweet apple mixed with cotton candy in a nauseating depth of foul perfume. There was a concentration of odors running under the bridge, the width of the river. I propelled around the abutment, hovering under the girder. This was their meeting point. A place of distribution. Hybrids came from all directions to this spot. Where they came from, I couldn't tell.

The immortal energy was stronger here too, but it was not alone. Another, unfamiliar scent lingered in the air. I sensed its potency on highway

M. It mingled with the immortal spirit on the bridge, as if the two beings met in the middle of the road.

Southbound highway M led to downtown Riverside. A likely hiding place, but with more buildings and homes to search.

To the north, nine hundred and thirty-three feet to be precise, highway M intersected with Summit Road. Beyond that there were no cross streets for miles. Square fields with crops of corn lined the straight path that led into the next county. As I stretched my mind to reach the open road, the presence I sensed on the bridge disappeared. It seemed to end at the abandoned farmhouse on the corner.

It was the last farm on Summit. Back in the 1930s, it was active. Today, a condemned sign was needed. The weathered barn was missing most walls and almost its entire roof. A smaller building beside it had already fallen upon its foundation. The gray, rotten boards piled in crisscross patterns atop one another. Trees, bushes, and weeds grew wild, covering the once-traveled gravel path. Windows were broken and stairs were atilt on the old porch that once welcomed visitors. An old tractor rested in its grave, rusted and covered in dirt and dust, with tall grasses hiding its engine.

The presence was heavy, but a rustling startled me. It came from two directions at once.

I broke the mental propel and stood back in the woods near the river, beside the large oak tree. The smell of cotton candy swept past me with a gentle breeze. The immediate sour aftertaste, so pungent in its depth, took my breath away. The odor was close, closer to my human body than ever before. It was potent and strong, eye watering and dangerous.

I was not alone. I could sense a hybrid was with me, or maybe more.

Like the scent of a skunk's spray in your face, I was intoxicated in its presence and felt myself falling into unconsciousness.

Chapter 56
Emma's Story

Lucas was a gentleman.

He kept his promise to his dad and had me home well before midnight. Not to mention, he didn't drink, smoke, or do any drugs. Not that I saw, anyway.

The house was fully lit when he turned his beefed-up truck into the driveway. We could see the glow from the television through the open windows.

"Thanks for inviting me," I said when Lucas shut off the engine. "I had fun."

"Yeah, me too. My dad waited up." He nodded toward the house.

"Looks like it. So you guys don't have a great relationship, huh?"

"Not really. Let's just say, I've given him reason not to trust me." He got out of the truck, while I struggled with the door. Lucas noticed my troubles and opened it for me. I mumbled a thank you, and he continued. "I got busted. He kicked me out. Case was dropped, but we haven't spoken since. Well, until today, that is."

"That was you?" I asked after I climbed out of the oversized cab.

"He told you?" he snapped. "Figures."

"Uh-uh, no. I just heard a friend of Drew's got busted. It was before I moved here."

Lucas headed toward the side entrance of the house, and I followed.

"Sorry. I didn't mean to assume it was you," I continued.

He only grunted an acknowledgement in response.

Chester was barking before we reached the porch. He greeted me with a wagging tail and nudge to my hand. He planted his large body in front of me, blocking my movement and Lucas' ability to even step inside.

Weird dog, I thought, *must be the new house*. I grabbed his collar and tugged with no reaction. I pulled harder and tried to shift his body up and over, just enough to get him to move aside. Mosquitos swarmed around the exterior light and filtered in, while Chester played guard dog until he finally conceded. I heard a low rumble in his throat when Lucas was inside with the door shut.

I yanked on Chester's collar, scolding him at the same time.

"Your dog hates me, doesn't he?" Lucas asked.

"He's like that with everyone."

"Not with me," Neal's voice piped in, as he and Aunt Barb joined us at the door. His smile beamed from ear to ear. The normal pleasantries of "Did we have fun?" filled the air along with "Wow, you're home early," which I knew was directed at Lucas more than me. Aunt Barb's gentle hug meant she was happy I was fitting in.

Minutes later, with Lucas and Neal gone, I said goodnight to my aunt and headed off to bed feeling content.

I can do this, I thought. I could move on.

Chapter 57
Ben's Story

Benjamin! Get a grip! Molly's voice pierced into my thoughts and kept me conscious.

I focused on my surroundings like I was taught back in training. It had been decades since I used tracking for any mission on earth. The large oak shielded my human body from open exposure to others. Its thick trunk split low like two seedlings grew side by side, intertwining their lives together.

It was a portal to my world, an escape route in the fold of the tree that only authorized immortals could travel. Humans that attempted to cross would find they left their human bodies behind. It would be an earthly death for them, with an unhappy ending, since entrance to my world without approval never ended well.

Victor could not use our portals without detection, and he knew that. While I could sneak back into the maze of tunnels within my world to move quickly and effortlessly from one area to the next, Victor had to rely upon speed and human technology for travel.

I noted the whereabouts of each distinct odor, each lingering spirit and sensation I felt. I was surrounded. Pungent, sour smells loitered at six positions around me, evenly spaced to perfection. This was not a random act. It was not the actions of a person or animal from this human world.

This was a hybrid army.

I forced myself through the mental barrier of the weakest one—the one with the least offensive odor. Hybrid barriers were not difficult for experienced immortals to break. Getting past the smell of their decaying spirit took willpower. Ignoring their personal story posed a greater challenge, especially since my focus had been in aiding humans.

The weakest hybrid scent was from the smallest mortal in the group. He was an older man that was originally unwilling to give in to death. Fear overtook him when diagnosed with cancer years earlier. He prayed for a miracle, for a second chance at life, to correct all the wrongdoings he had done during his seventy-one years on earth. He was frail and weak when Victor converted him. Most importantly, he was grateful. He expected to make amends with his loved ones, but he didn't understand what he was giving up in return.

Free will.

He stood firm at my two o'clock, ready to attack when the order was given, though his spirit was filled with misery. I felt his remorse for the human actions of simple misjudgment. He could have spent more time with his family. He could have focused less on frivolous things that wedged them apart. Swirling feelings of regret filled him. They were locked beneath the controlling power of his creator. He was a puppet forced along at the hand of evil. He wanted freedom. He wanted death.

All I had to do was remove Victor's tether, and the hybrid would be released. For now, his soul was still alive. It wouldn't be long before it decayed completely, and he could no longer be saved. The old man's remorse was enough to get him authorized and into rehabilitation. In time, his soul would heal and he would be well again, able to reunite with those on the other side.

The tether to Victor was thin and aged. The man was converted years earlier, not just recently. The old man's weakness meant Victor felt safe to loosen his hold and add more soldiers to his army. The hybrid wasn't strong enough to be a threat, Victor told him, which pushed the old man deeper into despair.

Feelings of worthlessness ruined spirits, even if they weren't human any longer.

I could sever the connection to Victor, if only I could get him within my grasp. I trained for this. I rehearsed the process in simulation exercises hundreds of times, at The Farm. Except, no field agent implemented it on earth.

There was never a reason to.

Distant voices interrupted my eavesdropped thoughts on the old man. The hybrids were suddenly on alert. The sound was a half mile away, in the direction of the abandoned farmhouse at the corner of highway M and Summit Road.

A man spoke first, followed by a woman's laughter and more

conversation. She was flattered by his advances and thanked him for his help. Her car broke down. Her voice sounded younger than his did. "I'm sure I can help," he offered. He told her he was a mechanic.

I wanted to propel to her, but leaving my body even for short stints of time was unsafe within a pack of hybrids and without knowing Victor's whereabouts. Destruction of my spirit meant total elimination. I could slip into a portal and escape. Although my goal was to release the hybrids, not run from them. Most were so brainwashed, they were unaware they were being held against their will.

To be sure the young female voice was not Emma's, I reached out to Molly. She reported that Emma was safe at home, updating me that Claire recovered from her poor performance earlier in the night. Molly's tone was light and airy, unlike her normal, snippy response.

When the man down the road suggested the girl accompany him to his home for tools, I felt tension within her thoughts.

Her comments were random and disjointed.

His response was soothing and persuasive.

She was reluctant and offered to stay by the car. He advised against it. "It's not safe out here all alone at this time of night," he said.

A hybrid moved. Then another.

As hard as it was, I had to focus my attention on the army around me. The girl would need to wait. The man was probably harmless, anyway.

When another hybrid shifted, I had to concentrate.

One by one, they began to close in the circle around me. It would be impossible for them to sense me. Only another immortal, a strong immortal, would know where I was.

My thoughts shifted to Victor. He had to be orchestrating this, even though I didn't feel his presence. The only other beings here with me were hybrids. I outlined the plan of attack. I could easily take them. Molly could call out a distraction and remain safe at home. The old man would not be my first target, but instead, my last. I felt a slight possibility he would come to my aide when he realized what I was. I could take out the three hybrids to my left before the ones behind me figured out what was going on. I'd start with the one directly in front of me. He was the largest, strongest, youngest hybrid within the pack. Except, he was not the leader. That title was held by their creator.

I'd work counterclockwise and hope the old man would meet me on the other side of this tree. As the last one, I could save him. I could throw the remains of his soul into the portal. It would be out of my hands then.

Molly's screeching voice interrupted my plan of attack. *Benjamin! Benjamin... it's him. It's Victor!*

Everything stopped. *Where?*

He's with the girl near the bridge.

The voices I heard?

Yes, she answered. *And, Benjamin? The girl is Stephanie.*

What would she be doing out here at this time of night? I eavesdropped on Stephanie's thoughts and realized he coerced her into the empty barn. Instead of a sexual assault, his intent was conversion.

Healthy human to hybrid.

The only difference was Stephanie Carlson's contract was not up. Victor moved beyond the worst of crimes. He was now taking lives. A crime punishable by extinction.

"Let me go!" Stephanie's weak voice screamed, as I searched for the portal near the barn. I streamed her thoughts and visions, watching when Victor compelled her to silence. Once she was calm, he wiped his brow and pulled out a switchblade.

He was in his mid-forties with shoulder-length dark hair and a receding hairline. His mustache and beard were neatly trimmed and clean. He wore a leather jacket, black jeans, and a red, collared shirt. A cross hung against his hairy chest from a thick, gold chain. He was physically fit and humanly strong. Though I knew his strengths were enhanced like an athlete on steroids. No one ever saw his human façade, until now.

Molly lifted her shield in thought and called his name in a disguised voice.

He stopped and turned toward the door, knife in hand. She called again and again. He spun around and around, searching for the source.

Stephanie was nervous.

Molly didn't identify herself, or the agency. Her distorted voice echoed his name at a pitch only Victor heard. After all, we needed to take him in alive. The distraction was all I needed to enter through the portal behind Stephanie.

Despite Molly's attempts, he heard me coming.

Instead of taking on the attack, he fled in a flash, leaving Stephanie and me alone in the dilapidated barn.

Chapter 58
Emma's Story

I checked the time on my phone.

Melissa wouldn't be happy that I kept her waiting. I was running thirty minutes late. I sent her a quick text, but she didn't respond. That was never a good sign. She couldn't be that mad, could she? It was a long drive from Westport. Shouldn't she understand that?

I picked up my pace. Hawthorne Mall wasn't huge for Chicago standards, but it was big enough. I walked the upstairs corridor and realized I didn't remember driving there. This mall wasn't our usual meeting place, either.

We planned to meet at a restaurant near the middle of the mall. Funny. I couldn't remember its name. I ran down the flight of stairs as fast as I could. When I reached center court, I lost my speed and was suddenly walking in slow motion.

A familiar-looking man sat at a bench alone. When I approached, he stood and everyone around us disappeared. He was the man in my dreams. The lights around us dimmed except for a spotlight focused on him. He was in the same wool overcoat as before, though he no longer had his pipe.

"Your parents are fine," he said.

"I… I miss them," I whispered, tears already building in my eyes.

"I know. That's why I sent him." He removed his hat, holding it near his heart. "He cares about you deeply, Elizabeth. Be patient with him. You will be rewarded for your efforts."

Before I could speak, he vanished. The lights brightened, and people buzzed around.

A wave of panic awoke me.

I couldn't remember the man's face, but being called Elizabeth felt strangely right.

Chapter 59
Ben's Story

Molly and I stood before Commander E at headquarters.

It was an hour after Stephanie was safe at home with an agent on guard outside her window. Other than her recalling car trouble and a stranger coming to her rescue, we blocked out the memory of being abducted and taken to the abandoned barn. No sense in messing with her already-fragile mind.

Our detailed report with images of Victor's human disguise was distributed to regional directors within the Midwest. Briefings were scheduled in key communities suspected of harboring Victor and his hybrids. A platoon of trackers was dispatched to the farm fields on Summit Road, but as everyone expected, Victor and his crew were long gone.

Commander E recognized my performance in front of his peers. Molly was similarly commended for her offsite participation. She was composed and confident during the meeting. As soon as we reached the hub to leave our world and return to Westport, she became quiet and reserved.

You don't have to do this. I can handle this on my own, I said to her in a conversation I shielded from Pete Jorgenson, who escorted us.

Molly was silent, as we walked to the gate.

Jorgenson shared his comments with us earlier. Commander E left it up to Molly. She could take a leave of absence, though we both knew that meant she would go into hiding in our world.

Images of the abuse Molly suffered at the hands of Victor crossed her mind and flooded into mine. Even though I encouraged her to put the past behind her, she was unable to. Her feelings for Victor, both good and bad, lingered.

She stopped mid-stride and began to shake. In the years I worked with

Molly, she never hit rock bottom like this. Not even close.

Pull yourself together, I told her.

It's like it happened yesterday, Molly said without shielding her thoughts.

Molly, I recommend you reconsider the commander's offer to remain here. At least temporarily, Jorgenson responded. *Benjamin can handle this.*

No, I'm fine. And I don't want to go into hiding, Molly snapped.

I've notified Bianca. She's ready and able to provide companionship for Benjamin.

Wait a minute, I interjected. *I do not need a companion. There's a team in place in Westport already… even* if *Molly chooses to stay behind.*

Jorgenson shook his head. *Your onsite team is made up of sleepers. They are not experienced—*

They're field agents, and they have *experience,* I said, cutting him off. *Bianca* doesn't *have experience.*

Benjamin, calm down. Jorgenson's voice was soothing. *Poor word choice on my behalf. Yes, your team's experienced. Frankly, the Prestons have more fieldwork on their resumes than most other agents in the vicinity. However, not one agent within a fifty-mile radius of Westport has this* type *of experience.*

Pete, Molly said, with more confidence than I saw from her since Victor surfaced. *No one does. There are only a handful of agents that have had combat to begin with. And not one single agent has ever battled Victor.*

Yes, but Bianca's trained for such combat. You both know that Sleeper Agents don't endure the vigorous simulation exercises that Special Investigators do.

Molly's shoulders drooped. She remained silent.

Molly, I appreciate your concerns, but this is out of my hands. Commander E has authorized the implementation of Bianca. She's been on standby ever since the bulletin was posted.

What? I asked.

Whenever you need her, she's ready. It's your call. Either of yours, he answered.

I'm fine, Pete. Please let Commander E know that I am fully capable of putting my personal feelings aside for the betterment of the team.

Jorgenson looked at Molly. Their eyes connected until the thought exchange was complete. Molly would return to the front line with me. Jorgenson gave her a hug, and then turned to shake my hand. *May you succeed in your mission,* he said and left.

Molly's face was pale and her shoulders slouched when we returned to my house through the portal. She slumped into the white leather armchair that enveloped her weak, human body. She was exhausted, nervous, and anxious. Yet, I knew she would never give up.

The attic was converted to a regional office long before Molly or I ever stepped foot in Westport. Within minutes of our return, Claire and Marty arrived, as did Grant and Ava Preston, Molly's fake parents. Each sat around the marble top, oblong table as silhouettes of other dormant officers in the area appeared around us. Commander E addressed our group, briefing everyone on what Molly and I already knew. He was cautious, leaving out confidential details above their security level, but still gave enough information to put us all on alert. Our security level was raised to red, a level not seen during my tenure.

When his speech concluded, I knew it was simply a matter of time before Bianca joined us. What capacity that may be, I wasn't sure. It all depended upon Molly. And for now, Molly was not at her peak.

The group dissipated slowly. News of Victor was difficult to absorb. Most, if not all of, the agents in the area never experienced firsthand the workings of one of our most notorious criminals. Shock ran through everyone, as did commendation to Molly and me for our quick wit. Though it wasn't recognition I wanted at that moment. I wanted to see Emma.

I had to see her.

I hated the stalking feeling I got every time I eavesdropped in on her. When her thoughts were quiet, I felt the need to confirm she was safe.

I propelled to her house and hovered over the window. Chester raised his head from his spot on the bed. He rolled his eyes, and then put his head between his paws. *You're a sap, man,* Chester said in thought. *She's fine. I've been here all night. You're right. Something's wrong with Lucas. In all my years, I've never experienced it either.*

Chester was an agent for a century. He specialized in youth, in helping children and teenagers in the aftermath of losing a parent.

He saw it all. He was solid and stable.

Except he didn't have experience with Victor, either.

Chapter 60
EMMA'S STORY

MY SECOND WEEK AT WESTPORT HIGH SCHOOL WAS BETTER THAN THE FIRST.

At least, I felt better about it. When I walked down the hall, people smiled and waved. Claire waited for me every day for lunch and each afternoon for soccer practice. Things fell into a routine. I turned in all of my assignments and made up the last of the quizzes I missed in calculus.

Being caught up was a satisfying feeling, though I still missed Highland Park.

"Claire reminds me of you," I told Melissa when she asked how I was doing. Melissa and I spoke almost every night and texted several times a day. Mostly it was small talk about school or soccer. I told her about the team I joined in Westport, and she kept me up-to-date on people we knew. I told her about the team I joined in Westport, and she kept me up-to-date on people we knew, especially Matt."You should come for a visit," Melissa suggested.

"I know. I want to, um… well, I'm not sure I should ask my aunt. At least not yet."

"Yeah. I'd ask my mom, but I know she won't let me drive there," Melissa said. "Hey… we're going to a football game at Northwestern in a few weeks. Wanna come?"

"Umm… I'll have to ask," I said. A college football game, out of state? There was no way Aunt Barb would agree to that. At least, I didn't think so. "I'll let you know."

We both knew that meant no.

I couldn't get the idea out of my head, as I worked on my pencil sketch in art class. I wondered if Aunt Barb would say no. Then again, maybe I shouldn't even ask. I could just tell her I was visiting Melissa. I didn't think Aunt Barb would call Melissa's mom.

Or would she?

"Emma, you're so quiet today," Hannah said. She and Claire chatted most of the class about anything and everything. She drilled Claire about Drew for a half hour, before moving on to TJ and Molly's break up.

"Ah… no reason," I answered and looked up. Lucas glanced at me and smiled.

"Are you going to the football game tomorrow night?"

"Um, I'm not sure," I answered, refusing to look up.

"You should. Claire, you're going, right?"

"Of course," Claire answered as the teacher instructed us to pack up our supplies. "Emma, you can ride with me."

"Okay."

"Did you get your homecoming dress yet?" Hannah asked without looking up.

Claire glanced at me, and then answered. "Not yet. How 'bout you?"

"Yup. I got it in Chicago when my mom and I went to Emma's—"

"What does it look like?" Claire cut her off.

Hannah paused and looked away briefly before describing her dress as short and strapless in metallic-silver taffeta.

"When is homecoming?" I asked as the bell rang, acting as if I didn't figure out she was talking about the Chicago trip for my dad's funeral.

"In a couple of weeks. You have time to find a dress. You know, your aunt's boutique at the Inn has really nice dresses. Maybe she'll have something for you," Hannah said as we walked out of the classroom.

"Oh. I don't think I'm going," I said.

"You have to. Everyone that's anyone goes to the dance," Hannah said just before the three of us parted ways.

I hurried down the hall, Hannah's thoughts fluttering in my mind. It was flattering, being "in" with the popular crowd. On the other hand, it meant I couldn't go to the dance alone. Thoughts of Ben entered my mind. It was silly, actually. Getting my hopes up was a guaranteed letdown. He would never ask me to the dance. Especially since Stephanie Carlson targeted him all week.

I strolled into literature class and took my seat as the bell rang.

I dreaded literature. It meant lots of reading of old historical novels by authors that wrote in a language too difficult for me to understand. Mrs. Moore called the class to attention, as my mind began to wander.

Did Ben like Stephanie? I never saw him smile or flirt with her. He seemed to tolerate her.

Mrs. Moore's irritating voice interrupted my thoughts. "Their writing is exceptional. Their stories have messages we must decipher. This is why American literature is so interesting and one of the reasons I love it," she said, and then paused for a moment. The silence was eerie. "Reading classical literature is my passion." She looked around the room and pointed to no one in particular. "My wish for each of you," she smiled before she completed her thought, "is that you will achieve a passion for literature after this semester project."

There weren't any weird teachers like her back in Highland Park. At least, none that I knew, anyway. She obviously loved her job. I, on the other hand, was not interested in literature. I found it boring. I loved to read, but I liked modern novels by authors that wrote about topics I enjoyed, not ones with hidden messages and old English I had to interpret in order to understand it. I was told we would study Romeo and Juliet this year, which I heard was a good section. But this project was not.

Mrs. Moore counted out sheets of paper and handed them out by row. The girl in front of me, whose name I didn't know, passed the stack back to me. As I grabbed my copy and turned to pass the rest back, I noticed Ben for a split second. He sat three rows to my left and two seats back. Our eyes met momentarily; at least, I thought they did. Maybe I just hoped for it. He certainly didn't acknowledge me in calculus first period that morning.

The class was distracted by the handouts, with small chitchat going on in various corners of the room. Mrs. Moore spoke loudly after handing out the last stack of papers, "Okay, settle down, class," she said and proceeded to explain the project. It sounded more like a sales pitch on how wonderful early American literature was.

I scanned the list of authors and suggested titles. Most I never heard of, or had any interest in reading. *Maybe Hemingway*, I thought. Mrs. Moore's voice jumped me back out of my daydream.

"These authors and their books are on hold in the library. Any of their work is acceptable. If you are having difficulties selecting an author, perhaps I can help." She paused slightly as the bell rang, finishing in a louder voice, "Any book by these authors. It doesn't have to be the ones listed. Have a good day!"

I grabbed my things and headed out. Great. A long novel assignment. Literature used to be one of my least favorite subjects.

Suddenly, I hated it.

Chapter 61
Ben's Story

I spent the past three nights on patrol.

My human body was tired and weak. A little rest was all I needed. Instead, I ran on adrenaline. Searching for Victor was a full-time job. Molly returned to school and a somewhat normal life. Claire was assigned to Emma, and all seemed well in Westport.

Except that it wasn't.

Agents patrolled the county in human form and in spirit. At one point, there was one operative located every one-thousand square feet. After forty-eight hours with no sign of unauthorized immortals, no scent of any hybrid, and no essence of Victor reported, most agents were sent home. Molly held herself together by day, but when alone at night, I heard her petrified thoughts, even with guards following her every move.

I glanced up at the cafeteria ceiling and saw the spirits of two immortals who propelled to the high school. A utility van parked on North Avenue housed the bodies of six agents that rotated shifts of school surveillance without human detection. It was the second lunch period out of three. The lunch hour that Emma and most of her friends were in.

I got there late, after checking in with one of my operatives that patrolled the premises. He was stationed at the school after I compelled the police chief and claimed there were threats in the area and a campus presence was wise. Comments, thoughts, and fears crossed the minds of kids when uniformed officers arrived Monday morning. By Thursday, however, only one policeman remained since the chief couldn't justify more.

"The threat level has declined. There's been no direct mention of Westport, and the only visible activities in Riverside have been dismissed as graffiti. I'll keep one officer on duty, but I suggest you implement a closed campus," the police chief said. The principle had no choice but to agree.

And all I could do was watch.

It caused sleepless nights for Molly and restless days for me, as I sat through high school courses thinking of all the places I should be searching for Victor. Work was constantly on my mind, to the point I didn't hear the teacher call my name in art history earlier that morning. Molly's screeching voice in my head snapped me back to reality. She fed me the answer the teacher was looking for and told me to focus.

She was right. I needed to balance things in order to succeed.

I glanced around the cafeteria. Juvenile behavior bounced from table to table. Lunch was a show-and-tell of social status at Westport. The haves and the have-nots segregated by linoleum at rectangular, white laminated tables with bench seating.

Molly gossiped and laughed with Stephanie Carlson at the same table every day. It was in the second row beside Hannah, Claire, Emma, and their extended group of girls. Foreign-exchange students sat closest to the cafeteria doors with brainiacs, druggies, and drama queens filling in the rows in between.

Window seats were unofficially reserved for the school jocks. Lucas, TJ, and some football players flanked one end, while my soccer teammates covered the other. Testosterone ran rampant. It was forty minutes of hormones, insecurities, and an occasional card game for most of the guys. For me, it was a chance to listen in on everyone's thoughts.

Hannah dominated the conversation as usual. Emma obediently listened, responding at appropriate times with an occasional nod, or an, "Oh, really?" to the gossip Hannah liked to share. Emma glanced behind her, and then up at the ceiling, before her eyes met mine for a split second. It wasn't the first time she checked me out, but it was just as flattering.

"Have you ever felt someone was looking at you, but there was no one there?" Emma asked the girls after Hannah was finally done with her story.

Ben, did you catch that? Molly's thoughts replaced my shock. *She's more perceptive than we thought.*

I swallowed the invisible lump in my throat. Emma's thoughts were clear. Even though she couldn't see the agents, she could feel their presence.

"I know exactly what you mean!" Hannah exclaimed. "The other night I was home alone studying and I was sure someone was standing behind me. You know, like I heard breathing or something. But the house was empty."

"Hannah, you're so gullible!" Claire said. "It was probably your brother."

"No, I swear I was home alone."

Lucas threw a crumpled napkin at the girl's table, landing it on Claire's tray. Laughter erupted, as the paper ball was tossed back with a few new ones the girls made. Lucas smiled at Emma. He intended to get Emma's attention, and it worked. It got the conversation started between the two tables with flirtatious looks and comments whipping back and forth. In a few minutes, the volume would be loud enough to draw the attention of the lunch ladies who supervised behavior in the cafeteria, and soon the paper toss would be over.

Drew flirted with Claire. Justin smiled at Hannah. Stephanie glared at Lucas, while he winked at Emma. I heard everyone's thoughts as well as their spoken words. I could tolerate all the hormonal hopes until it was Lucas thinking about Emma. I took a deep breath, gritting my teeth as I listened to his inappropriate comments.

Emma was flattered. Obviously, I needed to work harder to change that.

Chapter 62
Emma's Story

I had study hall eighth period.

In the weeks I'd been at Westport, few students actually stayed in the assigned classroom during that hour. Instead, they approached the teacher and asked for a pass. I noticed she made each student sign a sheet before handing them a laminated card.

Going to the library to check out the books for my literature assignment seemed like a good excuse I thought, as I approached the teacher. She told me the rules about leaving, made me promise to return, and handed me the get-out-of-study-hall pass in case I was found wandering.

The library was more impressive than I expected. The glass doors opened to a modern two-story area with tables and chairs and rows upon rows of books. It was refreshing, actually. Displays of new releases and top-selling books welcomed visitors at the entrance. They were propped up on easels with multiple copies below. I felt like I walked into Barnes and Noble, not the Westport High School library.

While it was comforting, it was incredibly intimidating. People moved about like they knew where they were going. They walked with a purpose, as I loitered near the door.

Where would I possibly find these reserved books?

After glancing around, I noticed a circular island and a woman behind the counter. I waited my turn and then asked where to find the reserved section. The confusion I felt must have been written on my face, as the librarian pointed to the loft area above and behind her.

"That's in Room A," she said. "There are reserved rooms along the east loft area. The western end has tables for study purposes, but please be aware of the quiet zone areas. They are marked."

I nodded and thanked her.

The only thing missing was the Starbucks counter.

I opened the glass door and walked in. It was quiet, and I was alone. I started scanning the section displayed for Mrs. Moore's class, picking up a book here and there to read the back. Nothing popped out at me. Mom would have been good at this. She loved to read. After scanning more than half the list, I saw Hemingway and picked up one of his books.

I heard the door open behind me, but I didn't bother to look. I started reading the cover and the teacher's notes on *A Farewell to Arms*. At least I had heard of this author.

"Hemingway, huh?" a deep voice said behind me. I jumped. "Oh, sorry, Emma, I didn't mean to scare you," Ben said as I turned to face him.

"No, it's me… I was just deep in thought, I guess," I said and looked into his eyes. They were brown like milk chocolate.

He pointed to the book in my hand, waiting for a response I didn't give. "I wouldn't have guessed you to pick Hemingway," he said.

I chuckled to myself, and couldn't help but notice how at ease I felt with him. Even though he was virtually a stranger, a boy that I spoke with for a few minutes combined. "Honestly, it sort of jumped out at me. I didn't know who to pick, but I'm going with it." I smiled at how stupid that sounded, as the words met the fresh air.

He looked into my eyes, holding me fixed for a second. "Things jump out at me too…" he said, still looking at me. "Once and awhile."

I looked away first, back to the book in my hand. "So, who are you picking?"

"Hemingway," he said with confidence and without hesitation.

"Really? But you… I mean—" Heat rushed to my cheeks. He looked up at me with a smirk, and I stumbled over my words. "You don't look like the type that would pick Hemingway." I smiled. It was my weak attempt at flirting. Was my face red?

Ben's smirk turned into a full grin. His teeth were exceptionally white.

"And what type would I be?" He picked up one of Hemingway's books.

"Um… well… let's see." I scanned the other shelves and took a deep breath. "I'm sure I can pick an author to match your personality." I didn't know where my newfound confidence came from, but I went with it.

"You have no idea."

I shook my head. Laughter filled the air. "Not a clue. I told you I picked Hemingway because it jumped out at me. I never heard of half these authors before." I motioned toward the bookcases. "Literature is not my favorite class."

"It's okay… but Mrs. Moore is weird."

"I thought I was the only one that felt that way!"

He smiled.

"So why did you pick Hemingway?" I asked.

He appeared serious. "I knew someone." He pointed to the book I clutched in my hand. "*A Farewell to Arms* was her favorite."

Her? A look crossed his face. Was he sad? The light, airy feeling in the room vanished. I knew he had a girlfriend.

"It was a really long time ago, actually." He reached for another book from the reserved stack. "Hemingway has a lot of books. If you want suggestions, I could help you pick some out."

"Umm… maybe." I didn't want to sound desperate.

"Do you have soccer practice today?" He took a seat at the large, round table in the center of the room as I answered yes. "It's a short season, isn't it?"

"Yup. Only three or four weeks." I sat in a chair on the other side of the table.

"When's your first game?"

"Saturday morning."

He opened the cover of Hemingway's, *The Old Man and the Sea*.

"You going? I mean, to watch your sister?"

"Yeah, yeah. I'll go." He turned pages so quickly that he couldn't have read them. "Claire and I are pretty close."

"That's nice." I paused. "Claire's a good player."

"Eh, she's alright." I couldn't tell if his monotone meant he agreed with me, or not. As I tried to guess his reaction, he looked up. His chocolate brown eyes were warm like hot cocoa on a cold day. I felt drawn in and didn't want to look away. "You're right. She is good. Just don't tell her I said so." He winked, and my heart pounded out of my chest.

Chapter 63
Ben's Story

I'm impressed. You finally gave that girl a glimpse of the real you, Molly said.

I sat in Spanish class, last hour of the day. *Eavesdropping again?*

I wouldn't, if you would tell me. Instead, I have to resort to reading Emma's thoughts.

Nice. I shook my head as I half listened to the teacher's lecture.

Actually, she's beaming from ear to ear. I didn't need to try very hard.

You're awfully bubbly when you delve into my personal life, I said. *How ya doing? Seriously?*

The mood changed as her thoughts slowed. *I'm good.*

You sure?

Yeah. I'm sure. I knew her well enough to know she wasn't. *How would you feel if I let Jorgenson bring someone else in?* she asked, after moments of silence.

Someone? Or Bianca?

Benjamin, you know that part's not up to me.

Molly, I can handle this. I don't expect you to go on patrol, but I will not work with Bianca Beringer. My words were firm, as my blood pressure rose. *I would never have guessed you'd change your mind and suggest her. You've never liked her. What're you thinking?*

Molly was silent for a minute, and then finally responded. *You're right. I'm being ridiculous.*

Damned right, I had this.

Chapter 64
Emma's Story

The next week flew by.

Ben was at the library every day, in the same room. We didn't make plans to meet there. It just happened. We talked and studied, then talked some more. We worked on math problems assigned in calculus class and laughed about Mrs. Moore's quirkiness until the librarian hushed us.

Ben had a great smile, and I found myself completely comfortable with him.

When Claire asked if I'd go with her to the boys' soccer game Thursday night, I eagerly agreed. Minutes after kick off, we were seated in the student area of the bleachers next to Hannah and a bunch of girls she introduced as girlfriends of soccer players. All but the redhead. She was definitely a wannabe, or the team's biggest fan. She called out every player's name. Or, at least it seemed like it. When she yelled for number twenty-three, Ben's number, I paid closer attention to her. I couldn't help but admit she was pretty. After a few minutes, I realized she was loud and as annoying as the juniors a few rows behind us. The rowdy guys that chanted "Go-Westport-Go," which matched the words painted on their bare chests.

We scored, and fans erupted with whistles and cheers. When the applause died down and people took their seats again, Lucas arrived. He said hi as he sat in front of us.

Claire smirked at me, and I felt my cheeks getting warm until Hannah nudged me with her elbow. It was then that I noticed Stephanie and Molly at the chain-link fence in front of the parents' section. I wasn't sure how long they were there, but Stephanie was focused on the field, while Molly stood with TJ.

"They're talking again," Hannah said.

"That's good, right?"

She nodded.

By the time the game was over, we won by three goals and everyone went to Rusty's to celebrate. Ben sat in the corner booth with a few other players I never met before. He smiled at me and for a second, I thought he would ask me to sit with him. Before I could get my hopes up, Stephanie scooted in beside him.

I ended up at a table with Claire, TJ, and Lucas, watching Stephanie giggle and lean into Ben.

I should have known Ben and I were just friends.

Chapter 65
Ben's Story

She could hate you. Molly smirked.

I sat in calculus Friday morning.

At least she thinks of you as a friend.

Nice. Really nice, I retorted. *This is because of you and your friend, Stephanie. That girl has issues.* Coach Vieth was busy demonstrating a solution for the math problem in the next chapter, so I tuned him out. I could easily look up the answer later, if it proved relevant.

I preferred watching Emma.

When class was dismissed, I timed my exit so I could talk with her. Drew was on my heels, as we reached the hallway. He got her attention first.

"You comin' to my party tonight, Emma?" Drew asked. I knew she was going without listening to her response.

Drew dominated the conversation, while we walked with the crowd. It was meaningless chatter not worthy of my time. When we reached Emma's locker, she stopped.

"I'll catch up with you later, Emmie," I said.

"Emmie?" Drew questioned as we continued down the hall. His voice grew louder than necessary. "You got a pet name for her?" He laughed.

I shook my head and chuckled. We parted ways, and I headed toward class.

"Hey, Ben." TJ caught up to me on the stairs.

"How's it going?"

"Good. Hey, listen. Don't call her Emmie." His tone was firm.

"Say what?"

TJ stopped at the top of the stairs and grabbed my arm.

"Don't call her that," he said as I turned to face him. "Her name's Emma."

His thoughts were as firm as his tone. Emma's mom called her Emmie. I glared back but stopped short of compelling TJ. Kids coming up the stairs interrupted our moment, as we blocked their path. Seconds later, TJ was heading toward class and I stood still, dumbfounded.

It wasn't often someone put me in my place. I couldn't remember a time when someone did since I was an immortal. That was a risk most humans wouldn't attempt. Though I couldn't imagine TJ knew what he was getting into. As I proceeded down the corridor, I realized I was never put in my place as a human, either.

Well, then it's about bloody time. Molly's sarcasm filtered into my head.

I ignored her and scanned the comments in student's head until I heard the voice I was searching for. Emma was talking about the sleepover at Hannah's later that night. Once I heard her thoughts, I was also able to see what her eyes saw. It was an extension of our abilities that took more concentration, but I felt it was worthwhile now. At least she wasn't dwelling on the name I called her. Claire and Hannah sat near Emma in Spanish class.

I glanced around her classroom as best as I could through her sight of vision. No random thoughts of TJ or me. Just girl stuff. Clothes, makeup. Drew's party. Football game. Sleepover.

I exited her mind and walked into art history class.

"What's up with your boyfriend?" I asked Molly and sat beside her.

She glared. I didn't care; I was irritated.

"He's not my boyfriend," Molly said in a low voice. Her teeth were clenched, yet she maintained her pretty posture, in line with her popularity status.

Other words to describe TJ came to mind. Molly's Boy-Toy was at the top of the list.

Stop it! she scolded.

When my verbal abuse got on her nerves, she envisioned slapping me.

"What would you like me to call him?" I said aloud, so other students could hear me.

"Stop. We broke up," she said. Her human cheeks turned pink, as the girl in front of her turned around. "We're just friends."

"Friends with benefits?" I blurted out. I shouldn't have, I realized. Several people glanced at Molly.

"I hate you," she replied as the bell rang.

"No, you don't. You love me."

I shielded myself, as the teacher called the class to attention. No need for the other immortals to hear what I was thinking. I scanned the student body looking for TJ. He was in class. His thoughts were clear, minimal. No anger. He listened to the teacher and the material being discussed. It was like his comment to me no longer mattered. Except that I couldn't get it out of my head. I wondered if he felt more than protection toward Emma. Maybe Molly knew that. Was that why she ended their relationship so soon after Emma got here?

Molly sat in perfect posture, listening to the boring lecture, taking detailed notes. When she caught my glance, she rolled her eyes.

Go figure. Still mad.

I loosened my shield and thought, *You'll get over it.*

She sighed heavily and focused on the teacher.

When the forty-two minute class finally ended, I felt as free as an escaped convict from jail. "Sorry," I said as we walked out of class.

"It's all right," Molly answered. "They need a little drama now and then. It keeps the gossip fresh."

We walked a few feet in silence. *You really like TJ, don't you?* I asked in thought.

Yes.

More than you wanted to?

She nodded.

Then don't be a fool. Get him back.

Chapter 66
Emma's Story

Friday night.

Drew planned a party. Hannah suggested a sleepover. And then, there was football.

Ben was at our usual table in the library during study hall, but we weren't alone. He spent the period working on calculus homework with ear buds in his ears. It was an easy assignment, so I didn't have a reason to interrupt him. Not to mention my ego wouldn't let me ask a stupid question.

Claire, Courtney, and I met at Hannah's house to get ready before the game.

Aunt Barb was thrilled with my friendship with Hannah. I overheard her talking on the phone about it to Hannah's mom.

It was the first time I really felt part of the student body. The National Anthem played as we walked in. When Aunt Barb raised her hand to wave at me from the parent section of the stands, Lisa shook her head to stop her. A huge smile crossed both of their faces.

The game started, as we found seats wedged in between some guys in front of us and juniors behind us. There was a definite social hierarchy here, and it felt good to fit in. Ben strolled in after us with some soccer players. I couldn't help but watch him. He still made my heart skip a beat, even if he and Steph had a thing.

Claire called to Ben, but by the time he made his way through the crowd to the student section, there was no seat by us. Conveniently, Stephanie found him, though I think she followed him. She grabbed his arm and clung onto it as they found a seat in the section beside us, a few rows closer to the field.

For once, Molly wasn't her sidekick. I almost said the words aloud when Claire did.

"I thought they were inseparable."

"Me too," I said and laughed.

A few minutes later, Molly walked in with a blonde I hadn't seen before.

"Who's she?" I asked Claire, pointing toward the stranger.

"Huh. No idea." She had a blank look on her face.

Molly seemed to stay with the blonde. They were dressed for a night out, not for a football game in school colors like the rest of us.

The blonde looked older with shoulder-length straight hair and bangs. She wore tight jeans low on her hips with a fitted, black jacket clasped at the waist. Even from the bleachers, I could see the sparkle of belly-button jewelry.

She was incredibly attractive. Guys turned their heads, confirming my thoughts.

Molly and her friend squeezed in with Ben and Stephanie. I watched the introduction and handshakes. For a second, I thought Ben glanced up at me.

When I blinked, I realized he wasn't even looking in my direction.

Chapter 67
Ben's Story

"What are you doing here?" I asked through clenched teeth.

We stood in my attic conference room. My heart pounded with the anger I held back for hours since the voluptuous woman appeared as Molly's sidekick at the high school game. If I were human, I'd be on the verge of a heart attack.

"Darlin', why are you so angry?" Bianca touched my arm.

"Before you get upset, Benjamin, I invited her," Molly interrupted.

My jaw ached and my blood pressure rose, as I turned to glare at Molly.

"Molly's right. I wouldn't have come unless you needed me. And clearly, you do." Bianca's flirtatious smile crept in, as she leaned toward me.

"Seriously, Molly? You invited her?" I couldn't believe the betrayal I felt.

I shielded Bianca and tethered my thoughts to Molly. *You knew how I felt about bringing her in. You knew I had this under control, and yet, you called Bianca in?*

She hung her head in silence.

Bianca realized we were in conversation that excluded her. She tilted her head at me, and then finally spoke. "Would the two of you like some privacy?"

"Yes," I answered before Molly ever looked up.

Tears already formed in Molly's eyes when Bianca slipped into the portal and out of the room.

"I had to. You don't understand. You don't realize what Victor is capable of."

"Molly, I appreciate that. I appreciate your concern and your care. But I don't appreciate you going behind my back and arranging a new partner for me when I've told you how I felt." I stared at her. I couldn't recall ever being this angry—as a human or an immortal.

"Bianca comes highly recommended, Benjamin. Pete thought she would be a good fit."

"Right, a good fit. You know how she is. You've seen her with humans. She has no regard for them. She has no respect for others, including you," I said louder than even I expected. I paced the length of the room and then returned to where she stood, solemn and weak. "And, frankly, Molly, I don't have time to babysit her, look for Victor and the hybrids, and try to have some relationship with Emma. Maybe you need her, but I don't."

I stormed out of the house without giving her a chance to reply.

***

I shouldn't have, but I went to Drew's party. It was what was expected of me and with my time so limited, juggling between all of my responsibilities, I had to. When I got there, the party was in full swing.

Emma had a drink in her hand, as she talked with Hannah and Claire. The girls looked pretty comfortable, sitting cross-legged on the couch. Eavesdropping on their conversation, I knew they weren't talking about anything that mattered. Not to me, anyway.

I took a shot of vodka when Trent passed it to me, and a second one before handing it to Lucas. To my surprise, Lucas shook his head and waved his hand to pass. TJ mumbled something under his breath about Emma that no one heard, but I was able to hear his thoughts. Lucas was trying to impress her, I learned.

Great. I didn't need that today, too. I chugged the equivalent of another two shots and gave the bottle to TJ.

Claire buzzed into my thoughts. *She's not that into Lucas.*

Not into him, or not that *into him?* I retorted. *Ah, never mind.*

Umm... so where's Molly and who was she with at the game?

Bianca, I answered. *She's with Bianca. I'm sure they'll make a grand entrance sooner or later.* The words barely came to mind when they strolled in, looking more like porn stars than high school students. Guys gawked at them. Their thoughts were louder than the girls' giggles.

Molly and Bianca mingled, while Stephanie loitered near me and Drew played bartender.

When Emma finished her beer, Lucas brought her another. After a shot and another drink, my blood pressure rose. What was Emma doing?

I beelined toward her. I couldn't help myself.

"Emma, you've had enough," I said.

Benjamin, settle down. Molly's thoughts pushed through my barrier.

"Hey, man," Lucas interrupted. "Just one more." He stood eye to eye with me.

"I think she's had enough."

Benjamin, stop. You're making a scene.

"I think she can make up her own mind," Lucas retorted. His piercing eyes were a weak attempt at intimidation.

Don't do this, Benjamin.

"And I think she's had enough." I stood my ground, fists clenched by my side.

Lucas raised his hands to my chest to push me, as Emma yelled, "Stop it!" She stepped in between us, placing her left hand on my chest, and her right on his. With her touch, I was able to download her feelings, the pain my behavior caused her and the disappointment she suddenly felt in me. She said she was fine and wanted another drink. Looking me in the eyes, she told me it was none of my business.

It was then I realized I went too far.

Chapter 68
Emma's Story

"What the hell was that about?"

Leave it to Hannah to be the first to speak after the uncomfortable incident that caused TJ to pull Lucas outside and for Ben to leave.

"I, ah… I don't know. One minute Lucas is getting me another drink and the next Ben is telling him I had enough." Even as the words flowed from my mouth, I found them hard to believe. My hands shook when I reached for the beer Hannah handed me. I was never the center of attention before, and I definitely never had two guys act like that around me.

"Just drink," Claire said under her breath. She tipped her bottle of hard lemonade into my beer. I took a sip and attempted to return the bright smile on her face, but I couldn't. After Hannah rejoined the group in the living room and whispers of Ben and Lucas filled their conversation, I asked Claire what was up.

"I have noooo idea. I haven't seen Ben like this. Ever."

After a few minutes, everything went back to normal. Someone turned up the music, and Drew handed out shots. TJ and Lucas came back inside, and Molly introduced us to a foreign exchange student, Bianca. She explained where Bianca was from and how long she was staying, but I was too distracted to pay attention.

I couldn't figure out if Ben liked me, or was just a jerk. While everyone got drunk, I got sober. Not that it was a bad thing. I was suddenly uncomfortable. After a visit to the bathroom and a break on the deck, I joined Claire at the island.

"There you are!" Claire's smile could light a cavern.

Lucas came up beside me and placed his hand on mine. "Hey, sorry about that," he whispered over the loud music.

I turned toward him and found our faces inches apart.

I wondered if I was as red as I felt. My heart started to pound in my chest. I knew he would kiss me if I wanted him to. I just didn't know what I wanted.

"It's okay," I said, but it was clear he didn't hear me.

He leaned closer, his lips nearing mine before he turned his ear toward me.

I caught my breath and repeated the words I whispered earlier. I watched him nod, but he didn't remove his hand until Drew gave him a beer.

Chapter 69
Ben's Story

I awoke on the leather couch in the attic conference room.

My neck was stiff and my head pounded—the disadvantage of being in a human body. I sat up, stretched, and applied pressure to the webbed area between my thumb and forefinger on my left hand. The dull ache at the crown of my head began to vanish. Tilting my head from side to side, then from front to back, relieved the pain in my neck. Though only the physical strain went away.

I still felt the tension I created with my behavior the night before. It was something that replayed in my thoughts over and over again, which was why I crashed on the sofa instead of going to bed.

After leaving the party, I met Jorgenson for a nightcap. Actually, I strolled into Rusty's Anchor for a drink, and he intervened. It was the first time Pete Jorgenson came to earth in decades.

"The pitfalls of being a handler," he said when he sat down beside me at the bar. "I go where you lead me." He ordered tequila from the bartender I previously compelled to serve me since I didn't bother to use a disguise.

There were only a few people playing pool and a young couple shooting darts when I got there at midnight. The place cleared out by that time, even on weekends. Jorgenson warned me not to go in, not to act like an angry, foolish human. His orders were direct and firm but I shielded myself, blocking out his unwanted thoughts. It was bad enough having Molly's comments floating in and out, I didn't want to hear it from him, too. However, blocking him meant I left him no choice but to hunt me down himself or alert the commander that I went rogue.

I was being stupid, and I knew it. Being in human form for extended periods of time tended to warp reality for us immortals. Our emotions heightened and our behaviors mimicked that of the earthly world inhabitants. We got so wrapped up in the human lifestyle that we lost sight of the bigger picture, of our world and our mission. It was why most agents' contracts were limited in duration.

This was something that never happened to me.

Jorgenson and I drank until closing time. He admitted sending Bianca, despite my dislike for the woman.

"Molly begged the commander not to send her," he said. "When Commander E asked my opinion, I couldn't think of anyone better suited than her." He poured two shots of tequila from the bottle and handed one to me. "And I'm not sorry about it."

Disgusted, I knocked back the caramel-colored liquid. My human body soaked up the alcohol like a sponge cleaning up a spill. Bianca Beringer was a good agent. No doubt she would be a great agent, someday. I just didn't want to be the one to help her reach that goal.

"You don't like her because she scares you," he said with a chuckle.

His words cut into me like a knife. I tried to shield my thoughts, but the alcohol and anger lessened my powers, and I slipped. He was right. Bianca scared me. She was sharp, witty, and most men found her irresistible.

"I'm not interested in Bianca Beringer," I told him.

"So you've said."

"I've turned down her advances."

"I know." Jorgenson poured another round of tequila.

"She just won't give up," I said and drank the shot he pushed at me.

"Bianca always gets what she wants."

"Not this time," I answered, though we both knew that wasn't true. Bianca was attractive and determined. If I was being truthful with myself, she was the only woman that turned my head in the seventy-plus years since I lost Elizabeth. Now that I found Elizabeth in Emma, I couldn't risk losing her again.

Jorgenson was kind after he read my thoughts about Bianca. He suggested I take a few weeks off. "To regroup. You've been here a long time. Longer than most agents. You could use a little time off," he said. Despite how great that sounded, we both knew it wasn't a good idea. Victor was lurking in Wisconsin and me being the only agent in centuries to have identified his essence, I couldn't leave. Not now. Not until he was caught.

Victor was suddenly my priority, and Bianca was the best operative to assist me.

***

Commander E's call ended the pity party my human side celebrated.

"Benjamin," his strong voice hailed. An image of the dark-skinned man appeared in a hologram over the conference table. "What the fuck are you doing?"

I stood at attention. "I apologize, sir. I got out of hand."

"You're damn right. Under no circumstances do you break protocol like you did last night, son. You can't compel the whole town because you're pissed off." Commander E sat at the mahogany desk in his office.

"I understand, sir."

"And I can't afford to have Jorgenson flying all over hell to pick up the pieces from your mess! You're not the only field agent he handles." He clenched his hand into a fist and pounded on the desk. A crystal golf ball jumped with the impact.

"Yes, sir. I understand. I apologize, sir."

It wasn't the first time Commander E admonished me in my years on the job, but it was the only time I saw him this angry. I wasn't myself. Letting my heart lead me to and around Emma was screwing up my career.

"Your priority has shifted to Victor Nicklas and the gang of hybrids in the Midwest. Another one surfaced this morning outside a nightclub in Chicago. I need you to get your head out of your ass and do your job. If you want to spend time with Elizabeth or Emma, or whatever the hell she calls herself in this life, don't let it interfere with your priority."

"Yes, sir. I understand. Thank you," I answered.

"Benjamin," he said and leaned forward in his seat, his forefinger firmly pointed in my direction. "If she begins to interrupt your progress on this case, I'll have her contract cut short. *Do you understand*?"

"Loud and clear, sir."

Before I finished speaking the words, Commander E shut down the link and his hologram disappeared.

There was no other choice. I had to refocus.

Chapter 70
Emma's Story

"I can't believe Ben told Lucas you had enough to drink last night."

Hannah's words still rang in my head, as I drove home the next morning. "I didn't realize he was so parental," she said. It was the topic of conversation hours after Ben left the party and again when the girls woke up at the sleepover. I was relieved when Hannah shushed the subject in front of her mom, as she flipped pancakes for breakfast.

No one understood what got into Ben, not even Claire.

***

Aunt Barb was sitting at the dining room table when I walked in a little after nine o'clock. Her hair was up and her glasses were low on her nose. It was a familiar look for a Saturday, I realized. Papers were scattered on the table, alongside plastic bags filled with small parts. I guessed they were screws or bolts for whatever was inside the two large boxes on the living room floor.

"Good morning, honey," she said. Her tone was always warm and welcoming. "Did you have fun last night?"

"Yeah, it was good. The girls are really nice," I answered. "What are you working on?"

"Oh, this? It's a shelving unit for the closet in the laundry room." Her smile turned down before she continued. "I overestimated my patience with putting it together. Not to mention, I really need two people to install it."

"I can help you after my soccer game."

She took a sip of coffee and shook her head. "You're a darling, but I've already called Neal. He'll come over with Lucas."

I was silent.

"Lucas is moving back in with Neal," she said, even though I didn't ask.

"He's been living with his mom, right?"

She nodded. “Just since his arrest on the Fourth of July.”

“What was he arrested for?” I asked, innocently.

“Possession of marijuana with the intent to distribute.”

“The case was dropped, right?” I asked.

“Yes. I stayed out of it. I don’t know what loophole the attorney found, but it was enough to get the judge to drop the case. Obviously, Neal was thrilled. No parent wants to see their child in trouble, but it doesn’t look good for an officer to have a son with a criminal record, either.”

“Yeah, I guess.”

Aunt Barb proceeded to tell me the story of how Neal’s wife left him when Lucas was four years old. “Charlene had troubles. They probably shouldn’t have married at all,” she said. “She was in and out of rehab for years and finally, Neal gave her an ultimatum to fix herself or leave.”

“She left them?” I asked, unable to imagine how terrible Lucas must have felt, knowing his mom deserted him.

Aunt Barb nodded. “She went to Vegas. Neal got a couple of postcards, at first. After a while, the cards and letters came back undeliverable. He had no idea where Char was for years. Then one day, she just showed up… a few years ago. She lives in Riverside now.” Aunt Barb took another drink of coffee and glanced at the clock. “You better get ready for your game.”

“Um, yeah,” I said and headed to my room. As bad as things were for me, at least I wasn’t abandoned.

By the time I had my uniform on and was ready for the game, Neal was busy reading the instruction sheet.

“Neal’s invited us for dinner at his house tonight,” Aunt Barb said when I told her I was leaving.

“Okay,” I answered. Not that I had a choice.

“Is that alright with you?” Neal asked. “You don’t have plans or a big date tonight, do you?” I noticed wrinkles near his eyes when he smiled.

I laughed. “No. No plans tonight.” My cheeks got warm.

“Good. Do you like bratwurst and burgers?”

“Yeah, that’s fine.”

Lucas was pretty lucky to have a dad like Neal, I thought, as I drove to the soccer field behind the high school.

Chapter 71
Ben's Story

I KNOCKED ON THE DOOR TO THE UPPER FLAT IN RIVERSIDE.

A female voice echoed in my head. No other voice or thought came from inside the apartment. I knew Lucas left, but since I was already there, why not meet his mom?

Charlene Tillman opened the door wearing tight jeans, a tank top, and no bra. Dark rings circled like crescents below her bloodshot eyes. I didn't need to be immortal to know she was hungover.

"Can I help you?" she asked. Her voice was meek and insecure.

"Hi. Yeah, I was looking for Lucas. I'm a friend of his," I answered, extending my hand. I loved the traditional American greeting.

"Oh. I'm Char… Lucas' mom." She shook my hand, and the download began.

"Is he here?"

She let go of my hand as the data received flowed through my mind. Thoughts of her childhood, her love for Neal, and her need for drugs flashed in front of me like a slideshow on high speed.

Pain, embarrassment, and addiction hit my chest. I looked down. I couldn't meet the eyes of the woman that suffered so much. A cross tattoo rested atop her foot. It was grayed and stretched, not like the crisp image it had once been. It was used and overlooked, like Charlene felt.

"No. No, he left already. He went to some soccer game, I think."

"A soccer game?" I asked, confused. "We, ah… we don't have a game today."

"Ray?" She turned behind her, looked up the empty staircase, and called a second time before facing me again. "Oh, that's right. He left, too." She fidgeted with the handle of the door. "I think Lucas said soccer. Umm… girls' soccer."

Char's memories were sorting and organizing in my mind like a computer server filtering files by topic. Childhood, school, and girlfriends flitted by. She was pretty, young, and popular. A cheerleader with lots of friends and a popular football player for a boyfriend.

"Do you know where the game is?" I asked, buying time.

She looked confused and for a second, I felt sorry for her. Years of drug use slowed her thoughts and reactions. Not to mention, it aged her both physically and mentally. She looked a decade older than Neal did, and they were the same age.

"In Westport. Umm... he's going to his dad's after that," she said and shook her head. "You know... he only lived here a few months. Decided he's going back... to his dad's."

I nodded, as more memories from her high school years rolled through my head.

"Got some girl back there, I think."

"Stephanie Carlson," I said.

"No. No... I'm sad, too. You knew Stephanie?"

"Yes, I do."

"Such a sweet girl. So terrible how she died." Char looked upset, but no thoughts crossed her mind. She hugged the door, resting her cheek against it.

Died?

"I'm sorry, Stephanie didn't die," I said.

Her dark eyes rolled up and to the left, focusing on the corner of the porch ceiling behind me. Her lips were taut and emotionless, as if in a trance. She was silent.

Quickly, I propelled myself inside her apartment and looked around. Besides the clutter of unopened mail, newspaper, and dirty dishes in the sink and on the counter and table, there was nothing out of the ordinary. The apartment was empty. Incense burned in a tray near the door at the top of the stairs. Ashes from past burns stacked upon one another, filling the crevice of its bamboo holder.

The apartment had traces of male and female scents. There was one bedroom, with an unmade queen-sized bed and dresser. The living room was long and rectangular with a couch on the opposite wall from an old, box-style big-screen television. The galley kitchen and snack bar hadn't been cleaned in days. Despite her calling for Ray, there was no male present, nor a scent of anyone beside Lucas.

I returned to my body before Char noticed my frozen stance.

"Mrs. Crandon?" I asked, regaining her attention.

"Call me Char," she said. "I haven't been Mrs. Crandon in years."

"Okay, Char. Stephanie Carlson was at school yesterday. She's not dead." *And I should know*, I thought to myself.

She blinked slowly, opening her eyes already affixed in my direction. "Yes, dear. I know. But when she does die, it will be a terrible thing. Now, won't it?"

Her thoughts whipped through her mind and into mine faster than I could keep up. I reached toward her to touch her hand resting on the door, but only seconds worth of files downloaded before she broke the connection, moving her hand away. I couldn't make out what she was thinking and with the lost connection, I would never know.

"Do you know if the soccer game is at the high school?" I stalled.

"Why yes, dear. He went to Emma's soccer game." Her motherly tone was unexpected.

"Emma's game?" I asked, prolonging my exit.

"Of course. Why wouldn't he? After all, Emma's his girlfriend, you know." She smiled, though her eyes refocused on the spot behind me.

I shook my head. She didn't notice.

"If I see him again, who should I say stopped by?" she asked. Images of her courtship with Neal sorted into files in my head. A mixture of love and deceit layered between lust and dishonesty, until I realized she tricked Neal into marrying her.

"Ben Parker," I answered.

"Ben Parker," she repeated to herself even after she shut the door, and I heard her count the thirteen steps to return to her apartment above.

Lucas' mom was messed up. Her memories continued to flow and filter in my mind. They were disorganized and irrational. She took drugs, any and all she could find. From friends and strangers. She was an addict since she was nineteen, about the time that Neal went off to college and she stayed in Westport. Waiting.

When he returned, he didn't come back to her. He set his eyes on someone else and someone after that. He dated several girls but never called her. She was distraught and unhappy. Her doctor diagnosed depression and prescribed medication she refused to take. She was confused and vulnerable.

Worst of all, she was revengeful.

By the time I reached my truck parked around the corner from her house, I knew more than I wanted to about Charlene Crandon Tillman. Memories of her life filed in chronological order in my mind. The longer I sat there, the more I learned.

Char lived in fear. But why?

I searched for the memory buried deep amongst all the rest. The one underneath layers and layers of useless thoughts and images of trivial things set to camouflage the truth hidden deep below. Like peeling an onion, I removed each membrane one by one, so as not to damage the recollection it held.

When I reached the core, even I had to catch my breath.

I released my shield and shared what I learned with my team.

Suddenly, we were all in danger.

Chapter 72
Emma's Story

"Emma, you're starting center-stopper today."

Coach Vieth's voice startled me during warm-ups. He turned away before I could respond. Being new to the team, I was still trying to fit in and was thrilled with the opportunity to play the position I did back in Highland Park.

"Brinn, you're on the bench," the coach told a brunette on my team. His words were loud and caught the attention of a few girls stretching nearby. Brinn rolled her eyes as soon as he looked away.

"Prove yourself. It'll shut 'em up," Claire said after a few glares and hushed whispers. She was right. Besides, this was just rec ball. Our high school girls' soccer season wasn't until spring. Fall was simply a chance for Coach to monitor skills and for us to get touches on the ball. Our win-loss record meant nothing. At least, on paper, and since soccer was one thing I really excelled at, skinny, little Brinn and her posse of friends weren't going to deflate my confidence.

Nine minutes into the game, I had my chance to shut them up. Our opponent got a breakaway thanks to a turnover by Brinn's best buddy. I didn't think about it, I just reacted. I blocked the girl's pass and regained control for our team. It wasn't the only time I saved her mishap. By halftime, she actually complimented my skills and thanked me for being there.

Claire started the game off strong, but after a few minutes of sluggish runs and missed shots, Coach pulled her and sat her on the bench. In the huddle at halftime, Claire looked pale, and while I wondered if she was sick, there was no time to ask her.

When I jogged back to my place on the field, I noticed Lucas leaning on the chain-link fence near the parents' section of the bleachers. The stands were bare, except for a few people scattered about. Lucas smiled and waved when I looked at him, and I found myself grinning as the ref blew the whistle to start the second half.

Chapter 73
Ben's Story

Local agents had already assembled in the conference room by the time I arrived.

Concerns flooded the group. I couldn't blame them. They were trained for surveillance, to revive a human not scheduled for transition, to redirect someone temporarily lost or off their life path. They were not trained for physical combat, especially against one of our history's most notorious criminals.

Unfortunately, we all knew combat was inevitable.

Claire was at the high school soccer field when my announcement went viral. She returned response in thought and reluctantly stayed undercover at the game.

It's better for you to maintain cover right now, I told her. *Besides, I need you to keep an eye on Emma since I can't.* She agreed and decided to link in via thought for our meeting. I knew it would be unsettling to hear alone, but I hoped she didn't let it show.

Bianca interrupted me before I could reach out to Molly, who hadn't arrived yet. "She's having a late breakfast with that strapping boyfriend of hers."

"Ex-boyfriend," I corrected.

"Not after last night." She smirked. "Molly had quite the night, I must say. Of course, I enjoyed myself as well."

I sighed. I really didn't care to know about Bianca's personal life. Before I knew it, however, she displayed a video of herself partially unclothed. I severed the transmission before seeing who she was with.

"I didn't need to see that," I said.

She shrugged as more agents arrived and took seats at the conference table.

"You shouldn't have left so early, Benjamin," she said. "It could have been you instead of that boy." She batted her eyes and placed her palm on my chest.

I removed her hand.

"Don't ever touch me again," I said under my breath, and then called the meeting to order.

***

"Charlene Tillman appears to have been in contact with Victor Nicklas." I blinked, releasing a hologram image of her current appearance. I displayed the most flattering photo first. It was the only one in which she wasn't intoxicated or under the influence of narcotics. She combed her hair, wore a touch of makeup, and had a bright smile. It was the day she returned to Wisconsin and knocked on Neal's door. She was gone for a decade and happy to be home, though Neal and Lucas didn't reciprocate the emotion.

"Char's memories were disjointed. Audio and visual files of the same moments were kept in different files, as were locations and scents," I explained. "Despite that, I was able to put together a few pieces of this puzzle." The hologram image changed to Char as a baby, then progressed to different ages, from childhood to high school.

"For all practical purposes, her life was normal—on track—during these years," I said, scanning the eyes of the agents present. Most of the group registered a moderate to high level of fear, while only two of us had none. Bianca and me.

"Gaps in sequential memories prevented an accurate recap of her life from age nineteen to present," I stated. "However, what we extracted gave us proof she encountered Victor at least once during her lifetime, specifically while living in rural Nevada."

An agent raised his hand and then asked, "How could Char have camouflaged her memories in this manner? It doesn't seem common amongst humans. Have you ever experienced this before?"

I shook my head. "No. I've not seen a human do this. It's one of the reasons I believe she has had—or possibly still has—connection to Victor."

"What other reasons do you have?"

"We retrieved the following footage, which takes place a few miles south of Tonopah, Nevada." I blinked, and the hologram of Char hovering above the table switched to the image of a rundown tavern. The exterior doors opened, and we were led inside as if we were actually present at the time the event occurred.

Char was scantily dressed and sitting at the bar beside a black-haired man in a suit. There was no audio sound with the video, but having seen it before, no sound was necessary to understand the danger.

The bartender we identified as Ralph, poured bourbon for the man, then a second for Char after a few words and a flip of her hair. She raised her glass and tipped it against his. The stranger never moved. He didn't return her toast, or turn to face her.

Words were exchanged, but without sound, I could only guess what was said by reading Char's lips. I rotated the hologram, spinning it on its invisible axis like a person turning in their seat to see around the room.

The bar was empty except for the three of them. A clock on the walk read seven minutes past four o'clock. An old-fashioned desk phone in a deep red color sat on the counter with its receiver off the hook. Beside it were dusty bottles of whiskey, gin, and vodka. The stranger stared at the heavyset tavern keeper, but neither moved. Char did her best to flirt with the overdressed man, but her attempts went unnoticed.

When Char turned her attention back to Ralph, he didn't move. The coloring in his face disappeared, and his cheeks sagged and thinned. Ralph's skin drooped and hung low to his neck until it simply slid off his face entirely.

The stranger's eyes bore into the keeper while Char watched.

Silence filled our conference room as the tavern owner's shoulders dropped in the hologram. Movement under his brown plaid shirt startled Char, as she visibly jumped. It was clear she didn't speak. The bartender held onto the rim of the counter separating him from the evil before him. His hands turned to bone, as the skin and fat that once surrounded his pudgy digits were now bare.

Within seconds, his body melted away to a standing skeleton frame that buckled under its own weight without the support of muscles and joints. A pile of clothing rested on the floor where the man once stood.

Char turned toward the stranger, as the video ended and the hologram disappeared.

Agents in the conference room gasped. Claire was mentally shaken, as she watched in thought from the huddle during halftime of her soccer game. After several minutes of uncomfortable stillness, questions arose from every corner of the room. Most I had no answer for.

"The man in the video is assumed to be Victor. Without sound, without the ability to smell his essence, it is only speculation. However, there is no other rogue immortal with his powers roaming the earth at this time," I said.

Chatter amongst the crew began. "Ironically, his disguise with dark, wavy hair is similar to his most recent appearance."

"Do you know if this was a single encounter with Char?"

"We do not. What you see is all we know at this time," I said.

After assigning tasks to agents to monitor Char, I ended the meeting and dismissed the team.

"We need to shield these details from Molly," I said to Bianca. "No sense in alarming her more than she already is. Push comes to shove, she's our bait."

***

Attending Claire's soccer game was expected of me and I needed to keep up appearances, despite what was really going on. I saw Lucas at the fence when I reached the bleachers.

"Hey," I said, though our eyes never met.

He grunted a response.

"Man, I'm sorry about last night," I said. "I had too much to drink." I placed my forearms on the top of the fence and leaned onto them for support. Faking a hangover was unnecessary. My human body gave me the real thing.

I almost didn't hear Lucas' response as the thought of tequila rushed in and out of my mind with a sense of urgency.

"You were totally fucked up, man." Lucas laughed. "It's alright. Everyone needs to let loose once and a while."

"Yeah," I said and nodded. If only he knew. "I just wish I would've stopped after Drew's." I shook my head slowly.

"No shit?" He turned to look at me. "Whad-ya do last night? You look like hell."

"I feel like it too. Tequila's not my friend."

Lucas chuckled under his breath and watched the game. Emma passed the ball to a forward, who ended up turning it over further down the field. She was focused on the game. I shouldn't have expected any different. Three minutes left.

When the ball was passed near our side of the field, Emma noticed me. For a split second, her thoughts reflected the night before with anger and confusion over the scene I made.

"Well, hey, I gotta go," I said and turned to Lucas, extending my hand. "Friends?"

He shook my hand and nodded.

The downloaded files from Lucas were lengthy and disorganized but not as informative as his mother's. I scanned them again and found no concrete evidence to explain the peculiar feeling I got around him.

Chapter 74
Emma's Story

"Thanks for coming," I said.

Neal and Aunt Barb waited for me at the sidelines. They greeted me with compliments and made small talk with my teammates' parents as people passed by.

Lucas lingered near the fence.

"I'll meet you at home, honey. Neal and Lucas are setting up that shelf." Aunt Barb beamed with excitement. I guessed it was a combination of the new house and spending time with Neal. After a quick hug, they left.

"So you're an athlete, too," Lucas said once we were alone.

"Huh?"

"You're not just a pretty face."

My cheeks burned. Fortunately, I was probably already red from running in the game and didn't need to worry about looking as embarrassed as I felt.

"I didn't expect to see you here."

"My dad said he was coming. So I thought, why not?" His smile softened the rough edge of his look, not to mention personality. "Do you need a ride home?"

"No. I've got my car. But thanks." I gestured toward the parking lot and instinctively, we both began walking.

"My dad thinks he needs some help with your aunt's shelf."

I nodded. "Are you coming over?"

"Yeah. If that's alright with you."

I held back a grin.

"Um, yeah. That's fine." *Better you than me*, I thought.

***

By the time I was showered and dressed, the shelf was installed.

"I'm making lunch," Aunt Barb called to me when I reached the kitchen.

Neal was nose deep into the refrigerator while Lucas sat at the island, looking uncomfortable.

"Why don't you run to your mom's after lunch and get your things?" Neal said to Lucas as he handed him a can of Coke.

"Yeah, sure," Lucas answered, popping open the can of soda.

Aunt Barb placed a platter of sub sandwiches on the counter, and Neal took a seat.

"Lucas is moving back to Neal's house." Aunt Barb restated what she told me earlier and everyone filled their plates. Then looking at Lucas, she added, "If you need any help, I'm sure Emma won't mind giving you a hand."

I shot her a look, but she wasn't facing me to notice.

"Actually, you need to give Ray his truck back," Neal said. "Maybe Emma can follow you to Riverside, so I don't have to see your mom." The latter part he mumbled under his breath, and I wasn't sure if anyone else heard him, but me. "You don't mind. Do you, Emma?"

I shook my head and took a bite of my sandwich. How could I say no?

"Don't forget dinner tonight," my aunt added. Neal eagerly agreed.

Great. *Another joint meal*, I thought, and finished my lunch. After helping my aunt clear the table, Lucas said he was ready to go.

"I'll follow you," I said, standing in the driveway, keys in hand.

"Have you been to Riverside before?" Lucas asked.

"No. And I have no idea how to get here. So don't lose me."

"Then you better keep up." His firm look turned to a smirk.

***

I remembered Aunt Barb vaguely pointing to a road near Lake Bell that led to Riverside. Except Lucas went a completely different route, and I found myself running yellow lights in downtown Westport just to keep up with him.

Outside the city, the road was narrow and hilly with large trees and leaves in shades of fall colors. The picturesque pathway followed the southern edge of Lake Bell with glimpses of the water far below. The flowing, scenic route gave way to city streets and small houses when we reached Riverside. Sidewalks and shops lined the curb with large flowerpots on the corners and flags that hung from lampposts.

The only stoplight in town changed from yellow to red after Lucas went through it. He turned left and pulled over next to a brownstone building with a sign that read, "Carmichael Corporation." I made a mental note to ask Aunt Barb about it when I got home.

Hmm. I glanced behind me and expected to see a grocery store, but only noticed a diner named Priscilla, a hair salon, and the post office. *My mind must be playing tricks on me*, I thought. The light changed, and I turned to follow Lucas.

The back bumper of Ray's truck read, "Black smoke don't mean it's broke." I didn't understand what it meant, but as Lucas pulled out in front of me and the vertical pipes in the truck's bed puffed out exhaust, I figured it out.

Lucas turned left and then right, before pulling over to park alongside a fence behind the Carmichael plant.

The brown brick houses looked the same on this block and matched those on the blocks around it. All the buildings were made of the same colored bricks, and I wondered if it was on sale the year these homes were built.

I parked behind Lucas and turned off the engine. Suddenly, I felt uneasy. I didn't know much about Lucas' mom, but what I heard didn't sound good.

There was no reason for me to worry because the upstairs apartment was empty when we arrived. McDonald's bags and wrappers were scattered on the table along with papers and beer cans. Lucas tried to clean up the garbage, though it didn't matter.

"Sorry about this," Lucas said when he caught my glance.

"It's fine." Plain white walls surrounded me. A brown suede couch was across from a large TV. Lucas filed a duffel bag with a couple shirts that were lying on the arm of the sofa.

"You can sit if you want. Watch TV." He looked away, as I turned to face him. He reached for the remote, clicked a button, and the television buzzed to life. "I'll be a few minutes."

When Lucas pulled out a plastic tub from behind the chair, a cat meowed and rushed past me, startling me.

"She scared you, didn't she?" he asked.

I laughed. "Yeah."

"Sorry. She's uncomfortable around strangers."

I nodded and looked around. I could relate. "Um… did you want some help?" I asked. "I mean, I don't mind."

"No, I got it. I don't have a lot, but I really don't want to come back for it."

"That's fine." I followed him to the hallway and stood in the doorway of the bathroom as he grabbed his toiletries. I wasn't paying attention to what he was doing and turned into him. "Oh. Sorry."

He smiled as my hand rested momentarily on his chest. "Not the kind of lifestyle you grew up with, I'm guessing."

I didn't know what to say, so I said nothing.

"Don't worry. I'm not like this. My mom's a mess. My dad was pretty strict."

When he leaned closer, I knew he was going to kiss me. Even though I was sure I only wanted to be friends, I didn't pull away. Voices on the stairs interrupted our kiss before it even began. He turned away quickly, as if not wanting to get caught in the act.

"Hey, I've got a friend over," Lucas said as a thin woman put a plastic grocery bag on the already-messy table. "This is Emma."

"Emma, this is Char, ah… I mean, my mom," Lucas said and then pointed to an overweight man. "This is Ray."

Char gave me a hug, like we were long-lost pals. "I've heard so much about you."

"She's prettier than you told us," Ray said and shook my hand. He held it longer than I expected, cupped in both of his hands. When he finally let go, he said, "Did we interrupt something? You two need some privacy?" His voice was gruff.

"Ah, no," I answered quickly.

"I'll just be a minute," Lucas whispered in my ear, and then headed to the bedroom.

"So Emma, tell me… You a senior, too?" Ray asked as he took a seat at the table.

"Yes."

Char unpacked the bag she brought in, placing two bakery boxes in front of Ray. "Emma, honey, would you like a brownie?" I started to say no, but she continued before I could object. "My friend has a bakery in town. Makes the best brownies for me. Here. Try one." She held open a white box under my nose. The aroma of chocolaty richness floated toward my nostrils, and I couldn't resist.

"Okay," I said and helped myself. A sheet of waxed paper separated what looked like multiple layers of square brownies as thick as they were wide.

"I'll get you some milk." She put the box down and left.

"Lucas said you just moved here," Ray continued, ignoring Char. His thin, black hair was slicked straight back, defining a receding hairline.

"Yes. From Illinois." I took a bite of the brownie. It was chewy and moist, just like my mom used to make, with mini chocolate chips, less the walnut chunks. Mom never put nuts in her recipe. She said Dad didn't like them. I didn't mind, I realized as I finished the small square.

I took a drink of milk from the glass Char handed me.

"You need ice-cold milk to wash it down, I always say," Char added. She helped herself to a brownie, pushing the box toward Ray, who waved his hand at her.

"What part?" Ray asked. "Chicago?"

"Highland Park."

"Here, Emma, have another," Char said in between chews, holding the box in front of me again.

I shook my head.

"Aren't they tasty?" she asked, her eyes widening as she spoke. I reluctantly took another. I couldn't resist and didn't want to hurt her feelings.

"These are really good," I told her.

"I know. Every once in a while, you need a nice treat. I always tell Ray that. Isn't that right, dear?" She turned to look at him, but he ignored her. His pink shirt was opened enough to see a thick, gold chain on his neck.

"Highland Park… yeah, I've been there." Ray's eyes were fixed on mine, though he appeared deep in thought. "Deerfield Avenue. There are some car dealerships there. Or is that further south?"

I finished the milk and placed the empty glass on the table.

"Oh, dear. You need some more," Char said to herself and turned toward the kitchen.

I waved her off, but she went anyway.

Ray ignored her, as Char hummed in the kitchen. "You by the car dealerships? On Deerfield?" Ray asked.

"Oh, sorry. That's south of me," I answered, flustered.

"You moved in with your aunt, right?"

Char returned with my glass refilled, as Lucas walked in. "Lucas, have a brownie." Char held up the box to him. She looked like a pusher.

"Did you have one?" he asked me.

I nodded in response to both Ray's question and the one from Lucas. I was getting confused with the amount of attention given to me. I glanced at Lucas, wondering if he was done yet. He shook his head and gave Char a dirty look.

"You just feel so good getting a treat like this, don't you, Emma?"

"Um, yes. They're very good."

"Take another. They're small," she said. I looked at Lucas, hoping it was time to go. "Lucas, I got another box, just for you, dear."

He ignored his mom's comment, kissed her on the cheek, and said,

"Let's go."

I nodded. He put the strap from the duffel bag on my shoulder, grabbed the plastic tub, and headed down the stairs.

"Bye. Nice meeting both of you," I said, waving my hand in a brief goodbye.

***

"Want me to drive?" Lucas asked after we loaded my trunk.

I shook my head and got in the car. Why would he drive my car?

After a few blocks turning left and left again to get back to the main street, I started to feel funny.

Dizzy.

I didn't realize it at first, but I felt lightheaded. What would it be like to fly?

Lucas stared at the road. Didn't he know I was looking at him? Huh, he was cuter than I thought. Well, not Ben-cute. Definitely nicer, though. Nice mom, too. And Ray was friendly, too.

"Slow down!" he snapped at me.

When I turned back to look at the road, I realized the cars in front of me were at a stop.

I slammed on the brakes. My heart pounded in my chest as I caught my breath. "What's wrong with me?" I thought to myself. When I heard the words in my own voice, I guessed it was aloud and not just in my head.

"You're a bad driver. That's what's wrong with you."

I chuckled and turned to look at Lucas after confirming the stop light was still red. He laughed and told me to turn ahead. It was a different route than what we came in on.

I got the giggles. Gut busting, couldn't breathe, couldn't-stop-laughing giggles.

By the time he told me the light was green, I had tears running down my cheeks and my stomach ached. I wasn't even sure what was funny. Nothing actually. Maybe I was getting sick. I didn't feel well. I didn't think. Or did I feel great?

Different, I decided. I felt different, like I was free.

I wanted to be free. The seat belt strap that crossed my body bothered me. I tugged on it, pulling it off my chest while I tried to focus on the road. City blocks turned into country fields.

There would be a farm ahead on the left, a tall, white house with a green roof.

Wait. What?

"You drive like a granny," Lucas said. I think he said it twice. I picked up my speed and told him I wasn't a granny. This time I couldn't remember actually hearing my voice.

When the road curved, I knew I was close to the farm where Julia Kensington lived.

Huh? Who was Julia?

"Slow down." Lucas raised his voice. "Just pull over. I'll drive."

"No. It's my car. I'm not letting you drive my car." I took the hill a little too fast and felt my stomach lurch, as the car reached the crest and swept down the other side. The shocks absorbed most of the sway, but my insides took a second or two to readjust. It was the same feeling I got on the rollercoasters at Six Flags.

Oh! Six Flags. I went there with Melissa and my friends back home. Matt.

I missed Matt.

I slowed the car down and tried to focus. My eyelids were heavy.

"What's gotten into you?" Lucas asked. I felt the tension between us as if his eyes were boring into the side of my head.

"I don't know," I whispered.

"You're baked. Did you have some of those brownies?"

"Those gourmet brownies your mother got from the bakery? They were soooo gooooood. Almost better than my… my… my mom's." I caught myself and swallowed the lump in my throat. I didn't want to cry in front of him.

Wait. Baked? What did he say?

"You're totally high!" he chuckled. "That's awesome."

"What? What do you mean?"

"Just what I said. Turn here. You can't go home like that. My dad'll fucking kill me. I'm already in enough trouble without getting blamed for this, too. Turn right."

"Huh?" I turned where he told me and then again, past a house that looked familiar on a road marked, Dead End. "Hey, does Drew live back there?" He nodded. "Where are we going?"

"Just park over there."

"Where? There?" I asked, pointing to a small opening between the bushes on the wooded hillside. Taking my hand off the steering wheel wasn't a good idea. The car suddenly had a mind of its own.

"Here!" Lucas's tone turned irritated. He mumbled something under his breath before he grabbed the wheel. I panicked. "Pull *around* the tree. Then no one will see your car."

The gravel path was covered in leaves, with grasses and weeds taking over the crushed, thinning stones. I stopped beside the tree, but after Lucas looked around, he told me to inch forward. When he seemed pleased, I shut off the engine and he got out.

He was on my side with the door open before I had the seatbelt unlatched.

I was stoned.

And I liked it.

Why didn't I do this before?

Lucas reached for my hand and helped me out of the car. He didn't step back to give me space, though I wasn't uncomfortable being this close either. His lips were touching mine before I knew it. I should have seen it coming. He closed the already-small gap between us, and I leaned back against the doorframe. I tasted his breath in my mouth and felt winded when he stepped back.

"Come on," he said. I followed him down the gravel path that was probably a driveway in another life. I touched my fingers to my lips. His kiss was different from Matt's, or any other kiss I ever had. My lips tingled. Maybe it was me.

The last house on the dead-end road looked vacant. We walked up the leaf-filled driveway to a dark brown two-story with white trim. An image flashed across my mind.

"It used to be white," I said.

"What?"

Huh? "Never mind." I shook my head and wiped my forehead with the back of my hand. Where did that come from?

I tagged behind him as he went around the house to a section of bushes under an empty window flower box. He knelt down, stuck his hand under a patch of leaves, and pulled out a small, metal box containing a house key.

"Whose house is this?" I whispered after he unlocked the side door and let us in.

"My grandpa's."

I nodded and walked around. The kitchen counters were bare. Sheets covered furniture in the small living room that faced the lake. The stairs were to the left, I thought, and turned to confirm their presence. I was overwhelmed with a déjà vu feeling. I couldn't understand why.

"How long has your grandfather been…?" I started, but he cut me off.

"He's not dead. He's in a home." He glared at me for a second and walked to the kitchen.

"Ooohhh.... This is *Neal's*... dad's... house." I knew Neal's dad was in a home. Aunt Barb told me that.

Lucas ignored me and opened the bottom drawer beside the stove. He pulled out two plastic red cups and a bottle of whiskey. "Want some?" he asked, though he poured a cup and drank it back before waiting for my reply.

I shook my head. "I don't think so."

"You're probably right. You're already stoned," he said and smiled.

Was not. Oh, yeah. I was.

"If I knew you wanted to party this afternoon, I would have had a brownie." He opened the cabinet below the sink and knelt on the floor. Reaching inside, he pulled out a small baggie and pipe with duct tape on it.

"I wasn't planning to party today," I mumbled.

He stood up and walked closer to me. I giggled.

"You probably need to sober up before we see my dad."

"Huh," I grunted.

"Or I need to get high too," he said and chuckled.

I raised my eyebrows, almost hoping he would. I hadn't felt this great since before Dad died. He sat on the counter, opened the bag, packed the dried, leafy contents in a small pipe, and lit it with a lighter.

I watched in fascination. There were a few football players back home that smoked pot, but I never watched them, or joined in, for that matter.

He inhaled, and I smelled the sweet aroma. He handed it to me without a word, and I mimicked what he did. Taking a deep breath, I choked. My throat felt constricted, and I coughed. He laughed. Tears formed in my eyes. After I caught my breath, he coached me. "Hold it in for a second," he said the next time I tried.

"I'm not feeling anything," I told him. He didn't answer.

He had pretty eyes. Not dreamy like Ben's, but pretty.

I giggled. Boys weren't supposed to be pretty.

"Yeah, we can't go home for a while," he said and took a hit.

"Oh-my-god. My aunt'll be so pissed. When are we going home, anyway?"

"I dunno. It's early."

"Where's my phone?" I panicked and patted my pockets until I felt where I left it. Checking the time was difficult. The numbers blurred even though I held it in my hand sturdy.

He slid off the counter and put his arm around my waist when I started to sway. Despite the chuckle brewing inside me, I welcomed his kiss. I put my hand on his chest, and he pulled me closer. I tasted marijuana mixed with whiskey on his tongue. His hands roamed my back, and I found myself walking backward until we reached the couch in the living room.

I felt woozy and floating. Things moved in slow motion. Lucas leaned me back on the sofa and kissed my neck. When his lips found mind, they were more gentle. He stopped and looked at me. "Will you go to homecoming with me?"

I nodded, my heart pounding in my chest. "Ye-yes." My voice cracked.

He kissed me again, and his hands wandered from my side to my chest. I didn't care. I was fully clothed. His fingers soon found bare skin when he lifted the edge of my shirt. He rested his hand on my stomach, as his lips wandered to my neck. I wondered what I should do now. The gentle tickle was relaxing. I didn't want the sensation to stop and eagerly kissed him back when our lips met again. His hand wandered upward, sneaking under my bra until it reached my breast. I tingled at his touch.

This wasn't like me, but it felt good.

I should stop him. I just couldn't bring myself to do it. Deep down, I wasn't sure I wanted to stop. It was the first time in weeks I didn't feel the pain of loss. I felt accepted.

His fingers scanned the waistband of my jeans as if teasing what he planned next. I definitely wasn't ready for that. My reactions were slow. I tried to reach for his hand. Instead, he pulled mine toward him, placing my palm on the bulge in his pants.

I jumped when my phone buzzed, signaling a text message. Lucas barely noticed. When his phone vibrated in his pocket, I giggled.

"Wait," I said, pulling away. This was moving way too fast for me. My words stopped him like disconnecting a lamp from its power source. "I can't do this."

He sat up, cleared his throat. "Okay."

My phone buzzed again and his vibrated, almost at the same time. His eyes were somber as he answered the call.

"Hey… yeah." He cleared his throat again. "Just hanging out. What's up?" He glanced at me. "Yeah, okay. I'll be there. See ya." When he ended the call, he said, "Drew's having people over. Let's go."

"To Drew's?"

He nodded.

"Right now?"

His eyes widened, as he nodded again. "Unless you want to stay?"

"No… do you have a bathroom here?" I headed toward the kitchen as if I knew where it was.

"Yeah. Turn right," he answered from the living room. "Hey, Em? I'm gonna call my dad and back out of dinner." His words were muffled behind the closed bathroom door.

I straightened my hair, wiped the smeared eyeliner from under my eyes, and put on a fresh coat of lip gloss. Suddenly, I wanted to go home.

My phone buzzed again, as Lucas locked the house. It reminded me that I hadn't checked it the times before. Melissa's picture popped up on the screen, notifying me of her incoming text. I couldn't read the words very clearly, so I couldn't reply.

"How long does this last?" I asked.

"What?" He looked at me after he hid the key amongst the plants. "Your high?"

I nodded.

"I dunno… I'm fine… You're not?"

I shook my head and walked beside him down the driveway.

"Don't worry. I'm sure it will wear off."

"You're *sure*?" I questioned. "Wha' does that mean?"

"Nothin'… I mean… I don't know… I'm not sure what's in the brownies."

I glared at him.

He chuckled. "Well, not exactly. Don't worry. You'll be fine."

Great.

We walked in the middle of the road in silence, past where I parked my car. A patch of dense trees blocked the view of the lake.

"So what did you tell your dad?" I asked.

"That Drew was having people over, and you and I were stopping there for pizza."

"And?"

"And what? He's fine with it… We'll do dinner another night, I guess."

Halfway to the corner, partially hidden behind thick brush, was another driveway. "Who lives here?" I asked as we walked by a house between Lucas' grandfather and Drew's. It was a single-story cottage with similar siding to the Crandon house with white-and-red shutters.

"No one."

I shot him a look.

"It's been empty since I can remember."

"Really?" I was surprised and even more shocked as my feet carried me toward the house in a light jog.

"Where are you going?" he called when I was already there. My right eye twitched, but I swore a light flickered in the window. I shouldn't be doing this. Should I?

"Are you sure it's empty?" I yelled.

He nodded and waved me back. I ignored him.

I peered into the window and jumped when my phone vibrated. Texts buzzed. Calls vibrated.

"Hi Aunt Barb," I said, answering the phone.

"Just checking you and Lucas are skipping dinner with us. Right?" she asked.

"Oh… Yes... Sorry. I should've called. Ah… Drew's having people over… I guess they're ordering pizza."

"You're not there yet?"

"Um... No… Just walking up to the house," I lied.

"Okay," she said, hesitating before speaking again. "Did Melissa reach you? She called here."

"No. Well, yes. I guess. She just sent me a text but you called, so I didn't read it yet. Why? Is something wrong?"

"No, not at all… Okay, honey… Well, I'll see you later, then… I love you."

"Me too," I said and ended the call. Guilt ran through me. At least I didn't need to go home. I wondered what Melissa wanted if she called my aunt.

Lucas looked impatient and motioned me back. "Come on. We're free for the night."

"Okay, okay," I mumbled, joining him in the road. I scanned the list of text messages as I walked, but I found myself swaying into Lucas. He grabbed my phone and put it in his pocket.

"Give it back!" I attempted an evil look, and then laughed.

He grinned. "Come get it, if you want." He raised his hands above his head, tempting me to dig in his pockets. I smiled but didn't take him up on it.

"Fine. Have it your way."

He grabbed my hand, as we reached Drew's front door. Lucas let us in without knocking, pulling me along, hand in hand.

I heard Drew's voice first. "You made it!" he said and gave Lucas a high five.

"Emma," Drew said. "Look who's here."

I wasn't surprised to see Claire sitting on a stool at the island, but I didn't expect to see Matt beside her. I felt my face go pale and was suddenly sick to my stomach. Melissa jumped out from behind Drew and screamed my name.

"Surprise!" Lucas held up the hand connected to mine and leaned down as if to kiss me. Instead, I turned my head.

"Wha-What… are you doing here? Oh-my-god!" I said to Melissa.

"I know. I couldn't tell you," she said.

"Hey! Missed you," Lewis, Melissa's boyfriend, said and then gave me a hug.

Out of the corner of my eye, I saw Matt stand up. The look on his face was cold, though he attempted a weak smile when our eyes met.

By the time Matt reached me, I was crying, full-blown tears.

Chapter 75
Ben's Story

"She saw you," I said to Bianca after Emma left the window of the vacant house on Lake Bell. "You realize that, don't you?" Bianca Beringer was smart, beautiful, and incredibly annoying. Yet, I promised Jorgenson I'd give her a chance.

She put her hands on her hips and cocked her head to one side.

"You shined, Bianca... when you came through the portal. Did you do it on purpose?"

Her hard eyes softened.

"I know you've got field experience. You have to know how to contain the aura when you shift." I tried to control my voice.

"I... I..." Bianca began. "I didn't think she was that perceptive."

"She's high right now. Of course she's more perceptive in this state of mind." I raised my hands in the air and quickly dropped them to my side. "Exactly what experience have you had in the field? I mean, come on, Bianca. This is rookie 101 training here." I wiped my brow.

"I... I'm sorry," she whispered. "I didn't realize she'd be here. I didn't think anyone would be here, actually." Bianca seemed sincere.

I paced the old living room with the window overlooking the lake. It was calm and peaceful, a typical fall day on the inlet. Though its serenity didn't relieve my anger.

"Where are we, anyway?" she asked aloud, while her thoughts filled with other questions. *And why are we here? I thought we were on the trail of the hybrid?*

Bianca and I spent the afternoon interviewing the new hybrid detected in Chicago. It was a woman, first one in a century, according to Commander E. She didn't offer any new locations from the man captured a few weeks earlier, though she did provide an image of one of Victor's previous disguises, buried deep in her memory.

I took a deep breath and exhaled slowly. "This is where I grew up. The house I lived in when I met Elizabeth… err… ah, Emma," I said. "And to answer your other questions, we *are* tracking Victor. The sighting the hybrid had was down the road a-ways. I wanna check on Emma first." I looked her in the eyes. "You can stay here, if you want. I'm going over to Drew's for a few minutes."

She nodded. "I'm really sorry," she mumbled. Her thoughts were apologetic. It wasn't like Bianca to be humble. She lived a rather privileged life, born to wealthy German parents. She was accustomed to getting most everything she wanted. That was, of course, until her life contract ended abruptly when she was twenty-four years old. She was filled with rage ever since.

"If you're with me… it's on my terms. Got it?" I stared through her eyes to her soul. Her shielding power was impressive but not good enough to block me. I watched her spirit genuflect as her human shoulders dropped in surrender.

I turned and left the house, knowing full well she was in tow.

Chapter 76
Emma's Story

There was something about the way Matt looked at me that reminded me of the day we broke up, Labor Day weekend. His weak smile didn't make up for his sad eyes.

Disappointment encompassed me like thick smoke. First Melissa's, "You've changed," comment followed quickly with a, "But that's okay," remark and then there was Matt's avoidance. His mediocre hug when I arrived reminded me of our final words that night on the island.

"Don't let Westport change you," he said back then. It seemed like eons ago now. The memory of that tearful goodbye haunted me. As the evening at Drew's progressed, I started to feel more like myself. Gone was the lightheaded, dizzy feeling I had. It was replaced by a layer of guilt so heavy my shoulders ached. A permanent image of Melissa's expression burned in my thoughts and seemed more defined as I came down from my high.

Melissa's laughter caught my attention. She cozied up on the couch with Lewis, a beer in hand, and chatted away with Drew and Claire. Molly and TJ sat at the island with Trent. I felt isolated and out of place. It was like the first time I went to one of Drew's parties.

I walked out to the porch to seek refuge. The bright moon cast a shimmer over the dark water. I pulled my sleeves down to my wrists. The fall air was crisp. I wished I had a thicker sweater with me, I thought, when I heard his voice.

"I didn't expect you to fit in so quickly," Matt said, leaning against the porch railing exactly like Ben did a month earlier. I wished it were Ben. He left already. "I mean, I'm glad you did. But I… ah…um… well, I guess I didn't expect you to have a boyfriend already."

"I don't," I blurted out, even though I knew what it looked like. I walked toward him, wanting to reach out to him, to touch him. I raised my hand the way I used to, just before he'd pull me into his arms, but when I realized he wasn't even looking at me, I quickly lowered it.

"Melissa said you had some-*thing* with a guy. I thought she said his name was Ben."

I tilted my head. That wasn't exactly what I said to her.

"I met him," Matt said. "Ben. Seems nice."

He glared at me. I turned to look at the dark lake. It was black outside, except for the ripples in the water. I bit my lip, not wanting to cry. I wrapped my arms tight across my chest.

Silence.

I glanced at Matt and looked away quickly. Why did I hurt so badly again?

"Tell me you're not dating Lucas."

"I… ah…" I said. Then, anger crept in. "What do you care?"

"I do care. I came here to ask you to homecoming. Then Melissa said you were interested in some guy, but I didn't think it was Lucas. What's up with that?"

"I… I don't like Lucas," I said, and then mumbled, "not like that. Not really."

"So you didn't come to the party together? And you're not hanging out… or going to the dance with him then?" Matt's direct question sobered me up completely.

"I… I am… but…"

"But what? He's always in trouble. You know that, right?"

"He's not like that."

"Emma, he got arrested for drugs."

I shook my head.

"Distribution, Emma. Not just using. Drew talks about him *all* the time. He's like the local dealer at your school."

"You don't *even know him.*"

"I don't have to, Emma," he said, turning to face the water. "And to think I was worried about you. I volunteered to help Lewis and his dad today, just to see you."

I swallowed the lump in my throat. "You should talk."

He turned back toward me and said, "What does that mean?"

"You've got Aimee. You took Aimee… *who I hate*… to the dance and not me."

"As *friends*!" He raised his voice.

I was silent. Friends?

"You dumped me two weeks before homecoming. What did you expect me to do?"

Tears welled in my eyes. "My dad died. What did you expect from me?" I clenched my teeth, fighting back the anger and waterworks.

He sighed and when he spoke again, his voice was soft. "I know that, Emma. I tried to be there for you." He reached his hand toward my arm, but I pulled back. "I'm sorry. I didn't mean to make you cry."

I covered my face with my hands and took a deep breath.

This time, when Matt pulled me close, I let him. He wrapped me in his arms and apologized as I cried. But as soon as his hold loosened, I escaped to the house and took a hit of pot when Lucas offered it.

Chapter 77
Ben's Story

So this is where you encountered Victor?

I nodded and motioned for Bianca to keep her thoughts silent. We propelled into the barn on Summit, where I rescued Stephanie Carlson. No sense in risking communication, verbal or mental, for Victor to overhear. I could shield my thoughts and stream in only those I wanted to hear, but I wasn't certain of Bianca's abilities and couldn't take a chance.

The dilapidated barn looked the same as it did weeks earlier. We inspected inside and out, circling around the building and house, but no scent was found and no energy was present. I led Bianca to the back of the farm's property along the river in hopes of picking up the odor. There was none.

We skimmed the water's edge and headed east toward Kensington's farm, the barn where I first picked up the sweet cotton candy and green apple scent of a hybrid.

The property was still and quiet. No lights were on in the house. While Kensington typically retired shortly after dark, this was about thirty minutes earlier than normal. His Chevy truck was parked in the driveway and not in the garage. Keys were under the driver's visor, but it had been at least a day since the engine purred.

I motioned for Bianca to cover me, as I propelled to the house.

Once inside, the bitter sour smell of hybrids overwhelmed my senses. At least a dozen scents mingled in the living room and kitchen of the old farmhouse. Some old, others fresh.

I summoned Jorgenson after clearing the house and confirming its vacancy. *"Any new transitionees unaccounted for?"* I asked.

"Negative. Not in the US, that is. Why? Wha-da-ya got?"

"Some suspicions. Can you download George Kensington's file?"

Waves of sound preceded Jorgenson's confirmation that it was sent. I began streaming critical dates beginning with his life contract. He had three years left before completion. He wouldn't even exhibit any symptoms. It would be a major heart attack, dead before he hit the ground. But he was not on his deathbed now.

So where was Kensington and why were there so many hybrid scents in his house?

Chapter 78
Emma's Story

I stood alone in the park.

It was the same playground where Mom and Dad took me, a few blocks from my old house in Highland Park. The trees were taller and thicker than I remembered.

Moms pushed preschoolers on the swings. Elementary-aged kids ran across the bridge and spun the steering wheel on the upper deck of the play structure. Children and adults mingled around the grounds, but there was no sign of the man in the wool coat.

He called me here, didn't he?

Yes, he did. At least, that was what I told myself.

I leaned up against the tree and waited. I didn't see him or hear him, but when he appeared, I wasn't startled. His fedora peered around the tree first.

"I'm happy he's found you, Elizabeth."

"My name is Emma," I whispered.

"I know." He didn't look at me. He focused on the children on the play set instead.

"If you know my name, why then, do you call me Elizabeth?"

"Do you see that girl with brown pigtails over there?" He nodded toward the child on the wooden bridge.

"Yes."

"In a minute, she's going to fall. She will slide under the railing and land on her wrist."

"What? We must help her!" I started to move, but I felt resistance holding me back. I looked at the man beside me. He wasn't moving. His hands were tucked into his pockets. It was the same wool coat he wore before.

"Sometimes you know what will happen, but you cannot interfere," he said, solemnly.

We watched the girl fall from the bridge, as he predicted. I looked at him when the girl's mother rushed to her side. Other mothers scurried over to help. The girl wasn't moving, but her screams intensified as her mom touched her arm. I could feel her pain in my own wrist and shuddered at the thought of her injury.

The man in the wool coat glanced in my direction. "It wasn't her time. Today, she will live. She will live until she reaches thirty-nine years old when she will die in a car accident, hit by a drunk driver. She will leave behind a husband and two children."

I shook my head. "I do not understand."

"There are things you are sensing, but you haven't trusted your instinct." He looked back at the girl on the ground and the chaos around her. He shook his head, as if listening to another conversation. Raising his right hand, he held it parallel to the ground, palm facing down. He mumbled a few words I couldn't understand. His eyes were closed, and he nodded. A second later, his hand was back in his pocket and his eyes focused on me.

"She will be fine. Her mother was a bit overwhelmed. She now has the direction she needs."

I watched the mother lift the girl to her feet and brush her off. She held her child's hand as if checking for bruising, before the girl ran off to the swings.

"You... you just..."

"Yes, I did."

"But... wh-who are you?"

"Just remember to trust your instincts. The rest will come. I have good things in store for you, Elizabeth."

"But what if I don't want Matt to come back to me?" I blurted quickly, sensing our time together was coming to an end.

He smiled and shook his head. "It is not Matthew that's been waiting for you. Use your instincts."

A light fog slowly surrounded us, and he began to fade.

"Wait... don't go!"

"Don't worry, I'll be back," he said, and then vanished.

***

I awoke Monday morning earlier than normal. My dream woke me up, and I found myself unable to fall back to sleep. Aunt Barb was already downstairs. I heard the clinking of plates and guessed she was making breakfast. She was a morning person and even though she often left before I did, she always had a plate of food waiting for me.

After showering, I dressed quickly and found a stack of hot cakes, syrup, and sausage on the island as Aunt Barb read the morning paper. I didn't have the heart to tell her I didn't need—or want—this much food every morning. I feared it would hurt her feelings.

Instead, I dug in, and thanked her for making it. As usual, she gave me a kiss and headed out before I finished. When she was out of the driveway, I dumped my breakfast in Chester's bowl. He eagerly devoured my leftovers.

Early mornings at school meant empty halls. I liked this time of day when there was peace and quiet, and no one rushed about. I actually had a chance to think clearly, as I delved headfirst into my locker.

I smelled him before I saw or heard him.

It was a cool and fresh scent, like crisp air I imagined breathing in atop the highest mountain. I turned when I heard Ben's deep, pleasant voice. He was just inches from me, the closest I had ever been near him. He leaned around the door of my locker with his masculine hand holding the top edge like a shield, separating him from me. His fingernails were perfectly oval and neatly trimmed.

My heart skipped a beat when our eyes met. A gentle smirk flashed across his face.

"Aren't you supposed to have tons of pictures taped up in your locker?" Ben asked after he swung my locker door open wide and peered inside.

I looked away briefly, trying to contain my smile. My heart skipped again with the realization that he was talking to me, and not to someone else. "I guess I didn't get around to it yet."

The hall was quiet, with only a few kids at the other end. We were basically alone.

"I thought you'd have pictures of your boyfriend posted. Matt, is it?" he asked. "I mean, what would he think if he knew you didn't have his picture plastered up for all of us to see?"

My lips betrayed me, and I grinned. "Um… Matt's not my boyfriend." I grabbed my books without looking at him. I was afraid I'd blush.

"Oh." He hesitated for a second and then continued. "Well, I just wanted to apologize for the other night."

I glanced up at him.

"I was out of line. You're free to drink as much as you want. I shouldn't have said anything… It's none of my business."

I stared into his cocoa-brown eyes and reached to close my locker door, but he didn't move. My fingertips grazed his shirt, and I imagined a rippled stomach underneath. He always looked nice. His deep red shirt complimented his tan skin and dark brown hair. I wanted to touch him, but quickly cleared my thoughts.

We were just friends, if that.

"Thanks," I said, still holding the door. I felt the blood rush to my face. My stomach felt a little queasy.

"Can we start over?" He extended his hand. I reached for it and nodded.

"Friends." His grip was firm, yet comfortable, like a good fit. I couldn't deny how attracted I was to him. I never felt this way about Matt and especially not about Lucas. My cheeks had to be fuchsia. Get control of yourself, I thought.

He smiled, still holding my hand in his.

"So did you finish the homework for calc?" he asked after letting go of my hand.

"Yeah… and you?"

"Pretty easy."

"I thought so, too."

He glanced behind me, and then said, "You going to the library for study hall today?"

"Yeah, I'll be there."

"Good. See you later," he said and left.

Would he really ask if he just wanted to be friends?

Chapter 79
Ben's Story

It was made official Monday morning.

The front page of Westport Gazette featured a photo of George Kensington in the lower right corner. The caption said his daughter reported him missing Sunday afternoon when she found his house vacant, doors unlocked, and a partially eaten sandwich on the table.

According to the article, the police department asked citizens in the area to be on the lookout for the five-foot-eleven inch, eighty-two-year-old man. He had a slender build and thinning, gray hair. "He left his vehicle behind, so he couldn't have ventured far on foot. He walks with a slight limp," Detective Neal Crandon was quoted. "Anyone with information is asked to come forward."

I knew Kensington was in good health, except for arthritis in his joints, but that wasn't life threatening. His daughter concurred no signs of dementia was ever present and likelihood of him wandering off on his own, on foot, was slim. The police conveniently omitted those facts in hopes of diminishing public fear. I read Detective Crandon's thoughts when I stopped at the station with the excuse of paying a parking ticket, the day before. I disguised myself as an elderly man and struck up a conversation with the desk sergeant on duty. He divulged more than he probably should have about the case, and I didn't even have to compel him.

Detective Crandon's thoughts gave me enough information to know the police suspected foul play, even though he never joined in the conversation.

I spent the better part of Monday sitting in class, but listening to Bianca's briefings as she dove into the records of all residents in or near Summit Road, where George Kensington lived and where hybrids congregated in the past. Bianca proved to be a good investigator, rather tenacious in probing files and minds of those involved. It was a task I never enjoyed, the tedious footwork of research.

Molly shot me an occasional comment about being bored playing human and kept away from the action of the case, but when I returned images of TJ, Emma, and other friends we'd made, she agreed her protective surveillance services were required at the school.

By the time I reached the cafeteria, Emma was seated at her usual lunch table with Claire and a bunch of girls. Lucas watched her intently, though he never left his dominant post with the rest of his football buddies. Surprisingly, Emma's thoughts didn't focus on him. Instead, her mind bounced from classes to friends, to her aunt, dress shopping, and, occasionally, to me.

I overheard her telling Hannah and Claire about my earlier apology after they recapped the original Friday night party scene. A memory I wanted everyone to forget. If they didn't get past it by the end of the day, I'd have to compel them.

Emma was physically embarrassed, as Hannah asked about Lucas. Her face reddened. She looked around the cafeteria and glanced at me for an instant. Her thoughts traveled back to her locker that morning, though she had no remorse for getting high with Lucas and didn't tell her friends about her fight with Matt.

I was so busy eavesdropping on teenage drama that I almost missed Bianca's update on the large farm across from Kensington's.

The title lists the owner as Henry Nichols, Bianca said. *Benjamin? Are you listening?*

Yes. Go ahead. Nichols.

But the taxes have been paid by a corporation.

What corporation?

CJ Morse and Company. They're a farm equipment distributor out of Chicago.

Did you say Nichols? Henry Nichols? I asked as I returned my tray to the cafeteria kitchen window, my lunch uneaten.

Yes.

Can you get a list of everyone on CJ Morse's payroll?

I can have Jorgenson do it.

Head back to headquarters. You'll get more accomplished in the office and in less time, I said to Bianca as the bell rang. *I'll meet up with you tonight. I've got a soccer game after school, so say nine o'clock?*

Bianca agreed.

Looks like you're making headway. Molly piped in her comments.

Yeah, I think we may have a lead, I answered, following the crowd of students through a set of double doors. My mind circled with memories of seventy years of cases that would take time to sort through.

Well, good luck with what's next, Molly said.

Whadda ya mean? I turned down a corridor and bumped into Stephanie Carlson.

"Oh! Hey, Ben. I've been looking for you," Stephanie said with a bright smile.

Her arm touched mine, and I sent Molly a nasty remark. By the time Stephanie verbalized her thoughts, I knew she would ask me to the homecoming dance.

"Unless, of course, you have a date already," she said and then chewed on her lower lip.

Benjamin, say yes. She needs someone right now, and you can't go without a date, Molly interrupted.

"I thought you and Lucas…" I said to stall and to make Molly nervous.

Really, Benjamin? Molly continued. *Don't be a muppet. That poor girl put herself out there. The least you can do is respond politely.* Molly's British accent surfaced as her frustration level increased.

"No, um… he, ah… well, we broke up," Stephanie's cheeks flushed when she spoke. Her thoughts flittered with jealousy toward Emma. "We can go as friends," Stephanie added before I could reply.

Stop it, Benjamin. Just say yes to that poor girl.

I smiled. "Okay. Sure. Sounds like fun."

"Great." Stephanie beamed, and then casually touched my arm. "Sorry for running into you," she added. "Well… gotta go."

I nodded. She turned and hustled back to Molly, who conveniently lingered with a few other girls down the hall. Squeals of laughter echoed.

Great. Stephanie Carlson asked me to the dance. Claire chuckled in my thoughts, Molly thanked me, and Jorgenson made snide comments from headquarters.

What did I get myself into?

Chapter 80
Emma's Story

Ben smiled when I walked in.

He was already in the library, in the same chair at the same table in the reserved room as the week before.

I took a seat across from him and smiled back. If only he asked me to the dance instead of Lucas. I pulled out the Hemingway book, *A Farewell to Arms,* for my report.

"Still reading that?" Ben asked, raising his eyebrows.

I nodded, uncertain if he thought I wasn't a good reader, or if he was just trying to make conversation. "It's kind of slow moving. You know what I mean?"

He chuckled.

"What?"

He shook his head and smirked. "Nothin'."

"What?" I asked again and reached toward his arm, my fingers barely touching his skin when I realized what I was doing. For some reason, I felt completely comfortable with him.

He laughed.

"What's so funny?" My cheeks felt warm.

"It's just… Well, I thought you'd love it. That's all," he said with a grin. "Sorry. I guessed wrong."

I shot him a look. I didn't understand if what he said was a good thing or not.

"It's a good thing." He placed his hand on my forearm. "Really."

I jumped when I heard the squeak of the door as it opened behind me. Ben removed his hand from arm, and his smile turned flat when he greeted Lucas.

"Hey, Ben," Lucas answered. "Em, I've been looking for you."

I felt sick to my stomach. I didn't do anything wrong. Did I?

Lucas took a seat beside me and dropped his backpack on the floor.

"So, I've got early practice and my dad's working late. Wanna grab a burger? Or something? Later?" Lucas asked in a low tone. It wasn't quite a whisper, but I could tell he wasn't trying to broadcast it in front of Ben, either. I wondered if he saw Ben's hand on my arm when he walked in. I still felt the tingle where Ben touched me.

"Umm… maybe," I answered, glancing away. Ben went back to reading his book for lit class, and I suddenly felt uncomfortable.

"If you can't, that's fine," he said with sad eyes. "I can always go back to Char's. I'm sure she'll find something for me. I mean, you know… she's got that special bakery she goes to." His full-blown smile made me laugh.

"Okay, okay. Let me check if Barb minds, though. She usually makes dinner… or has something ordered for us."

He leaned forward and put his hand on my knee. "Or you can invite me over for dinner."

My cheeks burned. I was confident they were flaming red. Ben didn't look up from his book. Thank God. "I'll see what she says," I answered.

Lucas winked at me, and then pulled out a textbook and notebook. He ruffled through his backpack, digging deep in its pockets until he found a pencil. He didn't strike me as a studious football player, but then again, I really didn't know him.

"You finish the homework in Spanish?" Ben asked Lucas.

"Yeah. You?"

Ben nodded.

"Are you in the same class?" I asked.

"Yeah, next hour," Lucas answered.

"Spanish Six?" I questioned.

"AP." Ben leaned back in his chair.

"You in six?"

I nodded. They were both in a more advanced class than I was? I never thought they were stupid, but I excelled at Spanish.

"It's okay. If you need any help, I can be your tutor." The smirk on Lucas' face kicked my competitive drive in high gear. It was too late to change Spanish classes, not to mention that would be a bad idea. The only thing I could do was get better grades than either of them in the classes we had together.

The rest of the week sped by.

Ben was absent for several days with the stomach flu according to Claire. Lucas walked me from history to art class each day and sat with me in the library during study hall, though I picked a different table than the one I shared with Ben.

At one point, Lucas put his arm around the back of my chair and leaned forward to whisper in my ear. I laughed when he told a joke. When I realized the librarian was staring at us, I shushed Lucas. Instead of stopping, he started making fun of her outdated glasses. I tried not to chuckle, but his mimicked expressions gave me the giggles and fueled his laughter.

"Mr. Crandon, you either need to settle down or move to a non-quiet zone," the librarian said. I glanced up at her briefly. "You too, young lady."

It wasn't like me to be disrespectful and while I suddenly felt slapped in the face, it was clear Lucas didn't care. He nodded at her, mumbled something I couldn't hear, and packed up his books.

"Come on." He grabbed my backpack from the floor and led me past Stephanie Carlson. She glared at me when she saw me with Lucas. It wasn't the first time she looked at me that way. She and her friends stared at me during lunch after it circulated that Lucas asked me to the dance. It was obvious they were just like the Aimee Wilkinson clique I left behind in Highland Park. Every school probably had a group like them. I just didn't like being their enemy. Of course, being their enemy meant they forgot I was *that* girl—the one whose parents died.

Lucas wasn't my first choice for a date to homecoming, but with his popularity, I was sure to fit in. Not to mention, it gave my aunt something to talk to her friends about. She seemed more excited about the dance than I was.

Thursday night she took me shopping when I told her I didn't have homework. A boutique in Westport had a selection of dresses in the window. Even though I was skeptical, I went along with her idea and tried them on. I should have known she wouldn't steer me wrong. She ended up buying me a strapless cocktail dress. At least, that was how she described it when she called Hannah's mom.

Before history class started on Friday, Lucas leaned forward and whispered, "What color is your dress?" It was obvious Aunt Barb told his dad, too.

I turned in my seat to face him.

"It's black on top and a fuchsia floral print on the bottom." I didn't realize

I spoke with my hands until he smiled.

"Sounds like a lot of dress."

"No," I said and hit his arm gently. "It's strapless and..."

His smirk made me stop talking. My cheeks burned.

"So I need to match to black and fuchsia? That's a pink, right?"

I nodded. "Yeah. Bright pink."

"Okay."

"Oh. My aunt said we could have pictures at our house on the lake. Or, at the Inn, I guess. Unless you—"

"Yeah, sure. I'll talk to Drew and TJ," he said and looked away as people began to take their seats in the row beside us.

"Who's Drew going with?" I couldn't see myself hanging out with Molly all night.

"He's asking Claire."

"He's what? When?"

"Shhh..." He stared at me as the bell rang. "Today, I think. Got cold feet the other day," he whispered. "Don't tell her."

He'd better do it quick. I couldn't keep that secret for long.

Chapter 81
Ben's Story

Bianca's research led to more questions than answers.

It also led to numerous dead ends, which elevated my frustration level. If I didn't know better, I would've questioned if it were staged. Knowing Bianca was on my team just meant this had to be the making of Victor and we were on his trail, regardless of how cold it felt at times.

Before my encounter with Victor weeks earlier, the last confirmed sighting was in Chicago back in 1997. There were other suspected locations reported across the United States and in London, though no agent was able to validate Victor's presence. Los Angeles, Indianapolis, and Reno were amongst the cities listed, but without an obvious pattern, Bianca quickly dismissed them.

I, on the other hand, couldn't.

Bianca and I spent the better part of the week investigating the tangled web of corporate ownership and suspected cities where Victor was spotted. CJ Morse and Company was located outside of Chicago, forty-four miles from where the last hybrid was detected. The farm equipment distributor was owned by a holding company based out of Las Vegas, but the address provided turned out to be a vacant lot.

The only useful information we found was that Henry Nichols was on the board of directors for CJ Morse. Except, Henry Nichols died of natural causes in 1991, at the age of eighty-three.

"He calls in every couple of weeks," the manager told us after I compelled him. "Stops by for annual meetings, but not often in between."

"Where does he live?" I asked.

He shrugged. "He has several houses."

"And where would they be?"

"Well, ah… there's the condo downtown, a mansion in LA, one in Vegas, and one in London. Oh, and some new place in Wisconsin."

"Where in Wisconsin?"

"I'm not sure." He hesitated a second. "North of Milwaukee."

"What does Mr. Nichols look like?"

"I don't know. I never met him."

"What?"

"The meetings are private. Held offsite. I've never been invited."

A shiver sensation rippled through my neck when Jorgenson dispersed additional information. As suspected, there was nothing unusual about Henry's transition back to my world, or his evaluation. He was cleared for future lives and departed shortly thereafter. He was born and raised in Westport, on the farm on Summit Road that appeared to be in the center of the hybrid sightings. Henry had no children, no heirs to carry on the family farming business.

"Have you ever met the other board members?"

"No sir."

So who was impersonating Henry Nichols at CJ Morse and who was the forty-something-year-old man that worked the farm now?

Chapter 82
Emma's Story

Friday night's football game was in Green Bay.

No one I knew was going. Well, except for Lucas and TJ, who played in the game, and Hannah, who cheered, but they rode the team bus. Claire said she and Ben had some family thing and were going out of town for the weekend, which left my Friday night free.

Aunt Barb and Neal attended every game and encouraged me to join them. I considered it for a second until I heard they were going with the Lamberts. I just couldn't see myself hanging out with adults all night.

I didn't mind staying home. Of course, after an hour on my computer, I was bored. I stared at my phone and realized I hadn't heard from Melissa all week. Not that I called her either. The last time we spoke was at Drew's party last Saturday, and it wasn't like old times. She came up to surprise me. Instead, I surprised her. I was high and hanging out with Lucas, the local bad boy.

Melissa didn't say she was mad, but I could tell she was disappointed. She gave me the I'm-being-polite-because-I-have-to smile and hug when we said goodbye that night. The one she'd give Aimee Wilkinson, if she had to. Deep down, I knew I changed and even though Melissa said she understood, she really didn't.

How could she?

It wasn't like I got drunk or high all the time, I rationalized, staring at the phone. What would I even say if I called her? I was sorry? That didn't seem to cut it.

Melissa was my best friend, and I couldn't stand to lose her. I swallowed the lump in my throat and pulled up her number. After a minute or two of rehearsing in my head, I hit the send button and waited for her to answer. I could tell by the tone of her voice when she said hello that she wasn't her normal self.

"Hey, it's me," I said meekly. "I just wanted… well, I'm so sorry about last weekend. I shouldn't have… I mean, I wish I could do it over again." I babbled it all out so fast that I didn't wait for her to answer. "I really miss you."

"Oh-my-god, Emma, I'm so glad you called. Are you okay? I mean, really *okay*? I've been *so* worried."

Tears welled in my eyes. The sound of her voice brought back memories of my old life. It was suddenly a comfort to the loneliness I didn't even realize I felt.

She told me about school and friends I used to know. I told her about the dance and my dress, but left out the after-party at Trent's and anything about Lucas. When she mentioned Matt, I promised to call him and apologize, even though I knew I'd chicken out and send a text instead.

"What are you doing this weekend?" I asked.

"Oh! Tomorrow's that game I told you about. Remember? The one at Northwestern, against Wisconsin. I'm sorry. I should have mentioned it last weekend. I didn't think your aunt would let you go."

"It's okay. She probably wouldn't," I said, recalling the conversation I had with Melissa a few weeks earlier. "Who's going?"

"Lewis, Matt, Jenna—a whole bunch of us... It's not too late. You should come." Her invitation was tempting, and I really wanted to go.

That wouldn't fly with Aunt Barb. Or, would it?

"It's okay. I understand," she said. Her tone was lower than normal, and I knew I disappointed her.

Again.

Chapter 83
Ben's Story

I expected a quiet weekend.

An away football game meant no party at Drew's house Friday night and with most of the guys headed to the Badger game on Saturday, I was confident slipping out of town wouldn't be a problem.

Bianca and Molly were assigned to monitor the farm owned by the dead guy on Summit Road. Molly wasn't happy about being excluded from the research earlier in the week. This was my way of appeasing her, though neither was happy about Bianca playing babysitter.

Things on Summit were fairly calm all week. Nichols' farm was quiet after Kensington disappeared. The hum of engines was silenced, and the mass of staff reduced to two and both were human. The forty-year-old man that lived in the house hadn't reappeared all week, though sleeper agents in the area were on the lookout for anyone matching his description.

My fake aunt and Molly's parents were assigned to inspect the homes on Lake Bell, looking for the man impersonating Henry Nichols.

It was simply a matter of time and patience. Neither of which I had.

Claire and I charted the reported Victor sightings across the U.S. and London. Dates and times when the calls came in seemed disjointed in the data Bianca provided. Nonetheless, we set our course in hopes to recreate Victor's travel plans. Chicago in 1997, with London next, followed by Los Angeles, Indianapolis, and Reno.

While I was undercover in Tucson, Molly took small assignments in two of the cities listed, but she refused to take any missions in London. Now that I knew she died there, killed by Victor, I understood why.

Yet, if Victor were hunting Molly for centuries, something wasn't quite right.

Aftermath

***

London was cold and rainy when Claire and I arrived Friday night. The vicinity where Victor was last reported had no sign of his past presence. Not that I was surprised by that. Tracking agents came to the same conclusion years earlier when the suspected location was first called in.

The address was within a short distance from a popular portal in this section of town. It was across from the underground station and in line with heavily trafficked methods of transportation, both for the human world, and our own. Four red phone booths lined the sidewalk. At one time, portals were plentiful in London. Practically every corner had a telephone box, as the English called them, and every box had a portal. Advances in technology meant fewer telephone boxes were necessary, and immortals had to hide portals in other ways. It was unfortunate for immortals who wished to travel quickly without detection. A bright red box on the corner was readily identifiable and easily used. Dark alcoves and thin lines separating facets on buildings were less noticeable to rookies on assignment and caused more questions to witnesses during congested hours.

Claire popped open an umbrella, as we walked down a narrow side street. It was an upscale section of town, opposite of where Victor killed Molly more than a century ago. I zipped my jacket and lifted the collar to prevent the rain from beating against my neck.

This city block bothered me. All the cities on the list bothered me, for that matter. The fact that I couldn't pinpoint why was a feeling I never experienced before undercover. I could tell something was wrong, but being unable to decipher the pieces of the Victor puzzle put me on edge. Lost in thought, I realized I shrugged off Claire's offer to share the umbrella and quickly thanked her, apologizing for being so distracted.

Even though this wasn't my first visit to London, I didn't know the city very well. Something told me I wouldn't find Victor hiding out here. The streets were clean and buildings well maintained. Flower boxes hung beneath windows, housing the remains of the past summer's blooms. All was in order here. Streets were safe, even in the dark evening hours. It was opposite of where I thought Victor would be.

I expected him to be in hiding in sketchy sections of town where graffiti adorned the walkways and neighbors were strangers. I pictured him in a rundown building, dirty with years of pollution browning its once-pristine brick. It would be fitting for the likes of a rogue criminal, like the dilapidated barn on Summit where I found him before.

Sophisticated surroundings weren't what I envisioned. Then again, it was only a sighting. Maybe he was just passing through.

My head swarmed in questions with no answers.

If I were Victor, I'd pick the largest city, the most populous area, and hide in plain sight. I'd blend in with the crowd. Be part of the mass, not in the open where people would notice me. I wouldn't make friends. I wouldn't know my neighbors. I'd hide in alleyways, not in wealthy sections where my presence would be known.

We walked more than a block when I realized I shielded myself from outsiders, including Claire. She stopped a few feet back, though I didn't see it at the time.

"Ben! Ben!" Her voice grew louder. "Ben!"

"Sorry." I turned to face her.

Then it dawned on me. Victor wasn't hiding. He was living among them.

"Let's get a drink." I motioned to the pub across the street.

We sat at the bar, disguised as a middle-aged couple. Claire glanced at me when I ordered us pints of beer. "Could I at least get a glass of wine?" she asked. "I'm not fond of dark beer." Thoughts of disappointment flooded her mind, as the older gentleman tended to our order.

It wouldn't be fitting for our cover, I answered and shared an image of our disguises, two commoners.

She rolled her eyes but kept still.

The pub was arguably one of the oldest in London. Heavily decorated with photos of former generations, the walls held memories of past dances, brawls, and even a murder back in the early 1900s. The soul had since left, though the energy footprint that lingered shared the brutal attack in more detail than what was comfortable for Claire.

My thoughts turned to Molly and the suffering she endured at the hands of Victor, also known as Jack the Ripper to the media. The murder here, though not too much later than Molly's untimely death, was not at the hands of Victor. The criminal in this case was caught, sentenced, and reincarnated.

Aside from the knowledge I had of the establishment, the décor was inviting, warm and cozy. The look on Claire's inexperienced face was less than soothing. Her thoughts bounced from confidence to fear and back again in mere seconds. She sipped the beer she didn't want and snacked on the pretzel nibs that sat in a small bowl between us. The massive wood counter saw better days, but the dings and divots in its finish were stories of their own I chose to disregard.

There was a sensation I was unable to ignore. It haunted me like a black cloud hovering and smothering my breath. It was there the moment we walked in, though I tried not to notice. The old structure had my mind working overtime.

I finished my beer and nodded to the bartender for another. Music on low kept the silence between Claire and me bearable. I could tell the mid-fifties man mentally questioned who we were when he refilled my mug.

"Cold night," I said, hoping to stop the thoughts in his head and ease Claire's mind.

"Yup," the bartender answered and leaned on the counter, toward us. His hands were spread wide, as if stabilizing himself against the mahogany bar. "You from here?'

"Nah," I said, and then put my hand atop Claire's. "The wife and I are just in town for the weekend." I squeezed her hand gently and, when I removed mine, a silver band was wrapped on her ring finger. I picked a city at random in rural England and called it our home. "Just visiting for our anniversary."

Claire smiled at him, and he seemed pleased with my answer. He focused on her eyes to the point I had to stop her before she compelled him. It wasn't common for a human to stare so long at an immortal, but when they did, a compulsion could automatically engage, something my rookie partner didn't realize. Without an intended message during the compulsion, her random thoughts would have been downloaded to the human, a breach of contract.

After I broke the connection between them with a gentle nudge to the bartender's hand, Claire gave me an apologetic look. "Can I get you anything else?" he asked, snapping back to attention. "We got bangers and mash."

"Perfect," I said.

***

In the brief moment my hand touched the bartender, I learned he had a wife who left years before and an only daughter that he never spoke to. A section of his memory was lost, however. A large gap in time was missing from the files I extracted, which could mean something or nothing since the contact was brief.

I paid the tab and made small talk with the bartender, while Claire was in the loo. A few tables of people still lingered toward the back of the pub, though most already ate and left.

"Hey," Claire said as she returned to the seat beside me. Her pale face lacked the bright smile she regularly displayed and, without reading her thoughts, I could tell the rookie had a problem.

Claire glanced at the woman in a red dress that took a seat at the table near the door. She sat alone. I could tell she was human. Her hands shook as she held the menu in front of her, and I guessed she was a smoker or an addict coming down from a high. Her clothing was not as conservative as the other female customers were. Her dress was fitted and bright compared to the drab colors of those that preceded her.

"I think she's a hybrid," Claire said.

"Can't be," I answered firmly. "Her vitals are normal. No scent, nothing unusual. You're probably reading the absence of drugs."

Claire chewed on her lower lip, as she glanced back and forth between the lady and me. I put a tip on the bar and nodded to Claire.

"You folks have a good night," the bartender said, making eye contact with me. He stared at me without blinking, as if expecting to be compelled. He had to have met our kind before. He'd been compelled and expected it from any immortal he met, which made me believe Victor had been here, maybe even recently.

I nodded in response and paged Bianca for Henry Nichol's London address, but she didn't answer. I forgot about the woman in red, as thoughts filled my head about Victor.

When I reached for the door to leave, I absentmindedly bumped the chair of the woman in red, knocking her purse to the floor. I stopped and turned, immediately kneeling down to pick it up.

"I apologize. I was distracted," I said to her.

Her eyes met mine briefly before looking down as if embarrassed or afraid. No thoughts crossed her mind. "That's… that's alright."

I handed the black bag back to her and met her eyes a second time. Like the bartender, she stared back an unusually long time as if compelled before. I touched my hand to hers and wished her a good evening.

Once outside, I shared my findings with Claire. The woman in red was not a hybrid, but she knew where to find them.

We were on the right track.

Chapter 84
Emma's Story

As I drifted off to sleep on Friday, I wished myself back to the park.

I wanted to see the strange man in the gray wool overcoat. He smiled at me in my last dream and told me to trust my instincts. Not that I understood what he meant.

Suddenly, I found myself sitting on the swing again. I rocked back and forth. The sun warmed my face, and the swing's slow momentum lulled me into a quiet place. I had so many unanswered questions—like who the man was and why I dreamt of him so often. Was I supposed to know him?

When I felt a presence, like a shadow hovering over me, I knew the man was there.

"You called?" He looked the same as he did last time.

I stopped swinging and stood quickly. "I… I want to know who I need to be patient with. And why you call me Elizabeth. And what is your name?" I rambled, getting everything out all at once.

The air was cool, cooler than when I was alone.

"He is in your heart, Emma. You prefer to be called Emma, don't you, Emma Elizabeth Bennett?"

I nodded. "Yes, thank you."

"It is he that must be patient now. You will find him. You are getting closer. Simply trust your instincts." The man looked toward the empty, wooden play structure.

"What does that mean?"

"You will soon learn of things that may be difficult to comprehend." He paused for a brief moment, staring ahead of him. Clouds grayed the sky, and a cold breeze swept up around us. "You must be willing to listen. The answers will come from within."

I looked down for a second. When my eyes searched for the familiar man again, he was gone.

Chapter 85
Ben's Story

I can't believe Claire didn't fancy the bangers and mash.

Molly's sarcastic tone interrupted my thoughts. Claire and I crossed the street. It was after bar time by London standards, and most pubs were already closed. Molly eavesdropped earlier and knew Claire didn't care for the traditional British dinner.

That's why I should have gone with you, Molly continued. *I would've enjoyed a good British meal.*

Is that right? I shook my head.

Well, it was worth a try. Sitting on the sidelines is rather boring.

I'll keep that in mind. Claire and I turned onto Piccadilly.

Oh… just so you are aware, Emma chose not to attend the football game with her aunt as originally planned, Molly said. *However, she's fine. I propelled around her house to ensure it's fully secure. Chester reported she's asleep. Happy?*

Yes. Thank you, I answered. Claire chuckled. *Hey, tell Bianca I need the London address for Henry Nichols. She didn't answer her page earlier.*

I'll have her send it over; she just got back. She spent the evening with Trent again. I think she's hoping for an invitation to the high school dance.

Claire smirked at the comment. We stood at an intersection beside another couple. The streets were mostly quiet and vacant. A few men waited for the light on the opposite corner.

At least Bianca fit in.

Are you enjoying London? Taking in the sights? Molly asked as the pedestrian light turned green.

It's nicer than I expected… at least the area where Victor was allegedly spotted. Claire and I continued walking.

Hmm… I noticed it changed since I lived there, Molly said.

I thought you refused to take any missions in London. Claire looked at me with suspicion in her eyes. *Are you holding out on something?*

No. But I did manage to squeeze in a day trip. It was wonderful being back.

What? I slowed my pace.

When was this? Claire asked. Her tone turned serious.

Um, several years ago.

What time of year? I questioned.

Winter, I think. No, perhaps spring.

Could it have been March? Claire glanced at me.

Like March 31st?

Perhaps. I can't quite recall. I was there just a few hours. Why so precise, Benjamin?

What assignment was this? I asked. Claire stopped mid-stride in front of Starbucks.

Oh, it was nothing, really. Commander E had me running from site to site, doing some training for new recruits. It was the first time I met Bianca, actually.

Bianca was in London?

Claire's face went pale.

Hmm… yes. It was a simple field excursion. There were a dozen or so trainees. I'm sure she doesn't even recall meeting me, now that I think about it. We weren't formally introduced until her induction following her completion, Molly answered. *What aren't you telling me?*

Molly finally sensed Claire's reaction.

Victor was spotted here on March 31st, fifteen years ago.

Where was this sighting? Molly's thoughts were lower than before.

Near Green Park.

Off Piccadilly? Her tone became sharp. Memories of her life with Victor flowed from her mind to mine. Images of a once-happy couple flashed before me like a slideshow. As Molly's gruesome death approached, I shielded Claire from the details. The scene resembled the street Claire and I just passed.

I thought he killed you in Whitechapel.

He did. But in our first life together, we lived on Half Moon. My friend… gosh, what was her name? She lived around the corner from us. Was it on Down Street? Oh, dear… I can't recall.

Down Street? We're headed to Down Street right now, I said, holding my breath. *Molly, I need to know everything. Where you lived. Where you visited. Dates. Friends. Acquaintances. Everything.*

Chapter 86
Emma's Story

I tossed and turned, waking up several times during the night.

The first time was after midnight when I heard the gentle hum of the overhead garage door, followed by footsteps on the stairs. Chester raised his head momentarily when Aunt Barb checked in on me and whispered goodnight. I must have dozed off quickly because I didn't remember answering her. An hour later, I was awake again. Lying in bed in the dark, all I could do was think about the football game at Northwestern. The one Melissa invited me to. The game everyone I knew was going to—even Lucas.

I should have asked my aunt. I fluffed my pillow and tried to get comfortable. Would she let me go? My mind traveled to what I'd do on Saturday night without Claire in town.

When I came up with nothing, I realized, I just had to go, too.

Chapter 87
Ben's Story

By the time we reached Down Street, it was too late.

Hybrid scents filled the air in the blocks surrounding the five-story building, but the flat was vacant. Opposite the fireplace was a plain black couch with a white, crumpled sheet, pillow, and blanket. The two bedrooms were empty. Beds were unmade, as if the occupants left in a hurry, some still warm to the touch. Remnants from the hybrids were everywhere. Clothes and personal items accounted for four men, all average height and build, based on sizes of shirts and pants hanging in the closet, though their wardrobe was minimal.

Molly watched in thought as we toured each room. She initially commented on how charming the residence was outside, but when she saw the bland interior white walls with cheaply framed mass-produced prints, she called it tacky. Red-patterned drapes flanked the bay window in the living room, with similar bright drapes in each bedroom.

I picked up a T-shirt from the laundry pile on the floor. It had DNA residue, which shared its original human owner, an Irishmen in his early thirties with previous signs of leukemia. A pair of dark jeans and a linen shirt found in the master bedroom belonged to a British man in his late twenties. He was the youngest among them, converted after cancer treatment proved unsuccessful. The other men had similar terminal illnesses at the time of their conversion.

"Here," I said, tossing Claire the pile of clothes that I collected.

"Eww. That's disgusting." She dropped it to the floor. "I can smell body odor on them. Why would you give that to me?" Her forehead wrinkled when she glared at me.

Molly's chuckle infiltrated our thoughts.

I waited. Couldn't she put the puzzle pieces together?

"Because," I answered firmly, hoping I didn't need to explain it, "they're not like the hybrids in Westport. Each of these hybrids was sick at the time of their conversion."

Claire's glare changed to a blank look when Molly elaborated. Humans in Wisconsin were stripped of their lives prematurely. Those in London were already terminally ill. Victor gave them a second chance. "Or, at least that's what he probably told them," Molly added.

I wandered through the empty rooms after clearing the apartment and dispatching the local Sleeper Agents to canvas the surrounding five-mile radius. Every piece of unopened mail on the kitchen counter, including the monthly rent, was addressed to Miss Mary Nichols. She was the woman in red at the pub. There was no sign of any human, no unknown scent or lingering presence.

Despite that, I was convinced this was Victor. He had to be using Henry Nichols as his alias. Who else could it be? And the woman, Mary, who was she really? Did he compel her to obey? How many other humans did he have at his disposal?

Reports from agents came in, ending my internal dialogue. Each of the four hybrids exited in opposite directions from the flat. All trails led to tube stations, London's underground subway, where their odor diminished amongst the electric current from the rail system. It was obvious they knew what they were doing, and I wondered how they knew we were coming.

***

With agents assigned to monitor the premises, Claire and I went in search of the other residences throughout London. The address of a Victor sighting proved to be a dead end. The two-bedroom flat was completely empty and on the market for sale.

Our second stop was Molly's first home with Victor, during her first life with him. It was a prestigious mansion on Half Moon back then. Centuries later, the building was converted to a hotel and there was no sign of Victor, hybrids, or any other immortal, for that matter. It was another dead end.

The employee at the hotel's front desk nodded as Claire and I walked out.

"Have a good evening," he said.

I thanked him and held the door open for Claire. The pre-dawn air was chilly and refreshing as Molly's thoughts relaxed. A faint, sweet cotton candy aroma met my nostrils momentarily.

A hybrid.

I tracked the weak, sporadic scent down the street and around the corner, Claire following behind. A small, concentrated dose of its odor caught my attention and then vanished. Like a drop of vinegar, pungent and strong by itself, yet weak and lost once mixed in a bucket of water.

The smell's source came from a residence on White Horse. I ordered Sleeper Agents to set up a perimeter around the building, while Claire and I prepared for entry.

Molly's gasp startled me, as she viewed the images in my mind.

What is it? I asked.

That's where my friend lived, she mumbled. *Oh… what was her name?*

I nodded to Claire, signaling I was ready, despite Molly's rambling.

Mary!

Her comment caused Claire to jump.

Mary? I asked. *You remembered her name was Mary?*

Claire chuckled aloud, and an agent beside her smirked. Molly really needed to shield herself with that kind of comment. It would ruin her credibility, if she didn't.

Yes. But I can't remember her last name.

Okay. Umm, mind if we proceed?

Sorry. I felt her blush, as she shielded herself from the others. Finally.

The home was a large, three-bedroom flat with two reception rooms, as Molly called them when I referred to them as living rooms. She walked with us, mentally, while we searched the premises. She was pleased to report this was the same home Mary lived in all those years ago. I commended her memory and laughed at her juvenile demeanor after we cleared it, having found no trace of a hybrid.

At sunrise, we had only one address remaining, the one Bianca provided for Henry Nichol's home on King Street. The residence was impressive from the exterior. Topiaries lined the second-story balcony, with flowerbeds hanging on black, wrought iron fencing along the wide sidewalk. Ivory bricks in staggering sizes and positions trimmed arched windows in a monochromatic color scheme. It was bright, clean, and classy.

Inside, the third-floor, open concept layout was equally awe inspiring. A baby grand piano sat beside a window in the oversized reception room overlooking St. James Square. Two bedrooms, each with private baths, were decorated in a modern, simple style with expensive artwork throughout the apartment.

While Claire and I checked each room, Molly bounced in thought from us to Sleeper Agents that joined us in our sweep. Her shriek not only caught my attention, but that of all agents within the empty residence. Everyone froze.

What? What is it? I asked, annoyed. Did she remember her friend's last name?

It's... it's... Molly stuttered. I scanned her thoughts and located the source of her sudden fear. There, on the bedside table, sat a small, antique photo frame with an image of a young woman with dark hair.

I rushed to the bedroom and picked up the picture.

It's me, Molly finally spit out.

Chapter 88
Emma's Story

"Drive careful," Aunt Barb said, handing me her credit card.

Convincing her to let me go to the Northwestern football game was easier than I thought. Of course, I gave her a made-up story that Melissa and I planned this before Dad died. It was sort of true I rationalized, as I left Melissa a message. We'd been talking about going since sophomore year.

I just didn't have a ticket for this game, and Melissa didn't know I was coming.

Guilt and exhilaration battled within me during the drive to the Highland Park Metra train station. I was excited and anxious to see my old friends and possibly make up with Matt. I owed him a better apology than the text I sent. Or, at least an explanation. Melissa would be ecstatic to see me, too.

The guilt of lying to my aunt fought my excitement, and I questioned if I should turn around more than once. I never lied to Aunt Barb before. Or anyone, for that matter. I might have withheld details a few times, but I had never outright lied the way I did today, and I wasn't sure I liked the sick feeling it gave me.

By the time I reached the Illinois border, I made peace with myself. It was only a little white lie. Right?

Driving the familiar Tri-State Tollway, I felt a surge of happiness. I was home again. I exited at Half-Day Road and made my way to the Metra station in plenty of time.

Waiting to board, I sent a text to Melissa. The late-afternoon train was scheduled to arrive in Evanston after kick off, but way before halftime. I thought about driving straight to the game, but I wasn't sure how to get there or where to park.

Besides, when Melissa and I went to Northwestern last semester to visit her brother at college, we rode the train. She was completely comfortable with it, so how hard could it be?

We took the Davis Street exit, I remembered, and walked a couple blocks to her brother's apartment. Though I wasn't sure I couldn't find my way there again if I had to. We turned right, and then left. Or was it left, and then right?

I was lost in thought as the recording stated the train's arrival at Wilmette. Two stops to Davis, I noted on the schedule posted in front of me. The train started to move again, and I typed another text to Melissa.

Relief swept over me when she called before I could send the message.

It was hard to hear her with the background cheers I guessed were in response to a touchdown. I realized I was talking louder than normal when an older woman on the other side of the aisle turned to stare at me.

The train slowed to a stop, and a college kid got on. He sat behind the woman.

After a minute or two of "Oh-my-god, you're coming here," and "How long can you stay?" Melissa's phone started to cut out.

"Em—come down, you'll need—train—Central—not Davis. Em? Em? Can you—me?" Melissa said, and the line went dead.

Did she say *not* Davis Street?

I leaned across the aisle and asked what stop was next.

"Davis Street," the woman answered with a heavy accent.

"Do you know if we passed Central Street?"

"Yes, it was the last stop," the college kid behind her answered.

Shit. Now what?

***

I stood on the Davis Street deck as the train departed, wondering what to do next.

Melissa didn't answer her phone. It went straight to voicemail. I sent a text, but wasn't sure she'd even get it, if her phone was turned off. Central Street couldn't be that far of a walk, could it?

I took the stairs to the street level and looked for a main road heading north. I frantically called Jenna as I walked briskly down the block, but neither answered. I sent Matt a text, too, but he didn't reply, and I didn't have anyone else's number in my phone.

Even though I didn't want to call him, I knew Lucas was at the game. My mind battled the pros and cons when I reached the next corner. With the sun setting and my lack of familiarity with the area, I dialed.

"Hey, Emma. Whas up?" Lucas sounded drunk or high.

"Hey. Are you at the Northwestern game?"

"Ahh... yeah," he said, but it wasn't convincing. After a brief pause, he added. "Why? Is my dad asking or somethin'?" His tone was casual and laid back, which fueled my anxiety.

"Umm... no. I'm not with your dad. Or my aunt, for that matter. I'm here. In Evanston." Panic began to set in as the streetlights illuminated brightly on each corner, confirming nightfall was imminent.

"Huh?"

I started to get impatient, my nerves on edge. "Just tell me... where you are? I'm sorta lost and getting freaked out."

"Why? Where are *you*?"

"I'm in Evanston. I was going to the game and missed my stop. I'm walking on some street downtown, and I don't even know where the football field is or where my friends are. I can't even reach them right now." I poured everything out without taking a breath.

"Hey, sorry, Emma. We're not at the game. We left." He said it so casually, I felt ill. "Who are you meeting anyway? That cute blonde friend of yours?"

"What? You mean Melissa. Did you see her... or Lewis?"

"Yeah, I think so. I don't think they're there anymore. We partied with them for a while, but didn't have tickets, so we left."

My stomach sank. Now what did I do?

"We're at some bar, if you wanna come here," he said. He continued talking, but his voice was muffled and it didn't sound like it was directed to me. "Where's this place again?"

"Lucas? Are you talking to me?"

"Hold on."

"Wait. How'd you get into a bar?" I asked, but Lucas didn't answer. I continued walking until I reached the corner. The sun began to fade.

"Lucas!" I screamed into the phone after crossing the street.

"Hold on!" he yelled back.

Patience wasn't a quality I possessed. The streetlights brightened, and I realized I walked two city blocks waiting for him to answer me. Music and distant voices were all I heard on the other end as I waited. Not that Melissa or Jenna, or anyone else I knew, was trying to reach me.

"Emma?" Lucas finally spoke. "We're at some bar, off Clark and ah... um, where again?" he called to someone else. "Clark and Sherman. Wait. Yeah. Let me know when you're here, and I'll come out."

"Clark and Sherman?" I asked. "Where's that?"

"Where are you exactly?" Background voices were louder than he was.

"Um..." I stalled, looking at street signs. "Sherman and Church."

I heard him talking to someone else again, before giving me directions. "How did you get in a bar? I can't get in. I don't have a fake ID. Do you?" I couldn't believe it, well, yes, I could believe he had one.

"Ray's buddy got us in. He's pretty cool. You'll like him."

"Okay." I repeated the directions he gave me.

"Yeah. Text me when you're close. I'll come out. The door is off an alley. It's kinda hard to see," he said before the music and voices were silenced, and I knew he hung up. That, or we got cut off. Either way, Lucas was my only option.

I zipped up my jacket and picked up my pace. I knew better. I was putting my trust in him, and he was the last person that earned it.

Chapter 89
Ben's Story

It was my third visit of the day.

Claire was at the end of the bar wearing a bright red dress when I walked into the pub. It was the same tavern where we were picked up the hybrid lead the night before.

At first, Claire was reluctant. Later, she seemed comfortable in her straight brunette hair and Molly-like expressions. Assuming Victor frequented the place, we wanted to draw him out.

A thirty-two-year-old human male was putting the moves on Claire. He leaned close to her when he spoke, placed his arm on the back of her chair, and finally whispered a proposition. I watched it play out through the bartender's eyes before I came in. I peered into the pub owner's mind from the hotel lobby around the corner.

It was a long day of disguises in hopes to lure the hybrids out of hiding to get a lead on the infamous criminal immortal. Instead, it was human after human talking and drinking.

Earlier in the day, we thought we had a lead, but again, nothing. The address Claire downloaded was a vacant warehouse. Additional Sleeper Agents from around Great Britain were called to duty to aid in our quest. Some followed up on leads, others did surveillance, and Bianca continued to do research back in Westport.

Claire's impersonation of Molly was a last-ditch effort for the day. One that Molly protested. *Please let me do it myself, Benjamin,* she begged. I ignored her pleas and shielded Claire from Molly's thoughts to prevent influence. It was already after ten o'clock, and customers were retiring for the evening.

The bartender took my drink order, as I sat on the opposite end from

Claire.

Claire wasn't thrilled with the possible harm she was in, but she, too, felt it was a last resort before we moved on to other cities on the list of Victor sightings.

The human flirt that hovered over Claire jumped when the door slammed open. A short, slender man in his mid-twenties walked in. His eyes were focused on Claire, as he made a path toward her.

The bartender grumbled. It was clear he knew the young guy in the twill jacket and dark jeans. His unruly hair matched the brown in his coat.

He approached Claire, stepping between her and the flirt. If it weren't for my immortal hearing, I wouldn't have heard his warning. Claire's eyes met mine when I glanced to the end of the bar. The brown-haired man repeated himself. "You're in danger here. You must come with me." He reached for her hand, squeezing her wrist.

I read her thoughts as she downloaded data. He was a hybrid.

The human stood up, hovering at least six inches over the hybrid.

"Now hold on," the human flirt said. "Who are you? Molly, do you know this guy?"

Claire chewed on her lower lip for a second before I sent her my thoughts. *Molly wouldn't be nervous, so stop chewing. And second, yes. You know him. Lie,* I ordered.

She did as she was told and the human threw cash on the bar and left, mumbling. Disgust was clear on his face.

"We must hurry," the hybrid whispered to Claire. "He's coming."

***

I followed Claire and the hybrid down the street and into an alley.

"Who's coming and where are you taking me?" Claire whispered to the hybrid when they were behind a row of dumpsters.

Don't! I scolded. *He thinks you're Molly. Just get him thinking and download what you can.*

He's quiet right now. Nothing to download. It's like he's stripped of all memories.

I knew her rookie status would be a limitation. *Just take a deep breath and regain your confidence. What would Molly do at a time like this?*

The hybrid didn't speak until they were securely hidden from view behind a row of large garbage cans. Releasing her from his grip, he said, "You have to leave. He's watching you."

She shook her head.

Go with it!

"Who's watching me?" Her voice was low and soothing.

"You have to leave the city. Go into hiding. Back where you came from."

Claire was still for a moment. She took a deep breath and put her hands on her hips. "Oh, you're being silly. I just got here. Why would I leave so soon?"

Beads of sweat pooled on the hybrid's forehead. "You don't understand. You're in danger here, Molly." Fear filled his eyes. "A few of us were watching for you. But if I get caught, I'm dead. Do you understand? You need to leave before he finds you."

I felt Claire's pulse increase, as the hybrid grasped her upper arms and shook her when he spoke. "We've been waiting for you for years." I didn't need to see her eyes to know the fear in them. "You must go."

Before Molly could eavesdrop, or any agent on site could read Claire's thoughts or listen in on her conversation with the hybrid, I shielded them. I wanted to take him down, but I was reluctant to move too quickly. He had no memory and, once in custody, the likelihood of him disclosing anything helpful was slim.

Claire was silent, too shocked to contribute, I guessed.

Watching through Claire's thoughts, I saw the hybrid's eyes soften and shoulders droop in response to her silence. "You don't know, do you?"

She hesitated, and then croaked out a, "No."

He loosened his grip and closed his eyes. For a split second, an image of a mid-twenties dark-haired man popped into the hybrid's thoughts. Before Claire could register who the man was, the thought was gone.

"I'm here to protect you," the hybrid said. His eyes were wide open and focused on Claire. "My job was to watch for you. To warn you to leave."

"How? Why?"

I propelled to the window ledge several feet above her and searched for the nearest portal.

"I've been here for almost ten years. There's another one… like me. A Dual, we call ourselves, because Mr. Nicklas thinks we are loyal only to him. But we're not."

"Victor—"

"Shhh!" the hyrid scolded. "Don't say his name."

"I… I'm not sure I understand," Claire whispered. A narrow doorway on the opposite side of the alley housed an old portal that didn't appear to have been used in decades. If need be, I could easily get Claire to the safety of our world and out of the grips of this double-agent hybrid.

"The other one... like me... he... well, he follows Mr. Nicklas." The hybrid shook his head, as thoughts slowly converted to words he spoke aloud. He struggled with communication, and I guessed some human abilities were stripped from him. Abilities he would never regain, like adverse effects from a lobotomy.

"Follows Victor?" Claire questioned.

The hybrid nodded. "Yes. He's security detail for Mr. Nicklas. We aren't allowed to call him by any other name." He blinked slowly, regained his focus, and continued. "Mr. Nicklas doesn't know we report to Aberthol."

"Who's Aberthol?" Claire mumbled her words.

The hybrid squinted, his eyebrow wrinkled. "He's the one who sent me."

A crease formed in the middle of the hybrid's forehead as he stared at Claire.

"I thought you knew," he said after moments of silence. His voice was low.

Claire shook her head.

"He's Mr. Nicklas' son."

A drunk human stumbled into the alley and fell, knocking over a metal garbage can. The startle caused Claire to jump and me to release the shield surrounding us. Their conversation ended abruptly, as both turned toward the commotion. When I looked back at them, Bianca slipped through the portal and ran to Claire's side.

The hybrid fled, and I followed. He led me through the alley, around the corner, and into a tube station. The hybrid was fast, but he lacked the speed and intelligence of immortals. I was inches away from grabbing him in a deserted section of the underground transit system, when Molly's voice pierced my thoughts.

Ben, its Emma! Hybrids are after her in Chicago.

My heart pounded. I could reduce my pulse rate, but that would require precious seconds I couldn't spare. Not yet, at least. Not until I got Emma to safety. I instructed Molly to stay in the safe house in Westport, though I knew she wouldn't listen to me.

By the time I slipped through the portal, Molly was already there.

Chapter 90
Emma's Story

No–no–no–no–*no*! My phone chirped. The lights flashed, and then nothing.

"Damn it!" I mumbled aloud. Now how would I get ahold of Lucas?

I was on the corner of Clark and Sherman, just like he told me. Except there was no bar on either corner, and he didn't answer his phone the three times I tried before it died. Lucas said something about an alley, didn't he?

All I saw was a travel agency, a shoe store, and a tall business building.

The sky was grey and the air cool without the sun. A few people passed me on the street. They walked with purpose, and I guessed they were headed to the fancy restaurant around the corner. I loitered, uncertain which direction to turn. Traffic was thinning, and most of the angled parking spots were empty as I strolled by.

When I turned back, I noticed a few people a block behind me. The group was loud and looked to be college-aged guys. I wondered if they came from the bar where Lucas was. I thought about heading toward them, to see if there was an alley or an entrance that I missed, but as I watched them from the corner, something told me not to.

The sky darkened. I hesitated, unable to take my eyes off them. One guy was pushed into the empty parking spot in the street, while another staggered forward, catching himself before he fell. Their voices carried in the still air, louder than the distant sound of a car horn and police siren.

I took a step closer to the darkened building behind me, hovering in the safety of its awning. But as the group continued toward me, increasing their stride, my heart began to race.

The tall one in the middle raised his arm and pointed at me. Someone whistled, while another yelled out, "Hey, where you goin'?"

The creep's words echoed behind me as I hastily crossed the street, sprinting in front of a car, and then jogging to the opposite corner. Clark Street was darker than Sherman, with buildings on one side and only one streetlight mid-block. There was no sign of a bar, or an alley, or whatever Lucas said there would be.

Stuffing my fists in my pockets, I walk-ran down the sidewalk. I was warm under my jacket, despite the fall evening breeze.

"Hey, wait up!" the creep called.

I ignored him.

When I reached the streetlight, I checked over my shoulder. Reflections loomed in the bookstore's window behind me. Glimpses of his friends running to catch up caught my eye before I again focused straight ahead.

"Yeah! You! Wait up! Where you going tonight?" the creep yelled.

"Want some company?" someone else asked, followed by more voices and words I couldn't decipher.

Someone laughed a deep growl. "Wanna party?"

"You shouldn't be alone out here." The voices sounded closer.

The desire to run was overwhelming. I didn't want to look scared.

"Never show fear," Dad once told me. Of course, he was referring to sports. *"Don't let your opponent know you're afraid,"* he said when I was smaller than the guard that defended me in basketball.

"Okay, Dad," I whispered, as if he were there with me.

A gentle breeze carried the scent of fried food. It was suddenly a comforting, safe smell, and I found myself charging ahead. The illumination of the red-and-yellow sign shined in the distance.

Just one more building, I thought. McDonald's had never looked so good.

Out of the shadows, in a gap between two businesses, a heavyset woman appeared, wrapped in a long, beige sweater that looked too thin for the cool October evening. I jumped, stalling on the sidewalk momentarily.

Her warm eyes met mine briefly and, for the tiniest of moments, I felt better. At least I wasn't alone any longer.

The woman passed by, as the creep caught up. Words flew between them and, for a second, I worried for her safety. Would the pack of drunks harass her, too? As much as I wanted to stop and help, a little voice in my head told me to run.

Before I could listen, he gripped my upper arm and spun me around to face him. Cold eyes met mine, and chills ran through my veins. I found myself unable to breathe as he stared at me, and his friends spoke to the woman.

"Hey, where you headed?" he asked.

"Um... I, ah..." I stammered and looked down. Everything about him was dark. An unzipped ebony jacket exposed a charcoal, button-down shirt tucked into ink-colored jeans. A gentle shake later, I felt compelled to look into his jet-black eyes.

"You really shouldn't be alone out here at night. A pretty girl like you."

"I... I have to go," I said, though I didn't move. His eyebrows rose, as his pupils dilated. Even his complexion was dark, not like the fair ivory skin I had. Something told me not to look him in the eye, but I couldn't look away.

"No, you don't. We haven't even partied yet."

"I need to go," I said, struggling to get out of his hold.

"Leave her alone," a deep voice from behind me called out.

A startled look crept up on the creep's face, and he let go of my arm. Before he could change his mind, I turned and ran into the arms of my hero.

It was Ben.

Chapter 91
Ben's Story

Emma's heart rate was elevated when she fell into my arms.

I didn't expect this kind of greeting and wasn't prepared for the reaction my human body disclosed. Outwardly, I was awkward, afraid to touch her. My palms got clammy, and my breathing accelerated. Inside, I wanted nothing more than to hold her and sweep away her fear, to tell her who I was.

"Sorry." She pulled back. Tears flowed down her cheeks.

"Hey... what's going on?" I asked in the most soothing voice I could muster, given the hybrids nearby. Molly, disguised as an older woman, detained them momentarily. She kept her identity hidden, so as not to scare them away prematurely.

"These... these..." Emma whimpered before wiping her eyes and clearing her throat. "I'm sorry. It's just that my phone died, I was lost... and then, these guys started following me. I... I was scared. That's all." She gave a weak smile, but I heard her thoughts when my hand rested on her arm. She was happy to see me, and it wasn't just because of the situation.

I looked to the group of hybrids crossing the parking lot. They stood tall and confident, walking in a pack with the biggest one in the middle, slightly ahead of the other two. I nodded in their direction. "These the guys?"

She glanced at them. "Yes."

"Go inside and wait for me."

She nodded, and I watched her until she was safely in the restaurant. Molly remained in disguise, lingering between two buildings and near a portal, a safe distance away.

"Hey. The girl's with us," one of the hybrids called to me. *The balls of these guys*, I thought. Not that it surprised me.

I shook my head. "I don't think so."

"Yeah? Well, I do," the blond-haired one answered as he moved closer to me.

A dozen agents that Molly summoned surrounded the hybrids in inconspicuous spots around the parking lot. Three were atop the two-story building next door, a handful were hidden between cars, and some were crouched behind bushes lining the parking lot. Several were even in plain sight on the sidewalk and in the restaurant.

What are you doing here? I asked in a frequency they would be able to hear. *And what do you want with the girl?*

The tall one, clearly the alpha by his position of lead hybrid amongst his two flanking rank, stopped mid-stride. *Something's wrong,* he said to his buddies. He glanced around, not knowing the voice came from me.

You're right. Something's wrong. Where's Victor?

With the mention of his name, the alpha hybrid nodded and the three dispersed in opposite directions, my team in pursuit. Frankly, I was getting tired of chasing hybrids, but I knew we needed to capture these guys. The tall one was not here to warn us like the one back in London.

This one was out to kill.

***

Emma watched from the window in McDonald's entry. As I approached her and our eyes met, she smiled. It made leaving my team in London worthwhile.

"Hungry?" I asked.

She hesitated, but I insisted. Having held her in my arms minutes earlier, I knew her last meal was pancakes her aunt made for breakfast.

"So what are you doing here?" she asked after we got our food and sat down in a booth. "In Evanston, I mean. I thought Claire said you had some family thing." She took a bite of her chicken salad.

"We did. Have some family thing. In Libertyville. My buddy and I are headed to a party down the street." I nodded toward a couple at a booth on the other side of the restaurant. "And you? How did you get lost here in Evanston?"

I listened intently to her story. When she finished, I suggested calling Lucas and began to dial before she could protest.

"Lucas. How are ya?" I said when he answered. "I heard you're here in Evanston. You with TJ and Drew?"

"No, they went back already. Where you at?"

"I'm just getting a burger, but I'm headed to a party in a few."

"Oh. Yeah. We're headed to the city now. To some club."

"Really? That's cool. Who's with you?" I asked.

"Trent and some buddies of Ray's. You know? My stepdad. This guy's got some club downtown and doesn't care that we're minors. You wanna come?"

Tracking what Lucas was up to interested me, but when Emma's eyes met mine, it didn't matter. "Yeah, hey. I'd love to. But I've got friends waiting for me. Oh. And hey, I've got Emma here. She's been looking for you. Her phone died or something. Here she is," I said, handing over the phone.

Lucas was hanging out with his stepdad's buddies. Something wasn't right about that.

On it, Molly said in response to my thoughts. I didn't even have time to issue orders.

You shouldn't be doing fieldwork, I retorted. Then again, I camouflaged her from the action in London, so she likely didn't realize the full impact of her exposure.

Let it go, Ben. I know about the hybrid in London.

I should've known the girls would talk. *I'd prefer you let tracking agents follow Lucas. You need to go back to Wisconsin, or at least meet Emma and I at the safe house.* She sneered. *Okay, fine. Do it your way. But I'm going on record as having directed against it.*

Parker? Jorgenson's thoughts interrupted our conversation. *Commander E agrees with you, but there's no other available agent with Molly's experience. Bianca and Claire have subdued the hybrid in London and are detaining him now. By all expectations, we believe Victor to be in London, so if Molly's up for it, let her do it.*

Yes, sir, I said, knowing I already lost the battle.

I ignored Emma's conversation with Lucas. He'd let her down. At least I wasn't the one to break the news he was a loser.

Lucas did it himself.

Chapter 92
Emma's Story

Lucas was a jerk.

"I called you, and you didn't answer. Emma, they were my ride. I *had* to go," he said.

I shouldn't have trusted him. And the worst part was that I couldn't even complain to Aunt Barb about what happened since I wasn't supposed to be here. What if I wouldn't have run into Ben? I mean, really? Lucas just left, when I was on my way to meet him?

"Look, we're at a house just a few blocks from the bar. We can come get you," he said, then added, "if you want."

"No, thanks," I answered and hung up. I was steaming mad, and Lucas knew it. Even if Ben couldn't take me back to my car in Highland Park, I knew there were trains running most of the night. I just had to get back to the Davis Street station, that was all. I picked at my salad, as Ben finished his burger. I wasn't hungry anymore.

The couple Ben knew on the opposite side of the restaurant glanced our way. "Looks like they're ready to go," Ben said. The auburn-haired girl smiled back, and the guy nodded. They looked to be about our age, or maybe a little older.

"Oh." It suddenly dawned on me that he wasn't here to be my knight in shining armor, though he played that part well. My little crisis interrupted his plans for the night. "Sorry. Thanks for rescuing me… and for dinner."

He put his hand on my arm. "Don't go. Come with me… it's just a few friends, and then I'll drive you back."

"Um… my car's in Highland Park."

"Okay, then I'll drive you to your car. Later."

My heart raced, and I was sure my face was bright red.

Of course, I had to accept his offer.

Chapter 93
Ben's Story

Emma blushed easily.

I reached for her hand, as we crossed the street. Reading her thoughts, I was flattered. I held back my smile, made small talk, and occasionally glanced at the Sleeper Agents that I introduced as friends. They followed us the two blocks to the safe house on Clark. The single-family home on Hinman was much nicer, but with looming hybrids in the area, I couldn't risk the distance. For now, the rundown, three-story, brown brick home would do. Not to mention, it was more realistic for a college party than the grandma-style Cape Cod.

Music thumped as we neared the safe house. Two agents on the porch greeted us when we arrived. They were rookies like Claire, but with other responsibilities. One tracked immortals, and the other did reconnaissance missions. The house was filled with agents from all divisions and tenures, a result of the Victor sighting and hybrid scare earlier that evening.

The tall building housed three apartments, one per floor. Doors were heavily guarded. Indestructible walls and unbreakable glass prevented unauthorized entrance. It was common in all safe houses. The only way in was with security clearance—something Victor would never receive. Even the portal in the attic was monitored.

"Hey, Ben!" a seasoned agent said, though we never worked together before. "Want a beer?"

"Sure. Emma, did you want one?" I asked, not letting go of her hand.

She nodded in response, although I felt her reluctance. I introduced her to the girls on the couch and the guys playing beer pong. She smiled and courteously asked and answered questions better than I expected, being the stranger in a group.

"Parker!" Pete Jorgenson's spoken voice surprised me. I turned to see my handler with an open Guinness.

"Hey. Haven't seen you in ages," I said, shaking his extended hand. "Pete, this is Emma." Jorgenson's appearance was a youthful twenty, without the receding hairline we were accustomed to back in our world.

"Emma, good to meet you." He reached for her hand and kissed the back of it.

A bit over the top, don't you think? I glared at him.

"It's nice meeting you too, Pete." Emma blushed.

"It's about time Ben brought someone to one of our parties." He winked at Emma, and then continued. "You don't look like a beer-drinking girl. How about a hard lemonade?" He didn't wait for a response. Instead, he turned toward a girl in the kitchen, who opened a bottle, poured its contents into an ice-filled plastic cup, and handed it to her.

"So, Emma, tell me about yourself. How did you and Parker, here, meet?" he asked, not skipping a beat.

I glared at him again.

Emma's rosy cheeks turned fire red, and she looked to the floor.

"Oh, I don't mean to put you on the spot," Jorgenson said. "I'm just happy he's found a girlfriend."

I was about to scream in his thoughts, when Emma regained her confidence. "Actually, Pete," she said, "we're just friends. Ben was my knight in shining armor tonight. He found me wandering and lost… with no cell phone."

"Is that right?"

She nodded, taking a sip from her drink. "How long have you known Ben?" Emma asked.

"Seems like forever," he responded, glancing my way. He took a liking to her spunkiness, which was good for me since it allowed me to fix Emma's phone and check in on my team. It was a window of distraction that Pete took advantage of. He and Emma began whispering and laughing.

What did you find? I asked Molly after learning that Claire and Bianca had everything under control back in London.

I followed the alpha's scent back to a house on Astor, she answered.

Any sign of the hybrid or his pack?

One was caught. Two are at large. He's being held in the city, she said. *The house has been cleared. I'm going in.* I watched through her eyes as she opened the wrought iron gate, climbed the handful of stairs, and entered through the double doors. The foyer was rich in detail with wide, cherry trim. To the left was a long sitting room. A Victorian loveseat in dark blue was against the wall. Rose-colored wing chairs sat at the window, separated by a pedestal table with an old, hand-painted red lamp.

As Molly ventured deeper into the room, she noticed a buffet near the open staircase. Atop the chest were antique photo frames filled with pictures of men and women. Her heart thumped faster, as she glanced at the collection. Memories of the London apartment filled her thoughts.

A picture of a young, dark-haired man with an older gentleman caught her eye. She picked it up and stared into it, though she didn't speak her thoughts. Others were of the same younger man in various stages and outfits. Some looked hundreds of years old, while others only decades. She opened the top drawer of the chest and found dozens of loose prints. Molly shuffled through them and again found the image—the same photo—of herself.

Her heart skipped a beat, and she gasped. This time, it was because the note in pencil on the back read *Mom.*

Chapter 94
Emma's Story

The lighthearted look on Ben's face disappeared.

His eyes squinted, and his smile was gone. Ben went from mingling around the room for an hour, like the party's host, to staring intently at the guys at the beer pong table. The game temporarily stopped, and I wondered if something happened.

As soon as the thought came to me, Ben looked up and winked.

Even though he didn't hover at my side, he was still incredibly attentive. I felt like a married couple that kept tabs on one another at an event—glancing at each other occasionally, nodding when they wanted a refill, or signaling when it was time to leave. Mom and Dad did that, I realized, as I watched Ben move to another group of people near the door. He shook hands with one guy, then looked over at me and smiled.

"He was quite popular in high school," Pete whispered when he noticed my stare.

I chuckled. Pete would have talked to me all night. I was sure of that. He was nice, polite, and funny. He told me story after story about them growing up together, followed by joke after joke. He had me laughing so hard, tears welled up in my eyes, which caught Ben's attention and brought him quickly to my side.

"I found a charger for your phone," Ben said after he pulled me into the empty kitchen.

"Great. Thanks." He was more accommodating than I was used to.

"Here." He handed the phone to me.

I shook my head, bewildered. "Where's the charger?"

"It's already charged. See? Full bars," he answered.

"Wow. That was fast!"

"Now you can call your friends whenever you want to leave."

My heart pitter-pattered and I paused, trying to formulate the right words. "I'm not ready to go yet," I finally said.

"Good. 'Cuz I don't want you to leave either." A smiled crossed his face.

I was lost in his chocolate-brown eyes.

He leaned toward me, and I was sure he would kiss me. I hoped he would, anyway. He moved closer, and I felt his breath on my cheek. My heart raced, and my palms got clammy.

As his lips neared mine, a dark-haired girl barged in from the back hall. Her entrance startled me, and the moment between Ben and me was gone. I could tell the girl was crying as she mumbled an apology when she saw us. It looked like she was crying. Seconds later, she was wrapped up in Pete's arms.

"Was that Molly?" I asked.

"Um, no," Ben answered.

I looked back to the girl, realizing she was shorter than Molly and had curly hair in a different shade.

"What happened to her?" I asked, more to myself than to him.

Ben shrugged. "I'm not sure. Come on." He grabbed my hand and led me out of the room.

The guys playing beer pong asked if we wanted to join the game. Before we could respond, Melissa called and arranged to pick me up. Ben gave her directions and within a few minutes, she was there.

Even though he held my hand when we walked out, Ben didn't try to kiss me again.

Chapter 95
Ben's Story

The last thing I wanted to do was put Emma in a car with her human friends.

I had her in a secured location and all to myself. Well, almost all to myself, before Molly blew it.

"I'm so sorry, Benjamin," Molly pleaded to me minutes later. "I wasn't thinking."

"Obviously!"

"Not clearly, anyway," she added. "I was just looking for someone to talk to."

Molly was calm given the circumstance and even though I was angry for her poorly timed entrance and initial lack of disguise, I completely understood her emotions. I didn't understand how she could have left a child—Victor's child—behind all those years ago.

"I had no idea the baby survived," she said to me in the third-floor conference room of the safe house. We were alone in the soundproof room that rookie ears couldn't penetrate.

"You didn't check?" I asked, irritated. "You died when you were pregnant with Victor's baby, and you didn't realize the baby survived?"

She looked to the floor, silent.

It wasn't like her to be absentminded. "Molly, how far along in your pregnancy were you… when Victor killed you?"

She shook her head. "I don't know. It was so long ago—"

"Think!"

"Six, seven months. Maybe. Benjamin, I'm not sure."

"And it didn't dawn on you to check what happened to the baby?"

"I was a human going through transition and admissions. I wasn't in any frame of mind to think about that."

"What about later?"

"What *about* later?" She repeated my words sarcastically.

"Did you ask about it? Did you wonder what happened to your baby?"

"No, Benjamin. I didn't." Molly tilted her head to one side and glared at me.

"What kind of mother are you?"

"How dare you, Benjamin Parker Holmes. I am *not* a mother!" Molly's piercing eyes flared, and I knew I hit a nerve. "What about you? Did *you* ever think about your son, Danny?"

"That's not even a comparison!" I knew she had a point. I took a deep breath. While I checked in on Danny several times since my death, I wasn't regularly following his life path. He had another decade left in his contract and when the time came, I'd be there.

"Funny how the rules are different for you, Benjamin!"

Pete Jorgenson appeared in the doorway. His presence silenced us and lowered the anger level within the room.

"Knowing what happened to Molly's child wasn't her responsibility. It was the job of her Admissions Counselor to know what happened to the fetus. My staff is already on top of it and, right now, it appears to have been reported as too gestationally young to have lived. We have no record of assignment. No immortal spirit listed on the books," Jorgenson stated.

"What does that mean?" Molly asked, though we both knew what that meant. It meant the baby could have only survived if Victor gave it life. A life different from that of a human, but not quite that of an immortal.

It meant Molly's son was out there for almost two centuries with immortal abilities we weren't even aware of.

A son Victor named Aberthol.

Chapter 96
Emma's Story

Monday morning, I awoke before my alarm.

Chester wasn't ready to get up when I stepped into the shower. The weekend was a whirlwind, and I couldn't wait to get to school and see Ben.

"You're up early. Did I miss something? A meeting at school, maybe?" Aunt Barb asked. She was making pancakes when I walked into the kitchen. Instead of her already-showered-and-dressed morning look that I was accustomed to, she was in a pink silk robe and fluffy slipper-sandals.

"No. Just up early." I helped myself to a glass of orange juice. Glancing at the microwave, I noticed it was an hour earlier than my normal breakfast time.

"I thought maybe there was some homecoming thing this morning," she said, her back to me as she flipped the hot cakes on the griddle. Her hair was down and even though it didn't look like bedhead, it wasn't neatly combed or styled.

"No… I couldn't sleep anymore. Sorry I woke you." I gave a weak smile and took a sip of juice. I couldn't tell her I was anxious to see Ben because then I'd have to admit I spent Saturday night with him at a party and not with Melissa like I told her. Well, I did meet up with Melissa later that night, so it wasn't totally a lie, right?

"Don't worry. I always get up at this time," she said. "Oh. I almost forgot." She looked excited for a second, and then went to the mudroom to grab something. "Can you watch the pancakes? They should be done," she yelled from the other room.

I did as she asked and turned off the griddle.

When she came back, her arms were full of things that made no sense to me. "I dug these out for you," she said with a smirk.

I didn't understand what I would do with a bunch of clothes, but I grinned in response and fixed my plate with a short stack of pancakes and syrup.

"Neal said everyone dresses up this week. For homecoming. Hat day, eighties day…" She rambled on and on about how they had spirit week when she was in high school too. She held up a striped pair of leggings, a grey, off-the-shoulder sweatshirt with matching headband, a brown cowboy hat she said Uncle Rob once wore to a costume party, and an ugly black-and-white checkered sweater. "I thought you could use these for your dress-up days this week," she said, pleased with her effort. "If you want. You don't have to."

"Thanks, Aunt Barb," I said and gave her a hug.

"I always loved homecoming week."

I took a bite of pancake to avoid answering. Unfortunately, it encouraged her to talk about her high school days in Westport. I barely listened, picking at my breakfast.

"I thought kids today went toilet papering. Seniors decorated the houses of juniors… Does that still happen? Or was it just my generation?" she asked.

"They still do."

She clutched her coffee cup with both hands and took a long drink. "Didn't you want to participate in that?" she asked, putting the cup on the counter between us.

"Maybe."

"Neal said Lucas was going out last night."

"I'm not sure," I mumbled. Lucas and I hadn't spoken since Saturday. I was still mad he didn't meet me in Evanston like he told me he would, but I couldn't tell her how he ditched me.

Aunt Barb's eyes opened wide, like she wanted to say something. After a brief pause, she spit out, "Just so you know, I'm fine with it—if you want to go, that is. I know it's past the city curfew and everything. Neal said officers just look the other way. Well, of course, unless there's trouble."

I nodded. "Okay, thanks."

***

I got a good parking spot in the student lot when I arrived at school that morning.

The cowboy hat Aunt Barb gave me slipped down on my forehead, the brim covering my eyes when I put my backpack inside my locker. I heard voices around me, as kids started filling in and the first bell rang. It was our warning we had six minutes until first period.

Aftermath

When I pushed the hat out of the way, I noticed Ben at the end of the hall, talking with Drew and a bunch of guys I recognized from the soccer team.

Everyone was wearing a hat, except Ben. Drew wore a bright green one that looked like it belonged to a Peter Pan costume. Another guy wore a tall, pointed hat, like a giant, striped cone on his head, while someone else wore three baseball hats, one atop the other turned in different directions. When they neared me, Drew yelled, "Nice hat, Bennett!"

Ben nodded. His eyes met mine briefly, and I thought I caught a glimpse of a smile before I turned away, feeling my face flush already. My heart skipped a beat like it did Saturday night, and I couldn't help but remember that almost kiss. Well, my hopeful almost kiss, that was.

I jumped when I heard a voice behind me.

"Hey, I stopped at your house," Lucas said.

"Oh." I glanced at him, and then looked away.

"Your aunt said you left early. You know, I can drive you to school."

"That's okay. I can drive." I grabbed my books and avoided making eye contact.

"Lose the hat."

"What?"

"It looks stupid," he answered. His expression was serious.

Screw it. I glared at him.

"You're still mad at me, aren't you?"

"Yes." I felt a twinge of satisfaction that he knew I was angry.

He smirked. "You'll get over it," he said, and then leaned down to kiss me. I turned my head, but not fast enough. His lips caught the corner of my mouth. Lucas turned and left quickly. When I looked up, I realized Ben was watching.

The rest of the week sped by. Most people dressed up and, despite Lucas' instruction to lose the hat, I kept it on all day and opted to wear the leg warmers on '80's day and the ugly sweater the next. Ben never dressed up, and neither did Lucas. Claire did, and so did most of the girls I knew.

At lunch, Lucas acknowledged me with a nod or smile, but never sat with me. I didn't expect him to, and frankly was happy he didn't ask me to join his boys' table either. Ben noticed me a few times, but we never had a chance to talk.

In study hall on Monday, Lucas stopped me in the library and made me sit with him. Well, of course, not physically forced me to sit with him. He gave me sad eyes, and I caved in.

"You can't be mad at me, Emma," he said. He justified leaving me stranded in Evanston by telling me he didn't have a car and was at the mercy of some guy I never heard of. "Emma, you didn't even tell me you were coming. I couldn't make everyone stay. I had to go with them. Abe was my ride. Besides, you ran into Parker, didn't you?"

I wanted to scream at him. I mean, boyfriends didn't do that kind of thing. Right? Then again, Lucas wasn't boyfriend material and of all the boys I met, he was the last one I wanted to date.

"Some guys were following me—" I began.

"I'm not surprised. I'd follow some hottie on the street, too." His grin was contagious. "Come on, Em," Lucas said, touching my hand.

I could have stayed angry longer. He was a jerk, leaving me, but he was right. He didn't know I was going there, and I wasn't planning to see him. I called him for help when I couldn't reach Melissa.

After I forgave him, I realized how I was manipulated, which made me mad at myself.

Later, I wondered if he would have felt bad if he knew how scared I was and how creepy those guys were. No matter what, I knew Lucas wasn't someone I could rely on.

Tuesday, Lucas walked me to study hall, so I couldn't look for Ben. Wednesday, Ben was out sick. At least that was what Claire said when I got up the courage to ask.

On Thursday, Lucas had a meeting with the football coach during study hall. I went to the small reference room where Ben and I met weeks before. I worked on my calculus homework and sat alone. Before I knew it, the period was almost over and there was no sign of Ben. When I left the library, walking through the main section on the first floor, I found Ben sitting with Stephanie. Figured. She chatted non-stop and even though he appeared to be listening intently, he looked up and smiled as I passed by.

That night, Neal and Lucas stopped by with carryout pizzas for dinner. I was surprised when I opened the door and saw Lucas and his dad standing on the porch. Aunt Barb worked late, getting home mere minutes before they arrived. It sounded like she called them, though she didn't tell me that. My aunt whipped up a huge salad, while Lucas and I set the table.

It was becoming a habit. Dinner with the Crandons was a weekly—or more often—event. It justified to me all the more reason why I couldn't stay mad at Lucas for long. Well, I couldn't let him know he irritated me, anyway.

What bothered me the most was that he didn't even seem to notice how I sacrificed my beliefs to forgive him.

"Emma, have you been out toilet papering this week, too?" Neal asked as we sat at the dining room table.

"Um, no," I answered, swallowing a bite of salad.

"You can come with us tonight," Lucas added.

"Oh, you should," Aunt Barb said. "We had so much fun homecoming week… when I was in school." I dreaded hearing her reminiscent stories of high school that I heard earlier that week. Lucas grinned at me, and then rolled his eyes as Neal joined in. Finally, I agreed to go.

An hour later, Lucas and I headed to his house two blocks away to pick up his car. Neal told Lucas that a guy should drive, even though I offered, which meant walking to his house. It was already dark and cool when we headed out the door.

Lucas didn't reach for my hand the way Ben did the other night. Then again, I balled my hands into fists and shoved them into my pockets, where I stuffed the hat and gloves my aunt insisted I bring along.

I couldn't get Ben out of my mind. He seemed so genuine compared to Lucas.

We walked the first half in silence. After we turned the corner, Lucas began to talk about plans for after the dance. "Trent's having people over. You know… a sleepover. Couples." He paused and looked at me, but I glanced down at the sidewalk. "I said we were in."

What? I shook my head. "I, ah… I'm not sure my aunt will go for that." I hoped she'd be against it. "Besides, Claire invited us girls to her house."

"Well, you can *tell* Barb you're at Claire's…"

"No, I don't think so. I mean, your dad's not okay with it, is he?"

"What's he gonna do?"

"Say no. Ground you," I said and then added, "Kick you out, again?"

He shrugged. "I dropped it on my dad. He didn't say much."

I felt sick.

"Don't worry. It's cool."

"What exactly did you tell your dad? I mean, I'm surprised he'd agree. And what about Trent's parents? Will they be there?"

Lucas laughed at first, and then answered as we reached his house. "I told him everyone was staying. Girls in one room. Guys in the other. You know." He smirked. "I lied. Besides, he won't know."

He unlocked the side door of the house, and I took a deep breath.

"Car's open. I'll grab my keys." He nodded toward the blue sedan parked in the driveway. "Unless, of course, you want to see my bedroom." He raised his eyebrows and gave me a lopsided grin.

"Ah, no. Claire's waiting for me at Drew's." I definitely wasn't ready for what he implied.

"You're right. We've got the weekend." He winked and headed into the house, returning with keys in hand.

"Ray offered up toilet paper he has at work. We gotta pick it up," he said, starting up the engine. Ten minutes later, Lucas pulled into an auto body shop in Riverside.

Ray was just as friendly as the first time we met. Creepy, but nice.

"Emma, good to see you," he said, putting his hand on my back. "Come. Sit down. Lucas can load up the trunk. Let's talk." Ray motioned to a burgundy leather chair with studded accents. It was across from an oversized desk with scattered papers and antique-looking pictures. I was completely uncomfortable, like I was called to the principal's office.

I sat anyway.

"So, Lucas tells me the two of you are going to a dance at the high school this Saturday. His mother wants to take pictures. She'd like you to come to the house. Okay?"

I nodded, afraid not to. His piercing eyes never left mine.

"You know. The typical: Smile for the camera. Pin on a corsage. That sorta thing."

I wasn't sure where the courage came from, but when I found my voice, I said, "My aunt is having everyone at the Inn. All of our friends will be there. At Lake Bell. Maybe you'd like to come, too?"

He nodded slowly, his oversized lips pulled taut in a frown. He looked deep in thought, and then raised his eyebrows before he spoke. "Lots of people, you say?"

"Um, yeah. I think so. TJ will be there with Molly. And probably Trent… but I'm not sure who Trent's date is."

"Molly?" Wrinkles creased his forehead.

"Yes. She's TJ's girlfriend," I said. "Long, dark hair."

Again, he nodded slowly.

"You're welcome to come. My aunt is… Well, I'm sure she won't mind if you and Lucas' mom come."

"At the Inn?" He seemed interested. A wave of excitement flashed through his eyes.

"Yeah. Carmichael Inn. Four o'clock."

"Okay," he said. "We'll be there." I was relieved he seemed happy. He gave me a brief grin, as Lucas came back into his Ray's office.

"Hey, look who I found loading up his car," a dark-haired guy said. He followed Lucas into the office and gave him a gentle shove. He looked older than Lucas, about mid-twenties, with curly hair he wore trimmed short. Despite his tough, rugged look and leather jacket, his eyes seemed kind.

Ray mumbled something under his breath when the tough guy noticed me.

"Oh, sorry. I didn't realize I was interrupting." The guy smiled. He looked familiar.

"Hey. Be polite, not your normal selves," Ray interjected, while Lucas punched the guy's shoulder. They acted like brothers fighting over something meaningless. "Abe, this here's Emma. She's Lucas' girlfriend, so be nice to her."

"Umm… hi," I said and stood up. I didn't have the courage to correct Ray. Worst of all, his comment didn't seem to bother Lucas.

Abe extended his hand, and I placed mine in his. I expected a handshake. Instead, he leaned down and kissed it. My thoughts immediately went to Pete and the house party on Saturday night, followed quickly by the memory of that almost kiss with Ben and the girl that interrupted us.

Odd, but something about Abe reminded me of her.

Chapter 97
Ben's Story

I'd been waiting outside of Drew's house for over an hour.

Claire said Emma and Lucas were on their way. There was no need for me to join the stupid ritual prematurely. TP'ing was the last thing I wanted to do, tonight or ever, but as any good agent, I complied with expectations in my undercover role. I was just procrastinating joining my so-called peers.

A crackling of leaves and branches brought me out of my daydream. I spun around and propelled to the security of the large oak tree branch twenty-two feet off the ground. I glanced down and saw a lone deer several yards away, hidden in the thick woods across the street from Drew's house.

I held position, quiet and still. I counted souls in the vicinity; eight teenagers in Drew's house, including Drew, Claire, Molly, and Stephanie. Drew's mom was sound asleep in her bedroom on the second floor. The other homes on the dead-end road were vacant. Approximately one half mile away, a car headed in this direction held three souls, all male. Another vehicle, three quarters of a mile from my position, had one individual. It turned eastbound, as I watched from my perch.

Another crackle had me scanning the woods and not the streets.

An essence of something non-human floated amongst the trees. A brief breeze carried it to and around me. It was not the sweet sickly odor of a hybrid that I grew accustomed to here in rural Westport. Instead, it was more of a sensation rather than a smell. As my mind circled it round and round, attempting to gather the memory in my recordable brain, another noise distracted me.

When I looked behind me, I saw Bianca approaching, having used a portal nearby. She didn't see me or sense me.

I should have called out to her, but something stopped me. Watching her from a distance, I noticed her casual stroll through the trees. She slowed her pace and looked over her shoulder before proceeding forward again. She looked left, then right, stopping, starting, and walking backward. She stood still for a moment, and then spun slowly around. I felt it best to stay silent.

The deer I saw earlier suddenly spooked, leaping over a fallen branch and out of sight. Bianca jumped with the slight noise its hoofs made on the dried leaves. As her breathing slowed and her heart rate returned to normal, the essence I felt earlier came flooding back.

It was stronger this time and more intense, almost mesmerizing and sickening.

In the distance, I heard the sound of rubber on gravel, but my mind was wrapped around the immense presence of something I never trained to battle.

Around me, like a fog, I was overwhelmed. As soon as it came, it left.

I shook my head, hoping to shed the daze I was in. When I felt clear again, I realized a car pulled into Drew's driveway, followed by another. Looking below and around me, there was no sign of Bianca or anyone else for that matter, human or immortal.

Not that I could tell, anyway.

Chapter 98
Emma's Story

"Ray's kinda creepy," I blurted to Lucas, as we drove to Drew's house. "I mean, he's nice. Just a little different." Once the words were out, I couldn't take them back.

His chuckle relieved me. "He's intense."

"He called me your girlfriend." I paused, hoping to gauge his response. When he didn't comment, I said. "We're just friends, you know." My voice sounded weak, even to my ears. I didn't want to be his girlfriend, but I didn't want him mad at me, either.

"Yeah. Whatever."

After a few blocks of silence, I said, "I invited him to pictures before homecoming."

He glared at me. "Why'd you do that?"

"Umm... because I thought I should." He was focused on the road again, but he didn't answer me. "He said your mom wanted pictures," I explained. "I thought it would be easier if they came to the lake, instead of us going there."

He nodded, and then sat silent for a while. The thump of the music in the car was the only noise. Finally, he spoke. "My dad doesn't like him."

I didn't respond.

"He thinks Ray's trouble."

"Why?"

He laughed. "Because he is."

Huh?

"Ray doesn't have much respect for cops, you know?" He glanced my way, and then stared at the road. "I got the pot from him."

"Oh." Why would he tell me this?

We drove again in silence before he said, "I never told anyone that."

Our eyes met for an instant. "I won't tell."

He smiled, and then turned into Drew's driveway. "Good news is that Ray's giving us the booze for Trent's party on Saturday."

Great. Another lie I'd have to keep from Aunt Barb.

Chapter 99
Ben's Story

A few hours spent TP'ing was more than enough.

The old Hamilton read eight minutes past two o'clock when I last glanced at it.

"Just a few rolls left. Might as well finish them," Drew said, tossing one to me and another to Lucas. It was the last house of the night, down from Trent's.

Emma and Claire helped with a house nearby, some soccer player they knew, but once the trees were satisfactorily covered, they decided to go home. "We're cold," Claire told me when I raised an eyebrow. The October air was chilly, so I couldn't blame them. Claire volunteered to take Emma home since it was obvious Lucas had no intention of leaving.

I unrolled a tail of the tissue and tossed the roll up at the maple tree beside the house. It was on the edge of the cul-de-sac, adjacent to the farm titled in Henry Nichols name. The farm that was quiet and almost vacant since old man Kensington disappeared, and I had my encounter with the hybrids.

The roll unraveled, leaving a trail of white streamer in the upper branches before falling back down, landing on a limb fifteen feet above ground.

Lucas was around the corner, at the front of the house, while Drew was busy decorating bushes like it was Christmas and the toilet paper was tree garland. Neither would see if I suddenly jumped up to the branch and loosened the roll from its ledge. Of course, I could leave it up in the trees, but a good stretch would loosen my stiff legs. Not to mention, extraordinary athletic abilities were one of the things I enjoyed most about being an immortal.

As I leaped in the air, the unforgettable, sweet scent of a hybrid caressed my nostrils, immediately followed by the bitter apple aftertaste. I hesitated, lingering longer in the air than I should have.

"Shit, man! How high can you jump?" Lucas yelled when I descended.

Damn it! I should have left the paper in the tree.

"You've got some vertical." Lucas chuckled. I'd have to eliminate his memory. I hated this guy as it was. Now, he was making me do more work, too.

When I landed back on the ground, I was suddenly in the spotlight of an exterior light that turned on unexpectedly. Lights aimed on the front and sides of the house brightened our work and exposed the three of us.

Drew yelled to run and Lucas scattered, me in tow. We weaved between the mature trees and jumped over small, fallen branches and twigs until reaching the perimeter of the property. Drew hurdled the fence that separated the private residence from the adjacent farm.

Lucas swore as he stumbled over the barbed wire fence, landing in the post-harvest soil. When it was my turn, I could smell the blood on the barbs and dipped my forefinger in it. A tiny drop was all I needed to know his blood type was rare. What was alarming was that the red and white blood cell counts were not in proportion for a healthy human. I was ten yards from the fence when I realized some of his oddly shaped cells were affixed to a component I hadn't encountered before.

In order to test it further, I'd need another sample.

"Parker, come on!" Drew yelled as I sprinted back to the fence.

"I dropped my phone," I answered and bent down to the ground. With one hand on the barb, I gathered a second droplet and notified my handler.

On it, Jorgenson answered, and I turned back to the guys.

Chapter 100
Emma's Story

I touched up my lip gloss and glanced in the full-length mirror, waiting for Lucas.

The image staring back at me was better than I ever looked before. Then again, with Aunt Barb, the little touches were everything.

She woke me up that morning earlier than normal.

Two hours later and after a mani-pedi, I was seated in a swivel chair at the salon. A trendy-looking, twenty-something-year-old stylist swept my hair into a cascade of curls. An older woman attended to my makeup. She said it would complement my bright blue eyes. She was right.

I loved the look staring back at me.

When the doorbell rang, I was lost in thought of past dances. Chester flew off the bed, dragging my comforter with him. His bark echoed, as I followed him down the stairs to greet Lucas and Neal.

"You look… great!" Lucas said. His wide grin made me feel pretty.

"So do you," I said. Even though I didn't like Lucas in that way, he was attractive all dressed up. "You matched my dress." I smiled, noticing his black shirt and fuchsia-striped tie.

Aunt Barb insisted I pin the boutonniere on Lucas' shirt, even though I was nervous I'd stick him. Lucas stood patiently as I tried, only for the pink rose to flip over on itself. She snapped photo after photo of what drew laughter out of everyone but me. I was suddenly overwhelmed with embarrassment, my hands shaking as I tried a second time and stuck him.

Lucas cringed, and then recovered.

"Sorry," I mumbled.

When Aunt Barb suggested I place my hand under his shirt as a guide, it worked. Though I was completely uncomfortable touching his bare chest with my fingers.

A few photos later, with a corsage on my wrist, we were on our way to the Inn.

Lucas and I drove separate from my aunt and Neal. Once alone, he asked if I reconsidered staying at Trent's overnight. He didn't seem happy that I planned to stay at Claire's house, like I told him the first time he asked. Instead, he changed the subject and offered up some girlie drink Ray gave him.

"It tastes like fruit punch," Lucas explained. "I guess it's really good. He thought you girls would like it better than the whiskey he gave me."

"Okay. I'll try it later. Claire's brother is designated driver, I guess."

He didn't answer, and I wondered what he was thinking.

We were the first to arrive at the Inn, which wasn't surprising to me. Aunt Barb directed staff the minute she walked in the door, confirming locations and times for our dinner and hors d'oeuvres for the parents.

I was used to it, but Lucas seemed uncomfortable. He put his hands in his pockets, took them out, and then put them back in again. Pacing the length of the room, he occasionally stopped to look out the window. The room was used for business meetings and weddings and had a private balcony overlooking the lake. Neatly trimmed mature trees offered shade and still gave incredible views, especially at sunset.

I wondered if Lucas was nervous about Ray and his mom coming.

Photography gear was set up in the corner of the room. A middle-aged man and a young woman set up equipment. He adjusted the height of a tripod, while she angled umbrella lights toward a white backdrop already in place.

"I'd like the entire group lined up on the balcony, shot from below. Then another pose at the water's edge," Aunt Barb told them.

Neal and I chuckled about my aunt's obsession with perfection.

"I think she's got OCD," I said.

"It *is* her job to make events memorable, Emma," Neal reminded me.

I nodded. I liked Neal. He was calm, while my aunt seemed so high energy.

"The garden would be nice for smaller groups or couples' photos, too," my aunt said to the middle-aged man. She pointed out locations across the property.

"She's over the top," I whispered to Neal, who grinned, tight lipped.

A few minutes later, Claire and Drew arrived, followed by Justin and Hannah, which seemed to please Lucas. Kids and parents filed in one after another, and I found myself losing track of who was there and who wasn't. Claire and I posed for photos with our dates and friends, snapping more than we'd ever need.

As Claire and I sipped on non-alcoholic spritzers, I noticed Lucas greeting a blonde-haired woman near the bar. I didn't realize it was his mom until I saw Ray nearby. Part of me couldn't get over him giving Lucas the pot. What kind of stepdad was he?

"Wish me luck," I whispered to Claire, and then joined Lucas.

Ray winked at me, as he shook my hand. "Good to see you again," he said.

Char gave me a hug. Even though her eyes were bright and clear and she looked much better than the first time we met, she was boney under the black, boxy dress that hung from her shoulders.

"Lucas. You gave her the corsage already!" Char said, irritated.

"Um, yeah, Mom. I gave it to her when I picked her up." He never called her Mom, and I wondered if Ray had a talk with him about it.

"It's alright, Char," Ray answered in a calming tone.

"No. No, it's not," Char objected. "I wanted pictures of the pinning." She reached up to touch Lucas' pink rose, but Ray held her shaking hand down.

"My aunt took pictures. I can get you copies." I interjected, and then regretted it.

"It's not the same. I didn't see you pin it on!" she shrieked.

"Mom, please," Lucas began and took a deep breath. I couldn't get over her insistence.

"Don't *please* me, Lucas Victor Crandon." She glared at him.

"Charlene, keep your voice down. We don't need to draw attention," Ray said. Then, turning to me, he added, "Emma, I'm sorry about this. She gets like this... once in a while."

An old, gray-haired man in a pinstriped navy suit approached Ray and whispered in his ear, while Char mumbled to Lucas.

"Mom, stop already. I knew this was a bad idea," Lucas said, more to me than to her.

Ray nodded at the man and then addressed Char. His voice was low and firm, but I couldn't make out the words. The gray-haired man walked through the crowd of kids and parents, exiting through a set of double doors, just as Ben walked in, looking incredibly attractive. They must have bumped into one another, because as soon as Ben saw him, he stopped and turned around.

"Emma? Emma, what do you think?" Lucas asked. His eyes were wide.

"Sorry. What?"

"I suggested you and Lucas pose. You know. *Pretend* you're pinning on the flower-thing. Make Char *happy*, would ya?" Ray's snarky tone made me uncomfortable.

"Oh, yeah. Sure. Okay." I was caught daydreaming and clearly scolded. Ray wasn't the person I wanted on my bad side.

"Outside. Hurry up. Let's go," he said with a sense of urgency.

Even for him, it was awkward, but I followed Ray anyway.

Chapter 101
Ben's Story

Stephanie barely stopped talking since I picked her up.

It was nervous chatter that continued aloud and in her head. The mere minutes she was outwardly quiet, she chewed on her lower lip. It was then that her random thoughts were the most entertaining and the most annoying, especially when they included me. *I can't wait for everyone to see us. We look great as a couple.* And the best of all, *I hope he kisses me in front of Lucas.*

Fat chance I'd do that.

Thinking of ways to get even with Molly for not warning me was a great pastime while in the midst of Stephanie's company. At least daydreaming about other things would prevent me from hearing Stephanie's irritating voice and her juvenile thoughts.

By the time we got to the Inn for pictures, I was mentally exhausted. I did everything a good date was supposed to do. I met her parents, gave her a corsage, posed for pictures, and opened the car door, but I avoided holding her hand. I didn't need to download any more information.

As we walked in the door, I smelled a hybrid. Stephanie was irritated with my inattentiveness, but I didn't care. It wasn't like all eyes were on us, or anyone would announce our arrival, like they did in the Cinderella-type of movies she envisioned in her head.

I offered to get us drinks and went to the parking lot instead. I followed a man resembling a younger version of George Kensington, the farmer that went missing. I was sure it was him and guessed Victor converted him to a hybrid.

The parking lot was full. Aside from the usual customers, thirty-plus kids and their parents descended upon the Inn for the photo op. The hybrid's scent led me to the far corner to the last row near the woods, where a lone Audi sat idling with two passengers.

Even though I was sure the man I saw was Kensington, I needed confirmation to appease the paperwork generals. Before I reached the car, the scent vanished, leaving me questioning if I was losing my mind.

Backup's on the way, Jorgenson confirmed. The Prestons, Molly's undercover parents, were heading over as part of the homecoming festivities, anyway. Even though tracking hybrids wasn't their forte, having someone was better than no one when dealing with Victor.

The driver rolled down his window when I reached him. "Can I help you, young man?" The man was the same age as Kensington, with similar gray hair, but he wasn't the same man. His wife stared at me with bright wide eyes that disclosed her fear. Both were human. Their hearts raced as a result of my approach.

"Sorry. I thought you were someone else," I answered solemnly. "Have a good evening."

The man nodded and rolled up the window, as his wife asked what I said. She suffered from undiagnosed Alzheimer's. He'd have a long road ahead of him, I thought, as I called off the backup and headed into the Inn.

Stephanie gave me a stern look when we met at the bar.

"Sorry. Bathroom break. Did you want the punch? Otherwise, I heard they've got some spritzer," I said, trying to be attentive.

"Yeah, sure. Spritzer." She smiled. Even though she didn't say it aloud, when Stephanie searched the room, her thoughts screamed, *Where's Lucas?*

I didn't mind, actually. She wasn't my first choice for a date, either. As a gentleman, I went through the motions, getting her a drink, posing for pictures, and mingling with her friends. She wasn't nearly as compromising when I suggested we get a photo with Drew and Claire. Instead, she rolled her eyes and pointed out someone else she knew.

Molly, what's your ETA? I asked.

She's already on your nerves?

I took a deep breath.

Okay, okay. I sense your irritation. We're three minutes out, she answered. *Oh, by the way, nice job stalking the elderly couple. You actually fell for a bait and switch?* I heard her chuckle in my head as I sipped on a 7UP and Stephanie talked about where she got her dress.

"You look really nice," I told her. After all, it was expected.

Benjamin. Behave! She's actually a nice girl, Molly scolded.

By the time Molly arrived, the photographer called everyone for a group photo. Stephanie grabbed my hand and led me out to the balcony. I was a pawn in her game of chess. She directed which way to face, and what side she wanted to be on. The photographer ordered people to smile and clicked away.

A gentle breeze blew by, carrying the familiar scent I grew to hate. Bait and switch again, I thought, when the smell quickly disappeared. I would have left to check the area, but as the photographer moved everyone to the stairs, I saw Emma and lost all interest in hybrids.

If my heart were able to stop beating, it would have.

Brunette curls framed Emma's ivory cheeks that pinkened when I said hello. Her eyes glanced away and then back at me. Time stood still. My mouth was suddenly dry and my palms sweaty. I was sixteen again, like the first time she spoke to me at the island on Lake Bell. Emma was more beautiful than Elizabeth was on our wedding day.

My mind wandered back to that day when I stood at the altar of Holy Name Church. Elizabeth walked toward me, a smile plastered on her face. Her white satin dress clung to her curves. When her father raised her veil and her blue eyes met mine, they sparkled. We recited our vows, and I promised to love her forever.

It was why I was here.

Stephanie nudged me, and I snapped back to reality. "Let's move by Molly," she said.

Instead, I floated a different idea to the photographer. Suddenly, he had another lineup in mind and I found myself settling in beside Emma. It took all of my self-control not to tell her who I really was. I envisioned sweeping her up in my arms and kissing her until she remembered, but I didn't.

Like a dog marking its territory, Lucas wedged himself between us. It was obvious he caught our glances. Emma tensed when his hand touched her. I really needed to do something about him.

It aggravated me that Emma let him back into her life after the incident in Evanston. Then again, I understood the need for her to keep peace and maintain whatever family she had left, despite how unconventional a family that was.

The thought stirred further irritation that Jorgenson couldn't diagnose the component in Lucas' blood sample.

It mutated, Jorgenson told me the day before.

What do you mean?

I mean, the sample didn't contain any abnormal components like you indicated.

What? It was there, I answered.

But it wasn't present when the sample was transported through the portal and checked in at the lab.

Which means?

It means he's normal. We've got it under observation, just in case.

Have you seen this before? I asked, though I already knew the answer was no.

Sorry, Ben, Jorgenson said, his tone low and sympathetic.

The photographer snapped a few shots, while a couple of guys cracked jokes behind us and parents mingled in clusters lakeside.

Barb Carmichael chatted with Drew's mom. TJ's dad talked politics with Grant Preston, while Stephanie's mom stood by my aunt and commented how pretty the Inn was at this time of year. "Perfect for pictures," she said.

The October afternoon was unseasonably warm, which brought everyone outdoors and had the dads talking about golf like it was still summer. I'd have to remember to thank Jorgenson for holding back the cold front originally forecasted for the weekend.

When Lucas leaned closer to Emma for the photo, I cringed. I began to wonder if Neal and Char were normal. Well, human, that was. I remembered how abnormal Char's mind was, but I chalked it up to drug addiction, not rare components in her bloodstream.

Jorgenson, I summoned. *What's Lucas' blood type?*

O positive, he answered seconds later. *Why?*

Do you have record of Char's blood type?

We don't keep any records on that. Benjamin, despite your observations, she's never hit the radar.

That was what I was afraid of.

Wait. Are you questioning if she's Lucas' biological mother? he asked.

I wasn't, but—

That's been confirmed, he said.

And paternity?

Nothing's in the file.

I loosened my shield and called to the agent posing as Molly's dad. The photographer continued snapping away. *Grant, do you keep medical records on police officers?*

Yes, he answered instantaneously. He was a physician at Westport Memorial. I told him what I was looking for and watched as he excused himself from the conversation with Tom Lambert.

The photographer dismissed the kids, and we dispersed. Staff circulated with trays of appetizers and beverages, as small groups of people took their own photos in the garden, on the stone patio, and at the lake.

Stephanie instructed her mother to take pictures of her, Molly, and several other girls in every setting and in a variety of poses, while I joined the rest of the guys hovering close enough not to get in trouble, yet far enough away not to get assigned a task. One poor guy wasn't paying attention and got too close. He was suddenly juggling multiple phones and cameras, ordered to take pictures. I felt his pain when his date complained that he didn't tell them to say cheese and as a result, she wasn't ready. "My eyes were closed!" she whined.

Even Stephanie rolled her eyes. I guessed that was what Molly meant when she said Stephanie wasn't that bad. Until now, I couldn't believe anyone could be worse than Stephanie was.

TJ nudged my arm. "Lucas hid some vodka in the bushes around the corner."

"Let's go." We casually backed away from the group and took the path past the staircase and out of view. A brown paper bag was tucked among a patch of impeccably trimmed, knee-high shrubs. TJ poured a healthy dose of the clear liquid in his half glass of coke, and then poured some in mine. I stirred the cocktail with my finger and took a sip. Vodka and 7UP wasn't my first choice, but neither was pretending to be a teenager again.

"Coke's not much better with it," TJ said when I glanced at him. "I think Lucas has whiskey for later. You going to Trent's?"

I nodded as Molly asked where we were, and TJ rattled off who expected to be there.

Nervous TJ will share something? I teased.

No. Okay, maybe, Molly answered, though she didn't need to be. TJ talked about the party more than anything. I really wasn't interested. I had other things on my mind, like watching Emma. Considering TJ was a good guy, I acted like I cared.

We headed back on the walkway, where the uncomfortable aroma of a hybrid met me head on. TJ never noticed, but the scent was overwhelming once we rounded the edge of the staircase. The crowd of kids and parents was thicker than when we left, which made locating its source more difficult.

I scanned the group, looking to pick up where the scent came from. When TJ noticed my look, he casually pointed toward the gazebo. "Molly and

Steph are over there. Hey, Trent's here. With that foreign exchange student."

"Yeah. I see 'em."

"I say we stay here until summoned otherwise," he said and chuckled.

I nodded, still searching for the hybrid. Nothing seemed out of place. Human thoughts appeared normal.

No sign of it over here, Molly said from the left side of the premises.

I don't smell anything either, Claire answered from the patio on the opposite end.

It seems to be coming from the lake. By the pier, in front of me. As the thought came to mind, I noticed Emma heading straight into it.

I told TJ I'd be back and went after her, crossing through grass patches that didn't look like they were ever stepped on before. When I circled around a group of giggly girls and another cluster of parents, I sensed the essence of something non-human. It had to be Victor. Where could he be hiding and why?

Emma reached the building at the shoreline and turned out of sight. I picked up my pace, navigating the winding sidewalk past more teenagers. When I thought I was clear of anyone that could slow me down, Lucas' mom took a step backward, bumping into me. She was uneasy in her heels and practically fell.

"Oh, dear! I'm so sorry," Char said when I caught her.

"It's fine. Are you alright?"

"Yes. Yes. Oh… I know you." She grabbed my hand in both of hers. "You're that sweet boy that stopped by the house. You're friends with Lucas." She turned sideways to look at Neal and some black-haired man who faced the other way.

I nodded, and the download processed. Disjointed files loaded sporadically, same as last time. I hoped I'd learn something new, or uncover a hidden map. No luck.

"Ray! Ray! This is…" She attempted to get the attention of the dark-haired man. "What's your name again?" She looked at me.

"Ben."

"Ray, this is Ben. He's friends with Lucas," she said to him. Ray didn't turn or answer her until Neal gestured in my direction. Neal's relief when Ray stopped talking would have been evident even if I couldn't read his mind. He immediately took a pull of his beer when Ray turned away.

"Yah-yeah. I'm Ray," he said, extending his hand to me. Ray was about Neal's age with a similar build, but a few inches shorter. He wore navy slacks and a starched white shirt with his sleeves rolled up, exposing a thick, gold-link chain on his wrist. He was the opposite of Char's disheveled look in her oversized dress. By contrast, Ray's thin, dark hair was neatly trimmed and combed perfectly in place. He carried himself with confidence, while she had none.

Before I shook his hand, I already knew he owned an auto repair shop and sold used cars on the adjacent lot in Riverside for the past seventeen years. He had a firm grip, but unlike other humans I met, I got nothing. No downloaded files other than those in his current memory, like the names and addresses of the three salesmen and two mechanics that worked for him. I got lists of interests and hobbies, even bank account numbers. Ray owned a couple of rental units, including the two-family house on Leonard Street where Char lived. He was with Char for four years, since the day she returned to Wisconsin.

Once our hands parted, all that remained were the memories of what I learned. None of the data I viewed was stored. It was like an old television without pause or rewind. Did Jorgenson ever see this before?

I was still dismayed when Ray asked, "You new here?" His eyes were so dark that I couldn't differentiate between his iris and pupil.

"Yes, sir," I answered like a respectful adolescent.

"Where from?"

"Libertyville, Illinois."

"Your folks here? Maybe I met 'em."

I shook my head, still evaluating him. "They couldn't make it."

He nodded, but remained silent.

"Well, it was nice meeting you," I said, starting to leave.

"Wait! Ray, could you be a dear and get a photo of Ben and Lucas?" Char asked.

"You don't need any more pictures, Char," Ray scolded.

"We always need pictures, Ray. Especially now. You said—"

"I know what I said. Yeah, okay, fine. We'll take more pictures," he answered to appease her. "Where's Lucas?"

Neal shrugged and everyone looked at me.

"I'm not sure," I answered.

"Oh, dear. Um, okay. Can you find him? Please?" Char pleaded.

"Sure."

As I walked away, I heard her whisper, "See, I told you he was a good boy." By the time I reached the water's edge, there was no lingering scent of a hybrid and no essence. The girls were taking pictures on the pier, with their dates nearby.

I watched from a distance, not wanting to interfere, yet unable to shake Ray's lack of download. At least Jorgenson saw it on the tetherstream.

When I turned to seek out Ray again, he and Char were nowhere to be seen.

Chapter 102
Emma's Story

Aunt Barb outdid herself again.

The Inn was a perfect place for pictures and scheduling the staff photographer was a nice touch she didn't tell me about ahead of time. Girls I barely knew thanked me for hosting the pre-dance event. "Oh-my-god, you need to do this again for prom!" one girl said.

While another added, "This is so pretty. You are so lucky to live here. I wish my parents had some cool place like this."

Of course, I couldn't correct them. I didn't actually live here. And being lucky was the last thing I was. Most of the girls heard I transferred because my dad died, but at that moment, I felt like that no longer mattered and they no longer treated me differently.

Even Brinn, who hated me the minute I took her starting position on the soccer team, was nice. She asked Lucas and me to join her friends at their table for dinner, but Lucas declined, leading me elsewhere. I was glad, actually.

Then it dawned on me. I was one of the super-rich kids everyone envied back in Highland Park. I was the kid that lived in the mega-mansion, whose parents hosted *the* party of the year. The girl everyone wanted to be or to be with.

These girls were jealous of *me*.

It was a revelation that took me by surprise, yet fit perfectly. I wasn't the outsider, not anymore. People that never gave me the time of day before suddenly talked to me. They were nice to me. Girls complimented my dress and asked where I got my hair done. Guys that never acknowledged me in the halls at school said hi.

The thought made me feel warm inside. The confidence I lost that day in the principal's office a few months ago was gone. As I followed Lucas to the far table filled with his football buddies and their dates, I realized I was me again. I was no longer sad, or scared. I was no longer angry with Dad for leaving me. I knew it wasn't his fault, and I knew he'd be upset with me if I dwelled on it too long.

Confidence rippled through me, as we passed Ben's table. When he noticed me, I smiled. Not a meek, shy smile, but a real one. One that I hoped would tell him I was interested.

I didn't care that Stephanie saw me, or that she turned to look at Ben, whose eyes sparkled as he smiled back at me. I didn't care that Lucas was ahead of me, impatient that I was walking too slow and not attentively at his side. Or whatever his annoyed look meant.

I was me again, and I knew it would be a perfect night.

Chapter 103
Ben's Story

Sorry it took so long, Grant Preston said.

He sat with a few parents in the lobby, while I had dinner in the dining room with the rest of the teenagers. The waitress placed a salad in front of me and asked if I wanted freshly ground pepper.

"No, thanks," I told her, and then glanced at Claire across the table. She moved lettuce from one side of her plate to the other. Drew didn't notice. His salad plate was bare, except for the slice of avocado he left behind.

What'd you find out? I asked Grant and took a bite. Stephanie finally finished cutting the mixed greens into bite-sized pieces. Like Claire, she moved food from one spot to another on the white china. She just wasn't trying to avoid the peppercorn ranch dressing, like Claire was.

Neal Crandon is type AB negative, Grant answered.

Wait. Lucas is O positive. Isn't he? I stabbed a forkful of lettuce and put it in my mouth, not realizing it was covered in dressing. I winced and ate it anyway, washing it down with a drink of water.

Yes.

How's that possible?

It's not. That's what took so long. I went back to the hard copy files at the police station and double-checked the lab reports. Neal has a rare blood type. As a matter of fact, the blood bank has several pints on reserve for him. Just in case."

I finished my water and waved to the busboy for a refill. The best way to overcome the toxicity of piperine, the component in black pepper, was to dilute it out with plenty of water.

I took another drink. *And this means…?*

It means Neal isn't Lucas' biological father.

Then who is?

Chapter 104
Emma's Story

"Are you heading out now?" Aunt Barb asked.

I found her in the bar near the lobby, sitting with a few other parents I recognized. Lucas already said goodbye to Neal.

"Yes. Thank you so much for doing this, Aunt Barb." Tears built in my eyes when the words came out. She gave a closed-mouth grin, and I noticed a slight quiver in her lower lip. She blinked rapidly and pulled me into her arms.

"Honey, you look so beautiful."

As tears overflowed and ran down my cheeks, I saw a brown-haired man in the hall staring at me. His arms were crossed in a familiar way and, for a second, he reminded me of my dad.

"You look just like your mom," she said. The man turned and even though all I could see was his profile, I was sure he was my dad.

I blinked hard, while Aunt Barb gently patted my back.

"I'm so proud of you," she whispered. The stranger greeted a man in a dark pinstripe suit with an old-fashioned hat and shiny shoes.

My voice cracked, as I thanked my aunt again. I tried to focus through watery eyes and caught a glimpse of red in the dark-skinned man's hat, like a spot or feather on the side.

Aunt Barb released me from her hug and held me at an arm's distance. "Your parents would be proud of you, too. You know that, right?"

"I know," I croaked. My throat burned, as I tried to form more words. I glanced toward the hall in hopes of getting a better look at the two men, but when my vision cleared, they were gone.

"Don't cry, honey," she said, wiping the wet streak on my cheek. "Wait. I don't want to ruin your make-up." She smiled and handed me a beverage napkin.

I blotted my tears away.

"Okay. So I'm not really good at this parenting thing, but here goes." She chuckled. "Behave. No drugs. No drinking. Definitely no driving if you're drinking." Her eyes widened, as she paused momentarily. "Just be safe. Make good judgments. Call me if you need me... or get into trouble... or anything. And most important, have fun."

"I will." With one last hug, I left.

It wasn't until I was walking out the front door of the Inn that I realized why the man in the hat looked familiar.

He was the man from my dreams.

Chapter 105
Ben's Story

Emma's dad showed up again, Molly said as I drove Stephanie to the dance.

What? How'd I miss that? I asked.

You were being a good date and saying goodbye to Stephanie's parents. It was right when TJ and I passed through the lobby. Brian Bennett popped in through a portal near the pub and just loitered in the hall.

"Mind if I turn the radio on?" Stephanie interrupted.

"Go ahead," I said. Music filled the silence in my car. Stephanie switched from station to station, looking for a tune she liked. As annoying as that was, it was better than listening to her mindless jabber.

Where was Brian's caseworker? I asked Molly.

She chuckled, and then answered, *Well, she's off the case now.* The rookie would be reassigned, probably on extended probation without possibility of a solo assignment for quite some time. If ever. Stupid mistake. *The best part is that Commander E caught him.*

What? What do you mean?

I mean, our fearless leader was here. In the lobby. At the Carmichael Inn.

You gotta be kidding. The commander hasn't made himself visible in what? Decades? Where's he now?

I believe he left. He took Brian back.

I can't recall the last time E checked in on one of our assignments. Can you?

No, Molly said. *But Benjamin, you should know… Emma saw her dad. She recognized him.*

That would be why E intervened, I acknowledged as I turned into a parking stall and shut off the engine. That, and because of Victor, and the abundance of hybrids and Lucas' blood. The reasons for the commander's visit were endless. Everyone was on high alert.

"... Ben? Did you hear me? Are you staying overnight at Trent's?" Stephanie asked, her squeaky voice a distraction from my conversation with Molly.

"Oh... No. Sorry. Can't," I answered, though my thoughts were still on Commander E and Brian's visit. And why I couldn't get a download from Ray. And what was up with Lucas' blood?

"O-o-o-h-h-h," she whined. "I was really hoping you were. I can. I mean, I told my mom that. You know... the girls were staying at one house and the guys were elsewhere. But, that's okay, if you can't. I mean... unless I can change your mind?"

She chewed on her lower lip and batted her eyes. That might change most guys' minds, but she wasn't going to change mine.

"Sorry, Stephanie," I said in my most sincere tone. "I can't." The sparkle in her eyes dulled. Even I didn't believe my lie. "My parents are coming into town, and I have to be home when they get there."

"Okay. Well, maybe you can stay really late?" She smiled, and I knew I was forgiven.

I nodded. I was definitely staying late—as late as I needed to keep an eye on Emma.

"Good." She leaned forward and kissed my cheek.

I turned in time to see TJ and Molly pull into the parking spot beside us.

"Ready to go in?" I asked.

"Sure."

Molly apologized, as I opened the car door.

Don't worry, Mols, I said. *Revenge is ever so sweet when its least expected.*

Chapter 106
Emma's Story

Lucas was already in the car when I went outside.

He revved the engine of his '80s-something Oldsmobile from the middle of the parking lot when he saw me exit the building. The sound of his impatience snapped me out of the sentimental moment I had with my aunt and made me realize how thoughtless Lucas was.

I didn't need him to walk me out, or open the car door like Justin did for Hannah a few spots down from where Lucas was parked. But revving the engine was no different than honking the horn from the driveway.

A guy that won't come to the door isn't worth your time, Emma, Dad told me the day before my first date with Matt. I smiled at the thought and remembered how embarrassed I was that Dad and I even had that conversation. At least Matt came to the door without being prompted. Lucas would never think of that on his own. Neal had to tell him to carry the groceries into the house, the first time they came over for dinner. Not to mention, Lucas wanted me to drive when we went out TP'ing.

It was suddenly clear. Lucas wasn't worth my time.

"Want a drink?" he asked as he pulled out of the parking lot. He motioned to a brown paper bag on the console between us.

"What? No!" I said, and then realized the tone of my voice was harsh.

"Wow. Aren't you a prima-donna?"

"Because I said *no*?"

Lucas was quiet as we drove the windy road back to Westport, which fueled my anger. When we stopped at a red light blocks from school, he reached for my hand, but I pulled it away. "I was kidding, Emma. Shit. Get over it."

"Seriously, Lucas? Didn't your dad give you the same lecture that I got?

About not drinking and driving?"

He rolled his eyes but didn't look at me as the light changed to green.

The silence that followed spoke volumes and gave me the confidence I needed.

When he turned into the parking lot, I took a deep breath and began. "Look. I like you, Lucas. But we are *so* different. Too different. This just isn't going to work. Between us, I mean," I said. "I just want us to be friends."

He shut off the engine and stared out the window.

"Just friends?" Lucas asked after a moment. Then he turned and glared at me. "You didn't act like you wanted to be *just friends* back at my gramp's place."

"You gave me pot brownies."

"No. Correction. You ate 'em yourself."

"Lucas, come on. You knew they were laced, and you didn't tell me."

"Whatever," he said, nodding toward a sedan a row over. "Trent's here with Bianca. Let's go." He got out of the car and slammed the door, greeting Trent like nothing was bothering him.

At least I told him how I felt. It wasn't my problem if he didn't like it.

Chapter 107
Ben's Story

"We should probably get a table. I don't want to get stuck with someone we don't like," Stephanie said when we walked into the decorated field house.

Molly agreed, and TJ and I followed like puppets.

After the girls analyzed which area they preferred and selected which table to drop their purses at, they headed to the ladies' room and left us on guard. Lucas strolled over with Trent.

"Where's Emma?" TJ asked before I did.

"Eh… she's somewhere," Lucas answered, not making eye contact with either of us.

Good. Maybe she wised up and dumped his ass.

Benjamin! Molly screeched in my head.

Okay, okay, I answered in defeat.

She walked in beside me. Seemed irritated, Bianca answered. *Not sure where she is now. I'm in the loo.*

Emma and I are to the left of the dance floor, Claire reported. *She's fine. She doesn't think much of Lucas, though.*

Join the club, I said and then realized I was in this seventeen-year-old skin far too long. I was beginning to use lingo from my teenage era.

Claire laughed. I peered into her thoughts and saw Emma smile. The girls were complaining about Lucas. I found myself unable to break the connection, enjoying every last negative word Emma said.

When Stephanie and Molly came back from the bathroom, they immediately headed to the dance floor. It was like earlier at the Inn. They were in a world of their own, and TJ and I were simply decorations they lugged along.

"I'm getting something to drink," I said.

"We can spike it, if you want. I've got stuff in the car," Lucas added.

"Nah, man. I'm fine," I answered, though TJ looked willing. "Besides, the cop at the door will get suspicious." I gestured toward the security guard the school had on duty. TJ was a nice enough guy. Hell, he put up with Molly, so he couldn't be all that bad. But when I saw him and Lucas leave the dance despite my gentle warning, I realized peer pressure was more convincing than common sense.

I was tired of these teenagers. If it weren't for Emma, I'd have skipped the dance and tracked Ray. It still bothered me that I wasn't able to retain any data when I shook his hand, and Jorgenson proved useless in explaining why.

Sorry, Ben. I have no idea. We've got nothing, was all Jorgenson said. No wonder Commander E showed up.

I hung out by the concession window, made small talk with Drew and Justin, and watched the teenagers grind on the dance floor, song after song. Back when I was alive, you could have been arrested for what these kids called dancing today. I was relieved Emma never danced with Lucas. I might have killed him if he touched her.

Hanging with a group of guys had its perks during the dance. It meant Stephanie danced with her friends and left me alone. I watched Emma and enjoyed the cold shoulder she gave Lucas. He headed to the parking lot more than once. First with TJ, and then with Trent. It got to the point that even the human rent-a-cop noticed. I was ready to smack him upside the head if he didn't figure it out.

By the third trip, the security guard finally told Lucas that the doors would be locked for the rest of the evening. "If you leave after this, you won't be allowed back in. Got it?"

Lucas nodded and looked apologetic. Once out of earshot, Lucas became the prick we were used to. "That fat fucker can't stop us. Wait until I tell Ray. He and his buddy, Abe, will put him in his place."

Trent laughed a gut-busting grunt, and the two knuckleheads fist-bumped. It was modern-day backslaps. They rejoined our group at a table, cracked jokes, and were their usual selves. Most guys liked them. Girls cringed.

I kept to myself, nodding and laughing at appropriate times, but not really paying attention.

Everything about Lucas bothered me—his blood sample that mutated to look normal, his mother's bizarre memories, and Ray's lack of download.

And then there was the abundance of hybrid scents. Was it every time Lucas was around? I couldn't recall. Though sitting at the dance with Lucas nearby, I didn't notice any peculiar odor.

What about Ray's friend? Lucas mentioned someone named Abe. Who was Abe?

Just when I thought I was onto something, the DJ dimmed the lights and slowed down the thumping beat to a mellow song, a sign the dance was coming to an end. I guzzled another bottle of water, watching people pair up and head to the dance floor. TJ asked Molly. Trent grabbed Bianca's hand. Hannah asked Justin, and Drew whispered in Claire's ear. Lucas went to the parking lot the minute Emma turned him down. Stephanie followed.

That left me.

Emma sat at a table alone, staring at her hands in her lap. She looked up as if she knew I was watching her. Her eyes lit up when they met mine, and I suddenly didn't care I brought Stephanie to the dance. I stood and crossed the room, Emma's eyes on me.

"Do you want to dance?" I asked.

"I... ah... I probably shouldn't. I mean, I'm here with Lucas," Emma answered, even though her thoughts screamed yes.

"I know, but I don't see him anywhere," I said, turning to look around in mockery. She did the same, and then smiled at me. It was the same expression Elizabeth used to give me every time I told a joke. "So, what do you say?"

Her eyes sparkled like they did when we were young. "Sure."

I reached for her hand and led her to the middle of the dance floor. Surrounded by her peers and all of our friends, I stopped, turned, and pulled her gently toward me. She didn't say a word, but I read her thoughts and gauged her heart rate. Emma was nervous.

Wanting to make a good impression, I kept a respectable distance between us.

"Lucas shouldn't have left you alone," I said.

She shrugged on the outside. Inside, her pulse increased.

I scanned the voices I heard in my head and settled in on his. Lucas was exactly where I expected him to be—in his car, smoking a joint. Within seconds, Stephanie joined him. She took a hit and then another.

"I think he went out for a smoke," Emma mumbled.

She smelled of jasmine. As much as I wanted to pull her tight, I resisted. I couldn't risk coming on too strong. Then again, being weak wasn't in my nature either.

"Exactly what do you see in him?" I asked the question I wondered for weeks.

Her body stiffened after the words came out. Suddenly, I regretted my forwardness.

"He's not that bad," she answered after she composed her thoughts.

We swayed to the song, close enough that I could whisper in her ear. "You're right, he's not bad. He's just stupid." Her tension eased, but didn't go away completely. "I wouldn't have left your side if I were your date tonight. Lucas is lucky to have you."

She sighed in my arms. "Lucas is just my date tonight. We're not... going out." She explained, like I had asked. Of course, I was happy to hear the words aloud.

"With the look he gives you, I'm pretty sure the whole school thinks you're a couple." I knew she didn't want to be his girlfriend. I pulled back enough to see her face.

"Well, you're here with Stephanie. Won't she be jealous that we're dancing?" she asked.

"Yes, she will." Stephanie would be angry.

"And you don't care?"

"No, I don't."

"Where is she anyway?" Emma scanned the dance floor.

"She's outside... having a smoke," I said with a look she understood.

"Huh." She nodded. "Does that bother you?"

"No."

"No to which part? Her smoking a joint, or hanging out with Lucas?"

"Either. I could care less what Stephanie Carlson does."

"Then why did you ask her to the dance?"

"I didn't."

"But—"

"She asked me, and I felt obligated to say yes. She wasn't my choice for a date tonight." I hesitated for a moment, and then continued. "The girl I wanted to bring already had a date."

She caught on.

"Right now, I'd say I'm the happiest guy in the room."

"Sometimes you can actually be sweet." Her eyes held mine.

"Aren't I always?" I chuckled, knowing how I treated her when we first met.

She looked at the floor. Emma was just as beautiful in this life as she was in the last.

"I guess I made a mistake by not asking you to the dance," I said when the song began its last chorus. "Once the song's over, you'll go back to Lucas instead of staying here with me."

Her heart rate increased, and her cheeks began to glow. A light pink hue filtered through her ivory skin.

"I wish you would have asked."

Before the moment was lost, before I could change my mind, I shielded my thoughts and kissed her. Her lips were as delicate as I remembered, and I was sixteen all over again, with the prettiest girl in school in my arms.

My palms got sweaty, and I forgot about everything but her.

Chapter 108
Emma's Story

I tingled when Ben's lips met mine.

It started in the pit of my stomach and crept up and through me like a volcano's eruption. Tiny sparks of electricity ran down my arms and to the tips of my fingers. It was unlike any other feeling I had. Matt's kiss was a dud compared to this.

I didn't know it was coming. One minute we were talking, flirting. Then the next, his soft, warm lips introduced themselves to mine, and I was lightheaded and dizzy when we parted.

The corners of his mouth turned upright into a full smile that reached his eyes. Dimples I never noticed before made an appearance.

"You look really spiffy tonight," he said in a soft voice.

"Huh?" I wasn't sure I understood.

He cleared his throat and repeated his words. "You look really pretty tonight."

The room felt as hot as a sauna. My cheeks were warm, and I didn't know what to say.

"I mean it," he whispered in my ear, as we swayed to the music.

I was uncomfortable. Aunt Barb said I looked nice and Dad often said stuff like that, but I never heard those words from a boy before, a *very* cute boy.

When his brown eyes peered into mine again, they touched my soul in a way that made my heart skip a beat. I wondered if this was what falling in love felt like.

"You're not so bad yourself," I managed to mumble.

The dimples returned with a full-size grin. Seconds later, our lips met again. This time, I was ready and anxious. Kissing him was my new favorite thing to do. He moved his hand from the small of my back to my neck as our lips opened, and I felt his breath in my mouth. His tongue grazed mine casually, as if proving it could, before retreating and sealing the kiss.

When the song ended, I was breathless. I squinted as the lights brightened, and the DJ announced the dance was over. Couples scattered, leaving Ben and I alone in the middle of the dance floor.

"Do I need to let you get back to Lucas?" he asked.

I shook my head. "I don't want to go with him. I'm not even sure he'll give me a ride to Trent's." Thoughts of our argument came flooding back, and I knew Lucas would be pissed if he saw me with Ben. Not that I cared. I just hoped Aunt Barb and Neal wouldn't be upset with me, too.

"I can take you there," he said, his hand on my back. "And I can take you home later. I mean, if you need me to."

"I'm staying at Claire's. Well, at your house, that is." I felt the all-too-familiar heat rise up my neck, and I hoped he didn't notice how red I probably looked.

He didn't say anything. Instead, he touched my cheek and gave me a quick kiss. My knees went weak, and I noticed Drew and TJ headed toward us. I wasn't comfortable with PDA back when Matt kissed me at the lake party. And this was double the attention, given I came with Lucas, and his closest buddies saw me kiss Ben.

"Where's Lucas?" Ben asked the guys when they reached us.

"I think he left," Drew said to Ben, then looked at me with a tight-lipped expression.

"Sorry, Em," TJ said with a smirk. "But it looks like you'll be alright." He raised his eyebrows quickly and winked.

I looked at my feet, and then realized I had nothing to be embarrassed about. I met his gaze and returned the wink. "Yup, I'm just fine. I guess that means he left with Stephanie?"

TJ pointed his forefinger at me and said, "You're right. I knew you were pretty bright. That's why I wondered what you saw in him in the first place."

We both laughed.

Chapter 109
Ben's Story

The hybrid aroma was overwhelming when Emma and I walked out to the parking lot.

I gripped Emma's hand and scanned the premises as best I could without leaving my human body. Emma's pulse rate increased and she smiled after my gesture, but I was too focused on where the hybrids were to delve into her thoughts. As long as she was safe beside me, that was all that mattered.

There were odors of at least two hybrids, but the further away from the building we walked, the less scent I smelled.

Molly, stick close, I said when she left the building. *I'm not sure if they're just out of sight or already gone. Where's Bianca?*

She left with Trent, Claire answered and got into Drew's car on the left side of the lot, next to the tennis courts. *There's no sign of hybrids over here,* she added.

"Looks like Lucas is still here," Emma said, pointing toward the opposite side of the parking lot, about twenty spaces from my Toyota. Lucas leaned against the passenger door of his car with Stephanie facing him.

"You ready for this?" I asked Emma.

She nodded.

The aroma increased the closer we got to Lucas.

There's no residual scent here, Molly said. She was at TJ's car next to mine.

Lucas nodded when Emma and I reached him. Stephanie turned to look at us, her eyes bloodshot. The sweet, sickly smell of cotton candy lingered around Lucas' car, but there was no sign of a hybrid.

"You going with Ben?" Lucas asked Emma, glaring at her. He glanced at our hands. Our fingers were intertwined.

"Yes."

Lucas took a drag from a cigarette and tossed the remaining half to the ground. The tobacco smoke blew back toward us with the light breeze. I stepped to the side to get out of its path and prevent inhaling the second-hand nicotine that could slow my abilities. I was happy I drank as much water as I did. It diluted the toxins that humans absorbed every day.

"You've got my bag in the back," Emma spoke up. I was surprised and impressed with her confidence. It was a change in her demeanor that I noticed long before I kissed her.

Lucas nodded to Emma and then said to me, "Steph doesn't need a ride."

With the mention of her name, Stephanie glanced up.

"I figured," I answered.

Another brief whiff of bitter apple filtered in like a Granny Smith on a cold, fall day. Its crisp bite touched my nostrils, and then diminished before my brain registered the direction it came from.

"It's just that… well, Lucas asked me," Stephanie whined. Lucas pulled her into his arms. He nuzzled his nose into her neck, and she squealed.

He had no idea I couldn't care less.

I looked at Emma and squeezed her hand. Her returned smirk read more than disgust. She understood we were both off the hook. I opened the driver's side rear door and grabbed the bag on the seat. "This yours?"

"Yes," Emma answered.

After shutting the door, I reached for Emma's hand and we walked toward my Cruiser where Molly and TJ waited.

"Good. Now Stephanie and I have space to spread out in the backseat!" Lucas yelled.

Emma tensed for a second until I put my arm around her. Lucas' thoughts bounced from making Emma jealous with Stephanie to being angry with me.

It appeared to be the first time Lucas was rejected.

Teenagers walking to their cars noticed us. Humans gossiped, while immortals monitored Lucas' behavior and measured his vitals. When Lucas' thoughts were angry, they were borderline violent and his adrenaline spiked. As the rage peaked in Lucas, so did concentrated droplets of the bittersweet hybrid odor. Yet, there was no sign of its source.

We're getting abnormal readings, Jorgenson said, observing the situation from the safety of our agency headquarters. *Now'd be the time to get a blood sample.*

Impossible. Besides, there's at least three different hybrid scents. They intensify and dissipate quickly. Molly and Claire concurred. *It appears to be circulating around Lucas. But he's not a hybrid. I confirmed his soul,* I told Jorgenson.

Emma and I reached my Toyota, and I tossed her bag in the back seat.

"Are you okay?" Molly asked. To my surprise, she greeted Emma with a hug.

"Yes. Perfect," Emma said. "Thanks, Molly."

See, Benjamin. I can be nice. Besides, it's about flipping time you kissed her. We've been waiting for this for how long?

This is cause for celebration, Claire added.

I turned away to prevent Emma from noticing my grin.

"Hey, you guys heading to Trent's party?" Molly questioned.

"Yeah, I think so. Right, Ben?" Emma answered.

"Yup. Let's go." I noticed Lucas and Stephanie already left, and so did all trace of the sickly sweet odor.

As I started the engine, I wondered if the hybrids were protecting someone. And if so, who? The more I thought about it, the more I realized the comings and goings of their presence even at the Inn. The concentration of scents began as parents congregated for pictures. Was one of them worthy of hybrid protection?

Pete, can you chart all of Victor's sightings—dates, times, and locations? And do a comparison against Charlene Tillman's past? I asked as I pulled out of the school lot. *Wait. And add Ray Tillman's whereabouts, too.* I reached for Emma's hand.

What have you got in mind? Jorgenson asked.

Call it a hunch.

Chapter 110

Emma's Story

Claire looped her arm through mine when I got out of the car at Trent's house.

"Omigod! You and my brother make such a cute couple," Claire whispered as we walked along the dark road and reached Trent's driveway with Ben and Drew behind us. There were a handful of cars, all lined on the same side of the dead-end street.

"You think so?" I asked.

She nodded. "He really likes you. I can tell."

Her words of encouragement made me blush. Again.

Trent's dad opened the door before we even knocked. "Keys inside the bowl," he said.

"We're not driving," Claire said.

"Okay. Boys, keys in the bowl," Mr. Hadley said to Ben and Drew. "No one drives home tonight. There are tents out back. I'm not condoning any drinking, but I know how you kids are. If you drink, you stay. Got it?"

"Yes, sir," Drew answered and complied, handing his key ring over.

"I'm not drinking," Ben answered.

"Don't matter. Keys in the bowl, son," Mr. Hadley grunted. It was the first time I met Trent's dad. He reminded me of Lewis' dad, but he wasn't nearly as intimidating. When Ben seemed reluctant, Mr. Hadley added, "You can get 'em back later if you can prove to me that you haven't been drinking."

With that, Ben dropped his keys in the bowl.

"Everyone's downstairs or outside at the bonfire." Trent's dad noticed the tote bag on my shoulder and the duffel Claire carried in. "You girls wanna change?" Claire nodded. "There's a guest room and bathroom down the hall, and another bathroom downstairs."

"Thanks, Mr. Hadley," I said.

Ben smiled at me as we parted ways.

By the time Claire and I switched into jeans and made our way downstairs, the guys were already outside. The lower level in Trent's house had a full kitchen and family room with a door that led to a stone patio with a fire pit in the middle.

Ben waved to me from the split-log bench beside the fire pit, as I stood in the doorway. He was holding a can of Coke in his other hand. Obviously, he was serious about not drinking and didn't care what anyone else thought.

"You girls gotta try this," Trent called from the kitchen. He pulled out shot glasses, lined them up on the counter, and poured a pink liquid into each. Molly, Bianca, and Hannah took one, raising and clinking their glasses to each other before slamming the contents. It looked like it wasn't the first time they did it that night.

"Tastes like Kool-Aid," Hannah said, following Molly and Bianca back outside.

I glanced at Claire. "Want one?"

She nodded, and we grabbed the remaining glasses. "Cheers!"

"Hey, we should toast to Lucas," Trent added.

"To Lucas?" Claire asked. "I don't think so."

"I agree. I'm not toasting to Lucas," I replied.

"He got us all the booze, man. Where is he? I thought he was with you?" Trent looked at me. When I shrugged, he said, "Okay. To us, then."

We clinked glasses and knocked back the fruity, spiked juice.

"Beer's in the cooler. Soda's in the fridge. Lucas' whiskey, and some other stuff, is in the box over there." He pointed to the table. "Help yourselves."

"So your dad doesn't care?" Claire asked.

"Nah." Trent shrugged. "Well, what he doesn't know..."

We thanked him, grabbed beers, and joined everyone outside. Ben greeted me and put his hand on my back. The gentle touch created a tingle like before, and I found myself leaning into him. I didn't realize what I was doing at first, but Ben didn't seem to mind.

"Wanna sit on the bench?" he whispered in my ear.

I melted. *Yes, of course, I want to sit with you*, ran through my mind.

I nodded, and we walked to the bench.

When we sat down, Ben put his arm around my shoulder, and I leaned into him. Hannah noticed with a shocked expression on her face. She mouthed, "What's going on?"

I replied, "I'll tell you later."

The fire's pop and crackle was louder than the sounds of conversations around us.

"You warm enough?" Ben asked.

"Yeah. You?"

"I'm good."

"You're not drinking a beer."

"Nah. I'm driving later."

"Oh."

"Besides, I'm trying to make a good impression." He smiled. I wanted to tell him it was working, but instead, I just smiled back.

Trent passed around the bottle of pink stuff and another of whiskey. Claire took a swig of the caramel-colored liquid and cough-choked on it before passing it to Drew.

Everyone laughed.

"She can't handle her liquor," Ben said soft enough that only I heard, but it looked like Claire glared at him anyway.

"Ben, you need to take a drink of this!" Claire said as if in response to his comment.

"No, thanks. I'll pass," he answered, and then added, "Besides, I don't want your backwash."

Drew laughed so hard, he spit out what he was drinking. Claire slapped his shoulder in a teasing gesture that led to him putting his arm around her. They made a cute couple, and I guessed she really liked him.

The laughter settled down as did the intense flames. The fire crackled as Trent passed the bottle of pink stuff to me. Trent asked TJ about Lucas when I took a sip of the fruity alcohol, but I didn't hear his answer. Aside from the orange glow, it was pitch black around us. I couldn't even see the moon under the thick covering of trees. It was quiet and peaceful, and I felt completely comfortable.

When someone suggested playing Never Have I Ever, I cringed. I hadn't played it before, but I heard enough stories. It was a sure-drunk game, especially if you got singled out. Of course, that was what Melissa's brothers did back in Highland Park. They would pick someone out and get them drunk.

"I haven't heard of it before. How's it played?" Bianca asked.

Hannah explained the rules and gave an example. "Never-Have-I-Ever sat at a bonfire in Trent's backyard," she said, smiled, and took a swig of the beer in her hand.

We complied, Ben sipping from his soda.

"Everyone has to drink because we're all here. So what I said was a lie. If what I said was true for you, then you don't drink. Got it?" Hannah asked Bianca.

"I think so," Bianca answered. "Okay, my turn. Never-Have-I-Ever drank a beer."

"This is going to be a long night," someone chimed as everyone drank. After a few rounds of toasts, it was Drew's turn.

"Never-Have-I-Ever gone to a dance with one date and left with another," Drew said.

"You're an ass!" Ben answered with a chuckle and glanced at me. We clinked cans and took a sip.

"Wait, wait," TJ said. "You need a beer. No soda, Parker."

Trent got up and headed inside, followed by Molly, who claimed to need the bathroom and Hannah and Justin, who needed more drinks. TJ and Drew suddenly vanished, and Ben and I were alone at the fire.

"Are you having fun?" he asked.

"Yes, are you?"

He nodded and lifted my chin. When our lips touched, my body sprang to life. Electricity flooded my veins. His hands moved to my back, as his tongue danced with mine. I was winded and wanted more when we parted, but by that time, everyone was back. Trent handed Ben a shot glass with a clear liquid in it.

"Penalty shot. No soda in a drinking game." Drew smirked.

The peer pressure was intense. The guys joked with Ben until he agreed to drink a shot of vodka. He mouthed *sorry* to me. I shrugged before he downed it. His eyes went wide, and he shook his head before handing the empty glass back to Trent.

"Good stuff, huh?" Trent asked. "Pepper-flavored vodka. Compliments of Lucas' stepdad, I guess."

"Yeah. Good stuff," Ben answered. I could tell he didn't like it.

After a few more rounds of the game, I excused myself in search of a bathroom.

Chapter 111
Ben's Story

People dispersed.

Emma went in the house. Justin and Hannah set up their sleeping bags in a tent. Drew and Claire decided to mix up more drinks, and Trent went in search of food, with Bianca and Molly volunteering to help. Even Mr. Hadley's thoughts were quiet. I wondered if he was gone or asleep.

That left TJ and me at the fire.

"I'll be right back," I said to him and headed into the woods. There'd been no sign of hybrids, which just egged me on. They had to be following Lucas.

Ben, we got something, Jorgenson said as I hiked out a few yards from Trent's house.

What's that?

First, there's nothing on Ray Tillman before Westport. Looks like he showed up about seventeen years ago. Only thing we have is what you already know about his auto shop.

He's older than seventeen, Pete. Where was he before?

I've got nothing. We need a download or his DNA. Something. Because right now, this guy doesn't exist.

Okay. Anything else?

Here's the part I think your hunch is about, Jorgenson teased. *It seems Victor was spotted in Wisconsin, at a tavern in Riverside, actually. About the same time Ray set up shop.*

Interesting.

I know. He's a man of disguise, Ben. Whatever you do, be cautious. He's had to have numerous aliases over the years. We even suspected him as a farmer in California a few years back but that fell through.

Farming?

Yeah. An agent thought he took over some dilapidated farm and got it operational. He had a pasture full of cows and produced thousands of gallons of milk. The community loved him.

And he staffed it with hybrids? I asked.

That was the thought. How'd you know?

Because the farm down the road has all the signs.

The one on Summit?

Yeah.

Look, Ben, need I remind you how dangerous he is? Jorgenson's voice was serious.

I understand... and I'll take precaution.

I'll send in a team. Be careful.

Ten-four, I answered, and Jorgenson broke the connection.

Listening for Emma's thoughts, I located her heading toward the kitchen. She had too much to drink, but she'd be safe inside the house with our human friends. I called to Molly and didn't wait for her response. Instead, I propelled into the trees in the acre of woods between Trent's home and the house next door. I could only spare a few minutes before my absence would be noticed. There was no sign of hybrids here.

Remembering where I picked up a scent before, I put up a shield and headed to the river.

Chapter 112
Emma's Story

I SHOULD'VE LISTENED.

Dad told me about the effects of too much alcohol. I stood alone in the dimly lit, upstairs kitchen. It was quiet here. My head was spinning, and I needed water. Melissa once told me to have water after drinking. "You'll feel better in the morning," she said.

"What about now?" I mumbled.

Uneasy on my own feet, I reached for a glass in the cabinet next to the sink. I tried to focus on the faucet as I touched the handle and turned on the tap. Everything blurred. My lashes moved slowly when I blinked. It was like windshield wipers that weren't working properly. Things didn't come into focus as they should. I followed the curve of the chrome faucet with my eyes from its base to the spout.

Before me, the gooseneck faucet came to life like a coiled snake, unfolding inches in front of me. I was frozen in place, afraid to move, unable to look away. The snake appeared to pull back, ready to strike. Its metallic, scaly skin glistened in the light from over the sink.

This couldn't be real.

I shut my eyes, squeezing them tight. Playing that drinking game was the stupidest thing I'd ever done, besides hang out with Lucas.

My head told me the snake wasn't real, but I was afraid to open my eyes in case I was wrong. I leaned against the counter and wished it away.

I didn't hear anyone come in. Was someone behind me?

Ben?

I felt the heat of his breath on my neck when he whispered my name.

No. It wasn't Ben. It was a voice I heard before, but I couldn't place. His words were wet and steamy. I opened my eyes as quick as I could. A woozy feeling overwhelmed me, as I refocused on the sink. The snake was gone. Water was running down the drain, not filling the glass in my hand. I moved the tumbler to catch the water.

"Huh?" I asked, glancing up to the voice behind me.

It was Ray.

He startled me.

"I don't like how you treated Lucas," Ray said. He moved closer, surrounding me. Placing his hands on the counter on either side of me, he pinned me in place.

I looked back to the half-filled water glass. My vision was hazy.

"His mother won't be happy you two broke up," Ray whispered in my ear, hovering around me. My cheek was dampened by his breath. Shivers ran down my spine. I focused on the cup in my hand. "I'll tell you what I'll do. I'm gonna give you another chance. To make it up to me."

"Um—"

"You tell me where Molly is, and I'll let you go," he interrupted. "Then you and Lucas can work it out, so Char never has to know. Understood?"

I nodded and he let go of the counter, placing his hands on my upper arms.

"Good. I thought so. Okay, now. Where's Molly?" he asked, gently rubbing my arms.

"I—I don't know."

"That's not how this is going to work, Emma. Elizabeth. Bennett." He rubbed my arms harder. The friction felt hot.

"She's here. I just don't know where she is this second. I left her at the fire. With TJ."

"TJ?" He let go of me. "Good idea… Good, good idea. I like you. You're pretty smart. I think you'd make a good asset."

I shut my eyes, wishing him away.

When I opened them again, he was gone. Water overfilled the tumbler in my hand, spilling over the sides. The cold wetness shocked my fingers and I dropped the glass, shattering it in the ivory, cast-iron sink.

Tears welled in my eyes. Did I imagine that?

Chapter 113
Ben's Story

I INCREASED THE DENSITY OF MY BARRIER.

In case the farm on Summit was Victor's hiding spot, I wanted to sneak in undetected. A subtle essence was evident as I moved closer to the river, to where the trees were older and the brush thinner. Like before, a gentle breeze whipped up the sweet, bitter fragrance from two distinct hybrids. The aroma appeared to be different from those I smelled at the high school parking lot. The pungent odor came and went with the wind, leading me west toward the abandoned farm where I rescued Stephanie.

Before going too far, I called out to Molly, loosening my shield temporarily. I wanted to tell her to head back to headquarters, even though I knew she wouldn't listen. Instead, I needed confirmation that she was safe inside of Trent's house.

Molly didn't answer.

I listened for her voice and heard nothing.

Claire, have you seen her? I asked.

No, but I'll check the bathroom, she said.

I heard other conversations. None included Molly. When I searched for TJ, I heard him talking with someone whose voice I didn't recognize.

"Is he alright?" TJ asked.

"Come. I'll take you to him," someone said.

Molly! I called. *Where are you?*

Nothing. I widened the perimeter and scanned for any female voice.

You're friends with Lucas, right? Stephanie asked in a high-pitched voice. Looking through her thoughts, I knew she was talking to a dark-haired man. I guessed she was in the road in front of Trent's house. I tried to read the man's thoughts, but I got nothing.

No sign of Molly, Claire responded.

She's not at the bonfire, either, Bianca added. *No one is, actually.*

Not TJ? I dropped the link to Stephanie and tried to get into TJ's thoughts. Nothing. Not even voices anymore. *I left TJ at the fire,* I told Bianca.

Ben, he's not here. I don't know where he went, either, she confirmed.

The effects of the pepper couldn't have blocked my scanning ability. Not that much anyway. I didn't want to head back unnecessarily. Especially when Jorgenson told me about the farm Victor ran back in California.

Damn it, Molly, I called to her again.

This time I picked up her thoughts and peered into them. Molly was with Stephanie on the side of the road, down from Trent's. Lucas was with them, as was an abundance of hybrid scents and other essences. The dark-haired man I saw earlier was with them. He appeared to be in his mid-twenties and greeted Lucas as if they knew each other. Lucas shook his hand and escorted Stephanie toward the house, leaving Molly with the stranger.

Molly stood frozen. Her heart rate was uneven, and her thoughts were empty.

I came to warn you, the man said to her when they were alone. He reached for her hand, holding both of hers in his. Despite the skin-to-skin contact, there was no download of data. *He's here. He's looking for you, and you need to leave now.* His voice was calm, his eyes gentle.

Molly shook her head. He continued, anyway. *There's no time now. I have so much to say. So much to ask you.*

I know you... You were there.

We don't have time right now. And I can't protect you. Not from him. The calmness of his tone left, replaced with a sense of urgency Molly ignored.

You were with Victor that night. The night he killed me in London.

Look. I'm sorry. I tried to warn you.

Who are you?

You need to leave, the man said and looked around.

Tell me your name. Molly's voice was low and stern.

He stalled, looked to the ground, and finally conceded. *Aberthol. They call me Abe.*

Molly's pulse quickened. *Are you...?*

Yes. Now, you must leave. He was impatient.

I can't. I won't, Molly said.

You must, Abe answered in a tone as firm as her stubborn one.

What about TJ? Victor's hurt everyone I've ever loved. I can't. I won't just leave without protecting TJ.

It's too late, Abe said, solemnly. *He already has TJ. That's just it. You need to go.*

No.

Mom! Listen to me. I don't care about TJ. I'm only concerned about your safety.

A noise from a raccoon below distracted me, and I lost the connection. When I regained it, Abe was gone and Molly was crying, holding her head in her hands.

Bianca reached her before I could verbalize a thought.

And then I heard Emma's cry.

Chapter 114
Emma's Story

Ben came up behind me as I stood in the kitchen, shaking. I turned into his arms and babbled how creepy Lucas' stepdad was.

"Ray was here?" Ben asked.

I nodded, my face buried in his chest. He smelled of cool breezes, and I felt stronger with each inhale.

"Let's get out of here," he whispered in my ear. His voice was firm. I looked up into his eyes and thought I saw a glint of anger.

Was he being protective?

Ben reached for my hand and led me to the foyer. He walked from the small table near the front door back to the kitchen where we came from.

"What are you looking for?" I asked. He was distracted and impatient.

"My keys. Where's that bowl?"

I shrugged.

"Never mind. We'll walk. I know a shortcut through the woods." He mumbled something about not going into the road, grabbed a flashlight from the counter, and led me out the side door. His grip was strong. He squeezed my hand as if I intended to let go as his pace quickened in the wooded hillside. My mother's anniversary band that Dad gave me on my sixteenth birthday spun sideways on my ring finger, cutting into my pinkie.

Ben waved the flashlight in front of us as we walked carefully, though he didn't say a word. After a few minutes, I asked where we were going.

"I had to get you out of there," he said matter-of-factly.

Curiosity got the best of me, "Why?" I asked, but before he could answer, I heard a noise and turned to look in its direction. *Probably a squirrel*, I thought.

"Come on, we gotta go." He tugged slightly on my hand.

"You're not going to tell me why?" I asked as he went from tree to tree. "You're soooo secretive, Ben Parker," I joked. I really didn't care where we were going. I was just happy to be with him.

Ben stopped for a second and looked at me. "Maybe I just want to be alone with you." His delicious smile convinced me his secrets didn't matter. "Let's keep moving."

I followed like an obedient puppy, though I hoped he didn't think of me that way. We weaved around and between a handful of trees. When I heard another noise, Ben stood still. He glanced left and then right, spinning me with him as he checked around us.

"Come," he whispered.

"Where are we going?" I almost demanded. I wanted to sound confident and not nervous. Suddenly, I wondered if being in the woods in the dark was a good idea.

He didn't answer.

"What are you looking for?" I asked as Ben slowed down near a maple. It looked the same as the last one.

"There's one around here." I almost didn't hear Ben's mumble.

"What?" I was trying to sober up. Or at least act like I was.

"A tree with a split trunk."

Huh? "A what?" I asked again.

He appeared to have found what he was looking for and tucked the lit flashlight under his arm. I stood off to the side and watched the direction of the beam. The light danced from the ground to the woods, from tree limb to tree limb, as Ben touched the bark and circled around the trunk.

In a brief glimpse, I thought I saw Claire and Molly standing a few feet away. But when the beam crossed a second time to where they were standing, I only saw trees. I blinked a few times and even though I thought I was sobering up, Molly and Claire seemed to disappear.

"Here."

Ben led me to the backside of the oversized oak. It looked like two small trees grew side by side with a deep crevice, merging the two as one. When we heard the sound of crushed leaves beside us, Ben froze. Panic settled in my chest, and I suddenly wondered if we were in danger. Voices echoed, and I was convinced I saw Ray and TJ.

Ben held me, as I backed into the tree trunk. Bark scratched my sweatshirt and was hard and jagged against my shoulders. He stepped closer. So close, his body blocked mine.

"Don't worry," he said.

What?

"Do you trust me?" he whispered.

I was in complete darkness. My heart began to race, and I no longer felt the wind or scratching of the tree against my body.

"Yes. Why?" I couldn't hear myself. Did I really say anything? I cleared my throat, but I didn't hear that either. "Ben? Ben?"

Everything will be alright, said a deep, confident voice in my head. I knew it was Ben's.

"Where is she?" I heard someone ask. Or did I?

Ben was talking to someone he called Kensington.

And then, nothing.

I strained to hear my own thoughts. The darkness was overwhelming. I couldn't tell if my eyes were open or closed. Even though I blinked and blinked, I couldn't see anything. Pressure in my ears increased as if I were on a descending airplane. A hum of static began and grew louder.

Then the floating started.

A breeze touched my cheek, and my head tipped back. It was heavy and uncomfortable. I felt the gentle momentum of falling, swirling through the air. Weren't my feet firmly planted on the ground?

Ridiculous. I was just anxious to be in Ben's arms.

Get a grip, I told myself.

Wait. I had done this before. The twirling was easy and slow, and I felt light as a feather, like the day I broke my arm when I was six years old. *The light called to me*, I told my mom.

She held me tight and drew a smiley face on my cast. "It was just a dream, Emmie," she said.

"No, Mommy. It was real."

"Emmie, don't be silly. You had a dream," she convinced me.

Suddenly, the memory was as fresh as if it happened yesterday. Thoughts of friends, my parents, Aunt Barb, and Ben rapidly flashed through my mind. Then I realized I couldn't hear any more sounds. Not the wind. Not even my beating heart.

What was happening to me?

I wanted to speak. I wanted to hear something. As I opened my mouth to call for Ben, his lips met mine. His hand touched my cheek, while the other held me tight. His kiss was intoxicating, tasting of cinnamon. I was dizzy and weak when we parted.

Aftermath

Was I dreaming?
I was pulled from behind.
And then, I saw the bright white light.

Chapter 115
Ben's Story

Hybrids surrounded us, but I refused to let Emma go.

"Where's your partner?" George Kensington asked, twenty feet in front of me.

"Back at headquarters, Kensington." I held Emma secure while I turned to face him.

"He's lying," a voice from the darkened woods answered.

"What do you want with her?"

"That's not your concern. Where is she?" Kensington asked.

"I don't know," I lied, not disclosing Molly's whereabouts inside a nearby portal. A portal so narrow that even Victor wouldn't notice it easily.

"Well, then. We'll take the girl until you find Molly for us," the voice said.

I recognized the Wisconsin sweatshirt before I saw its owner's face. TJ tripped forward, out from behind a tree, with Ray grasping his arm.

My suspicions were true. Ray was one of the aliases Victor used.

I turned to face Emma, kissed her lips, and stepped her backward into the crevice of the oak tree. It hid a portal to my world. Humans could only pass through the portal when they transitioned. Pushing a human completely through would cause earthly death. I held Emma on the edge, far enough into the doorway to protect her, but not too far to lose her.

Despite the distance between us, I could see TJ's eyes were glassy. I knew he was under Victor's control.

Emma's body tensed with the calling from our world. The spinning, swirling movement was her body's response to our world's invitation. She was not ready to leave this life. Her contract was not yet fulfilled, but Emma wouldn't know that. She would feel welcomed.

"Keep Emma out of this," I said.

"You brought her into this, Benjamin Parker Holmes," Victor said, inching forward.

A hybrid stepped to the side, making room for Victor inside their circle. I counted six in total, all evenly spread around, plus Victor.

"Yes. I know all about you. Your last life taken so abruptly... leaving your wife a widow. So you entered the academy. You met my Molly. You learned many skills, didn't you?" He paused, his eyes focused on mine. "I learned all of that from our little handshake, Benjamin," Victor continued. "You didn't shield yourself as well as you thought. Did you?"

I couldn't break his glare. His power was too strong. Even if I cracked the hold he had on me, I feared he'd notice my glance or read my mind. I had to trust my team was in place—Molly to the left and Claire to my right.

A deep chuckle erupted from Victor. "You can't do it. Can you?" he said, his eyes still fixed on me.

If only I could find his weakness.

"You can't break our bond, can you?" he asked. "Although, you have quite a bit of power yourself. Your commander should be impressed." He was silent for a moment. "You're just missing one thing."

Don't engage, I told myself.

"You shouldn't have gotten involved, Benjamin."

Immortals stood by, waiting for the precise moment to come forward.

"All I wanted was to reunite Molly with her son. We're a family. You see?"

"Is that how you remember it, Victor?" Molly's voice echoed. "Because I don't recollect family being of any importance to you." Her British accent was heavier than it ever was, in my presence, anyway.

Victor dropped a limp TJ to the ground.

"Molly, darling, there you are," Victor said, turning toward the sound of her voice. A brief silhouette was barely visible, as she teetered on the edge of the portal.

Victor would never enter a portal for fear of being captured. Physically, he could travel into and through our portals, because he was one of us. While our portals were not manned in person, they were monitored by guards ready and able to descend upon him should he choose to venture into the walls of our world. Victor knew that. That was what kept him alive all these years, undetected.

He simply never used them.

My hand tensed from holding Emma tight at the portal's entrance inside the oak tree. When I felt a push from the other side, I knew I had support.

Jorgenson's voice whispered in my head. *I've got Emma on this side, but it's only temporary, Ben. She doesn't have much time. Minutes. Maybe.*

That was all I needed. Minutes.

I released Emma but maintained my stance. Molly argued with Victor from the shadows of her doorway, while Victor pleaded she join him.

"You can finally meet our son, Aberthol," Victor said.

"Don't do it, Molly," I said. My request was ignored. Molly stepped out from the security of the portal. Fourteen feet separated her from the infamous Victor Nicklas.

"You killed me, Victor. In London," Molly said with angry tears streaking down her face.

Claire came out of the portal to my left, hovering close to its edge.

"Molly, Molly, Molly… *darling*!" Victor consoled, taking a step closer. I leaned forward, and then remembered not to break position.

"Don't '*Molly*' me. I'm not a naïve human this time."

Another step closer. "That's what I love about you. Don't you see? Molly, dear. This was my goal for you. I hurt you so you would become stronger. I broke you down, to make you tough. Don't you see? It worked."

Victor laughed, a deep rumble that made my skin crawl even though I wasn't human.

"Worked? Is that what you think? You needed to *train* me?" Molly's anger rose to an exorbitant level, greater than even I saw after decades of working together.

He stepped closer again. "Calm yourself, Molly. Please. You're making a scene. It's not respectable for a lady to behave in this manner," Victor whispered, stepping forward a second time. Only ten feet separated them now.

Molly glared at him. "Not respectable?"

"You know that's unattractive, darling. You, making a scene like that. Remember, it is important to make a good impression. Impressions are everything." Victor nodded. His dark hair lightened to a medium brown, taking on a boy-next-door style, short and parted on the side. His cheeks thinned, his skin tone tanned, and his smile warmed.

"Isn't this how I looked when you fell in love with me?" He grinned at her and unzipped his leather jacket. Opening one side, the fabric lining changed from black to brown, while it lengthened in his hand. Seconds later, he was in a tailcoat and pantaloons common in the era in which they met.

"Have you forgotten how much you loved me, Miss Molly?"

Molly's eyes narrowed, as she glared at the evil immortal that walked the earth for centuries. "You seem to have forgotten that you killed me. Victor, you *murdered me*."

Victor looked up to the trees and shook his head. "Yes. Yes, I did, and you have no idea how much I regret what I've done."

I felt Molly's anger at his words. "What kind of man *are* you? You killed innocent women. You were Jack the Ripper!"

"But you see, darling, I had to. I had to cleanse society. And you, darling... you needed to die, too." He paused and watched her reaction, as we all did.

"You're simply evil, Victor. How could you do that?"

"I am not, sweetheart. After all, I sent your son to stop you. Aberthol went to warn you to change your lifestyle. Yet, you didn't listen."

Molly's thoughts rapidly settled on the memories of her past life.

"You thought he was a john. Yet, he turned you down. Your temper got in the way. He gave you money anyway, but he asked nothing in return. When he came back again and again, you ignored him. You didn't listen to his warnings to clean up your act. A girl of the evening was no life for you. It was not respectable, Molly. And I wouldn't tolerate it!" His anger increased as he finished talking.

"Father!" Abe interrupted. "Let her go. Don't do this."

"Son, don't disrespect me. Know your place," Victor said as Molly looked on.

Ben, Emma's slipping. Jorgenson's voice filtered in.

"Victor, it's time to turn yourself in," I said with more patience than I felt.

His deep chuckle annoyed me less the second time.

"I mean it. You're not getting out of here. Look around," I suggested and took a step toward him. Bianca hovered in the portal behind Victor, to the right.

"Give yourself up," Abe urged. Hybrids lingered in the shadows, ready to act when Victor gave the word.

"Yes, Victor. Please," Molly said.

Victor took a few steps closer to Molly, in perfect alignment with the portal where Bianca hid. Molly reached for his hands in a gesture even Victor didn't expect. His expression softened. In that moment, he weakened. The regret for his actions was strong because he lost Molly, not because he felt remorse. His obsession with Molly was still overwhelming and his anger over not getting her back grew hostile.

It was a welcomed distraction. I glanced at Claire and Bianca, hoping they understood my idea. Without waiting for response or reaction, I lunged at Victor and my team followed suit.

We had him surrounded and overpowered physically. Tackling him to the ground, I rested my weight on his chest, while Bianca and Claire held down each arm. He flung his hands and kicked his legs, as agents descended in an attempt to keep him pinned down.

Mentally, we severed his thoughts from outside transmission, but not before he was able to signal to Abe and his hybrids. Our combined energy was tested as Victor struggled to get free.

Agents flooded the woods from nearby portals and battled the hybrids standing on guard. One by one, the hybrids were subdued, but Victor's willpower was still strong. Despite our barrier blocking his communication to outsiders, Victor's thoughts were loudly transmitted among us. He pleaded with Molly again, but to his displeasure, she held firm.

"Victor. Enough," Molly said. He winced as Molly's energy level soared and flowed direct to him in the tethered grip we had. "It's over. You know that."

When Molly spoke, Bianca's hold on Victor lessened. I raised my adrenaline on the mental rope connected to Victor to accommodate her slow release. Bianca's grip slipped. She glanced at Abe and Kensington; both were restrained by agents nearby.

Bianca's weakness was alarming and, for a second, I feared she'd break the link.

Benjamin, hang on. You can do this. You're stronger than Victor is. Always have been. Which is why I trust you. Commander E's voice filtered in.

"Bianca!" I called aloud.

Thunder rumbled in the sky above us, as shards of lightning exploded and struck trees nearby. The sudden outburst snapped Bianca's attention back to the team and the task at hand. Her eyes refocused on me, and she regained her strength. Together, our powers surged and Victor's energy subsided, weakening him in place.

A blue glow hovered around us. Its thick aura thinned to a series of wires woven in a crisscross pattern as intricate as a spider's web. Once Victor was covered from head to toe, Commander E stepped out from the portal. His voice was deep and stern when he addressed Victor.

"You disappoint me," Commander E said.

"Why is that, Ezekiel?" Victor answered in a cocky tone. "Or, do you still go by Zeke?"

Commander E removed his fedora and shook his head. "You had so much potential." He spun his hat in his hand. "You excelled at The Farm. You were top of your class." He looked to the ground, continuing to shake his head. "Very disappointing… you threw all that away, didn't you? And, for what?"

Victor's eyes narrowed, and anger built inside of him. Our combined unit's shield strengthened, as his powers fought for freedom. "You're jealous of me. You always have been, Zeke."

"Well, Nicky. That *is* what the commander called you back then, didn't he?"

Victor was silent.

No further explanation was needed. Images of an inexperienced Victor in training at The Farm with Commander E as a fellow recruit, filtered through all agents on site. Victor was indeed top of his class. He fell from grace shortly after his first solo field assignment. A dispute with a commanding officer escalated until Victor began a plan of revenge, despite Commander E's pleas not to. Learning the two were partners in the early years made the animosity between them understandable.

"We can continue our discussion on the other side. No need for everyone here to watch as we reminisce the good ol' days," Commander E said.

Victor shook his head. He wanted to fight it out here, where he had a chance to escape.

After one last glare, Commander E said, in a gentlemanly, polite tone, "I have some place to be. So, shall we?"

Commander E gave the nod, and I lifted Victor to his feet.

The blue wires grew, surrounding Victor's back and securing his arms tight to his sides. He groaned. His legs were strapped together. The glow from the netting pulsed as it tightened. The brightness illuminated the woods and the dozens of agents on guard. Victor's will broke when he realized there was no escape. The web around him compressed, and the wires thickened to an almost-solid shell.

My eyes met Molly's briefly before she glanced away. In one swift movement, I pushed Victor into the portal, into custody.

Bianca and Claire followed him through, while Molly ran to TJ, lying still on the ground. Only a few agents remained. The others returned to our world. Hybrid bodies turned to dust where they stood, as their souls returned home to our world. They were now free of Victor's control.

Abe stared at me. He was suddenly alone, without his security team of hybrids.

His thoughts were difficult to read. Years of practice with barrier blockers was evident. An obvious sign he worked with Victor for a very long time. I took a step closer, ready to react should Abe become a threat.

"I'm not here to hurt anyone. I came here to warn you," Abe said, raising his hands up, palm facing outward, in a surrendering gesture. Once I unraveled his weakened shield, I knew he was telling the truth.

"I understand that. Except your existence is not up to me," I answered.

"Ben, let him go," Molly piped in. "Abe's not like Victor. I know that."

I glanced in Molly's direction. TJ was alive, but groggy. Tears streaked her cheeks, and I felt her emotions. She pleaded for Abe's safety, while she held TJ's hand in hers, draining her energy to strengthen his weak body. He would survive with little to no memory of this incident. Molly, on the other hand, would need time to recoup. And time to get to know Abe.

I looked back at Victor's spawn and nodded in agreement. Before words came to mind, Abe was gone. I sent a few immortals to follow.

Keep a distance, I said. *Surveillance work until we formulate a strategy for his existence.*

Molly thanked me, as I darted back to the portal where I left Emma. Jorgenson pushed her back to earth, to a bed of crushed leaves.

Emma wasn't breathing.

Chapter 116
Emma's Story

I sat on the swing in the park alone.

It was eerily quiet and within seconds, the sky darkened. Wind swept up fallen leaves and swirled them around my feet. A garbage can tipped over in the distance. Papers were carried high in the air with the breeze, like helium balloons on a summer day.

The hem of my favorite sundress lifted, and I struggled to keep it in place.

Instead of seeking shelter, I stayed on the swing. The storm's anger rocked me back and forth. I wasn't afraid. I knew he would come.

I remembered him now. The memories were as vivid as if they happened yesterday. We'd met several times before. The first time, he pulled me from chilly water and dried me off. The second time, he lowered me from the noose hanging from the loft in my cousin's barn.

He scolded me both times for breaking the rules. "It's irresponsible," he said.

I knew he was right. It was a breach a contract, he told me, though I barely saw his lips move when he spoke to me.

Gusts of wind pushed the empty swings beside me and spun the merry-go-round. Trees swayed and bowed in respect of Mother Nature. The charcoal sky rumbled as if in warning, or to announce his arrival. I couldn't be sure.

Years passed since I last saw him. I mean, *really* saw him. He showed up in my dreams, I knew. That wasn't real. *This is*, I thought, as I sat on the swing, waiting. Where was he? What was taking him so long? I never had to wait like this. Before.

A fedora was his signature.

The temperature dropped, and I almost felt the wetness on my face from that first time he saved me. The day I chose to dive into the white-capped waters of Lake Michigan. Closing my eyes, I tipped my nose to the sky. I remembered catching the mist in the air, as waves crashed against the rocky shore.

I knew it wasn't graceful—plunging into the depths of the great lake, but it was what I wanted. I was pulled, tugged, and swept under the current, into the deep reservoir that held me captive until I met him. Until he lifted me to shore.

"Call me Zeke," he said that day we stood on the boulder, lakeside.

"I'm Emaline."

"I know," he answered, to my surprise. He was pleasant and well dressed.

It dawned on me then that I was in my nightgown when I dove in. When I looked down at my clothing, I realized I was wearing my best Sunday dress. It was clean and crisp, as if just pressed.

Zeke looked away. I knew it was him.

I glanced up the hillside to my house on top of the cliff. My sister, Catherine, was on the second-story balcony overlooking the lake. I waved to her. Why didn't she wave back? I didn't expect her visit. Why was she there?

"Because she grieves for you," Zeke said. I didn't recall asking him a question.

"Grieves?" Bewilderment filled my thoughts. "Why?"

"Because you left her. Unexpectedly, Emaline."

I nodded, and he said no more. I understood. It was a breach of contract.

Silence disrupted my daydream, as I sat on the swing. When I opened my eyes, Zeke was standing before me. Angry thunder diminished, and birds chirped. Gray clouds vanished, and the sky blued.

"I'm ecstatic you've found one another again," Zeke said. He was in a brown pinstriped suit with wide lapels.

I smiled. I understood. Again.

"Emma, dear, it is not your time," he continued.

I stalled. "They don't call you Zeke anymore. Do they?"

He was silent and unhappy with me. I didn't want to go back. After a moment, he shook his head.

"What do they call you now? Commander Ezekiel?" I pursued.

"Emma, it's not your time," he repeated.

I ignored him and stared at his shiny, wingtip shoes. "Why is it that you don't dress in the fashion of the current day? I mean, I'd love to see you in a sweater and slacks," I said. "Or... what about jeans? Yes. A dark denim. You would look really nice in dark jeans and a gray sweater. What do you think?"

He was getting impatient.

"Emma, you *must* go back."

No! I said in my head, but the words didn't verbalize aloud. He didn't want to hear them.

Zeke raised his hand to hush me. I'd been a problem for him for years. He didn't understand. I wanted to go *home*. I didn't want another life. It was selected for me.

The silence was compelling, and I knew I could never win against Ezekiel Cain.

When I finally conceded, he lowered his hand and stared off into the distance. He pulled a matchbook out of his pocket and began tapping his forefinger against it in an almost nervous twitch. The pastel pink cover had brown writing on it, though I couldn't read the imprint.

Children came from nowhere and filled the playground. The grass greened, and flowers bloomed. It was summer again. Laughter filled the air and for a slight second, I forgot.

He turned quickly in my direction. "You mustn't forget, Emaline," he said, tossing the matchbook at me.

I caught it and whispered, "I'm ready."

"Emma, this is not up for debate."

I shrugged.

"You must go back."

He was right. It wasn't up for discussion.

Staring off into the distance again, he pulled a small, waxed paper bag from his coat pocket, unfolded the flap, and shook out the contents into the palm of his hand.

"Rock candy?" he asked, helping himself to one and extending his hand to me.

I stared at the white, crystal nuggets and reached for a piece. The sugary goodness made my mouth water.

"There's more to do, and I have many things planned for you," he said.

I glanced at the matchbook in my hand.

"And for Benjamin," he continued.

Benjamin. *My* Benjamin.

"Will I see you again?" I asked.

He shook his head. "Only if you need guidance."

I looked into his eyes. They were dark like his skin. Yet, they were warm and sensitive.

"I don't suspect you will. Everything should be clearer now." He turned away from me, ready to leave.

"Do you have any last words of advice?" I asked, hoping to stall him.

He turned back to face me. "Steer careful on the road."

"I... I don't understand."

A grin crossed his face. "Don't worry. You will."

I didn't know why, but I felt peace with his words.

Pressure suddenly hit my chest. I winced with the pain, closing my eyes momentarily. When I opened them again, Zeke was gone.

The brown letters on the matchbook cover read, Danny's Bait Shop.

Chapter 117
Ben's Story

Emma's lifeless body lay still with her skin already cool to the touch.

"Come on!" I yelled and began chest compressions. I kissed her lips and blew air into her lungs, though she didn't respond. It wasn't her time. Her life contract was far from over, and a premature termination like this would mean a year or more of rehabilitation and immediate reassignment.

In other words, I would lose her again, even in my world.

"Benjamin, take it easy," Jorgenson said, putting his hand atop my clenched fist. I was showing human emotions I had difficulty controlling.

Jorgenson slowed the compression rhythm and counted to five. He signaled to me, and I blew air into Emma's purplish lips. Reviving a human wasn't usually this difficult. Our ability to heal with a simple touch was a skill I used thousands of times before. Emma's untimely death in a portal was not the typical rescue I was used to, and the length of time she was unconscious was longer than most I resuscitated.

Compressions began again, as Jorgenson counted aloud, "One-two-three—"

"Stop!" I said. "She's back. She's breathing." Emma opened her eyes and stared up at the sky. "Emmie, you're back!" Tears welled in my eyes. I blinked them away. Her eyes fluttered and closed. She mumbled something I didn't understand.

"What?" I asked, leaning closer to her mouth. "Em, what did you say?" She remained silent with her eyes shut tight.

"Emma, can you hear me?" Jorgenson asked, with no response.

I peered into her mind and stared at Jorgenson.

He shrugged.

She whispered, "Danny."

Chapter 118
Emma's Story

"Emma?" a calm voice broke through my dream.

I was drowsy, and my head ached. Memories jumbled in my mind. I wasn't sure if I was asleep or awake. I recalled the dance and Ben's kisses. I swore I saw Ben's friend, Pete, in the woods, and TJ lying against a tree. But even though fishing with Ben in a silver rowboat seemed incredibly real, I didn't remember it actually happening.

All I wanted was sleep.

The motion of being lifted, carried, and placed on a hard surface disrupted my rest. A bright light flashed into each eye, despite how hard I fought to keep them closed. A gray-haired man leaned over me and away. He repeated it again, as he pried open my other eye.

I didn't understand what was going on.

"No," I whispered, shaking my head.

"Shh," a woman's voice answered. "It's okay. You'll be alright." Someone held my hand, and people talked around me.

I was too tired to listen and wished myself back to sleep.

***

The honk of an old-fashioned car caught my attention. I stood on the sidewalk in front of Father's store. Julia's brother parked the truck down the street and waved for me to join them.

Julia Kensington was my best friend.

I climbed in and we headed to Lake Bell, where her brother's friend lived. Julia and her family lived on a farm outside of Riverside. She was the oldest girl, and the first Kensington to attend high school. Her four older brothers dropped out after eighth grade to work the farm.

It was summer.

Aftermath

Julia nudged me when we got to the island party. The cutest boy I'd ever seen was tying a silver rowboat to a tree nearby. He had dark hair and defined muscles in his arms. I blushed when I looked at him and quickly turned to Julia.

When the sun set and the fire crackled, Walt Crandon started telling ghost stories. Julia and I sat with a few other girls across from Walt and next to Benjamin Holmes, the cute boy I admired all evening.

Walt told a story about some boy that drowned in the lake and haunted the island. The other boys booed him, as he lowered his voice. When he jumped up and flung his arms around to spook us, I turned into Benjamin and buried my face in his chest.

My Benjamin.

Chapter 119
Ben's Story

Emma stirred as she slept.

She gasped and giggled a few times—even mumbled my name once. Her mind was working overtime. Random thoughts interrupted functional normalcy. They bounced from an image of Molly to a rowboat and back to the woods and TJ, before wondering where Claire was. Scenes rolled out in Emma's head faster than she could absorb them or understand their meaning. Past recollections played out in short spurts that even I had a hard time following.

When Emma's memories included our past lives together, I shielded her from outside readings. No need for Molly or Claire to hear Emma's thoughts. I monitored her vitals, checking Emma's heart rate and blood pressure with the touch of my hand. Our ability to heal humans in times like this was incredibly convenient. Of course, Grant Preston had to pretend to use medications in the hospital. Humans relied on them. Here, in the confines of my safe house, a simple touch to Emma's temple would minimize her headache. A gentle jolt of electricity to her chest would restart her heart, giving it sufficient energy to run at full capacity. The only thing I couldn't do was give her body the rest it needed after a predicament like she just endured.

That she'd have to do herself.

Sleep was vital for her full human recovery. Our house, the home I shared with Claire and Aunt Marty, was a perfect setting for Emma to heal. Jumpstarting Emma's heart wouldn't have happened without our immortal powers. She was dead too long for conventional medicine to have worked or for medical experts to continue to try.

Even then, she would have needed a miracle, which could only have occurred with one of my kind on staff.

Aftermath

Emma would recover. So would TJ. His injuries were less severe. Victor's compulsion withdrew much of his energy, except TJ's heart never stopped. He didn't actually die and come back to life the way Emma did.

TJ's sleeping, Molly said in thought as I sat in the corner chair of the guest room. *His stats are all normal,* she reported from her house a few doors down from mine. It was where she took TJ after the Victor incident. It could easily be explained should anyone ask. After all, Molly and TJ were a couple, so their peers would accept it. TJ's folks, on the other hand, may not approve of cohabitation, even if just for a night. Molly would cross that bridge if need be. For now, it gave Molly the ability to monitor TJ's wellbeing overnight.

Good to hear, I said. *How are you holding up?*

I've been better, she answered. Sorrow and relief were in her tone.

Molly was never one to let negative things linger. She simply moved on. She was positive and alert. Someone you'd want on your team. I did my best to build her spirit, but getting over something and someone this overbearing would take time.

Time we both agreed she needed.

You love TJ, don't you? I asked.

Her initial silence was the yes answer I expected. Without verbalizing a response, she concurred. Molly never fell in love with anyone other than Victor and doing so with a human, while she was in immortal form, wasn't acceptable. In her mind.

Molly, it happens all the time, I said in attempt to soothe her.

Not to me.

I know. It'll work out. Don't sweat it. Just remember to keep our existence—our world—a secret. We both knew that disclosing what we were was the biggest infraction an immortal could make. A mistake that could cost Molly her badge, not to mention immediate termination and a new life contract. Neither of which she wanted.

I-know-I-know-I-know, she babbled, unbecoming to her. *I promise not to do anything stupid.*

Good.

How's Emma? Molly asked.

Nice change of subject.

She laughed.

She's resting, but it's clear she remembers me.

Well, of course she does. What did you expect? Molly snapped. *You're the one that needs to be reminded that our existence cannot be disclosed. You know that, right, Benjamin?*

Yes. I know. Trust me. I know.

Good. And you've given her the cover story about the storm... looking for firewood in the woods—

Yes. And a tree branch fell. I haven't forgotten. It was the story our team contrived and shared with both TJ and Emma. It was loaded, rehearsed, and assumed to have minimal rebuttal after they'd awake in the morning. *Hopefully, it works.*

Since when have you been pessimistic?

I'm not. Just anxious.

I know. And you don't like lying to her, either. I get it. Don't worry. What did you tell me? Molly mimicked. *Oh, yes. It'll all work out.*

Goodnight, Molly, I said with a chuckle and severed the link.

Sitting in the chair, I watched Emma sleep. Her deep breaths were comforting. Humans had unexplainable flashbacks all the time. Especially those humans that were brought back to life. In a matter of a few hours, Emma's brain would recalibrate her disjointed thoughts into reasonable form.

As much as I wanted to wake her and catch her when it was possible she knew me, I mean, *really* knew who I was, I didn't. It was best not to.

Instead, I watched her sleep.

Chapter 120
Emma's Story

The water was cool on my skin.

Not cold, just comfortable. It was dark except for the glistening ripples in the lake. The light from the moon illuminated the shoreline and pier.

A splash beside me reminded me I wasn't alone. He surfaced in front of me. His short, buzz-cut hair dripped water, as he shook his head a few feet away. He smiled briefly before diving below.

We were close to shore, yet the water was deep. I bobbed up and down. My toes touched bottom, then sprang me up when I pushed off the lake's floor.

The water swooshed, as he swam around. His hand grazed my waist as he came up behind me, and I realized I was naked. He took me in his arms and spun me around. I was not embarrassed or uncomfortable.

"See? I told you the water would be refreshing," he said.

I giggled. He was right.

It was Ben.

***

I awoke with a start.

My head was heavy. I saw double closet doors in front of me and sat up quickly, swinging my feet over the edge of the bed. I had to wait for the woozy feeling to subside before trying to stand. It took a few moments for my eyes to adjust. The room was dark except for the faint light that filtered in through the window and the green glow of a digital clock on the table beside me. It was minutes past three.

I registered the sound of someone clearing their throat and turned to look. The outline of Ben came into focus. He was sitting in an oversized chair with his elbows resting on his knees. He yawned, and then rubbed his eyes with the heels of his hand before noticing my stare.

"Hey... you're awake," he said and walked toward me. He was dressed in the same white shirt and black pants he wore to the dance, though his shirt was unbuttoned, and his sleeves were rolled up. "How do you feel?" he asked, taking a seat beside me.

"My head hurts," I mumbled, touching my hand to my temple. Memories filtered back and forth, and I found myself unaware of what was real and what was imagined. *I had some crazy dreams*, I thought. "Did I... Did *we*... *skinny dip*?"

He raised an eyebrow and gave me a confused look.

"No. We didn't skinny dip last night." I almost heard a chuckle in his voice.

"Oh. Okay," I said, embarrassed for saying aloud what my wild imagination concocted. I looked down and realized I wasn't wearing the clothes from the party. I was in the tank top and plaid boxers I packed for my night at Claire's.

"Claire helped you." He met my eyes and continued, "Change your clothes, I mean. I swear I wasn't in here at the time."

Embarrassed again, I glanced around. "Is this the guest room? In your house?"

He nodded.

I felt a bit of panic. Where was Claire? And why was I in the guest room? Did I drink too much last night? Is that why I didn't remember getting here?

No. I didn't drink that much.

I was at the park. On the swings. Or was that a dream? Who was that old man I was talking to? I felt like I knew him. Why did he give me a matchbook and why I talking to him? Was he real?

Wait. What happened to TJ? He was slumped over, by a tree. Wasn't he?

Ben put his arm around me, and the rambling in my head stopped. I felt a calmness, despite the weird thoughts that ran through my mind.

"Where's Claire?" I asked, attempting to sound confident.

"She's sleeping. In her room," Ben answered.

"So, I, ah... I must have been pretty out of it last night. Huh?"

He nodded again and hesitated before answering. I almost wondered if he was trying to read my reaction before he spoke. "You hit your head pretty hard. You don't remember, do you?" His tone was sincere.

I shook my head.

"You were actually out for a minute. Like, out cold."

I definitely didn't remember that.

"Molly called her dad. He's a doctor," Ben said and held my hand. "Just to make sure you were okay."

"And TJ?" I asked. "I saw him in the woods."

"Yeah, he's fine. Went home with Molly." He was silent for a moment, and then continued. "Doc Preston left you some painkillers, if you need them," he said, pointing to a bottle on the table. "You were awake and talking to him. He said you didn't have a concussion, or anything. So we kinda overreacted, I guess. I was worried."

I saw a look of concern. His eyes never left mine.

"I feel pretty stupid." I whispered and hung my head.

"Don't," he whispered back, lifting my chin.

I glanced up at him, and he chuckled.

"What's so funny?"

"You're cute when you're embarrassed," he said with a smile. If my cheeks weren't already red, they would be in a second. I expected him to tease me. Instead, he leaned down and kissed me. The same sensation I felt the night before fluttered in me again.

"You should take these for your headache," he said, handing me two tablets and a glass of water. "And get some sleep."

Reluctantly, I agreed. I didn't want to go back to sleep. I wanted to stay with Ben. Of course, I couldn't tell him that.

"Did you sit in here the whole time?" I asked.

"Yes."

"Didn't you sleep?" I rested my throbbing head on the soft, feather pillow.

"Not really." Ben pulled the covers up and tucked me in.

I couldn't believe he didn't leave me. It was incredibly flattering, and I hoped my cheeks weren't betraying me.

"You know, you can join me, here," I said. After his eyes lit up, I knew that didn't come out right. "I mean—"

"I knew what you meant." He grinned and sat on top of the covers on the other side of the bed.

"Thanks for staying."

"There's no other place I'd rather be."

I turned to face him. That same tingle I felt when we kissed came back when he looked at me. He put his arm around me.

My body relaxed, and I drifted off to sleep.

Chapter 121
Ben's Story

I lay atop the covers fully clothed except my dress shoes, which I had slipped off and placed by the chair in the corner. My hands rested on my stomach, fingers locked as I stared at the ceiling. I could count sheep, but that never worked.

The sound of Emma's rhythmic breathing indicated she was asleep. I wanted to wrap my arms around her, to nuzzle beside her, to kiss her ivory neckline until she gave herself over to me.

Except, I couldn't.

She died tonight and came back to life. She needed time for her body to heal, for her to recover from the ordeal she went through. I was perverted thinking anything different. Even commanding rank wouldn't condone my behavior should I act upon my thoughts.

Did she really ask about skinny dipping? Could she possibly have remembered the hot summer day I talked her into baring all?

It was late enough to be dark, but early enough to get caught. The inlet was quiet and private. I told her, "No one will see." The July weather was humid, and a dip in the lake would be refreshing. I pulled off my shirt and dropped my shorts to the pier. I heard her gasp, as I dove in.

From a short distance away, I treaded water and watched as she removed the articles of clothing hiding her perfect figure. She glanced over her shoulder and threatened me gently. "Don't look, Benjamin. I mean it!" Her beaming smile was contagious, though I turned away to appease her.

I heard the splash behind me and after a few swooshes of water, I pulled her into my arms and kissed her.

We both lost our virginity that night, in the boathouse. It was weeks before our wedding, and I knew more than anything that I loved her.

Aftermath

***

I must have dozed off.

A circular motion on my chest, followed by two light taps, woke me. It was what Elizabeth used to do on lazy Saturday mornings before we had Danny. Except when I opened my eyes, it wasn't Elizabeth in my arms, it was Emma.

It was clear to me that she remembered our lives together, as she slept in my arms. Her thoughts were filled with disjointed memories she probably wouldn't understand. And even though she remembered bits of her life as Elizabeth, she was still Emma Bennett.

She also remembered our first life together. It was so long ago that I'd put those memories behind me. Emma clearly remembered the Victorian house where we lived and getting swept away in the current of Lake Michigan that cool fall day.

Emaline Elizabeth Rice jumped into the chilly waters on September 20, 1893.

I was due back days earlier. Except my schooner capsized in a storm and never returned. Emmie, as I called her back then, saw something floating in the water that evening and dove in the lake in hopes of reaching it. It would have been proof my ship was lost and that I perished. Emmie never reached the floating sail. She drowned instead.

Catherine, Emmie's sister, stood vigil at our home, day and night, awaiting word on both of us. It came when Emmie's human body washed ashore with the sail weeks later, a mile south of our home.

After rehabilitation, Emmie was reassigned a new life. With good behavior, despite her poor judgment and the breach of her contract, she was allowed some negotiations of her next life, selecting the Hudson family of Riverside.

"It's near Westport," she told me, back in our world. We were granted limited correspondence prior to reassignment.

I took a new contract in neighboring Lake Bell, as Benjamin Parker Holmes. There, in 1931, I met Elizabeth Emaline Hudson.

Lost in my own memories, I didn't hear Claire in the hallway. The door creaked as she opened it and Emma jerked awake, sitting up quickly. She pulled the covers tight to her neck, as if covering indecent attire.

"Catherine Rice! You startled me," Emma said, staring at Claire.

Claire looked to me, silent.

Chapter 122
Emma's Story

Once the words left my mouth, I couldn't retrieve them.

I heard a voice that sounded like mine, though what was said was clearly not what I meant. "I, ah… I'm sorry," I said and shook my head. "Claire." I rubbed my eyes and mumbled something about weird dreams in hopes she wouldn't think I was crazy. "I dreamt you were my sister." *And I dreamt about a boy named, Danny*, I thought.

A smile replaced the shocked look on Claire's face. I felt pretty stupid. Head injury or not.

"Well, I feel like your sister," Claire said. "I mean, after all, you *are* my best friend."

I returned her smile and hoped my slip up would soon be forgotten.

"You gave us a big scare last night," she said, giving me a hug.

"Yeah, I heard. I'm sorry," I said, massaging my head. "A tree branch fell, huh?"

"More like a limb," Ben added.

I looked over at him and realized he was fully dressed atop the covers.

"Well, I just wanted to check in on you. Go back to sleep. It's just after eight," she said.

"Where are you going?" Ben asked Claire. She was dressed in jeans and a sweater.

"Oh, um… Drew's picking me up in a few minutes. We're spending the day together." She smiled as she spoke, and I knew she was happy.

"You guys make a really cute couple," I said.

"Do you think?" she beamed.

"Yes, I do," I answered.

After Claire left, I realized I had been sleeping in Ben's arms.

"Are you hungry?" he asked. "How 'bout we get breakfast?"

When I turned to look at him, a wave rippled through me. It was as if I had known Ben before, not just the months since I moved to Westport, like for a really long time. Everything about him seemed familiar—his eyes, his smile, his look. "Yeah, I'd like that."

"Then, maybe we can go downtown, or catch a movie this afternoon."

I nodded, trying to hold back my smile. I felt content and happy. "Sure."

"Good. I'll let you get ready."

I dressed quickly, brushed my teeth, and ran a comb through my hair before we left.

"I'm low on fuel," Ben said when we reached the gas station in Riverside. He ran his credit card through the machine and hooked up the hose, before climbing back into the driver's seat. He reached for his Altoids tin between us. "Want one?" he asked.

I shook my head. "I'm more of a Mentos girl. Not Altoids."

He nodded and opened the tin. "Good. 'Cuz the box is empty. I'll have to pick some up before we leave," he said, turning to check the pump.

"I'll go in. Cinnamon flavor?"

"Yeah. I'll be right there," he answered.

An old-fashioned bell rang when I opened the wooden door. Inside, the walls were dark with a vintage look. Short, wood shelves filled the store, not like the tall, metal ones they had at Kwik Trip in Westport.

"Mornin', Miss," an older voice said.

I turned and noticed an elderly gentleman sitting on a stool behind the counter. "Good morning," I replied. Small, metal signs hung on the wall behind him, advertising old-fashioned soaps and cigarettes. *Very nostalgic for a small town*, I thought.

"Nice day out there. Unseasonably warm," the gray-haired man said.

"Yes. Very nice." I smiled at him and located the aisle with candy and mints. The charm of the doorbell rang again, and I guessed it was Ben. When the older man told someone to go to the stock room, I realized I was wrong.

I found the Mentos and scanned nearby rows for Altoids, but only saw mint. I placed the Mentos on the counter and was about to ask about Ben's favorite flavor, when the man put the Sunday paper in front of me, along with a Red Bull.

"My grandson's getting the Altoids for Benjamin," he said.

"Oh. How did… how did you know that's what I was looking for?" I asked.

"Your husband comes in every Sunday. Buys a tin of cinnamon Altoids, a coffee, an energy drink, and the Westport Gazette, early morning edition. 'Course, he's later than usual, today."

Husband? "We're not..."

"Ecckkk—I know. He told me he wasn't married. Now that I saw ya... I know. I know these things. He's had eyes on you forever."

I smiled in response.

The older man rang up the purchase, as a boy placed the Altoids on the counter and Ben came in. Before I could open my purse to pay, Ben dropped a twenty-dollar bill on the worn, wooden counter.

"You folks make a nice couple," the man said, handing Ben his change. "You don't have kids yet, do ya?"

"I, ah..." I was uncertain what to say.

"No. Not yet," Ben answered as I was still absorbing the question. Wait. Not yet?

"Well, you'll be good parents. I can see how much you love each other."

I felt my face flush.

"Most kids these days..." He waved his hand. "They get married for the wrong reasons. Then they divorce. No love there. Not like in my day, like my parents. Now, *they* were in love." The older man reached for a framed photo and turned it toward us. "These were my folks."

The aged, sepia photo was of a young couple. He was tall and good-looking with a short buzz-cut. She was pretty, with long, dark, wavy hair she wore pinned back on the sides. When I glanced back to the picture of the man, I realized he looked familiar, like an old-fashioned version of Ben. For an instant, I wondered if they were related.

"Very attractive couple," I said, looking at the older man across from me. Was there a resemblance?

"They loved each other. She never married after he died in the war. Died of a broken heart."

"I'm sorry," I whispered.

The man was silent, and I wondered if showing us the photo brought back sad memories. As I glanced away, I noticed his name tag.

"Thanks for sharing your story," I said.

Danny chuckled. "Anytime, little lady." He put the mints and Red Bull in a bag and handed it to me, while Ben grabbed the paper. "Can I interest you folks in some rock candy? On the house." He put a glass jar on the counter in front of us and pulled off the lid. He didn't wait for our answer. Instead, he used tongs and placed a small handful of crystal nuggets in a white, waxed paper bag. As he folded the top and gave it to me, something seemed strange.

"You come back soon," Danny said.

Once outside, I noticed the sign in the window. Danny's Bait Shop. I got back into the car and asked Ben, "Have you ever had déjà vu?"

He looked at me in a peculiar way and then smiled. "Have you?"

"I think I just did."

***

"Come on." I got out of the car in Aunt Barb's driveway. I jogged toward the staircase hidden by the bushes, lakeside. "I wanna show you something."

"Wait. Where are you going?" I was already heading down to the water. As I reached the landing and turned toward the last flank of stairs, I heard him call my name. "It's too late to go down there," he said. I thought I heard pain in his tone and wondered why he was being silly. After all, it wasn't dark yet.

"It's the best time of day to come down here," I said when he joined me on the boulder.

He stood behind me, wrapping his arms around me.

"Look," I said, pointing to a distant glimmer where the setting sun sparkled on the water's surface.

"You scared me," he whispered.

"Why?' I asked, turning in his arms. "It's not like I was going to jump in or anything." I chuckled at the absurdity.

"Crazier things have happened."

"You know, there's this old story about some woman who came here every night looking for her husband that was lost at sea," I said.

"Huh. Where'd you hear that?"

"My aunt told me about it. Something about this house. I think the woman lived here."

He was quiet.

"Well, it's just a rumor, anyway." A funny feeling came over me as I continued. "Apparently, she slipped on the rocks and got swept away with the current." My voice softened, and I wondered why it seemed so real. "They say if you see a distant sparkle of light, it's her, looking for her lover."

He hesitated at first, and then whispered, "It's just a story, Em."

"I know." In my heart, I wondered if there were any truth to it.

"Promise me you won't go near the edge."

Huh?

"Promise?" He looked concerned that I'd do something careless.

"I promise," I mumbled just before he kissed me.

Epilogue
Ben's Story

In all the years I was an agent, the Bureau never had an all-department conference, or a weeklong celebration. Nor speakers or entertainers like humans had during special events.

Then again, capturing Victor Nicklas was an exceptional feat worthy of that and more.

I missed most of the parties that took place those first days following the takedown. Instead, I chose to spend my time with Emma and simply listened in, remotely.

By Saturday, however, I found a few hours to sneak away and participate in the General Session, where Commander E attributed our success to my leadership. We were recognized hemisphere-wide in regional meetings and in the Nightly News.

The auditorium at headquarters was filled to capacity with standing room only that afternoon. All levels and ranks of agents congregated as the commander addressed the crowd.

He covered the details of Victor's lives, his tenure with the agency, and the years on the run, but it was Victor's capture that drew the most interest. Videos of that night in the woods outside Westport played on a continuous loop, while immortals cheered in the streets of our world.

Victor was admitted to a medical facility where agents could study him. Counselors worked to extract and evaluate the extent of his infractions. Final numbers of the souls he restrained was greater than any immortal could fathom. While his eventual existence couldn't be confirmed until all indiscretions were detected, it was unlikely Victor would ever be allowed to leave our world.

Molly was commended for her strength, both as an agent and during the multiple life contracts where she died at the hands of Victor. She smiled when Commander E awarded her the Purple Heart and announced Aberthol's pardon.

Without saying it, we knew the commander wanted to observe Abe on earth. The extent of his capabilities was unknown, as were his connections. Letting Abe live would let the commander monitor Abe's network of comings and goings, and see if immortal offspring posed a threat, or were of future benefit to the force.

Molly chose to ignore Commander E's underlying objective in hopes Abe's time would last long enough for her to get to know the son she lost.

A memorial service was held in our world for Kensington and the other hybrids whose souls were lost at the hand of Victor. Missing persons' flyers were taken down as cover stories flooded communities across the country. Cadavers replicating those humans lost surfaced in cities, putting an end to the misery their families endured and giving them closure for burial.

It was confirmed that Emma retained some memories of her past lives as a result of her near-death experience. But it was also determined that she was unaware of her actual pre-life existence. With mere speculation and without firm facts, she was not a threat and her life contract was still intact.

Claire eagerly accepted an extended assignment in Westport, to follow Emma not only through the final months of high school, but into her college years as well. She turned down a life contract opportunity, wishing to wait for Emma's next life, where Claire could be her sister once again. Claire's probationary status as a rookie changed to corporal rank.

Lucas found a note, in Ray's handwriting, the morning after the dance. In it, Ray apologized for the short notice, but said he was unexpectedly needed out of town. The thick, black ink didn't offer an explanation, or contact information. It didn't give Lucas or Char any indication of Ray's anticipated return. Instead, it simply said, "See you soon."

Char was flustered but quickly calmed when Lucas opened a brown paper bag containing thousands of dollars in cash. Neal offered emotional support for the disappearance of Lucas' stepdad, but it was Emma that Lucas chose to confide in. Their friendship strengthened and while I didn't like, nor understand, Lucas, I accepted the need for the two of them to bond. The unconventional family Neal and Barb created was the only family Emma had left, and I wouldn't do anything to jeopardize that.

"We've seen the end of an era, folks," Commander E addressed the crowd. "One that will go down in history!" Cheers and applause ended the session in the auditorium as Commander E waved to the crowd and exited the stage.

After everyone dispersed, I joined Commander E in his office where he poured each of us a scotch. The heavy, crystal glass with its ornate detail was reminiscent of his early-twentieth-century style, compared to the casual turtleneck sweater and slacks he wore. His youthful attire and neat appearance was opposite his norm.

"What gives?" I asked after taking a sip.

"What do you mean?"

"Your clothing. Your style's changed."

He shrugged. "Everyone needs a change once in a while."

I laughed. Commander E never changed. His rigidness was the one, trusted constant in our world.

"Okay. So I had a little encouragement."

"Encouragement?"

"Yes."

"Is this from some attractive woman I've seen you with before?"

He shook his head and took a long pull of his scotch. "Well, yes. She's very attractive. But you've never seen me with her before. She's not interested in me. In that way."

"Since when has that stopped you?"

"She's human."

"And? Need I ask again?" I chuckled, but he remained silent until I gave in. "When has that stopped you?"

"I want her as an agent."

"You're recruiting?'

"Something like that."

"And she has no idea, does she?"

He shook his head and finished the scotch.

"How long's her contract?"

He poured another glass and refilled mine before answering. "She's got years. I don't know. Thirty… forty, maybe."

"And you're recruiting *already*?" The thought seemed absurd.

He shrugged.

"Are you planning to cut her contract short?"

He didn't answer. He was done talking. I was able to read that Ezekiel Cain had been following this woman for several lives before he shut his shield and blocked me from learning too much.

"Enjoy your R and R." He raised his glass and toasted mine. "You deserve it."

"Thank you, sir," I said and finished the scotch. Extending my vacation a few years was granted, despite Commander E's attempts to lure me back home to head up The Farm. It was a high-level position, but it wasn't for me. Not now. Not after I found Emma.

"After that, we'll talk again," he said with a smirk. We both knew I'd be reassigned. In time. Whether it would be fieldwork, where I could stop in by Emma on a regular basis, or headquarters work, would be determined at a later date.

For now, all I knew was that I found my Elizabeth in Emma Bennett.

THE END

Acknowledgements

LOOKING BACK AT THIS INCREDIBLE JOURNEY, I CAN'T HELP BUT RECOGNIZE the people that supported me along the way…

To Rebecca, Courtney, Marya, and Dyan, thank you for believing in my story. I am truly blessed to be a part of your family.

To my husband, Michael, I couldn't have done this without you. Every step of the way, you were there for me and I appreciate that, more than you know. Love you, always! To my daughter, Brittany, and my son, Kyle, you are my inspiration and my strength. I love you both—you're the best!

To Diana Zawada, you listened to my ramblings, gave great advice, celebrated good times, and consoled me in down times. I can't ask for a better friend.

To the staff, students, and my friends at AllWriters' Workplace and Workshop, you helped make Ben and Emma's story better. To Author Michael Giorgio, your honest critiques were invaluable. Thank you for your guidance and friendship, and most of all, for your sarcastic humor.

To my friends and family, I appreciate each and every one of you. Your encouragement kept me going.

Lastly, to Mom, Dad, Eustice, and Sharie—who are probably celebrating this day in their Afterworld—this story is for you!

About the Author

Sandy Goldsworthy was born and raised in Sheboygan, Wisconsin, earning a Bachelor's Degree in Marketing from the University of Wisconsin-Oshkosh.

Her passion for putting pen to paper began when her high school English teacher inspired her to be more descriptive in her work. Ever since, Sandy has dabbled in creative writing, searching for that perfect shade of red.

Sandy's first novel, Aftermath, was signed by Clean Teen Publishing, in 2014.

When not writing, Sandy enjoys traveling, cooking, reading, and hanging out with friends and family. She resides in southeastern Wisconsin with her husband, Mike, two children, Brittany and Kyle, and their English Mastiff, Miles.

CPSIA information can be obtained at www.ICGtesting.com
Printed in the USA
LVOW11s0556110515

438003LV00003B/4/P

9 781940 534886